DARK HAVEN

By Brey Willows

2023

Butterworth Books is a different breed of publishing house. It's a home for Indies, for independent authors who take great pride in their work and produce top quality books for readers who deserve the best. Professional editing, professional cover design, professional proof reading, professional book production—you get the idea. As Individual as the Indie authors we're proud to work with, we're Butterworths and we're *different*.

Authors currently publishing with us:

E.V. Bancroft
Valden Bush
Addison M Conley
Jo Fletcher
Helena Harte
Lee Haven
Karen Klyne
AJ Mason
Ally McGuire
James Merrick
Robyn Nyx
Simon Smalley
Brey Willows

For more information visit www.butterworthbooks.co.uk

This trade paperback is published by Butterworth Books, UK

CATALOGING INFORMATION
ISBN: 978-1-915009-40-1
CREDITS
Editor: Nicci Robinson
Cover Design: Nicci Robinson
Production Design: Global Wordsmiths

Acknowledgements

A book is a piece of who we are as writers. A little piece of our soul sent out into the world to fend for itself. But before it makes that epic journey, it is brought to life by the people around it. I am fortunate to be surrounded by creative, kind, dedicated souls who understand what it is to throw your being into the world. My wife, Robyn, keeps me on track with her unshakeable, and often unfathomable, belief in me. The writers with whom we work have always been a source of inspiration, and as they're releasing their own books and flying high, I'm reminded that this is a journey we're taking together as much as we're doing it on our own. We are never alone, and to each and every one of them, I say thank you for sharing your creative soul with mine. And to the wonderful KC Lylark, thank you so much for the map at the beginning of the book. The nerdy kid in me who used to love them in the fantasy books I read is doing a happy dance. Thank you, too, to the ARC readers whose support and positivity help me relax a little bit before release day. And to our wonderful proof reader, Margaret Burris, thank you for catching all that little stuff that could pass us by so the book can really shine.

And thank you, most of all, to the readers who continue to follow me from world to world. Support like that nourishes a writer's soul.

Dedication

To my wife: my own dark haven, my safe place, my light when I can't find my way. You're my home for all eternity, in this life and the next.

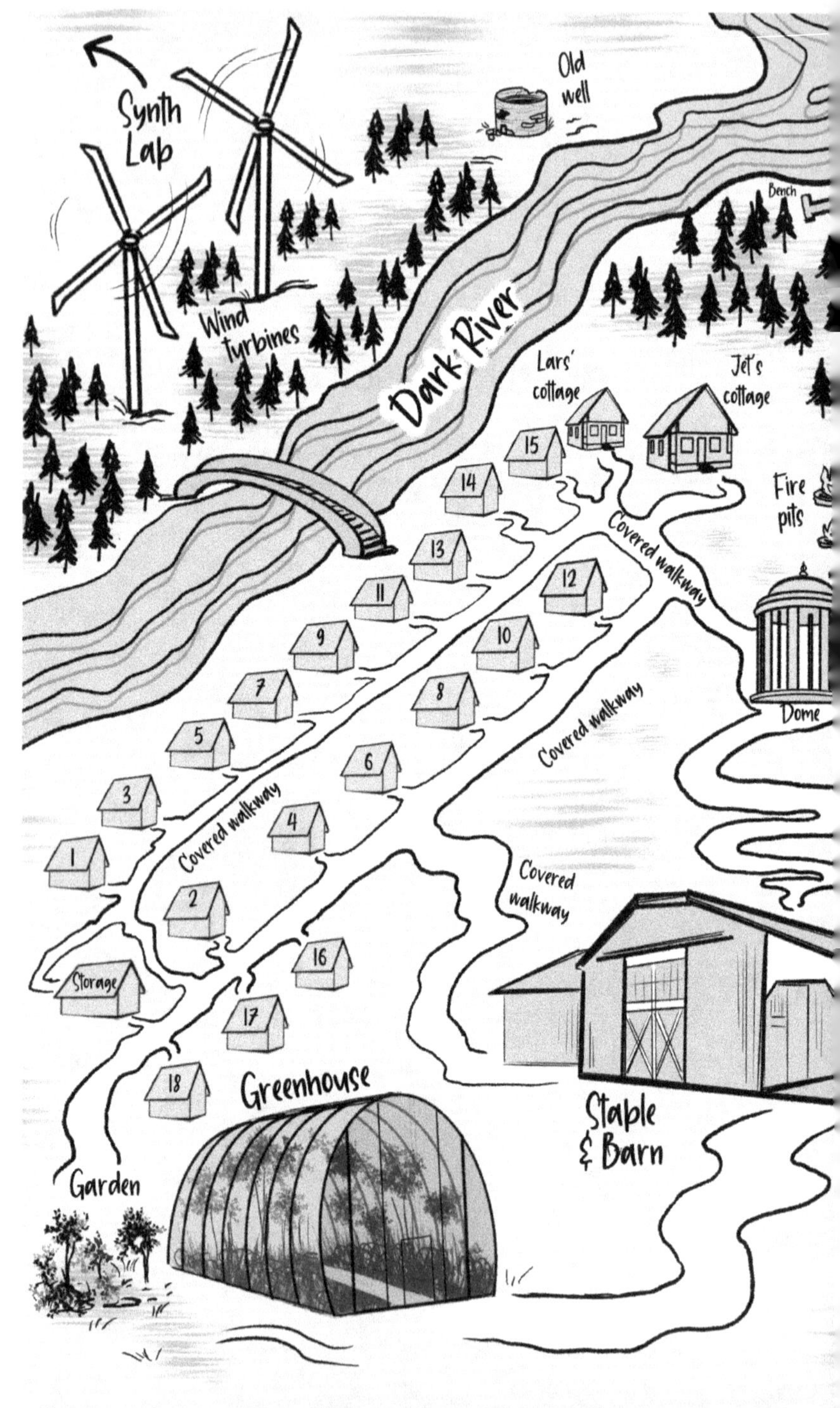

Synth Lab
Wind tyrbines
Old well
Bench
Dark River
Lars' cottage
Jet's cottage
15
14
Fire pits
13
11
12
9
10
Covered walkway
7
8
Dome
5
6
Covered walkway
3
Covered walkway
4
Covered walkway
1
2
16
Storage
17
18
Greenhouse
Stable & Barn
Garden

DARK HAVEN RANCH
250 acres
BLUFF BAY
Bench
Bench
Dock
Boat house
Lester's cottage
st
Two-story
Upper Story: Remy's Home
d walkway
Driveway
Buggy parking
Dark Haven
No Humans

Chapter One

"Hey, family!" Sage Samara gave her usual fluttering-lashes look at the camera on her phone as she posted her fourth ZimTak video of the day. "I'm on this super-secret mission, and you're going to absolutely die when you find out what it is. But for now, it's all hush hush! Wish me luck. Love you all!"

Sage hit stop and turned up the radio. So far, Bluffington had been a bust. It was pretty, if you were into trees and a zillion miles of fuck-all. But she was a city girl through and through and if her signal dropped one more time, she'd scream. Not that anyone would hear her.

"For real?" She slowed to a crawl behind an honest-to-god horse and buggy. The person riding it seemed not in the least bothered that Sage couldn't get past thanks to the curves in the road. "Seriously. Is this 1980?" At last, she saw her opening and threw the sports car into second gear. She glared at the driver as she went past, but they didn't have the decency to look over and see her irritation. "Whatever."

Two miles later, while singing at the top of her voice to the latest Zero Pitch song, she yelped as the car began to judder. She turned down the music and the steering wheel shook so hard, it hurt to hold it. "What the actual fuck?" She pulled over as far as she could, but there was no emergency lane, just a grass-covered ditch. She hit the video button on her phone. "You guys, seriously. Oh my god, I'm so stressing right now. I totally have to get to my super-secret mission, and my car has bit the big one. Hopefully I won't disappear like girls do in the movies while they're out in the woods." She widened her eyes and made a pouty face. "Better see what's up!" She ended the video and got out of the car with a deep sigh.

Her high heel sank instantly, throwing her off balance. When she tried to right herself, the other heel sank, and she was flung face first onto the ground. Into mud, actually.

She struggled out of her heels and crawled on her hands and knees to the car, where she pulled herself up using the side mirror. She screeched when she saw mud splattered not just on her face, but all over the top she'd only bought two days before. The more she tried to wipe it off, the more it smeared, eventually mixing with her tears of frustration.

A sound caught her attention, and she looked up just as the horse and buggy were passing. The driver didn't look over, but she caught the smirk on the person's face, even though there was a large brimmed hat shading it.

"Hey!" She waved, as though the person hadn't seen her. "I need some help here!"

The buggy kept on buggying.

She used the bottom of her blouse to wipe the dirt from her eyes and then looked at the car. The right front tire wasn't just flat, it was shredded. She looked back down the road and saw pieces of the tire marking the length of her inattention. "Shit."

She leaned on the hood and pulled out her phone. Surely she could still get a tow truck out here. She opened the map app and waited for it to pinpoint her location, but a gray bar with "no signal" across the front quickly dashed that hope. She couldn't very well call for a tow and say she was on some road in some ditch.

Tears formed, and she brushed them away. Okay, so she'd have to walk until she found a house. That buggy must have been going somewhere, and it couldn't be that far. Right? She pulled her suitcase from the trunk—glad it had four wheels—and locked the car even though it wouldn't be going anywhere. She stuck her feet into her ruined heels, swearing when mud squelched between her toes. She'd only hobbled about a hundred feet when she heard a car engine. She stepped into the middle of the road with her suitcase. No one was going to pass her by this time.

An old pickup truck with tinted windows, including the windshield, came into view and slowed to a stop well away from where Sage stood. No one got out.

"Who are these fucking people?" She huffed and sighed as she dragged her case toward the truck. She left the case directly in front of it so it couldn't drive off, then went to the driver's side.

"That your tire back there?" The person tilted their head. A large cowboy hat shaded their face, and the deep voice didn't give any indication of gender.

Sage looked at the pieces of shredded rubber in the truck bed. "Eww. Why would you pick that up? Yes, it's my tire. And I don't have any signal so I can't call for a tow, and this totally rude buggy guy drove right past me even though it was so obvs I needed help."

"Mm." The person opened the door and got out, motioning for Sage to get in the other side. "No spare?"

Sage rolled her eyes. "I needed the extra space for my stuff, and it seemed dumb to carry around something I wouldn't need." She felt her face flame at the knowledge that she did, in fact, need it. "Whatevs. Lesson learned, I guess."

"I'll put your case in the back. Hop in. I'll tell you where your car is, and you can call for a tow from the nearest hotel."

Sage winced a little as the person tossed her suitcase in the back with the shredded rubber. She pulled herself up and into the truck, which had an old-fashioned bench seat. Mud coated her jeans, and she tried to wipe it from her face again, only to transfer mud between the two places to make it worse. Once the driver got in, she could finally see them properly.

And promptly wished she could crawl back into the ditch and hide.

The woman was hot. Like, cowboy in chaps for a lesbian calendar hot. Butch porn hot. New York City didn't compare kind of hot. Her plain white T-shirt hugged a firm-looking body, and her roughed-up jeans were clearly authentic, not expensively trashed.

The cowboy hat covered short hair. She melted, just a little. Too much would seem needy.

"How do I know you're not a killer? I know there are plenty around here," Sage asked, trying for cute and sweet in lieu of sexy, since the mud definitely fucked that look up.

"You don't, I guess."

The woman looked her over, clearly unimpressed. "You're free to get out and wait, but you won't know that about the next person who comes along either."

That wasn't comforting, but at least the woman wanted Sage to stay with her. "All right then. I'll let you be my knight in shining armor."

The woman's eyebrow quirked, and she didn't say anything as they set off down the road. Sage continued to pick at the mud in her hair, dropping it out the window and stressing about how she was going to do her job now. This kind of exclusive came along once in a lifetime, and she absolutely couldn't blow it.

"Where were you headed?"

"The *VCN* conference, and then Dark Haven for a week." She tried to say it like it totally wasn't a big thing, even though it definitely was. Not that this hot butch cowboy would have any idea what she was talking about. Although, those eyes... With a start, she realized that the woman looked vaguely familiar, but she couldn't quite place her. The tinted windows, though...was that just for show?

The woman's expression hardened ever so slightly. "Right."

Was there a hint of judgment in that one word? Before she could get to the drama, the woman turned into a driveway with a small signpost that read Rac's Place. It led to a large farmhouse with several cars parked outside.

"You can make your call from here. Tell Rac your car is at the entrance to the old Rose Bower." The woman threw the truck in park, jumped out, put Sage's suitcase by the stairs, and then got back in the truck. All without another word.

Sage stared as she drove off. "So rude." What a shame too.

She and a woman like that would have made fire look cold with what they could do in the sheets. The screen door squeaked open behind her, and she turned.

"Hey there. Can I help you?"

The woman speaking from the shaded porch was tall and slender. She had shoulder-length braids and cheekbones that Sage would die for. "Yeah, hi. Um, my car got a flat, like totally shredded, and this woman gave me a ride and said I could use your phone." She held up her cell. "No signal."

The woman smiled widely, and Sage's knees went weak. *Fangs*.

"Of course. Come on in and clean up. Looks like the mud might have won the fight." She bent and looked at the suitcase. "Zipper is busted too. You'll have a time getting it open, and then you won't be able to shut it again. Should probably keep it closed till you get where you're going. I'll set some clean clothes outside your door."

Sage swallowed and gave her brightest smile. This was her first taste of the vampire world outside of the city. She could do this. "That would be amazing, thanks."

The woman lifted Sage's suitcase like it didn't weigh fifty pounds and then held the screen door open for her. The inside was simple, nothing fancy, but it felt like a place to relax in. If, of course, you weren't going to be dinner.

"I've got one room empty tonight, and you can take that. Any idea where your car is? I can call our local garage and see if they can spare anyone."

"The woman who dropped me off said to tell you," she hesitated, "well, to tell someone called Rac that it's at the entrance to the Rose Bower."

"I'm Rac, and that's all I need." She opened the door to a room. "Here you go. Come on down and have dinner when you're ready."

Sage closed the door and locked it behind her. That was dumb, but she couldn't help it. What were the chances of her staying in an inn run by a vampire just as she was about to go to their biggest conference of the year? She shuddered and dug out her papers of safe passage and laid them on the desk. She'd have to keep them on her all the time now.

The shower felt heavenly, even if there weren't any high-end soaps, and the clothes she found outside the door fit almost perfectly. She tugged at the burnout T-shirt and tried not to think about the possibility that the person who'd worn them no longer needed them. Ever again.

She made her way downstairs and noticed there weren't any pictures. No art, no decorations, no knick-knacks. There were lots of books, but nothing that was simply pretty. She'd always thought vampires were a frivolous bunch. With lifetimes of money, why not?

When she got to the dining room, it was empty except for Rac sitting there, flipping through a newspaper. She looked up. "Food?"

"Please. I'm starving." Sage sat down and poured a glass of water from the jug. Rac left, presumably to go into the kitchen, and Sage set her papers next to her glass, the red seal bright against the white tablecloth.

Rac came in and set down a chicken dish of some sort that smelled divine. Her gaze flicked to the paperwork and she gave a small nod, then sat across from Sage.

"I admit to wondering why a human would risk crossing this neck of the country." She tilted her head toward the papers. "Safe passage only helps if you have time to hold them up. Or if the vampire in question cares a blood cell for government documents. Not all do, you know. Especially here."

Sage murmured her appreciation of the food and took a quick photo. She could always post it later, when she had internet again. "I know, but I'm kind of an internet celebrity. People would totally notice if I went missing."

Rac's head tilted almost like a dog's. "And you think a vampire in the middle of vampire country cares about that, do you?"

"Well, yeah. Since you guys got the green light to be totally yourselves, which is awesome, by the way, everyone knows you have strict rules about who you can feed on and who you can't.

And perception is everything. You don't want to look like the bad-guy monsters anymore, and seriously, who can blame you?" She finished eating and took a long drink of water. "And besides, like, all my followers know I'm here."

Rac's expression was one of bemusement, but Sage was tired and didn't want to get into the whole vampire-human politics thing tonight. "I'm so beat."

Rac seemed to snap back from wherever she'd gone. "I called our local garage, but they can't get your car till tomorrow. They'll stop by here to get the keys, fix the tire, and then drive it over when it's ready. Keep you from standing out in the open."

"Wow, that's so fantastic. And kind. Thanks so much, really." Sage tugged on the T-shirt. "I love this. So retro."

Rac smiled enough to show the tips of her fangs. "Feel free to keep it. The person who wore it doesn't need it anymore."

A tiny flicker of fear finally made its way through Sage's illogical optimism. "Great, thanks."

Rac laughed. "Not because she's dead. Or even undead. She's pregnant with her third kid, and the likelihood she'll ever be that small again is as likely as I am to start eating Brussels sprouts."

Sage laughed a little too forcefully. "Obvs. Of course. Didn't even cross my mind." She noticed the paper Rac had been reading. "Oh hey, that's where I'm headed. The Vampire Community News Conference."

"Really." Rac leaned back in her chair. "Seems like a dangerous thing to do."

Sage rolled her eyes. "Yeah, for normal people, I guess. But I'm totally a vampire rights supporter. I even marched for equality last year with the New York Vampy Vamps." She grew irritated when Rac didn't look impressed. "Anyway, I run a ZimTak channel that has over a million followers. The VCN invited me to report on the conference for my peeps, so they can get a better understanding of how great you all are."

Rac nodded, slowly, her gaze never leaving Sage's face. It was intense.

"And then," she said, trying not to tap her fingers against the chair and make it obvious she was nervous, "I'm going to be staying at Dark Haven. I'll be there for a week, seeing how they live, what they're up to, all that. Like, modern investigative journalism. When I'm done, you'll have a million more people on your side."

"Do we need people on our side?" Rac asked, still as intense.

"Well, yeah. I mean, history has shown what happens when people turn against you." Sage rolled her shoulders. "I so need a massage. I hope the hotel has a spa."

Rac stood and shoved her hands in her pockets. "I'd be a little more cautious if I were you." She looked Sage over. "And I damn sure wouldn't get naked and wait for a vampire masseuse to work out my knots." She picked up Sage's plate. "Sleep well."

CHAPTER TWO

"I TOLD YOU, JET. This is a bad idea. Probably the worst you've ever had, and the devil knows you've had your fair share." Remy "Wind" Winslow ran her hand through her hair, wondering if it might all fall out by the time this was done.

"Oh, please. Wearing that corduroy jacket in the seventies was worse than this. Hell, wearing silk in New Orleans in the *seventeen* seventies was worse than this. It's a reporter, Wind. Just a silly vore who will give us some good press and then be on her way."

"Vores don't belong here. You know that. Everyone knows that. It's on the fucking sign on the fence." Remy indicated said sign to make her point. Below Dark Haven, it read: *Humans not welcome. Keep going until you've left Bluff County. Stop at your own risk.*

"What is it Saint Pete preaches? We were all human once and should be humble in the face of their ignorance and squishiness."

Remy laughed and some of the tension eased. "He doesn't say 'squishiness.' He should though. It would make his droning more interesting. The idea of a church for vampires is ludicrous."

Jet tilted her face to the moonlight. "I love this time of year. It's best when it gets dark at three in the afternoon."

Remy didn't respond. Talking about the light was a lot like talking about the weather. Mundane topics rarely required her attention. Silence surrounded them like a hug from a long-gone mother, and she breathed it in as she always did. The stars twinkled like magic sprinkled across the fabric of the sky, and she marveled at the way the constellations had hardly changed in all the years she'd been wandering this big blue floating rock.

"Thing is," she finally said, "I can't guarantee her safety, Jet. If she gets hurt here, if someone decides they're hungry, and she's a pest no better than a rodent, then we look bad. And with politics being what they are right now, that could be disastrous. If you'd seen her on the side of the road, looking as helpless and edible as a deer, you'd get what I mean."

Jet jumped down from her perch on the fence. "Then I guess you'll have to make sure she lives through it. Besides, she's covering the *VCN* conference first. She may not even make it this far."

"Let's hope," Remy grumbled, earning her a quick disapproving look.

"I know you don't like outsiders." Jet motioned to the extensive ranch spread around them. "I don't either. That's why I live in the middle of nowhere with a best friend who has the personality of a donkey with a burr stuck up its butt."

Remy harrumphed but didn't deny it.

"But, babe, these are crazy times. Ever since we came out of the proverbial bloody coffin, our world has been balanced on a knife edge. Not being in hiding, not having to change our names every few decades...it means a lot. And you were a huge part of making that happen. But," she crossed her arms and looked up at the sky, "we're still considered monsters. Humans can turn on us in a millisecond, and all the freedom we've been enjoying for the last five years can be ripped away. With the weapons and the technology they've got now, hunting us would become a sport." She looked back at Remy. "And we'd lose, eventually. No castles or caves would be able to give us sanctuary anymore."

Remy squeezed her eyes shut against the memories of what it was like to be hunted. "Yeah. Okay, I hear you. Entertain the blood enthusiast, make sure she doesn't die, get her out of our territory, go on with life." She stood and stretched. "Got it."

Jet nodded and walked off into the dark, whistling. "Have fun at the conference tomorrow. Do the kind of shit I'd do. It'll be good for you," she called over her shoulder.

Remy headed the other direction toward the barn. She didn't

want to think about the conference. She hated crowds and having to talk to people she didn't know or care about.

The cows were all in their pen, as were the goats. The nights were getting cold, and the compound couldn't afford to lose any livestock. As she passed the various cottages, she could hear signs of life here and there. No radios or TVs, since they didn't have that sort of thing at Dark Haven, but conversations and laughter spilled out occasionally, as did the sound of a violin coming from old Lester's place. His was farthest from the main lodge, right up against the forest. He came from a clan who'd lived in treehouses and being close to the trees made him feel a little less far from home.

When she returned to the main lodge and went upstairs to her place, she breathed a sigh of relief. Everything was perfect. They were safe, and things were simple. As simple as a vampire living in a human world could be anyway, a concept about to be put to the test by the internet personality coming to invade their space. Sage Samara was knockout gorgeous. Long, wavy blond hair complemented her fair skin and blue-gray eyes. She was small, probably not more than five foot two, and she could probably fit into sizes Remy hadn't fit in even as a child. She was overconfident and her sentences were ill-constructed, but that was part of language in this century.

There was something about her. Something interesting, if irritating. Something that felt familiar and yet utterly foreign. She should have taken her right past Rac's place to the train station and sent her packing. Humans didn't belong here. Not even really sexy ones. Maybe, especially, really sexy ones.

Remy fell into bed and groaned. This wasn't going to be over quickly enough.

***

"Attention. Attention, everyone. Please take your seats."

Remy found a seat in the back, in a corner near the door. Briefly, she wondered if the vampire on stage had always looked like an officious librarian. Taking on new personas was part of living forever, but somehow, Remy had a feeling that this vampire had probably been turned when she was handling the books in Alexandria before it burned.

She sighed and slouched in her chair, legs spread, taking up room. Maybe that way no one would sit next to her. A dead leg punch made her grimace and shift. "Asshole."

"Grumpy bitch." Lars Storm sat primly down beside her after he wiped the seat with a handkerchief. "You're looking like your usual, hot butch self. Nice tie."

Remy tugged at it a little. "It's a noose."

"A sexy noose. It sets off the pale bloodshotness of your eyes."

The room finally went quiet, saving her from having to come up with any more banter or admit to how uncomfortable she felt. It was only a shirt and tie, for fuck's sake. She was still in her jeans and boots. It was an outfit she wore often when she was out looking for a quick hookup. But that wasn't it, was it? It had nothing to do with the clothing and everything to do with why she was wearing it.

"Thank you so much for coming to the Vampire Community News Conference!" the officious librarian said, clearly not used to having to muster genuine excitement for a large gathering that didn't involve books. "As you know, this conference has grown year by year, and we've got nearly a thousand people here to discuss our political situation, as well as what's happening throughout our community. We hope you'll get involved in the break-out sessions and remember, there's karaoke and games tonight in the main ballroom."

Remy stopped listening and let her gaze sweep slowly over the attendees. Every age, every ethnicity, every build. The only thing they had in common was the fact that they were all vampires. Other than that, little held them together. Many of them, she knew. Some were friends, others acquaintances she'd met throughout the centuries. But there were plenty she didn't know. *The Vampire Community News* had been going for nearly a century, and the invention of the internet had made it even better. It was good to come together, even if they had nothing to talk about at the end of the day other than the best types of synthetic blood on the market.

Lars elbowed her in the side, getting her attention. "Idiot. They're calling you to the stage," he said softly, his head tilted so only she could see his mouth.

She stood without saying anything and walked to the front. Silence and gazes filled with curiosity and venom followed her. Of course, there were plenty of friendly faces in the audience too. That mattered. She took the mic from the librarian and inhaled deeply. "Thank you. As was said," she couldn't say by whom because she didn't know the woman's name, "I'm Remy Winslow. Five years ago, I was able to work with the government and an incredible team of vampires to get us equal rights and protections under the law, meaning we no longer have to live in the shadows. Bluffington has officially been declared a vampire state, and Bluff County has the largest contingent of vampires living out in the open in America."

"But we still live in fear!" someone shouted from the audience. There was a grumble of agreement.

"Fear is a choice." Remy's tone grew hard. "They've lived in fear of us for centuries, and rightfully so. We're stronger, faster, more powerful, and we hold their lives in our hands." She looked at the crowd, making eye contact, and winced internally when she saw the damned little faux reporter sitting in the second row, her eyes wide. "If we're going to live among them, out in the open, then we have to show them they aren't simply food. We can't just *tell* them we aren't a threat. We need to *show* them by how we behave. Many of us have human friends, human lovers. Don't forget that when things get difficult. When you're meeting over the course of the conference, remind one another what it was like before, and how things are better now."

"And what if we don't want to, Wind?" A vampire stood, his

shoulders back, his posture rigid, his dark skin offset by his white suit jacket. His eyes held decades upon decades of knowledge. "What if we want to live as vampires are meant to, as predators? You're asking us not to be true to our natures. You're asking us to change in order to fit into a society that reviles us." His tone was respectful, but the challenge was clear. The fact that he'd used her nickname meant he knew full well who she was and what *her* true nature had once been.

"You're right. We do have to change. But that's life, isn't it? No matter how long you've lived, you know that change is inevitable. Just because we don't age doesn't mean we don't change. You adapt to your environment, and *this* is our new environment. There are plenty of humans willing to feed the vampire community, especially in the cities. The synth blood is better than real blood most of the time now as well. You don't *need* to hunt anymore, and if we all stick to the new order of things, then we can continue to adapt, and change, and still be out in the open. They'll begin to trust us and see that we're not the monsters we've been made out to be."

The person who'd raised the question tilted his head to acknowledge her answer, but he clearly didn't fully agree. Remy scanned the room again, but vampires were notoriously hard to read. Most had learned to school their expressions long ago. "And if you're interested in leaving the world behind to live like you're back in the Middle Ages, you're always welcome at Dark Haven." She grinned and received some genuine laughter. "Seriously though, if anyone wants to talk to me during the conference, come find me. The conference coordinators have my schedule, and I'm happy to talk through any issues you may be having adjusting to life in the open. Maybe I can help, maybe I can't, but we're in this together, and together, we're stronger." She nodded when about half the room responded with the motto she'd used throughout their legal campaign. *Together, we're stronger.* She wasn't always sure it was true, but it worked as a rally cry. She gave a vague wave and left the stage.

When she was back in her seat, Lars gave her a side glance. "If I were a woman with very little self-esteem and a desire for a broken heart, I'd be all over you right now. So *commanding*." He gave a little fake shiver.

"Shut up or I'll tell Oliver you're still pining over him." She tilted her head toward Lars' ex, sitting at the front of the room.

"Please." He rolled his eyes and straightened the cuffs of his satin jacket. "I don't pine."

Remy checked her watch. "I've got a meeting." She leaned over and pointed. "See the blonde up there? Long hair, looking around like she's at Disneyland?"

He narrowed his eyes and nodded. "Those are some rosy cheeks. Does she know she's a steak in the midst of hungry lions on a vegetarian diet?"

It was an apt description, and Remy noticed the vampires directly around Sage glancing her way, their nostrils flaring at her scent. "Yeah, she knows and yet, she's clueless. If you have the chance, can you make sure no one decides she's too good to resist? She's some internet person, and she's here to show how well behaved we are."

He scoffed, not looking away. "They get dumber by the decade, I'm sure of it." He waved her away. "I'll keep watch. Meet me for drinks later."

Remy slipped from her chair and left the room to head to her meeting with the mayor in charge of the area with the most vampires per capita than anywhere else in the USA, although the coastal states were seeing a surge as well. Remy had written an article for the *VCN* suggesting that as vampires spread out they should always be aware of not being landlocked, thus making sure they had an escape route should one be needed. While she was hopeful and believed in the movement toward integration, she was also a realist, and human feelings were more volatile than hurricanes. That meant most vampires lived near water of some kind.

She felt someone at her side and groaned out loud when Sage looked up at her. "Shouldn't you be in the conference hall?"

"Hello again to you too. I'm doing great, thanks. And yes, I do clean up well, don't I?" She tossed her hair over her shoulder and gave Remy a flirty smile. "You seem like the person to know around here. I realized after we met why you looked familiar. You're the one behind all the laws. You looked totally different in your jeans and hat. But I googled you, and you're the rock star of vampires. Like, their president and queen and—"

"Queen?" If Remy could still get headaches, she knew she'd have one coming on. "I'm not any of those things. I'm an activist, and I managed to talk to the right people." She looked at her watch. "And I'm about to be late to talk to one of those people. Excuse me." She lengthened her stride, quickly leaving Sage behind.

"Rude."

She rolled her eyes as she heard Sage grumble behind her. She'd have to deal with her soon enough.

"Hello, darling girl. I've been tasked with making sure all that lovely blood in your veins remains there. I'm Lars Storm, the vampire with flare."

Remy blew out a relieved breath and headed to her meeting. Lars, for all his bitchiness, was a good man and took his human-vampire relations job seriously. Sage was in good company, and now Remy didn't have to worry about all their good work being undone because a foolish human didn't understand she was a kitten walking into an alligator swamp.

"Remy." The mayor held out her hand and shook Remy's firmly. "Thanks for taking the time. I know you don't like to leave Dark Haven."

Remy accepted the glass filled with crimson liquid and took a healthy sip. The blood coursed through her, giving her energy and making it easier to focus once again. Maybe she needed to evaluate her diet. Maybe she was getting anemic by only using synth blood. The heavy iron tang and faint hint of oranges told her this was the real thing, but she wasn't about to question its origin. "No problem, Dez. It's good for me. Reminds me why I started Dark Haven in the first place, and I can't wait to get back."

Dez Carmine wasn't as old as Remy, but she had political savvy and could play the game better than Remy ever could. They'd spent many nights together, drafting proposal after proposal and sitting with irritating bureaucrats, and they'd developed a close friendship built on trust and an understanding that shit could go sideways at any second.

"You've met the influencer?" The word sounded like food covered in dust.

"Twice. Once when she managed to shred her tire without noticing for about half a mile, and just now, when she seemed irritated that I didn't want to drop at her feet and tell her how great she is." She didn't need to say that she wanted to run her fingers through Sage's long hair. It wasn't relevant, and it wasn't going to happen.

Dez pulled up something on her phone and handed it over. "Then you're going to love this."

The video was of Sage talking animatedly to whoever was watching, telling them about her "super-secret mission" in vampire country and how she'd even stayed in an inn run by a vampire who'd given her fresh clothes to wear and made a wonderful breakfast that was "totally normal" food. She promised regular updates throughout the conference and even said she'd be interviewing attendees so her "family" could get to know them.

Remy handed the phone back. "Can we get ulcers? I think I'm getting an ulcer."

Chapter Three

Sage bit her lip and tried to do some deep breathing. This *wasn't* a bad idea. It was only scary because of old bedtime stories and bad movies. The reality was different, and she was a strong, independent woman who could hold her own.

She repeated it three more times before it started to seep in and soothe the nerves that had started from the moment she'd arrived at the conference. Rac had been intense, yeah, but she'd been nice enough. And Remy had given her a lift when she needed one, even if she wasn't much of a conversationalist and hadn't bothered to tell Sage who she was. They were vampires and totally like other people, which is what Sage was hoping to show the world.

But then there was the talk about humans being weaker, about them not just being food. That had set her pulse going. But it was after, when Lars had dragged her along to a community meeting about how vampires needed to get involved in keeping the roadsides clear of overgrowth that things had gotten strange. Bored, she'd said she needed the bathroom and would be right back. Lars, in the midst of an argument about some bush with thorns being used along the highways to deter motorists from stopping, had simply given her a quick nod and continued his gesticulating.

When she'd stepped outside the room, a small group of vampires were gathered in the middle of the hall, clearly in deep discussion, given their tense body language and whispering. They'd turned almost as one and stared at her. One had even taken two steps toward her, fangs out, eyes hard, before another had grabbed their arm and pulled them back.

"You shouldn't be here." One of the group looked her over, disdain clear in their expression. "You forget your place, vore."

Sage didn't know the word, but it didn't sound like a compliment. She backed away and bumped into the wall. "Sorry. Didn't mean to interrupt." She nearly ran to the bathroom and heard the soft laughter behind her.

And now she was locked in a bathroom stall, trying to get the image of the vampire's hungry gaze out of her head. She had safe passage papers and everyone in the cyber world knew she was here. And yet, she was considering getting in her car and driving like hell back to the city where she knew the rules. She heard the door open and tensed.

"Sage? You in here?"

So relieved to hear a friendly voice that she was nearly dizzy, she opened the door. "Hey, Remy. Just needed a pit stop, and all that talk about plants on the side of the road was a yawn."

There was no chance at all that Remy was fooled. Sage could see it in the way she looked at her, obviously checking for bite marks or something. "Yeah. Regular life can be dull at times. I'm having lunch with Lars. Want to join us?"

The invitation sounded far more like an obligation than a genuine desire to hang out, but she didn't care. "For sure, thanks. Maybe you could introduce me to some people who want to talk to my followers?"

"Mm." Remy held the door open for her and they started toward another room at the end of the hall.

Lars waved from a round table that already had a few people at it, and although she'd never admit it out loud, she was glad to know two people in this incredibly intimidating crowd. It was a novel feeling, one she didn't like in the least. She was always the one people were hesitant to approach or couldn't wait for time with. *She* was the star attraction. Here, she wasn't even a blip on their radar. Well, she'd just have to change that. She looked at the variety of cookies, cakes, and other nibbles on the buffet table, along with sandwiches and wraps. "Am I okay to eat this stuff?"

Remy placed a wrap on her plate, along with some chips. "It isn't made of human, if that's what you're asking." She pointed. "That's vegetarian, if you're asking something less insulting."

Sage bit back a retort because that was exactly what she'd been asking, then made the same choice Remy had, plus a couple cookies. She grabbed a bottle of water but stopped to stare at what looked like a water cooler full of blood, where people were getting themselves little paper cups.

"Now, that *is* what you think it is, and it probably wouldn't suit your palate." Remy gave a half grin and waved Sage ahead of her toward Lars.

Lars was mid-conversation when they sat down. "And now you'll think of me every time you eat a prune."

"Because they look like dried assholes." Remy sighed and took a bite of her wrap. "Must you tell everyone that story?"

"Too few people know. I find their lack of knowledge offensive." He looked past Remy to Sage. "And how are you doing, blondie?" He didn't wait for her to answer. "Everyone, this is Sage Samara. Viral sensation on social media. She'd like to interview us beautiful creatures for her thingy she does."

Indignation rose, and she didn't temper her tone. "Patronizing, much? My *thingy* has won both Shorty and Webby awards, and I've personally won an AIA award for Awareness Influencer of the Year." Normally, that statement was met with the respect it deserved. Now, however, she got a few blank stares, and Lars almost looked like he wanted to pat her shoulder. Remy gave a little shake of her head and continued to eat.

"Anyway," Sage said, pasting on a smile, "what matters is that I'm here to further vampire-human relations by showing my social media family how we can all get along. The idea is to humanize you so they can really see past the misconceptions."

"You're good with this, Remy? With us being 'humanized?'" a woman with a short black bob and rimmed glasses asked.

Remy set her half-eaten wrap down and pushed her plate away. "It's like I said in my speech this morning. We have to live with them if we want to live out in the open. We have to show them who we are, but we've gravitated to living together the way we always do. If we're separating ourselves, then we have to find another way for them to know we aren't a threat." She tilted her head toward Sage. "And like it or not, the world is now global in a way we've never known before. Information reach is exponential, and people like Sage are spreading it. Better to have her with us than against us and able to spread the truth instead of more myths and superstitions."

"Thanks, I think." Sage turned to the others. "So, who will be my first guest?"

Lars held up his hand. "I'm unofficial head of human-vampire relations here in Bluff County. I'm also the best dressed and classiest of my brethren, so it should be me."

Remy stood. "If anyone else is available to talk to Sage, I'd appreciate it." She looked at Sage. "Do us all a favor, though. Stay with Lars, and if you aren't with him, come find me." She motioned at the others at the table. "Or them. But be aware, Sage." She leaned down and lowered her voice. "Not everyone here is happy about the changes we've made, and they won't care about how popular you are or about those papers in your pretty little handbag. If you stray and forget where you are, and what you are, it could get you killed. You're in our world now." She moved away again and checked her watch. "See you all later."

Sage shivered at the warning and watched her leave the room. Moreover, she watched as plenty of other people watched her leave the room too. She had that strong, confident swagger that made femmes like Sage hot and bothered, and there was more than one girly vampire in the room who clearly wouldn't mind a night in Remy's bed. Of course, Remy probably wouldn't tell *them* that they could be someone's next meal if they wandered off without her. The thought made her flush, and she turned her attention back to Lars. "Let's get started."

By the time the day was over, Sage had seven interviews done, and they'd been lots of fun, as well as illuminating. She learned that synthetic blood, or synth as their community called it, was manufactured in labs run by vampires who knew what they were doing. Some labs did better batches than others, and while you could pick up synth at any grocery store that had vampire goods, most vampires got theirs delivered via Nozama, the giant distribution company. She decided it wasn't any different than the diet companies who delivered ready-made meals, and the vampire she'd said that to had laughed and said it was true.

She'd been a hit, and while none of them had been willing to divulge their actual age or where they were reborn, which were apparently sensitive topics, they'd been more than happy to talk about their day jobs. When she asked what myths they'd most like to dispel, the first had been that they were a danger to humans in general. The next had been that they were monsters, and the third was that they didn't have feelings. That one made Sage hug the vampire who'd said it, though the woman's grip had grown a little tighter than comfortable when they were close. She'd let go and hurried off, leaving Sage to remark to the camera about how deeply sensitive the vampires really were.

She already had another four interviews scheduled for the next day, and those vampires had come to her after watching from the sidelines today. The high of being appreciated and noticed had started to fade by the time she made it to her room, and it wasn't long before she was soaking in a hot bath, replaying the day's events.

She'd seen Remy a few more times, but she was always surrounded by people wanting her attention. There'd been a few heated conversations, which Remy had seemed to throw water on, and Sage had noticed more than one woman whose touch had lingered or who had stayed in Remy's personal space a fraction longer than others. And although Remy was always polite, she never seemed to take them up on their overt offers.

Sage ran her fingers over her clit and thought of Remy's muscular arms, the way her strangely pale eyes never left the person talking to her, as though she wanted to make certain they knew she was hearing them. She thought of the smell of her cologne, something woodsy and dark, and her clit jumped under her fingertips. It had been way too long since she'd been with someone. She had plenty of offers, for sure. Loads came in through her DMs, with pleas for a date, for sex, for romance, for adoration. She hooked up with a couple, here and there. Cute young butches who liked what she had to offer online. But Sage wasn't interested in more than a night or two. She had plans, and that didn't include someone needing more time than she had to invest in a relationship.

But damn. What would a night or two with a woman like Remy be like? She circled her clit a little harder. Would she be rough? A throw you down on the bed and take you like a top kind of butch? Or would she be a gentlebutch, all about laying you down and undressing you slowly? Sage moaned as her clit grew harder. She liked both versions, but the rougher one did it for her tonight. She cried out as she came, the feel of Remy's hands almost tangible on her breasts.

She shivered as the cooling water slid over her thighs. Not exactly a warm cuddle after a good orgasm, that was definite. She got out and wrapped herself in a huge, thick towel. At least this hotel was top of the line. As much as she wanted to try out the spa, she couldn't get Rac's warning about not being naked with a vampire out of her head.

She flopped onto the bed, shook out her damp hair, and flipped on the live video after she'd moved around enough to make sure the lighting was right. "Hey, sweet fam. I am so wiped out. What a huge day!" She watched as the hearts and hellos began pouring in. "I know I only checked in a couple times, but when you see the people I chatted with, you're totally going to understand!" She saw plenty of names she recognized as they floated past with endearments. "Aww, you guys are so sweet. And I know I've said it before, and I'm going to show you as soon as I get the vids edited, but vampires really are just like us. No different than the vegetarians, or vegans, or the folks who can't eat bread or sugar. It's just a dietary difference. In fact, I had lunch with them. Real food! Turns out, the whole thing about them only drinking blood is a myth started years and years ago by people swamped with fear. Nothing but a stereotype. Who knew?" She combed her fingers through her hair. "Remember, we're all about the love! Acceptance is good for the soul." She hid her yawn behind her hand. "Okay, another big day tomorrow. Love you all so much!"

She stopped the live feed and flipped onto her back. It took another hour and a half to respond to the various messages and comments on her videos of the day. There were several more vile comments to do with vampires not belonging among "good, decent people" and that they should never be allowed to flaunt who they are.

Sage never engaged with the trolls. They were only out for drama, and she wasn't about to feed into their negativity. Not to mention she hated conflict. It made her stomach hurt and anxiety flutter in her chest.

She crawled under the luxurious comforter and tucked a pillow between her knees. The thought occurred to her, for the briefest moment, that she was about to go to sleep with nearly a thousand predators in the rooms around her, but she shoved it away. That was prejudice talking, and she wouldn't give in to that kind of fear-based thinking.

***

She finished the last of her makeup and tilted her face this way and that in the light to make sure it was flawless. Her dreams had been full of women with long hair, sharp teeth, and sharper gazes. And there was Remy, arms crossed, watching as the women surrounded Sage. She'd wake up briefly only to fall straight back into the same dream.

She'd applied plenty of eye serum, and the notion that the women in her dreams weren't that different from many of the women in the conference made her squirm. Some of them were so beautiful. And they wouldn't get old and wrinkly. They wouldn't have to worry about getting stretch marks or a mom-bod. How could Sage possibly compete with that?

Not that she was competing, she admonished herself. There was no need to compete with other women. It was all about lifting each other up, even if the other women were vampires.

With a final check that her loose curls had fallen just right and that her lip gloss was glistening perfectly, she turned to go. When she opened the door, she nearly had a heart attack thanks to the person standing there about to knock. "Jesus!" Sage clasped her hand over her thumping heart.

"Well, we both rose from the dead, I guess. But nothing godly here." Remy leaned against the wall opposite Sage's door.

Sage looked her over and had to disagree. The black button-down shirt and baby blue tie looked hot paired with loose-fitting black jeans. If there was a lesbian vampire god, surely Remy was it. "Did you come to take me to breakfast?" Sage batted her lashes and pulled her shoulders back to push her boobs out just a little more.

Remy's gaze flicked to her cleavage and back up. "I came to see if you want to sit in on a political meeting."

"Oh." Sage gave a little pout. "That's not nearly as sweet."

"You'll find I don't do sweet." Remy motioned toward the elevator. "But we can stop for a cup of coffee and a pastry on our way if you're hungry."

Sage hooked her arm through Remy's and didn't pull away when Remy frowned. "You told me to stick with you."

"I didn't mean physically attach yourself like a limpet." She flexed her arm under Sage's hand. "But okay."

Sage thrilled a little at the small victory and at the way Remy's muscle felt against her arm. "So, is there a Mrs. Remy?"

"Subtle." Remy hit the elevator button. "I don't talk about my personal life, not that it's likely to stop you from asking about it."

Sage gave a little shrug. "I'm staying at Dark Haven so I'll find out anyway. If you won't answer that, will you tell me why some people call you Wind?"

Remy stiffened and gently pulled her arm away from Sage's grasp. "No. And please don't ask again. People who know, know. And that's where I'd like that to stay."

"So mysterious." Sage puffed out a bit of air. "Fine. I'll stick with talking to the vampires who are willing to discuss themselves. For now."

Remy shook her head, but there was a small smile on her lips. They went into the dining area, and Sage looked around for coffee. Remy nodded toward a bowl.

"Oh my god. Instant?" Sage poked at the container like it might become something better if she searched long enough. "Everything else has been so good. Why would you have instant coffee?"

"Just so you know, they drink instant coffee in most of the rest of the world on a regular basis. But we can go to the hotel café for the real stuff."

"Okay, but answer my question?" She put two different types of little Danish pastries on a plate and followed Remy to the hotel's café, where the smell of brewed coffee made her want to happy dance. Still, the café was nearly empty.

"Honestly?" Remy shoved her hands in her pockets. "We don't tend to drink it. Something about caffeine messes with our systems, sends us into a kind of hyperdrive. Young vampires on the club scene might use it for fun, and vampires on the day shift who need a harsh pick-me-up, but it's essentially a kind of drug. Even the decaf version has effects, minimal though they are."

Sage ordered and pondered that. "I wish it had that effect on me. I can have a cup right before bed and sleep like a baby."

"Did you get the interviews you wanted yesterday?" Remy perched on the edge of a table.

"I did! Thanks for asking. We had so much fun talking about favorite places and things to do. We even liked some of the same movies."

Remy took out her phone and glanced at it. "Good. Glad to hear it."

Sage bit her lip and looked around when Remy continued to pay attention to her phone instead of her. A woman was sitting at a table near the door, staring at them intently. Sage gave a polite smile, and in return, the woman bared her fangs slightly, her eyes narrowed.

"Yikes," Sage murmured, turning her back to the woman.

"What is it?" Remy looked up.

"That woman at the table just growled at me, I think. Do vampires growl?"

Remy frowned. "You mean she showed her fangs?" she whispered.

Sage nodded and was surprised when Remy turned around and faced the woman, not discreetly but clearly. The woman didn't bare her fangs at Remy, but her expression wasn't a whole lot of friendly either.

"Excuse me." Remy moved around the table to the woman. She leaned down and said something Sage couldn't hear, and this time, the woman did bare her fangs. Remy put her hand on the woman's shoulder and the woman flinched, her gaze not leaving Remy's face as Remy continued to talk to her.

Remy let go and stepped back, and the woman grabbed her bag and hurried out of the café but not before throwing Sage a look that could have melted stone.

Remy came back over. "Your coffee is ready."

Sage looked at the counter and quickly grabbed the latte and then added four packets of sugar before returning to Remy. "What was that all about?"

"Politics. Don't worry about it."

"I'm pretty sure I wouldn't want to meet her in an empty hallway." Sage sipped her latte. "Is she an ex? I imagine that's how an ex would look at competition."

Remy looked incredulous. "You think an ex of mine would find a human competition?"

Well, that stung in an unexpected way. "The heart is the heart. Jealousy is often irrational."

"Sure." Remy pulled open a door to one of the conference rooms, which was already full of people talking in small clusters.

It put an end to their conversation, and she had to admit she was glad. Any more talk about how she was in no way a suitable option for a hot vampire and she'd crawl back to her room in humiliation. Still, the situation had unsettled her. And apparently, baring your fangs wasn't polite behavior. Good to know.

"All right, everyone. Let's get started." Remy went to the front while Sage took a seat next to Lars.

"I'm going to hand over to Shelly today, and she'll run the meeting. You all know how much I hate this kind of thing." There was a titter of laugher and agreement. "But this meeting is important, and I want you to say what you have on your mind, even if you think the others won't agree with you—even if you think I won't agree with you, though we all know I'm always right." Remy grinned and tilted her head to acknowledge the disagreement with her statement.

She nodded at a woman waiting to the side, who stepped up to the mic. Remy took a seat on the other side of Sage.

The meeting was just as boring as the other one had been, and they were still talking about the roads and plants. Sage considered taking out her nail file so she could be doing something of use, but then the tone of the meeting changed, and she refocused.

"I know what we said about change being part of life. And I know how hard Remy and others worked to get us out into the open." The person speaking, a man with an honest-to-god mullet, looked around the room. "But I'm tired of seeing vampire stuff on the news all the time. Did you see the piece the other night about the teenager attacked outside a grocery store? The kid had gone in for something for his mom, and when he came out, a group of vores came at him with knives. Nothing long enough to get his heart, thankfully." The speaker motioned as though to take in the whole room. "That could be any of us, at any time. I don't think we're safer now that we're out in the open. I think we're turkeys waiting in a field for Thanksgiving and pretending the farmer is a vegetarian."

"What does vore mean?" Sage whispered to Remy, who just shook her head as she focused on the conversation.

"I think there are quite a few of us who agree with you, Bobby." Shelly looked at Remy. "And if I'm not mistaken, Remy has already written an article about this issue."

Remy stood, and although she looked relaxed enough, Sage could feel the tension coming off her.

"I wrote that article six months ago. And you're right, Bobby. We still have to be vigilant. I'm heading out to see that kid and his mom tomorrow." She hesitated. "Bobby, the thing we have to remember is that people get hurt all the time. Humans get mugged and stabbed in the street and always have. People with different skin colors to the ones they live around have been beaten, enslaved, and killed. We're no different, and just like everyone else, we have to ride out the tough times in order to get to the days where we're truly equal."

"But we could fight back, Remy." Another person in the room stood up. "Those other people were powerless to defend themselves. We don't have to be. That kid could have broken their necks and left them for dead, and it would have been self-defense. Why wasn't he allowed to defend himself?"

There was a murmur of agreement, and Sage started to stand, desperately wanting to weigh in. Lars put his hand on her leg and kept her in place.

Remy met people's gazes as she looked around the room for a moment. "Truthfully? Maybe he should have. But what then? He breaks the necks of four humans who have knives, and he makes it look easy. The cameras see it, and what's the spin in the news? Even a teenager is a killer, and the four men were right to attack him and try to keep him from hurting more humans. This is what happens when vampires are threatened; they're violent and deadly. They should be forced underground again, or worse, eradicated." She held up her hand at the angry muttering. "You and I know that's stupid, and ignorant, and wrong. We also know it's exactly what we've been battling for century upon century, and one misstep will send us straight back to that. Back to living in cities where we can't get to know people. Back to living in rural areas where the neighbors won't notice that you tend to stay out of the sun. Back to sleeping in caves and coffins instead of double beds in high-rise apartments and getting your blood from the local grocery store. Back to being hungry, being the local monster, being...alone."

There was silence as people digested that, and Sage could sense the tension brewing.

"But it's by bringing up these fears and questions that we can keep looking for answers and keep understanding what we're up against," Remy said. "Don't stop talking, to each other and to the people in charge. We're going to have dark times, but we can get through them, I promise."

She sat down, and Shelly picked up the next item on the agenda. But the tone had changed, and people were no longer invested. It wasn't long before Shelly sent Remy a look, and Remy just shook her head.

"Okay. Let's close the meeting, and remember to get in touch if you have further concerns or questions."

People filed out of the room having quiet conversations, but no one stopped to talk to Remy this time.

Lars took Remy's hand in his. "You okay?"

Remy took her hand back and gave him a quick smile. "Always.

I have a meeting with the Darwin clan. Watch after Sage?"

"I'm perfectly capable of taking care of myself, Remy. I don't need a babysitter." Sage crossed her arms and tried not to think of how scared she'd been the day before or how weird the incident in the café had been.

"Let's agree to disagree." Remy looked at her watch. "See you later."

Lars put his arm around Sage's shoulders and steered her toward the door. "Tell me, what did you want to stand up and say in a room full of frustrated vampires?"

Sage felt the heat rise to her face but pushed forward anyway. "I was going to say that not all humans are bad. That many of us are on your side and believe that humans who treat vampires badly should be held accountable, and if anyone wanted to come on my platform and say that, they'd be welcome."

Lars was silent for a moment as they passed groups of chatting vampires in the hallway. "That's very sweet, Sage. But, honey, you're not in Kansas anymore. They don't want to hear from the enemy. They want to hear from their leaders how they're going to fix things."

Sage shrugged off his arm. "But don't you see? I want to explain that I'm not the enemy. I want them to know we aren't all bad guys."

He stopped, his expression quizzical. "And you think by saying that plenty of humans aren't bad, vampires should then stop disliking humans as a whole?"

"Well, yeah." Sage had a feeling that wasn't the right answer, that there was something she was missing, but she had no idea what it was. "You can't lump us all together. That isn't fair. I wouldn't lump all vampires together."

He shook his head and waved toward the café. "And yet you talk about how great we all are and how you want to humanize us." He held up his hand when she started to protest. "Let's not go down this dark and bumpy road, darling. Let's have a sandwich and talk about where you got those fabulous boots."

Ordinarily Sage would be more than happy to talk about her boots, but the sense that she was being shut down as someone without the brain power to understand what was going on around her was so frustrating, she wanted to break something. Instead, she'd just have to show them. She'd get the interview videos done and get them out into the world. The resulting love from her followers would prove her point.

As she ordered her food, she couldn't help but feel like maybe she was finally out of her depth.

Chapter Four

Remy threw back the covers and moved silently out of bed. The woman still sleeping didn't stir, and Remy was glad. She poured herself a glass of high-end synth and stepped onto the balcony before closing the sliding door behind her. The cool air caressed her skin as she leaned on the railing in just her boxers and tank top.

The moon was full and she tilted her face toward it, letting the soft glow infuse her with strength. She'd needed a release after the fraught meeting, and a pretty city vampire here just for the conference had made it clear she'd be happy to be temporary company. The sex had been quick and hard, no romance or pretense necessary. Hell, Remy didn't even know her name, not that it mattered. She'd probably see her again at some point, at this conference or another, but the good thing about vampires was that they tended to live long enough that they understood monogamy was a silly idea meant for those who only lasted seven or eight decades.

She sipped her drink. Still, it might be nice to have someone to talk to. Someone to call and talk about her day with. Someone who was hoping she'd come home soon. She hadn't had that in a very, very long time.

The door slid open behind her, and she looked over her shoulder. The woman was stark naked, her arm resting over her head against the door. Her skin turned to pale marble in the moonlight, her breasts high and full. Remy swallowed the rest of her drink and went back inside.

When she woke next, she was alone. No note, no phone number. She smiled and stretched. Perfect. The second bout of sex had been less rushed than the first, and Remy could still feel the scratch marks on her back, which would be a good reminder when her day inevitably got complicated. She showered and dressed and headed to the conference room. Lars was already at a table with a hot cup of synth in a china mug. Few other people were down yet.

"Morning." Remy sat down opposite him and yawned.

"It is that." He eyed her and gave her a little grin. "Someone had an interesting night. You have fang marks on your collarbone, you know."

Remy winced. "Damn. I didn't notice." She buttoned up the rest of her shirt. "I'm leaving anyway. I'm going to see that kid and his family today, then I'm heading back to Dark Haven. Are you coming home or going into the city?"

He gave an elegant shrug. "I'll play it by fang, but I think I'll enjoy my apartment in the city. I feel like letting loose at Sang for a few days."

She blanched. Sang, a club exclusively for vampires and humans who had an obsession with serving them, had a reputation as a place for the macabre and vulgar. "Better you than me. That place still gives me the creeps."

"That's because you've never been the kind of vampire who likes that we're higher on the evolutionary tree." He took a sip of his synth and looked at her over the rim.

"It disturbs me that you think that's true, but I don't have time to argue evolution with you. Keep an eye on Sage for me, will you?" She stood and stretched and saw the woman she'd been in bed with a few hours before come in. She smiled and got one in return, and that was it.

"Of course, I'll keep an eye on our little oblivious butterfly of beauty. It's a good thing the conference is nearly over though."

She frowned and stopped her move toward the door. "Why is that?"

He looked around and then leaned forward. "The garden has

weeds, my love. Sage is but a molecule in the cosmos of crankiness surrounding us. There are rumors of someone new, someone interested in vampire evolution. I couldn't get a name, but I'll keep listening."

Remy sighed and shook her head. "Great. Maybe don't stay in the city too long?"

He nodded and waved her off. "Good journey."

It took Remy another fifteen minutes to get out of the hotel and to her truck, thanks to several conference attendees wanting a word with her about the schools in Bluff County being subpar and the need to bring in more vampire teachers. She promised she'd talk to the mayor about it and placed it on her mental checklist. Schools hadn't been an issue when they'd first segregated this part of the States as vampire territory because there weren't any kids. But then families started showing up, where at least one parent was a vampire or their child had become one, and they wanted a safe place to live. Where it used to be that you almost never came across a vampire with kids, now there were families all over the place.

And maybe if kids like the one she was about to go see had lived in Bluff City, they wouldn't be undergoing the trauma they were.

It took an hour before she crossed the city line and another half hour to get to the address she was looking for close to the state border. It was a run-down neighborhood, and kids were kicking a ball around on the street. When she pulled up in front of the house, they gathered across the road and stared. As she headed up the path, one of them called out, "Hey, are you a blood boiler too?"

She turned and faced them. With her arms crossed, she looked them over. It was a bully brigade. One main bully doing the leading, the other bullies behind him. They traveled in vicious little packs and always had. Nothing new there. She walked down the drive, aware that one of them had his phone out and was filming. "Now, why would you call someone names like that?"

"Well, are you? 'Cause if you are, then there are way worse names we can call you." The bully backed up a step, despite his bravado.

"Has it occurred to you that vampires are stronger, faster, and smarter than you? And that the only reason they don't attack is because they're also kinder?" She leaned forward slightly. "Personally, I wouldn't piss off someone who could take you out if you pushed them too far." She straightened again. "But it isn't like you hear about vampires hurting people or calling you names in front of your house, is it? Nope. That's you guys. Not them. Think about that. Which one is the monster?"

She left them standing there. It didn't matter that the video would go on the internet. What she'd said was true, and she wouldn't back down from that. If the message got through to even one human, it would be worth it.

She knocked on the door, and it was opened as though they'd been waiting for her.

"Sorry. Got sidetracked." She held out her hand. "Remy Winslow."

The woman closed the door behind her. "Selma Artillo. Thank you for coming. It's truly an honor to meet you. We've watched all your interviews on TV."

Remy followed her into the living room, where a young man lay on the couch, bandages around his mid-section and one on his shoulder. He struggled to sit up, but Remy waved him off. "Hey, stay down. No worries." She sat opposite him and declined the offer of a drink. They probably didn't have a lot to spare here.

"Why'd you come?" he asked.

"Jimmy!" Selma's tone was sharp.

"It's okay. Nice to meet you, Jimmy." Remy held out her hand, and he shook it. "I'm here because what happened to you is wrong, and I wanted to see how you and your mom are doing. Is there anything I can do to help?"

He looked at his mom and then at Remy. "You can get us the

hell away from the humans."

"Watch your mouth." Selma sat down next to him and caressed his hair gently. "I told you, we can't move. I have a job and moving is expensive. We can't just up and leave."

"Would you want to?" Remy asked, making sure the question was to both of them. "Jimmy, do you have friends here? Selma, do you like your job?"

They were both silent for a moment, and then Jimmy shook his head. "I've got a couple friends, but we're not super tight. School can be tough. Shit written on my locker and ketchup dumped on my desk. That kind of stuff." He shifted and motioned to his bandages. "If I'd been human, this would've killed me. The docs say that I'm not healing the way I should because the synth we're getting isn't quality. They gave me a supply of better stuff to get me through the healing."

"But if we lived among other vampires then I wouldn't worry about my child being stabbed on the street." Selma held his hand and wiped at his brow.

"Can I ask about your origin?" Remy asked. "I know it's intrusive, but I have my reasons."

"Jimmy's father went out with friends one night in a bad part of the city. They were mixing alcohol and drugs, and they got in an argument with a group of vampires also on a wild night out. When he came home, he was out of his mind. Screaming strange things and breaking whatever he touched. I realized what was happening, but we weren't fast enough. He bit me and would have killed me if Jimmy hadn't managed to pull him off me, but then he turned on Jimmy too. By that time, he was coming to his senses. He ran from the house, and we haven't seen him since."

Remy closed her eyes briefly. Turned without consent. If they found Jimmy's father, he'd be given a death sentence even though he was newly turned and didn't know what he was doing at the time. That kind of thing wasn't allowed any more. And if they found the vampire who'd turned him, the sentence would be the same.

"It's not a big deal. He was a bastard anyway." The waver in Jimmy's tone belied his words.

"I'm sorry that happened to you both. It shouldn't have." She looked at Selma. "Can I ask what you do for work?"

"I was a teacher, before I changed. But they fired me because they said they had to protect the children." She rolled her eyes. "Maybe it's true, I don't know. Now I'm cleaning offices downtown on the night shift."

Remy was always a little amazed at how the synchronicity of the universe worked sometimes. Occasionally it made her think there really might be some higher power out there. "It turns out we need vampire teachers in Bluff County. We're short-staffed and have more families moving in all the time. Not all the kids are vampires; some just have vampire parents, so there's a good mix and not a lot of the kind of shit you've just had to deal with." At the look of hope mother and son exchanged, Remy knew she was on the right track. "I can send some guys with a moving van to help you get loaded up and relocated. You'll just need to come down and do some house searching. We have a guest cottage at Dark Haven you can use while you search, and we'll get you working and back in school. How's that sound?"

"Fuck, yes!" Jimmy punched the air and then winced.

"Language!" Selma stood and pulled Remy into a hug. "I can't tell you what this means to us. Thank you so much."

Remy hugged her back. Two things in the world made life hell on a vampire. Isolation and hopelessness. This way, she was tackling both.

"Isn't Dark Haven some kind of weird cult thing though?" Jimmy asked. "No offense or whatever."

Remy laughed. "I'm sure a lot of people see it that way. But no, it's not a cult thing. It's a ranch spread over two hundred acres. We don't have internet or TV signals, and we're off-grid. We discourage the use of technology as a whole so we can continue to be present and part of the world around us. We live off the land as much as we can and keep mostly to ourselves. We supply our own water too, from the river that runs through the property and a reservoir right in the middle of the ranch."

"But you drive a car." Selma looked out the window. "And definitely not a hybrid."

Remy grinned. "True. We acknowledge that sometimes we have to do things in a more convenient way. Taking a horse and buggy all this way wouldn't be logical."

"What if you catch someone using their phone for ZimTak or something? Are they cast out?" Jimmy looked thoroughly enthralled.

"Nah. Everyone is entitled to live the way they want to, but there's no signal out there, so they'd be wasting their time. If they want to get their fill of modern life, they just leave the ranch and head to the city until they're ready to escape it again." She laughed when he looked a little disappointed. "See, no cult. Just a bit of the quiet life." She handed over the package she'd brought with her. "This is for you. It should help with healing and get you back on your feet in a day or two. If you know when you want to come to the ranch, we'll get everything in motion." She handed Selma a card. "And if you have any trouble, call this number. I've got friends in the area who can come help."

Once again Selma pulled her into a hug. "Thank you. We'll come down next week, if that's okay?" She looked at Jimmy. "I think we're ready to get out as soon as we can."

Remy nodded. "Whenever you're ready. Take care of yourselves, and I'll see you soon." She left the house and was glad there was no sign of the bully brigade. Hopefully she'd gotten through to at least one of them.

The moment she was out of the city, she could breathe again. The powerlines, car noise, music blaring, and general clamor of constant chatter made it so she couldn't think. The city felt like a tsunami of chaos that slammed through her brain, and she struggled to rise above the tide until it turned into just a buzz behind her. She drove down the tree-lined back roads and stopped when a small herd of deer crossed in front of her. Their ears twitched as they looked at the truck, sensing a predator nearby, and then they bounded off into the forest.

She never grew tired of the beauty of nature. It had saved her life on more than one occasion over the centuries when she'd felt so desperately alone she didn't want to go on. Immersing herself in the natural world had made her feel less like the monster she'd often believed she was.

When she pulled up to the gates at Dark Haven, the sense of home filled her and she relaxed. The firepit was going, and people were gathered outside. The moon was still mostly full and that always made for nights full of laughter and community. There were cheers and waves as she pulled up beside the main lodge.

Jet came over with a glass bottle full of her favorite synth and handed it over. "Welcome home, dark warrior. How went your travels? Or should I say travails?"

Remy snorted and took a long drink. "I miss the old way of language sometimes. Everything went fine. Anything I missed?" She strolled with Jet back to the fire and said hello to the others.

"Nice and quiet on the home front. The ones who went to the conference said there's a strange undercurrent though. What say you?" Jet asked, and the others turned to listen.

"I agree. There was something I couldn't put my finger on. There were the usual disagreements about whether we should have come out, how we're being treated, all that stuff. But no one said anything unusual to me." She thought about it. "Lars seemed to have some info to pass on though, once he gets back from his place in the city."

"If anyone is going to bathe in the oily gossip, it's Lars." The group laughed and the banter returned to normal.

Remy finished her drink and yawned. "I'm going to turn in. Remember that Sage Samara, the internet reporter, is going to be here tomorrow." There were grumbles, and the energy dipped. "I know. I agree. But you know how important outreach is to the changes we're going through, and I really hope you'll be nice. Or if not nice, then not in her way." She saw Jet grinning and subtly flipped her off as she ran her hand through her hair. "And remember, she's a guest. No biting or feeding on the pretty human." She made certain to make eye contact with everyone, and each person bowed their head in respectful agreement. "Okay. I'm gone. Night."

The main lodge was warm and cozy. Downstairs was open to everyone, and in the summer months they often congregated there, away from the direct sunlight. They shared meals prepared in the main kitchen too. It was a communal space that Remy loved having. She'd made the entire second floor her home. That way she didn't need to use the communal space if she didn't feel like company. It was spacious, and every room had windows that faced the forest. She undressed and slipped into loose sleep pants and a tank top, then sat in the egg chair hanging from a beam by the floor-to-ceiling window. She swung lightly, contemplating the last few days.

Sage. She'd be here for a full week, and Remy couldn't imagine how she'd get by without the phone that seemed permanently attached to her hand. Remy shuddered. She'd had a cell phone for a month before she wanted to chuck it into an active volcano. She hated being tethered to a virtual world. What mattered was the one she was actually in. She had a cell now but only used it when she was off the property, like at the conference. There were a number of contacts in the city who would come out to Dark Haven to give Remy a message, if it was necessary.

She let herself drift to sleep, images of Sage's flirty smile making her wish she could still dream.

Chapter Five

Sage groaned as the signal on her phone gave a final gasp. Thankfully she'd downloaded the map to get to Dark Haven. No being without directions this time, thank you very much. Huge trees on either side of the narrow, not-really-two-lane road created a kind of tree tunnel, and the sunlight blinked in and out so constantly, it made her dizzy. She'd filled up on coffee before leaving the hotel, and plenty of vampires had promised to give her a call the following week when she was back in the city so they could get drinks. Except for the slight weirdness here and there, she'd been back in her element, and her ZimTak numbers had gone viral. Nearly a million people had watched her interviews, and she'd had contact from corporate sponsors who wanted to place products in her videos or have her do little ads for them.

She shimmied a little in her seat, making the car drift over the line. Not that it mattered; she hadn't seen another car for at least ten miles. Glancing down, she pulled her lip gloss from the middle tray and heard a shout.

Her car had drifted into the other lane, and she was about to become intimately acquainted with a horse in her passenger seat. She yanked the wheel and pulled back into her lane at the last minute. The horse reared, and in the rearview, she saw the driver of the buggy jump off the wagon to calm it. Should she stop and apologize? See if they were okay? She shook her head and pressed the pedal down. She hadn't clipped them or anything, just given them all a little scare. And she was deep in vampire territory now. Lars had told her not to stop for any reason until she got to Dark Haven, and even though she was desperate to pee, she'd taken his advice to heart.

Only three miles later she pulled up at the Dark Haven gate. The sign directing humans to keep driving until they were out of Bluff County made her grimace. She lowered her window and shivered at the wind that gusted into the car. A press of the button brought on a husky voice that was more grunt that greeting.

"Hi. Sage Samara? I have a reservation."

"Be right there."

Sage waited, tapping her fingers a little harder with each minute that went by. There was a strange network of metal-covered walkways extending from the gate, which was wide enough for a car, and she assumed it went all the way to the ranch house, which she couldn't see from where she was. Finally, Remy strode toward her and swung open the gate so she could drive through. She waited until Remy had closed it behind her and then stuck her head out the window. "Where to, cowboy?"

Remy's expression didn't change. She had that same non-expression, not exactly a blank face, but...bland. "Drive up to the main lodge there. Park in front but leave your bags in the car."

Sage did as she was told, and Remy strode up shortly after Sage got out of the car.

"Bathroom first, please."

Remy motioned, and Sage quickly found what she was looking for, given the quirky little door carving of a bat sitting on a toilet.

When she came back out, she took the time to glance around. It looked like a ranch house should look. Lots of heavy wood furniture, blankets thrown over chairs, magazines on the table, and even a piano in one corner of the huge living room. Nothing in the least showy or vampiric, which was a bit of a letdown, really. She'd expected something more...gothic. Gargoyle statues and candles, or something. Remy leaned against the back of one of the big overstuffed sofas.

"Better?"

"There wasn't a single rest stop from the hotel to here. That's torture." Sage looked around. "Great place. Like something from the movies."

"Thanks." Remy pushed away from the couch. "Obviously this is the living room." She led the way into the rest of the house. "This is a communal kitchen. Every cottage has its own, but sometimes the people who live here like to come hang out together, especially in the summer months when it's particularly bright out for most of the day. We serve three meals a day for people who want to eat together."

"I wanted to ask about that." Sage leaned down to sniff something growing in a little pot in the kitchen. "There're a lot of questions about the reality of vampire life and the mythology. There are tons of articles out there, some saying they're dispelling myths, some saying those myths are the actual truth. It's hard to know what's real. One of those is about daylight. We've seen plenty of vampires out in the day, including you, but I noticed the multiple metal-covered walkways on my way in. So, what gives?"

Remy pointed. "The conservatory is open to everyone, but it's generally considered a quiet space. You can be around people but not around people." She opened another door. "Dining hall for big group dinners." She kept walking and opened another door. "Library. It gets a lot of use."

She sat down in one of the big leather chairs and Sage sat in the one opposite, though she couldn't stop looking around at the gazillion books on floor-to-ceiling shelves.

"The sunlight thing is complicated. Direct sunlight burns, no question. We stay in the shadows if we can, but we can handle short bursts. Say, in order to get from the house to the car. It won't kill us, but it will make us incredibly uncomfortable, and we'll have to heal from the burns, or in an extreme case, blisters. Being out in the daytime isn't an issue as long as we're not in direct sunlight. Hence, the covered walkways and multitude of awnings and such throughout the ranch. We are a little slower on the uptake with regard to energy though. A little more lethargic than we are after the sun goes down."

"So, no sunbathing in a bikini in Key West. Got it." Sage grinned and was glad to get a smile in return. "On a scale of one to ten, how much do people hate that I'm going to be here?"

"Twelve hundred." Remy shrugged a little sheepishly. "We like our privacy and as you saw on the sign outside, we prefer humans to drive on by. But it's only short term, and you've promised not to film anyone who doesn't want to be on camera."

Sage nodded. "Of course. Hundred percent."

"Remy!" someone shouted from the front of the house.

Remy frowned and headed that direction, and Sage followed.

"What the actual fuck, lady?" the person said when they spotted Sage coming in after Remy. Their fangs were visible, and there was a tint of rose to their eyes.

"Gabe, what's wrong?" Remy moved slightly in front of Sage.

"She nearly ran me off the fucking road! Scared the hell out of Pumpkin. It took me twenty minutes to get him to calm down enough to get us back." She looked around Remy. "What is wrong with you?"

Remy looked at Sage, her eyebrows raised in question.

Sage's stomach dropped. Not a good start. "I'm really, really sorry. I was reaching for something, and I hadn't seen anyone on the road for hours and hours, and I drifted..." She looked from Remy back to the woman named Gabe. "I'm really sorry. I figured if I stopped, it might only upset the horse more, and since I didn't hit you or anything..."

Gabe's jaw clenched. "I hope you pay more attention while you're here."

"She will." Remy gave Sage a stern look. "She won't be driving while she's here anyway."

Sage figured it was best not to argue in front of someone when she'd only just arrived, but that most certainly wouldn't be the case. "Again, I'm really sorry."

Gabe turned away without another word, and Remy shoved

her hands in her pockets. "Let's get you to your cottage."

She followed Remy out to the car. "You're not serious?" she asked when Remy slid into the driver's seat.

"You nearly killed one of my people on your way here. Let's not have you kill anyone while you're driving through the ranch." She held out her hand for the keys.

"Boring." Sage slapped her keys into Remy's palm. "At least this way I can look around while you're all safe and slow."

"Sure. Let's put it that way." Remy did, in fact, drive slowly through the property.

The slim covered walkways with slight overhangs on either side led from the cottages to a main covered walkway that led to the lodge, creating a kind of mandala effect. They passed a kind of parking lot with wagons sans horses. "What's with the no cars thing?"

"I'll tell you all about it over breakfast. Why don't you take tonight to get settled in?"

Sage tapped the clock on the dash. "It's eight o'clock. Are you all so ancient you go to bed before nine?"

Remy glanced at her, her expression unreadable. "How old do you think I am?"

Sage shrugged and noticed a pretty collie running after a ball someone was throwing. How ordinary. "I tried to google it, but there's hardly any history about you at all. Lots of people have theories, but no one has actually been able to trace you."

"Good to know." Remy pulled up in front of a pretty little cottage with a front porch that included rocking chairs.

"How adorbs!" Sage jumped out of the car and ran up the few steps. "It's like something out of a fairy tale."

White siding was offset by navy trim. Rose bushes lined the front, though they were at the end of their seasonal life and looked a little droopy. The rocking chairs looked handmade and huge trees were in the back.

Remy opened the door and waved her in. "It's one of our

smaller cottages, since it's just you. One bedroom, one bathroom, but spacious enough, I think."

Sage quickly glanced in all the rooms. The place smelled of pine and something else that was woodsy. It was sparkling clean, and the fire was already going in the fireplace. "I cannot believe I'm not showing my Zim family this." She took out her phone and moved through the house, starting to record.

"Okay, well, come over to the lodge in the morning for breakfast if you want, and I'll give you a rundown." Remy was already halfway out the door.

Sage turned the camera toward her. "How excited are you about having me here this week?"

Remy's eyebrow twitched but other than that, her expression didn't change. "So excited." She turned and left.

Sage sighed and turned off the video. She'd start again, because although the whole stoic butch thing was intensely hot, it definitely didn't film well. She started in the kitchen.

"Hey, fam!" She panned around the kitchen, keeping her face in the frame. "So here I am at Dark Haven, the mysterious vampire compound where no humans have ever been allowed before. I'm going to learn all about it this week, and I'll be sure to record lots for you. In the meantime, check out this gorgeous little place I'll be staying in." She continued the tour, exclaiming over little touches like the color-coordinated bedspread and curtains, and the basket of goodies on the kitchen counter.

"Okay, that's it for now. See you soon. Love you all!" She saved the video to drafts, then turned off the phone and set it aside. It already felt strange to be disconnected, but she could handle it. Getting her suitcase from the car and up the stairs was a little more effort than she was used to, and she had to wipe the sweat from her face after, but it felt good to do it on her own. In fact, it felt good to be doing all this on her own. She'd struck out for herself, leaving the comfort and safety of Canton to do something bold. She was killing it.

She unpacked and took a shower, and then curated the video so it was ready to post as soon as she had Wi-Fi again. She plugged her phone in and then looked around.

And the general sense of unease began to set in. No TV. No internet. No radio.

She lay on her back and stared at the ceiling. Okay. So it would be like a meditation retreat. People did that all the time. It would be fine.

For the first time she could remember, she curled up under the comforter before ten o'clock, a time she'd often just be getting ready to go out for the night. As she lay there, unable to sleep, she thought of Remy. Damn, she was sexy. She looked rock hard too. It had surprised Sage to see many rather ordinary-looking vampires at the conference. The general idea of them was that they were all super-hot, super cool, and had no physical flaws at all. But she'd seen plenty she wouldn't have given a second look on the street. Granted, no zits, but there were some who were overweight, some with wrinkles, and a couple even had gray hair. They must have been turned late in life. Of course, there were plenty of beautiful vampires who made Sage feel downright frumpy.

That brought her back to Remy. No wrinkles, definitely not overweight, and her hair was a thick, chestnut brown cut close on the sides and a little longer on top. Who had turned her? And when? The age thing had been deftly avoided, she suddenly realized. She'd have to pay more attention. She flipped over, and then flipped over again. Then she grabbed her phone and started looking through photos. At least it was something to do.

Eventually, she drifted to sleep.

She woke with her heart pounding, her hands shaking, and the feeling that she wanted to scream but she didn't know why. There was a sense, a feeling of something really, really bad about to happen. She pulled the comforter up to her chin and looked around. The fire had gone out a long time ago, and it was cold enough to see her breath. A long, unearthly howl outside sent shivers up her spine, and she pushed deeper into the bed. Then others joined it, and she whimpered. Wolves had been reintroduced to this part of the country not so long ago, and right now she was wishing it was otherwise.

She grabbed her phone, but there was no signal. No way to call for help, no one to know she was scared out of her mind. A shadow passed by her window so fast she wondered if she'd imagined it.

"This is how I die," she mumbled. "Just like every horror movie ever. Stupid girl thinks she's safe, and they find her body in the forest ten years later." Weirdly, it worked to make her laugh, in a slightly hysterical way.

Slowly, she wrapped the blanket around her and slid out of bed. Vampires. She was surrounded by vampires who didn't like humans so much that they lived in the middle of nowhere by themselves. Why on earth did she think this would be a good idea?

At the front window, she teased the curtain aside and peeked out. The very edge of a big open fire threw shadows across the main area. People moved around it, talking and laughing. She let the curtain go and sucked in a shaky breath. *Stupid.* They were night creatures. Of course they were up and around while she was sleeping. She must have been startled awake by them talking.

She went back to bed, continuing the positive self-talk. Even though it was completely logical, a niggle in the back of her mind wouldn't let it go. It had been *real* fear that had woken her. But maybe that was just her subconscious fight or flight, knowing she was surrounded by potential predators? That was probably it.

Still, she didn't sleep well for the rest of the night.

By morning her eyes felt gritty, and she thought about going back to sleep now that the vampires would probably, mostly, be going to bed. But she was only here for a week, and day one was already behind her. Needing to make the most of this, she stumbled out of bed and took an intensely hot shower to get the blood flowing. The thought made her wince. Maybe that wasn't a great idea. She shrugged off the negative thought and got dressed.

The morning sun was warm and the hint of frost was quickly burning off, turning to glinting water crystals instead. She inhaled, and the smell of cooking made her stomach rumble. She walked beside the covered walkway, glad to have the sunlight on her face.

A few people were headed into the lodge, and she smiled brightly and received a couple tentative smiles in return, which was a start. A woman with dark skin, long braids, and beautiful golden eyes held the door open for her.

"I love your skirt. What amazing patterns!" she said, looking at the colorful mosaic in the flowing material.

"Thank you. I got it in Jamaica a few years ago." The woman fluffed the skirt a little and then headed toward the drink table.

Sage looked around, uncertain what the protocol was. She'd been hoping for an invitation to sit with the woman, but no such luck.

"Well, hello there, intrepid adventurer. Welcome to Jumanji, where everything wants to kill you."

Sage's eyes widened, and she couldn't help but laugh. "Well, that's disturbingly funny." She held out her hand. "Sage Samara."

"Jet." She shook Sage's hand and then brought it to her lips and kissed her knuckles, her eyes never leaving Sage's face. "Welcome to our little piece of paradise."

"Christ on a crutch, Jet. At least let her have some coffee before you make her vomit." Remy came in with a kitchen towel slung over her shoulder and an honest-to-goodness apron with "Tell me my cooking isn't good. I dare you" printed on the front.

Jet let go of Sage's hand with a dramatic sigh. "That's Remy, always making sure we behave ourselves." She hooked Sage's arm through hers. "Come along. Remy is a terrible conversationalist and has the social graces of a gassy rhino, but she can cook like it's your last meal."

Speechless in the face of Jet's buoyant personality and rather dark humor, Sage gladly followed her to a long table with hot dishes full of eggs, sausages, bacon, biscuits, and gravy. There was also an urn with red splashes of liquid around it, and she quickly turned away to concentrate on piling her plate with the delicious-smelling food.

She sat at a table with Jet and quickly dug in. "Oh my god. Remy made all this?" The flavors danced on her tongue. "This is amazing," she mumbled around a mouthful.

Jet nodded and took a bite from her more modest portion. "It's good we can't get fat, that's for sure."

Remy came over with a mug of something and joined them. "Sleep okay?"

Sage hesitated.

"What? What happened?" Remy set her mug down and leaned forward.

"Nothing! I mean, I don't think. I woke up freaked out, like something bad was about to happen. But I think it was just people talking around the firepit. No big." She didn't miss the quick look shared between Remy and Jet. "Really, it's fine. Just being in a new place and overtired from the conference." She didn't mention the shadow she thought she saw by the window. She couldn't be sure, so it wasn't worth making a big deal over. "Anyway. Where'd you learn to cook like this?" she asked.

Remy picked up her mug and sat back, not looking convinced. "Under a chef in Paris. I spent a few years there, and she taught me what she knew."

Jet snorted and wiggled her eyebrows, earning a black look from Remy.

"Was the chef a vampire too?" Sage asked. "I imagine there are vampires in all walks of life. That certainly seemed to be the case at the conference, anyway. Although there were a lot of lawyers."

Remy looked around the room. "True. Right now we've got a banker, a painter, a woodworker, a chemist, and—"

"A candlestick maker." Jet grinned.

"And what do you do?" Sage asked. She liked Jet's fun, flirtatious personality, which was so at odds with the mostly serious vampires she'd been around at the conference. Including Remy.

"Nothing." Remy shook her head and took another sip from her mug, and it left a slightly red tinge on her upper lip. "She's a waste of space. She eats all my food and sits around the ranch all day acting like her breath doesn't stink."

Jet put her hand over her heart. "You wound me. Or you would, if I had a heart." She winked at Sage. "I'm waiting for someone to show me that I do."

Remy made a gagging sound.

"Seriously, I'm the ranch manager. I handle all the stuff Remy is too lazy or too busy saving the world to do." Jet stood and nodded at Remy's mug. "Top up?"

Remy handed over her mug. "I won't ever admit it to her, but this place wouldn't be the same if she wasn't here. She takes care of a hell of a lot more than she admits. In fact, she's the one responsible for you being here. She set it up because she's invested in the whole humans and vampires can get along thing."

Sage bit her lip. Somehow, the idea that it wasn't Remy who had organized this was a little deflating. That was silly though. It didn't matter whose idea it was. She was here now. She got out her phone, hit record, and propped it on the table between them.

"So, tell me about Dark Haven. What makes it so special?"

Remy took a deep breath. "It's our space away from the world. A place we can be ourselves, without any pretense or need to tiptoe around someone's fears. It's a place where people can have true, genuine silence. No buzzing of power lines, no car noise. It's a natural place of community, where we support each other and understand how hard life can be."

Sage frowned. "Because of discrimination?"

"Because life is awfully fucking long when it doesn't end." Jet sat down, looking serious. "Part of what makes human life precious is knowing it will end. Your time is finite. But when you never die, it can be like looking into a black hole of time and space, where you just fall in and in and in..."

Remy nodded, her expression softening. "And that's where community comes in. The fact that we can find each other a little easier now, that we can come together at places like this, and even at the *VCN* conference, helps a lot. It makes eternity a little easier to bear if you know you don't have to do it alone."

There was a heaviness in Sage's chest she hadn't felt before. "God. I never thought of it that way. Living forever, not worrying about disease or getting old, seeing new things all the time, that was what I've always thought. Probably what most of us think." She tapped the table next to the phone. "I hadn't considered that you'd feel like the only one, that you'd have to search out people like you. I can't imagine how Dracula felt, all alone in Pennsylvania. That's why this is so important. You're teaching us the truth."

Remy's expression didn't give anything away, but somehow Sage had a feeling she'd said something wrong.

"I think you mean Transylvania. Rather a long way from here."

Sage flushed. "Oh god. Of course. I knew that. Brain fart."

"This place is a retreat. We can come and go as we please, and the only rule is that we treat each other with respect." Jet grinned, lightly skimming past Sage's mistake. "And that we don't bring humans around."

"But why no internet? No grid overall?" Sage looked at her phone and noticed the lack of signal. "Why not have it and let people choose whether or not to use it?"

"They can choose to be here or not be here." Remy crossed her arms, and the T-shirt pulled tight over her biceps. "But I want this to be a refuge. If you don't have it, you can't use it, and you're forced to be here, with yourself. Read, go for walks. Ride a horse. Help with the ranch work, which is never-ending. But be present in this world, not a virtual one."

Sage bit her lip, unsure how to respond. She didn't find anything wrong with the virtual world, but it was hard to argue against being more present. But she felt totally present when she was telling everyone what she was doing as she was doing it too. It meant they were being present together, didn't it?

"Come on." Jet stood and held out her hand. "I'm your guide today. I'll show you around the main ranch and tell you all about Remy and her checkered past."

"Jet..." Remy's voice held a warning and the very tips of her fangs showed.

Jet held up her hands, one clasping Sage's "Down, boy. Kidding. Your secrets are always safe with me."

Sage followed her out and looked over her shoulder at Remy, who continued to watch them, her eyes narrowed thoughtfully. They stepped onto a covered pathway, and Sage forced herself to focus on the task at hand, instead of wishing it was Remy holding her hand to give this tour. "Show me around, Romeo."

Jet flashed a smile. "Onward, Juliet."

The hairs stood up on Sage's neck, and she looked around, that feeling of fear welling up again. But there was no one around, or at least no one watching her like they wanted to make sure she ceased to breathe. She gripped Jet's hand a little tighter and swallowed. She'd just have to stay in the sunlight, and never, ever be alone.

Chapter Six

THANKS TO TWO OTHER people helping, Remy finished the breakfast clean-up earlier than usual. It meant she could head across the ranch to the greenhouses to check on the autumn harvest. It was one of the parts of the ranch she loved the most. Watching things grow was infinitely better than watching them die.

As she strolled past the barns, she saw Jet, Gabe, and Sage by the horse corral, and Sage was gently petting Pumpkin's nose. The horse didn't seem to have nearly the misgivings the vampires around her did. She noticed Jet's hand on Sage's shoulder and a flare of irritation washed through her, which she quickly doused. Vampires had stopped claiming humans as their own the moment technology began to change the world. Word spread too quickly, and people were reported missing in a whole new way. It wasn't so much that they wanted to stop claiming them; they were incredibly useful for sustenance as well as companionship, though you had to be careful you didn't get too much of one and end up derailing the other. It happened though.

No. She had no claim on Sage, nor did she want one. But she knew humans like Sage, especially in today's world. They were so enamored of the myth come to life, of the mystery and glamour, that they fell in love, or what approximated it in this century, far too easily. Jet's attention could make Sage feel like she wanted to be her soulmate. But that wasn't going to happen. Jet might enjoy Sage for the week she was here, but she was too much like Remy in that way. She'd had her chance, and she didn't want another.

She opened the greenhouse door and breathed in the scent of life. The tomato vines were still looking healthy, though they were putting out a little less fruit. The melons had been harvested and cut back, so their little patch looked sad and empty. But the strawberries were in full, fruity blast and she picked up one of the small baskets they kept throughout the greenhouses so she could harvest some.

The door opened, and she looked over her shoulder. "Lester. Had a feeling I'd see you here."

He nodded and picked up his own little basket, then moved to the patch of zucchini next to her. "And I figured you'd be furthest from the noise."

She smiled and kept plucking the strawberries. "Isn't a whole lot of noise out there."

He shook a zucchini free of dirt. "You know what I mean."

"Anything I need to be worried about?" She sat back on her haunches and looked more closely at him. She only knew part of his story. It was rare they knew the whole picture when it came to anyone's history. But there was a stiffness to his shoulders today, a harder look that replaced his usual placid expression.

"Having a human here puts us all on edge. Some more than others." He glanced at her then continued his harvesting. "It brings back bad memories. I came here because it was a sanctuary, and I feel like it's been...tarnished."

Remy winced. "I'm sorry, Lester. I can see why you feel that way. I promise you, when she's gone, we'll never do this again."

He sighed and dusted off another, smaller zucchini. "I hope that's true, Wind. I don't know where I'll go if I can't have this as my home. I hear they're starting something similar up in Finland, but I don't like the cold."

She put her hand on his shoulder. "Please don't leave. This is a political move and nothing more while we try our best to make it so people know we aren't a threat and we can go about our daily lives in peace."

When he looked up, his eyes were full of ghosts. "There is no peace with them in this world, Wind. You know that." He stood, hooked the basket over his arm, and left the greenhouse.

Remy moved to a bench and leaned her head against the cold pane. She'd given in to Jet's reasoning and it still felt logical, but logic wasn't always the answer to a monumental problem driven mostly by emotion. She was working on bringing the two factions of the world together, and in the meantime, the home she'd built for her people could be torn apart.

So much for the serenity she'd been seeking in the greenhouse. She picked up the strawberries and took them back to the main lodge. Sage and Jet were nowhere to be seen, and that was for the best. Out of sight wasn't exactly out of mind, not when any vampire within a football field could smell the tang of Sage's blood, but at least the temptation wasn't visible. After dropping off the strawberries, she decided she needed some space, and she took the path past old Lester's cottage into the forest. As she walked, she let her fingertips slide over rough old tree trunks and the tops of ferns that were already dressed in autumn's sunset colors. Leaves crunched under her feet, and her soul began to settle.

Until she saw the scratches.

Nerves suddenly raw, she pressed her hand to the five gouges in the tree trunk nearest the riverside. They were deep and unmistakable. A vampire had come here in full rage. She moved slowly, looking at the other trees and finding even more. But when she saw there were differences, she knelt, unsteady on her feet. This wasn't one vampire in a rage. The claw marks varied between short and deep to long and shallow, clearly made with different-sized nails. Only a vampire in full turn would do this kind of damage. How many were there? By her count, at least four, possibly five. Vampires had no scent unless they were wearing one, and she didn't detect anything. Nothing on the ground, no footprints or dropped belongings, gave any hint either.

She went to the lake and sat on the stone seat one of the vampires had carved just for the space. They were dotted around the lake, sometimes single, sometimes in twos or threes. That vampire had long since moved on, wanting something less remote where his art stood out. Now, Remy stroked the cold stone under her fingers as she considered her next move. The ranch had a policy of live and let live, so to speak. They were close enough, but they didn't pry into one another's affairs. But she had to confront this somehow. If there were vampires going feral, she needed to know.

Especially with a human on the grounds. A human who'd been woken by the instinctive fear of being hunted, though she didn't consciously know that.

Remy leapt from the stone chair and ran back through the woods. If Sage died while she was here at the ranch, Remy would never forgive herself.

She ran to the barn first, but there was no one there. Feeling gazes on her as she flew past others who were working on the new buildings or in the gardens, she wondered which of those watching were the ones going feral. That would have to wait until she knew Sage was safe. The silos were empty, the horse corral didn't have anyone in it, and the entertainment area had a handful of vampires playing ping pong. Sunlight made her uncomfortable as she dodged people on the walkways and dipped into the warm rays, but it stopped the moment she was back in the shade.

She burst into the main lodge and looked around wildly. When she saw Sage and Jet at the table in what looked like an earnest conversation, she sagged against the couch. If her heart still beat, it would be hammering out of her chest.

"Damn, Remy." Jet looked up, concern clear in her expression. "What's wrong?"

Remy forced herself to move. "Sage needs to leave, and I need to talk to you. Now."

Sage frowned. "Hey, I don't know what's wrong, but I'm not leaving. I was told I could have the whole week, and I still have a ton of—"

"I don't care." Remy shoved her hands in her pockets. "You need to go."

Jet stood, her hands up. "Let's go talk—"

"No!" Remy motioned at Sage. "We can't leave her alone, and we need to get her out of here."

Jet grabbed Remy's arm and pulled her far enough away so Sage couldn't hear them. "What the hell is going on?"

"Ferals."

Jet's head went back like she'd been struck. "Where? How do you know?"

"Down at the river's edge. Claw marks all over the trees, and definitely by different vampires. Five, if I have to guess." Remy tilted her head toward Sage. "Make sense now?"

Jet sighed and ran her hand through her hair. "She can't leave now. It's too close to dark. We'll send her out first thing in the morning. You can follow her in the truck until she's past the county line."

Remy nodded, her stress easing in the face of Jet's simple plan. "Yeah. Okay." They went back to the table, and Remy sat down. "You need to leave in the morning, but you can't stay at your cottage. We'll bring your things here, and you can stay upstairs with me."

Sage crossed her arms, her expression defiant. "What's going on? If I'm in actual danger, I have a right to know."

Remy slammed her fist on the table, making Sage jump. "You don't have any rights here, Sage. I warned you, this isn't your world. When you signed up to do this, you agreed to do as we said. And we're saying you leave in the morning."

Sage looked at Jet. "But why?"

Jet took her hand. "There are things that we keep private, Sage. Things not meant for those outside our community." She held up her hand when Sage started to speak. "I know you're just trying to help. But we have our guidelines and rules, and they're not for public consumption, as much to keep us safe as it is to keep everyone else safe. You need to respect our boundaries."

The defiance went out of Sage's expression, and she sagged.

"I was so looking forward to this though." She looked at Remy with tears welling in her eyes. "I mean, you have forty vampires living on two hundred and fifty acres, and you're building more houses in order for more vampires to come live here. That's amazing. Solar power, your own water supply... It's amazing. I wanted to show people that."

Remy's throat worked but nothing came out. She'd said what she had to say and hated repeating herself.

"You got some great stuff while we walked around today, and I bet you can cut it and draw it out so it covers a whole week." Jet seemed truly sympathetic.

Sage gave a little shrug. "Sure."

"Let's get your stuff from your cottage. Come with?" Remy said to Jet.

Jet simply nodded. If they both acted as bodyguards then it was unlikely Sage would get attacked. Even in daylight they couldn't be sure a vampire who had gone feral wouldn't make a move.

Sage moved slowly through her cottage, dramatically sighing and saying how she'd miss this and that, even after only a night. Remy rolled her eyes and was going to urge her to hurry, but Jet stayed her with a hand on her arm. By the time Sage had repacked in the busted but still vaguely useable suitcase, Remy was ready to drive her out of town herself.

Instead, they went back to the main lodge, and Remy led the way up the stairs to her place. Jet headed off to do whatever it was she needed to do, leaving Remy and Sage on their own. As she unlocked the door, she tried to ignore the unease of having someone new in her private space. Jet came up here occasionally and once in a while, a vampire who was only there for a night or two might keep her company in bed, but other than that, it remained her refuge.

"Wow." Sage set her bag down and turned in a circle. "This is beautiful."

"Thank you. You can stay back here." Remy led the way, vaguely bothered when Sage touched a sculpture or piece of furniture along the way. She opened the door to the second bedroom. "I'll get some sheets for the bed."

Sage walked past her and looked around. "Everything is wood. There's so much wood. Jet's place is the same."

"We live off the land and make use of the forest in a sustainable way. Every place here has been built by us. I built most of the main lodge myself. The plumbing, the solar power hookups…we do it all ourselves." She didn't care that she sounded proud. She was.

"Wow. That's super impressive. I couldn't begin to understand how it works."

Remy didn't bother to respond. Most people in this century had little idea how anything worked unless they trained to fix something specific. Otherwise, it was a plug and a switch, and things just worked. She brought the sheets in and set them on the bed. "I'll make us lunch when you're ready."

"We're not going downstairs?" Sage asked as she fluffed a sheet in the air.

"No." Remy didn't need to explain further. Sage would be gone in the morning and then she could deal with the ferals without worrying about Sage's safety. She went to the kitchen, got out the makings for sandwiches and took a healthy swig of the synth she kept in the fridge. Calmed a little by it, she thought about how this place looked through Sage's eyes as she put the food together.

"I wish you'd explain. Just so I understand, that's all." Sage sat on a high stool at the kitchen bar.

"I'm sorry. I can't. I hope you've enjoyed your time, and I'm sure those interviews you've done will accomplish what you set out to do." She tried to be as kind as Jet in her delivery, but she couldn't quite manage the tone.

"It has to do with that feeling I woke up with last night, doesn't it? And with the way that woman at the conference looked at me." Sage's gaze was penetrating. "And what's a vore, by the way?"

"Yes, it has to do with the way you felt last night. No, it has nothing to do with the woman at the conference. And a vore..." She tilted her head and grinned a little. "It's vampire slang. Short for carnivore, or herbivore, or omnivore... You humans and all your weird labels around food. Someone started using it in the last century and it stuck. It's like..." She tore the lettuce into strips and laid it on the bread. "It's like calling an old person a geezer or someone from a poor neighborhood a thug."

"Except you're using it to indicate everyone but vampires." Sage sounded truly offended.

"Nah. We call the werewolves flea traps, and the elves are pole snobs because they're all skinny elitists." When Sage looked at her with wide eyes, she began to laugh. "I'm kidding. The elves died out years ago, and a werewolf would rip your eyes out if you called them names."

Sage frowned at her and spun her phone on the table. "Werewolves aren't real, are they? You're making fun of me."

Remy pushed the sandwich in front of her. "I'm teasing you; there's a difference."

Sage took a bite and stared at her thoughtfully as she chewed. "See? I don't know these things. And I'm really into paranormal culture." She ignored Remy's snort. "But the only way we're going to give real information to people, true information, is by doing what we've started here." She put her hand over Remy's. "Please don't make me go."

Remy closed her eyes, liking the feel of Sage's warm hand way too much. "It's for your own safety, Sage." She opened her eyes again and had to steel herself against Sage's look of disappointment. "If I could change that, I would."

Sage nodded. "Will you at least tell me why I'm suddenly unsafe?" She huffed when Remy shook her head. "Okay. So, what do I do in here for the rest of the day and night?"

"Well," Remy said, already regretting what she was about to say, "You could ask lots of questions and irritate me with your video stuff."

Sage perked up immediately. "Not a total win but I'll take the consolation prize."

Remy poured herself a glass of synth and put an orange slice in it. She didn't miss Sage's grimace, which was gone in an instant. She sat down with her sandwich. "All right. Shoot."

Sage hit record on her phone. "I'm not videoing this so you don't act like a nervous butterfly. We'll do sound only, and then I'll add photos and overlay graphics later."

Remy rolled her eyes and waited.

"Geez. With so much latitude, I don't know where to start." Sage took a bite of her sandwich. "Okay, Remy Winslow," she said, pushing the phone so it was directly between them. "You told me why this place is important. But you haven't really explained why *you* felt the need to start it. What brought you out here, in the middle of nowhere, in the first place?"

Yeah, this had definitely been a bad idea. She thought about her answer, and all the things she wouldn't say out loud. "I was tired, I guess. The world is fast, and I constantly felt like I was falling behind. I've seen every stage of technological evolution. From the first electric lightbulb in the eighteen hundreds to the first phone and first computer in the nineteen hundreds. Those were interesting and exciting, and it was fascinating to see how the world changed." She took a sip of her drink and saw Sage's gaze move to the phone instead. No matter how collected she pretended to be, there was still discomfort there. "But then, it exploded. Computers went from something that filled an entire room to something in people's homes. Cell phones were on the market, and suddenly you were never out of touch with anyone. In one hundred and fifty years, we went from beings who'd used fire, steam, and horses for most of human existence to plugging things in and never needing to *un*plug them. You never had any peace."

"You could turn it off though. Or leave it at home." Sage finished eating and pushed her plate away, but her gaze never left Remy's face.

"But no one wanted to. And if you did, you were seen as old-fashioned or out of touch." She grinned. "Plenty of other phrases you wouldn't be familiar with."

"Want to tell me how old you are now?" Sage grinned back.

"I don't." Remy picked up their plates and put them in the sink. "But I will tell you that I felt older by the day. And, god, the world got loud. You couldn't have a conversation without a phone ringing, or a TV blaring, or music so loud you could feel it against your heart, squeezing your soul from your body." She sighed and sat back down. "One day I was helping out at a homeless shelter, and someone handing out food stopped to chat on the phone, totally ignoring the people standing there waiting for the only food they'd get that day." She rolled the tension out of her shoulders. "That day I decided it was time to get some peace. Some silence."

Sage bit her bottom lip as she took that in, and Remy fought the urge to reach out and soothe the bruised flesh.

"Okay...I guess that makes sense, kind of. And that you decided against having internet and all. But you still have electricity from solar power, and that powers the well systems that bring in your water. So you haven't gone full Amish eco-warrior."

She'd clearly paid attention to the tour Jet had given her. Should she give her other reasons? Well, they wouldn't sound any stranger than an entire vampire community who lived off the land. "The other side of it is that I saw the effects of climate change beginning a very long time ago. I saw how mining and the creation of plastics would begin the breakdown, and then it sped up to a degree I hadn't even thought possible. So this ranch is meant to be self-sustaining when droughts and food shortages become more common."

"But you don't make synth here, do you?" Sage frowned. "You wouldn't survive out here without it, would you?"

"We're working on that, and we hope to one day have our own way to produce it using the systems we already have in place." Remy wasn't about to admit that they already had a lab at the far eastern edge of the property, and what they were coming up with wasn't all that bad, given they had to work certain hours to make use of the solar farm. She didn't need vampires knowing there was a synth lab out in the middle of nowhere, especially when things went bad.

"You said *when*." Sage looked at her expectantly and then like she was as smart as a dust bunny when she said, "You said *when* droughts and food shortages become more common. But we're nowhere near that, so aren't you a little premature?"

Remy shook her head. "You know, one of the things I don't understand about the world today is that so many people have a universe of information at their fingertips, but they use it to look at cat videos and to find out what the next fashion trend is." She went to the desk at the corner of the living room and came back with a file. "Since 2000, droughts have become longer, more severe, and more frequent. When there's a drought, the crops fail. And when the crops fail... Climate refugees are already in existence and have been for several years."

Sage bit her lip again. "I'll definitely look those facts up for my followers." She smiled. "Now, tell me why everyone looks up to you? They nearly bow when you walk by."

Remy blew out a breath, unsure how to respond.

There was a frantic knocking at the door and then it popped open. Lars and Jet came in, both looking upset, which was something, considering how vampires usually schooled their emotional reactions. But then, this was Dark Haven, and there was no need to hide.

"We've got a problem," Lars said, breathless. "I got back as fast as I could, but if there are any other Haven people not at the ranch, it may be too late—"

Remy stood. "What are you talking about?"

His eyes were wide. "There was a human-vampire fight in the city. About a hundred were involved, some killed and some turned. The government has called for a quarantine."

Remy sat back down. "What?"

Jet leaned against the door, looking paler than usual. "They're enacting martial law, Wind. All vampires must stay where they are, and the borders to the entire state have been closed. The military is at every point, ready to kill."

Remy rested her head in her hands. After all the work she'd done, after everything she'd tried to do to bring them together... They were gathered here, sitting ducks if the government decided to get rid of them all at once. Not to mention, on a much smaller scale, she had feral vampires and a human who couldn't leave the compound now. "Fuck. What have I done?"

CHAPTER SEVEN

SAGE BLINKED AT THE screen as she watched the news, which was changing so fast the banners at the bottom couldn't keep up. Remy had practically ordered Jet, Lars, and Sage into the truck, and she'd driven like hell to get into the city.

Lars had filled them in along the way, saying he'd been in the club when the lights had been switched on and the TVs had gone from sexy videos to the news. Within minutes the club had cleared out, vampires heading to safety as fast as they could. Lars had made it past the county border just as the military convoy was approaching. Not only had they closed the state borders, but they'd also positioned themselves at the various county lines as well.

They'd gone to the hotel where the *VCN* conference had been, and the parking lot was packed. Remy walked in first, and Sage saw the way the other vampires watched her, clearly hoping for guidance, for words of encouragement. But Remy stayed focused and when the desk clerk saw her, he immediately handed her a room key. She took it without a word, and they followed her to a large suite on the top floor.

If Sage had to describe Remy in that moment, words wouldn't be enough. She didn't swear. She didn't yell or even calmly ask questions. She was like a living statue: stiff, her expression blank, but radiating a power that suggested she could crush mountains if she wanted to. On the way there, Sage had sat in the squished back seat and gotten a few videos ready to load. She kept it on silent, figuring the last thing Remy would want was that kind of noise.

Now, she posted two interviews but decided to wait on the rest. As soon as she got Wi-Fi again, her phone began to ping with notifications. Remy threw her an irritated glance, and she put it on silent. Between reading the outpouring of messages saying they hoped she was safe and asking if she was back in the "real world" yet, she watched the news.

"In case you're just joining us," said the reporter, her hair blowing lightly in the wind, "it was at this stadium where a popular band was playing last night when a fight broke out. Initial reports said it was a simple skirmish between one human and one vampire. But it quickly became apparent that the two groups were there by previous arrangement and had planned the extreme altercation." The camera panned the front of the stadium, showing shattered glass that glittered like angry daggers spread over the sidewalks. Blood splatters created a gruesome picture.

"It's estimated that, at one point, nearly *a hundred* people were involved, and the hospital has reported that at least twenty humans were bit with the sole intention of turning them into vampires. All of them have been placed in solitary confinement until they can be controlled."

"Jesus," Jet whispered. "Remy—"

"Wait." Remy held up her hand, and her jaw clenched.

"Of the people involved in the chaos, only twelve humans have been arrested, and so far, no vampires have been caught or come forward. It is currently unclear how many of the dead are human or vampire, but given the abilities of the vampire, conjecture is that most, if not all, of the dead are human." The reporter came back on screen and looked into the camera, her expression deadly serious. "The president, when informed, said that although the new laws and changes had been made with the best of intentions, it was apparent we still have work to do. In order to keep the situation from escalating, he has decreed that all vampires will shelter in place—they're to stay at home or within their communities." She pressed her finger to her ear. "We're going to take you to Bluff

County, which has the largest vampire population in the US, where our reporter on the ground has just arrived at the militarized border."

Sage gasped when the picture changed.

Not only were there military trucks along the border, there was a tank. People in uniform, guns held at the ready, stood in a line across the road. The reporter in question was standing next to an official-looking military guy. "Are we to understand, general, that this border is closed? What if there are vampires who'd like to join the others in Bluff County?"

"All vampires are to shelter in place. They will not be allowed across the border, nor will anyone be allowed to leave." He spoke automatically, like the words were computer-generated.

"And what about the humans who live within or near the vampire communities or who may be visiting?"

A photo of Sage appeared on the screen, and she jumped up and squealed a little. "That's me!"

Lars nodded, looking tired. "It is, darling."

"It's just been confirmed that Sage Samara, internet influencer and noted vampire sympathizer, has posted two new interviews from her time inside the vampire conference, which suggests she's alive and well. But if she were to come to the border–"

"Ms. Samara knew what she was getting into when she decided to place herself within the Bluff County borders. Until the president gives the command, she will need to stay where she is. That goes for all humans living in or near vampire communities." Clearly, the general knew full well he was going to be asked about Sage and had an answer prepared.

Remy turned to her. "Sage, you need to do your thing. Show people you're okay and that you want to come home. I don't want it said you're a hostage or whatever fucking things they'll come up with."

Electrified by her part in this unfolding drama, Sage nodded, already thinking of how she'd word everything. "God, I'm so not camera ready. Is there a brush, or eyeliner, or anything here?"

The three of them simply looked at her, and she flushed.

"Yeah, okay. I'm going to go out on the balcony so I've got a better background."

Remy nodded, and they all turned back to the news.

Sage went outside and shivered a little in the cool air. She finger-combed her hair as best she could and pinched her cheeks a little to give them color. Actually, if she didn't look perfect, it would totally add to the vibe of what was going on.

She hit the Live button and smiled at the camera. "Hey, fam!" Instantly, her screen was flooded with people asking questions and saying how crazy everything was. "Guys, I know things are super surreal. I wanted to come on and let you know that I'm totally fine. I was at the vampire ranch and there's no internet there, so I haven't been able to check in. But as soon as we heard what was happening, we came rushing back to the hotel so I could let everyone know I'm fine, and that there's no reason to worry." She moved so her viewers could see Remy, Lars, and Jet in the other room in front of the TV. "I've had some time to get to know Remy Winslow, the vampire who helped get the laws passed so vampires were protected under the law." She shifted again so the camera only focused on her. "And to our president, I say: shame on you. You *just* passed this law, and now you're acting like the whole vampire community should be held accountable for a few vampires' actions. You're not holding all humans accountable for the actions of a few humans, are you? No. You're taking it out on the minority community, and that is so wrong."

She let her eyes grow glassy as she thought of the sad movie she'd seen a few weeks ago. It would play well on screen. "How can you say that we can live peacefully together when you instantly take such an extreme action?" She blinked and lightly brushed away the tears. "ZimTak family, if you believe in equality, if you believe that this is as unfair as it could possibly be, then I encourage you to start shouting about it. Tell the government that we're all just people. Tell them they're wrong and that we all deserve respect." She looked up to see the others moving toward the door. "Okay, I have to go. I probably won't have a connection again for a while, and since the news said I won't be allowed to cross the Bluff County border, I don't know when I'll be home again. Keep me in your thoughts, and remember—use your voices!"

She ended the live session and blew out a breath. That was certainly more intense than anything she'd ever done before. God, it felt good to be able to mobilize people. She glanced at her profile and gasped. *Four million followers.* She had a global audience. She laughed and twirled in a circle. When all this weird stuff was sorted out by the end of the week, she'd have the world at her feet. She'd be successful, and no one would ever tell her she was nothing ever again.

"Guess I'll get to stay at Dark Haven after all?" Sage grinned and raised her eyebrows, but deflated when they barely glanced at her.

"We'll figure that out later. I have some calls to make, and I'm probably going to need to be here for a while. Jet and Lars are heading back to Dark Haven, but I figure you'll want to stay where there's a connection to your world."

Your world. Why did that sting? She couldn't help but feel like she was viewed as an enemy. But she'd do her best anyway. She'd have time not only to load her interviews, but she could post them with plenty of messages to support the vampire cause too. "I didn't bring fresh clothes or anything."

"I'll take you shopping before we head back." Lars hooked his arm in hers. "Jet and Remy can sit here and stew. You and I will go get some pretty things."

Was that a grateful look Remy gave him? Did she actually want Sage out of the way? The notion burned, but she wouldn't show it. She tossed her hair. "Perfect. And then I can keep doing my part online."

Their response, which she'd thought would be enthusiastic and appreciative, fell flat. Remy and Jet went back into the room. Her shoulders fell. "Whatever."

The shopping trip with Lars was functional at best. Under ordinary circumstances, it probably would have been loads of fun. But the atmosphere was eerie. The parking lot of the mall was almost empty, and the few people working were busy watching the news on their phones. Sage picked out a couple different tops and underwear, but she too was constantly checking her phone as the notifications never stopped.

Lars was quiet, mostly speaking only when she asked him something. Finally, tired of her own company, she turned to him. "I know it's not good. But won't it be sorted out quickly? I mean, I'm really sorry all those people died, but they brought it on themselves by meeting up just to fight, didn't they?"

He sank onto a bench, his shoulders hunched. "If it were that simple, then yes, things would be sorted out quickly, my dear. But it isn't that simple. If we fight, we rarely lose. Turning humans is an offense punishable by death in our community. So we fought humans we knew weren't strong enough to win, and we turned some, knowing the penalty."

Sage sat beside him, considering that. "And if you found the vampires involved, and..." She swallowed, finding it hard to say the words out loud. "And they were killed, then wouldn't it show people that the vampires are trustworthy, that they can police their own?"

"It would be a start, yes. But fear is a motivator unlike any other. Fear hits the part of the brain that responds to survival, and rewiring that is nearly impossible. After something like this, people's fear of us, which was barely under control in the first place, will be extraordinary." He looked at the giant TV in the main hall, the news focused on the military zones. "Fear is what drives someone to call the military to corral anyone who is different. Fear is what gets bombs dropped on communities who have no escape."

The twisting pain of anxiety began in Sage's chest and radiated down her arms. She bent forward, her breathing getting harder and harder. Her vision narrowed and began to spin.

"Hey. Come on." Lars rubbed soothing circles on her back. "Breathe. Think of sunshine and your favorite beach. Think of the scent that always makes you happy."

Sea air. The beach where there were sunbeds already laid out for people. Cinnamon and apples at Christmas. Her breathing slowed, and her vision cleared. She sat back slowly and wiped at her eyes. "Thanks."

"Being in front of a camera is a big thing for someone who has panic attacks. You should be proud of yourself." He continued to rub her back almost like he'd forgotten he was doing it.

"Thank you. That means a lot. It was kind of a freedom by fire thing. I needed to get a handle on the anxiety, so I put myself in a situation where I had no choice." She stood and stretched, trying to release the tension flooding through her. "Should we go back?"

He nodded, and they headed toward the parking lot.

At the glass doors, a woman stepped in front of them. "Vore. You shouldn't be here." She bared her fangs, and her eyes were tinged pink.

Sage's chest tightened, and she gladly moved when Lars gently pushed her behind him. "She is here at Remy's invitation. She's a guest, and I don't imagine you'd want to face Remy if you insulted her guest any further."

"Remy is the one who got us into this mess!" The vampire's eyes went a deeper shade of red and spittle dropped from her fangs. "If we'd lived the way we always have then we wouldn't be trapped, waiting for the vores to take us out."

Lars crossed his arms and tilted his head. "Did she invite you to move here personally? Or did you decide to move here because you liked the idea of living out in the open? We are all responsible for our decisions, and if that includes moving into human society, then you should acknowledge that."

Slowly, the red turned pink and then back to white. Her fangs receded, and she ran her hand through her long auburn hair before looking at Lars again. "You're right. My apologies to Remy's guest." She glanced at Sage, who was peeking out from behind Lars. "I meant nothing by it."

Lars nodded. "We're all scared right now. Remy is at the *VCN* hotel if you want to go there and hear what she has to say."

The woman looked surprised at the calm invitation and then gave him a small smile. "Thank you." She turned and left through the doors she'd been blocking.

"Christ." Lars blew out a breath. "Let's go. I don't have the patience for any more of this nonsense."

Sage climbed into the truck and sat on her hands to keep them from shaking. "If you hadn't been there..."

He glanced at her but didn't respond. She didn't need him to. The woman would have killed her. For the first time, she felt truly afraid. She was in the largest community of vampires in America, and right now, they all hated humans. In a world of glowing embers, Sage could burn.

Chapter Eight

REMY AND DEZ STARED at one another on the Zoom call which the president had just left. Neither of them, it seemed, knew what to say. Even as Mayor, Dez hadn't had much sway.

Dez took a sip from her mug and cleared her throat. "Where do we stand? Let's lay it out."

Remy held up her hand. "One. He sees this as a political message without teeth, one meant to calm people down. Two. It doesn't make the vampires feel calm in any way, shape, or form, but he doesn't care about the fact that angry vampires are a bad idea. Three. He thinks it will go back to normal after this."

Dez leaned her head back on her office chair. "Four. If we force his hand, he'll need to react, so he wants us to stay in our place until this somehow blows over."

"And five. Synth deliveries will be allowed past the military checkpoints as long as everything remains calm. If it doesn't and he thinks military lives may be in danger, synth deliveries will be stopped. Which could then create a bigger problem, because then we'll have hungry vampires, which he doesn't seem to have taken into account." Remy rubbed at the knot in the back of her neck. "Why did he go through the whole thing in the first place if he didn't believe in it?"

"Political expediency. Doing something no other president before him has done, something utterly out of the ordinary. Now he's in, and he can use the brawl as a way to rein in that crazy liberal agenda." Dez sipped her drink again. "How are things there?"

"A powder keg with a lit fuse. I'd guess that eighty percent will stay calm, but the rest?" She shrugged. "There was some grumbling about us not being predators anymore right from the start. But we figured those were just growing pains. Lately, though..." She shook her head, thinking of the vampire who had wanted to rip a big hole in Sage's chest at the conference, and only because she was human. "I think there are vampires who regret the changes we've made."

Dez shrugged and narrowed her eyes. "Then they can go back to wherever they came from. They can go back into the shadows. We're not forcing them to be out in the open."

Remy nodded and glanced over her shoulder at Jet, who motioned with her head. "Okay, Dez. Sure you can't be here for this?"

Dez gave her a sad smile. "We've known each other for a long, long time. We both know better than to pretend anyone would listen to me when it's you they need to hear from. I may be the official face of our governmental body, but we all know who the real leader is."

"Fuck. I'm going to go back to Pennsylvania to be a real vampire." When Dez looked confused, Remy explained Sage's assertion about Dracula being lonely in Pennsylvania.

"Ha!" Dez shook her head. "And those are the people making decisions about our rights. You did good, by the way, having her go live and show she was not only fine but also fighting on our side."

"I don't know. If anything happens to her, shit will go sideways in a way we haven't seen since Henry was chopping off his wives' heads. They'll use it as a catalyst to take us out."

Dez turned serious. "Then you'd better make sure nothing happens to her."

They ended the call, and Remy rested her head on her arms. When had she become the fucking leader of the vampires' free world? She knew the answer, but it didn't make her feel any better. When she heard a shuffle behind her, she turned to see Jet leaning against the doorframe.

"That bad?"

"Nah." Remy stood, feeling as ancient as she was. "Way worse."

They headed to the largest conference room, which was standing room only. The moment the decree had gone through, there'd been a rush to get into Bluff County, and many vampires had managed to get across the border before the military's arrival. Remy leaned into Jet's firm hand on her shoulder for a bit of strength before she moved onto the stage. The room went silent.

"Thank you all for coming. I'm sure you had better things to do with your time, but this pyramid scheme will make you lots of money..." She grinned and received a few relieved smiles in return, and the tension dropped a little. "No? Very well." She pulled up a chair, too exhausted to stand for what was sure to be a long stay. "I'm not going to pretend that everything is okay." For a moment, she lost her train of thought when Sage and Lars quietly entered at the back of the room. God, Sage was beautiful. So innocent and positive. Traits she hadn't had herself in centuries. She forced herself to look away. "Everything isn't okay, and you have every right to be angry, to be frustrated, to be scared." She made eye contact with as many people as possible as she scanned the room, and few looked away. It was a good sign. "I don't mind telling you I feel all those things too. Maybe even a tad more, since I sat beside the president when he signed those documents protecting us." There was a murmur from the audience, and she held up her hand. "So don't think I don't understand. I do, and I'm doing my damnedest to fix things. I've already been on the phone with the president and our mayor here in Bluff County."

In the back of the room, she watched Sage raise her phone, clearly recording. *Fucking shitsticks*. Now she'd have to be careful how much information she imparted, because it couldn't be shared with the world. She had no intention of letting it be known how vulnerable they were. But she needed to be honest too. She looked at Lars and then tilted her head toward Sage. He gently lowered her arm and took the phone from her. Sage looked thoroughly put out, but Remy didn't care. There were no other phones being held up, no other cameras pointing her way. Vampires understood the necessity of privacy and secrecy without having to be told.

"First of all, the president has no intention whatsoever of this going any further. A week or so to make the humans feel like their safety was taken seriously, then the borders will reopen, and we'll go back to our lives." She'd started with the decent news because it was going to get worse. "Second, we need to abide by the decree in order to keep the situation from escalating. We play by the rules, and this goes away."

From the audience, someone shouted, "And if we don't?"

Remy looked around. "Then it will escalate. He didn't say what he meant by that, but I think we all have a pretty solid idea."

This time, the crowd began to speak loudly. There were shouted questions, angry statements, and several people were on their feet. Remy stayed seated and silent, and waited until they settled.

"That's what the president said. Now, here's what I have to say." She stared at the scratched stage floor for a second. "If you want to leave, if you have a place where you can go to be safe, then you're free to do so. We have a border on the water for a reason. Yes, there are some military boats out there, but we all know how useful they will be."

There were a few small chuckles. No one stood a chance against a vampire who wanted to move in the dark, especially across water. It was good to remind them they couldn't actually be held against their will.

"Many of you made the decision to come out into the open. Yes, myself and a few others stood up to make the world safer for us once it was acknowledged that we exist outside their mythology. But *you* chose to take a leap of faith and you decided to live in the light." She put her hand to her heart. "And your bravery is what has kept me going every day through the process. You trusted me, and I pray to whatever dark god created us that I won't let you down." She swallowed hard. "But if I'm going to be able to do everything

I can, then I can't be worried about a revolt either. We know how messy those have been in the past, and it sure as hell wouldn't look any better in this century."

"What do you need from us, Wind?" The man who'd stood up at the conference and said he felt like they were going against their nature now sounded like he was firmly in support of her. He was also wearing the deep purple armband of a clan leader. "You're right. We chose to be here, and we can choose to leave. How can we help?"

She blew out a long, relieved breath. It only took a moment to scan the room and see a few other purple armbands. An idea began to form. "First and foremost, I need everyone to stay as calm and as patient as you can. We have extra space at Dark Haven, and if anyone here has extra rooms or if you want a place to stay other than the hotel, please write down your name and contact details on the sheet in the back of the room." She smiled when Jet hurriedly pulled a sheet of paper from someone's notebook and slapped it down. "Second, I need you to wait this out with me as best you can. Talk to me, talk to Dez, talk to each other. If you still have a clan, talk to your clan leaders. We are not alone anymore. We're stronger as a community."

"And if we want to leave?" A woman from the back of the room had a child sitting next to her and a child on her lap. "Remy, I want my children to live out in the open, but more than that, I want them to live." She stroked the hair of the one on her lap. "If the situation becomes the worst it can be, if they decide to drop a bomb on us or come in and shoot us all down, I don't want my kids here."

Remy smiled in understanding. "If you want to leave, we'll make it happen. I'll work with the clan leaders, and we'll arrange a water relocation option. That goes for everyone here. If you want to go, then put your names on a separate sheet of paper." She nearly laughed when Jet threw up her hands and then grabbed another sheet of paper from the person's notebook. "And we'll let you know when we're ready to move on that front. Obviously, you're free to head out on your own through the woods *if* you have somewhere safe to go. But if you want the help of your community, then we're here."

"Wind." Someone at the side stood up to get her attention.

"Cadence." If Remy had been standing, she might have needed to sit down. "I wasn't aware you were back from Europe."

Cadence slid her long, wavy blond hair over her shoulder. "Lucky me, I got back the day before yesterday." She turned from speaking to Remy to speaking to the crowd. "Things are different in Europe. We're accepted as part of the community, and any humans who attack us are considered foolish and deserving of what they get. Whatever that might be." The coldness in her eyes left no doubt as to what that was. "Perhaps, Remy, we need to take a different tack. Show them that vampires aren't weakling humans to be pushed around or corralled like wild animals. Perhaps a show of force on our part is the only true way forward."

Damn her to hell and back again. "No, Cadence. Fear is infectious. Europe may be okay for the moment, but we all know what happens when humans are run by fear. It never ends well for us. Calm is the only way forward." She looked away, clearly dismissing her. "Okay, everyone. We have a basic plan. As things change, I'll keep you all posted. Clan leaders, if you could come chat with me, I'd really appreciate it." Remy stood, effectively ending the meeting. Everyone else began to move, and though the tension was still there, it wasn't as intense as it had been when she'd stepped into the room. If she could keep a lid on it, maybe it wouldn't blow them all to hell.

Speaking of hell. Remy gritted her teeth and didn't even pretend to smile when Cadence stepped in front of her.

"You're making a mistake." She twirled her hair around one of her fingers, like they were discussing the color of paint.

Remy leaned close to whisper in her ear. "If you ever suggest violence as the correct course of action in a group like this again, I will end you." She let a fang catch Cadence's earlobe, drawing blood and making her jerk. "Do you understand?"

Cadence gave an abrupt nod and stepped away. "Always good to see you, lover. Maybe you should think beyond your narrow little world view one day. Just a thought." She swept from the room, not speaking to anyone else along the way.

"Did you know she was back?" Remy asked Jet and Lars, who stepped up beside her.

"If I'd known, I'd have handed you the prettiest silver stake you'd ever seen and given you her address." Lars' narrowed eyes belied his lightly dark words.

"Likewise. Except I'd have made sure the stake was tipped in thorns." Jet shuddered. "She's the monster they think we are."

"Who is she? How do you know her? Does she really think vampires and humans should fight it out? Where is she from? I couldn't place her accent." Sage's cheeks were pink, flushed with excitement.

"Not now." Remy really looked at Sage and saw a beautiful human filled with young, strong blood. She was the epitome of what a vampire liked to hunt. "Jet, I need you to call Rac and ask her to come to the compound."

Jet flinched. "Is that really necessary? Surely we can handle this on our own, Rem."

Lars looked between them. "I'm missing something juicy if you're getting Rac involved."

Sage held up her hand. "You mean the innkeeper?"

Remy realized they hadn't had time to tell Lars about the ferals. "Claw marks. Five sets in the trees down by the riverside."

He blanched and leaned against a chair. "Oh."

"If everything else wasn't happening, then maybe we could handle it. But I don't have time, and I need you to keep an eye on Sage at all times."

Sage huffed and crossed her arms. "Wait a minute—"

"No. Not now, Sage." Remy sighed at Sage's hurt expression. "Please, just respect that there are things you don't understand and can't be involved with. I know you want to help, but right now, that means not giving me another thing to worry about."

Sage looked at the floor, her arms still crossed. "I'm not a *thing*," she mumbled, but that was the end of her argument.

"I'll call Rac." Jet pulled out the ranch's emergency cell phone. "When do you want her there?"

Remy looked outside. It was nearly dark. "In about an hour if she can."

Jet moved away to make the call.

"What can I do?" Lars touched Remy's shoulder. "I'm yours to command."

Remy smiled a little. "Can you stay here at the hotel and make trips to the ranch to let me know how things are going? I'd stay, but I think it would make people feel better if I looked like I was going about my normal business too. I need to be apprised of any new news and told if anyone wants to contact me. Like, say, the president to tell me they're sorry, but they're going to wipe us off the planet." She gave him a wry smile meant to take the sting out of the words.

"Why not just get an internet adaptor for the main lodge?" Sage said, looking between Remy and Lars. "I know you're all about not being connected, but it seems to me right now you need to be. Wi-Fi adaptors are really good compared to when you probably used them last. Plug one into your computer, and if there's a signal tower close enough, you'll be good to go. Then when all this is over, you can toss it into a volcano." She gave Remy a tremulous smile.

"It's a good idea, Rem." Lars gave Sage a little pat on the arm. "You don't need to provide it for the whole compound, just for your office. That way, you're in touch. I'll still play messenger boy." He grinned slightly and wiggled his eyebrows. "But you need to be available by email at the very least."

Remy groaned. "Fine. You're right, and you're no longer allowed to be alone together."

Sage smiled, and it lit up her pretty eyes. *For fuck's sake. Focus.*

"The key will be seeing if you can get one from Bluff County, since we won't be getting any deliveries for anything other than synth." Lars took Sage's arm. "We passed several tech stores while we were shopping. We'll come back with one before you leave for Dark Haven."

Remy had a brief moment to breathe before someone touched her arm. It was the clan leader who'd stood up.

"Wind." He bowed his head respectfully. "When you're ready, the clan leaders present would be happy to talk."

Remy looked past him to the five vampires who stood near the door. What she wouldn't give for an extra-large cold glass of real blood spiked with vodka right now. "Thank you. Let's talk."

Chapter Nine

Sage had so many questions and not nearly enough answers. Watching Remy sit in front of a room full of irate vampires and calm them down had been...magnificent. An old-fashioned word, maybe, but it fit. She was so collected, so sure of herself, and her kindness radiated from her as she assured people they weren't trapped and were free to leave.

On the way to the tech store though, Lars gave basic answers to her questions and seemed disinclined to talk for once, so she got online and researched the best option for them. She had an idea of the size of the ranch and knew where she picked up service, which meant she knew where one tower was vaguely located. When they entered the first shop, she explained what she wanted.

The guy at the counter shook his head. "I wish we had that kind of tech. What are you getting it for?"

"Dark Haven." Sage watched his eyes go wide.

He leaned forward. "For real? Bussin'. That place is a unicorn."

Sage nodded. "Right? I'm amped. Any idea where we can get what we need?"

He looked at Lars, who looked baffled, then back at Sage. With a shrug, he said, "If you can't help Remy Winslow, then you shouldn't be in Bluff." He pulled over a piece of paper and wrote down an address. "None of the other tech stores will have what you need. It's too advanced for this area, and Dark Haven is too big even for what you've asked for." He tapped the piece of paper. "But TimTam will totally hook you up."

Sage took out her phone and turned, and they took a selfie together. "You're the best. I'll let Remy know you helped us out."

His smile was so big it probably hurt. "That would be bussin'. Nothing like having people know you're on the right side."

They left and once they were in the car, Lars looked at her. "I live in the real world as well as at the ranch. I have a vague understanding of how technology works. But you walked in there like you were a gaming nerd on a quest. How did you know what to ask for?"

Sage waved her phone. "Remy said all people use the internet for is cats or something. But it's instant access to any information you want at any given moment. You just have to understand what it is you're searching for." She held up the slip of paper. "And it has a maps app."

They put in the address and were soon on the back roads of North Bluffington. They turned onto a long, winding driveway.

"Are all vampires rich?" Sage strained to look at the huge house at the end of the driveway.

"Not young ones. But if you live century after century, you tend to have a healthy appreciation of finance, and that money makes life far more livable."

"How old are you? Can I ask that?" she said.

He put his hand over his heart. "How rude. Only young people ask how old other people are." He fluttered his lashes at Sage. "I'm younger than Remy and Jet."

Sage sighed and opened the car door. "That's not an answer. It just raises more questions."

Lars pressed the doorbell. "And that keeps life interesting, darling."

A voice came out of the camera over the door. "Sage Samara? No way!" A moment later, the door was flung open. "This is cray! Come in, come in!"

Sage smiled at the young man who was so thin he might disappear if he turned sideways. His jeans and T-shirt were baggy, and he was barefoot. He also had eyes a lot like Remy's—a kind of icy bluish-white. She hadn't seen many of those and suddenly wondered if it indicated a certain type of vampire.

Lars also seemed taken aback. He simply frowned, his head tilted slightly.

"Drink? I mean, I know you don't want synth, but for your friend? Sorry! I'm Geno. My friends call me TimTam though." He looked between them, seeming a little bemused at their silence. "Sorry. Being totally extra, but I love your feed."

"Great to meet you, Geno. Sorry to just drop in on you like this." Sage glanced around. The house was an eclectic mess of trinkets, art, books, and computer parts.

"No worries at all." He led them into a living room. "I saw your last video. Wicked smart, showing them you're alive. Have you seen the fallout?"

She shook her head, and he waved them over to a computer on a glass table. "Check it." His fingers flew over the keys. "Viral, all the way. Even your backvids are viral. Vamps in every state as well as all over the world are reposting and adding their voices, just the way you told them to." He ran his hand over his shaggy hair. "You're slaying it."

Sage looked at the numbers and thousands upon thousands of comments on the various videos. Her heart raced as she tried to take it in. When Lars cleared his throat, she finally looked up. "Right. Your friend gave us your address. We need internet at Dark Haven until this blows over so Remy can—"

"Damn. Yes and yes." He practically ran from the room. "How many acres is the ranch, Sage?" he called from another room.

She looked at Lars. "Two hundred and fifty, I think?" When Lars nodded, she felt better. She'd been paying attention and was literally helping.

Geno hurried back in, his arms full of gear. "I can give you this to hook up yourself, or I can come out and do it for you." His expression didn't hide which one he'd prefer.

"I can plug and play, but I think that's beyond me." Sage eyed all the wires and boxes. "I thought all we'd need was a Stargazer

WISP."

He looked mildly impressed. "That would probably work okay, but they're super temperamental. Even fog can make them shut down." He hefted the gear in his arms. "This stuff is reliable."

Sage looked at Lars, who still seemed to be studying Geno like a science experiment.

"Yes, I think that's a good idea," Lars finally said. "But if you have your own transport, I suggest you follow us, as it may be some time before we come back from the ranch."

Geno set all his gear on the table and held up his finger. "I just need to gather some stuff. Can you hang for a second?"

Lars wiped at a chair and perched on the edge. "He needs a housekeeper."

"Maybe he has one, and they're just not very good. Or able to keep up." Sage lifted a discarded bra with cups of a size that made her back ache. "I'd guess the latter." After a few minutes, she turned to Lars. "I've only seen, like, two other vampires with eyes like that. Does eye color mean anything in the vampire world?"

"Sometimes. Very, very old vampires lose some of the pigmentation in their eyes when they live in the darkness for too long and it can lead to, well..." He waved toward the noise Geno was making elsewhere. "That's why you don't see them often. There aren't many vampires that old."

Sage gaped. "You mean to tell me that kid who looks my age and seems like someone I'd go to college with is the same age as Remy?"

"It would appear so." Lars crossed his arms and then his ankles. It was almost like he was making himself smaller. "And that we didn't know he was here is rather disturbing."

Before Sage could ask why that was, Geno shot back into the room. He put the things from the desk into a bulging duffle bag and then looked at them. "I've got an electric car in the garage, and it's all charged up, so I'll keep up with you no probs." He looked from Sage to Lars. "I don't suppose you want to ride with me, Sage? I'd love to talk ZimTak with you."

Lars shook his head firmly. "I'm afraid I'm in charge of her safety. No offense, but you know how it is."

Geno looked only a little disappointed. "Cool. Maybe you can come hang out some time." He hefted the bag over his shoulder. "I'm so jazzed I'm going to Dark Haven. I've wanted to, but I know Remy has a whole Amish Vampire vibe going, so I've never been. Didn't want to give her the ick, you know?"

He followed them out the front door and then headed off to the garage. They got in the car and waited, and he pulled out in a pearlescent Tesla Cybertruck.

Sage whistled softly. "That's custom. Two hundred and fifty thousand at least."

Lars shook his head. "I'm always one for extravagance but that seems outlandish, even to me."

Sage looked at the behemoth in the side mirror as it followed them. It caught the light, swirling colors and making it look almost like it was underwater. "I don't know. It's fully electric so it's environmentally friendly, and that kind of truck would probably survive an apocalypse. It looks like something you'd drive at the end of the world." She sat back, thinking. "It's probably the kind of thing Remy should have on the ranch for emergencies instead of that old beat-up thing she drives, which totally goes against her whole 'climate change is going to kill us so we should help out' thing."

For the first time in a while, Lars laughed. "That's true. I'm sure she's aware of the irony. But the truck holds a special place in her heart. I'm sure she'll tell you one day if you're a good little human."

Sage rolled her eyes. "Okay, so tell me about the woman who stood up at the hotel and challenged Remy. What's her deal?"

The smile left Lars' face like it hadn't ever been there. His eyes flashed slightly. "Her deal is destruction and chaos. She likes drama—"

Sage snorted a little, and he shook his head.

"No, not like you and I like a bit of drama. She likes the kind of drama that causes queens to have their heads removed from their bodies. The kind that means people die in droves and she laughs as the pyres burn."

His tone had turned somber, dark. There was something ancient in the way he spoke, and she shivered. "Not a dinner guest at Dark Haven then. Did she and Remy have a thing?"

He sighed. "That's not my story to tell. But if you come across her, Sage," he glanced at her, his expression deadly serious, "pray to your god that one of us is nearby. She hates humans with a passion I've never seen in anyone else."

"But wasn't she one at some point?" Sage bit at her lip. "It's something I've been wondering. Are all of you turned at some point? Or can vampires be born? Like that woman at the hotel today with her two kids. Were they vampires too? And if they are, will they ever grow up? Or will they stay that way forever, like the little girl in that super old vampire movie?"

Lars looked puzzled for a moment. "You mean *Interview with a Vampire*? For the love of petunias, honey, I have shirts older than that movie." He shook his head, looking distinctly put out. "Anyway, yes, those children were vampires, as was their mother. Once upon a time, vampires couldn't have children. As soon as we were turned, that was it. No more breeding, no more aging. But nature is a fickle beast. About a century ago, the *VCN* reported that there were a number of vampire pregnancies recorded by clans across the world."

Sage swallowed. "Evolution? You mean vampires are evolving?"

Lars tapped the steering wheel. "Seems to be, my lovely. And the children born vampires grow to a certain age and then stop aging, just as we do when we're turned. Most never age past about twenty-five. Maybe it will change one day as we continue to evolve." He shrugged. "That, my dear, is a highly kept secret and should never leave this car. If humans knew vampires could breed..." He gave out a long, low breath. "You think they hate us now?"

Sage put her hand over his, which was tapping more intensely on the wheel. "But they don't all hate you. Didn't you see what Geno was showing us? Millions of people are on our side."

His eyebrow twitched, and she flushed.

"I mean, on the side of the vampires." Although they probably didn't think it was true, she really *was* listening to what they were telling her. But she wouldn't stop helping either.

"Maybe so. I love your human optimism." He looked in the rearview mirror. "I think he wants us to pull over."

They moved to the side of the narrow road, but Geno's truck still took up a large portion of it. He jumped out of the truck with a box and cables in his hand. "There's a tower about half a mile that way." He motioned with the box. "I want to put this on it. We'll use it as a relay for the ranch. I'll be back in a minute." He loped off into the woods.

Sage blinked as he seemed to shimmer and then was gone. "Next question. Remy said that people could use their powers to help them get where they need to go. Do all vampires have special powers?"

Lars seemed to know what she was thinking anyway. "Yes, we all have powers. Some are more powerful than others."

"And can you—"

"Oh, look, he's back." Lars waved to him, as though he wouldn't see them waiting for him.

"Personal info is so out of bounds for you guys, isn't it?" she said, giving Geno a quick smile as he walked past her window, which she had cracked.

"Personal information is a way to give someone power over you," Geno called out as he was climbing into his truck. "And no one wants that."

Sage looked at Lars. "I take it super-hearing is a power?"

He nodded. "One of them. My personal super power is looking like I just walked off a catwalk no matter what time of day or night."

Lars flashed his headlights when they got to the ranch gate.

Remy came out to meet them, her gaze focused on the Tesla with black-tinted windows that pulled in behind them.

Lars jumped out and pulled her aside. Sage didn't hear what he told her, but she frowned and looked past him as Geno jumped from the truck, his duffle bag in hand. Remy stiffened and crossed her arms, her mouth set in a firm line.

Lars moved to Sage's side and pulled her further under the overhang.

Geno walked over, swinging the bag, a big grin on his face. "Remy Winslow, in the flesh."

Remy kept her arms crossed. "Valentino Shivante. You certainly haven't kept with custom. I had no idea you were in my own backyard, let alone still alive."

He dropped the bag and held open his skinny arms. "You can't possibly still be mad at me. That would be the longest grudge in history."

Remy dropped her arms and held out her hand. "You're a damn fool. Why didn't you come to Dark Haven?" She held him at arm's length. "You look ridiculous in modern clothes."

"And you look the same as you did when I met you. Every century you seem to just get more gorgeous." He squeezed her bicep. "But you're keeping even more gorgeous company these days."

Sage wondered if this was the same guy she'd just met. He had a soft accent, though she couldn't place it, and there was a light formality that definitely hadn't been there before. Even his body language seemed different, more...uptight, maybe. And unlike the other vampires, he seemed to have no deference to Remy at all.

Remy looked over her shoulder at Sage and Lars. "That I am. Come in and tell me why I sent these two looking for internet and they came back with the most irritating vampire on Earth."

Sage looked at Lars, who continued to look thoughtful, but there was less tension in his shoulders. At least that was something. For a minute, she'd been worried that they'd brought an enemy into camp. Was that a saying? She thought she'd heard it somewhere anyway.

"I'm going to go get Jet." Lars touched her shoulder gently. "You go on ahead."

Sage followed the sound of laughter into the dining room. Remy and Geno were already seated at the table with glasses of synth in front of them. Suddenly, she felt out of place. She turned to go upstairs. No need to force her presence on them.

"Sage."

Remy's voice stopped her and made her weak-kneed. What she wouldn't give to hear Remy say it while they were in bed together. She turned.

"Thank you. For the videos, for wanting to help, for bringing the exact right guy for the job." Remy's smile was sincere, and her gaze flickered over Sage for the briefest moment.

Not so brief it didn't make Sage want to crawl into Remy's lap. "No problem. Is it okay if I go upstairs? Or I can go back to the little cottage—"

"No." Remy's tone was sharp, and she winced. "Sorry. But I'm afraid you're stuck staying with me for a while. I hope that's okay."

Disturbed by Remy's abrupt assertion and equally glad to be told she'd be staying with her, she just pasted on a smile. "I'll manage." She headed upstairs wishing Remy had told her she could stay. What stories the two of them must have! They'd be so great on camera, but they were unlikely to give that side of themselves away.

Once she was in her room, she took out her phone, but there was no signal yet. *Yet.* Soon, there would be, and she could check in every day. Would that be okay with Remy though? She'd signed a contract saying she wouldn't post anything directly from Dark Haven. She bit her lip. But that was before, right? When things were normal and she was going home at the end of the week. She flipped onto her stomach and pulled up some of the photos she'd taken of Remy. Myth had it that vampires couldn't cast shadows, be photographed, or see themselves in mirrors. All of them were false, as far as she could tell. Lars certainly appreciated any mirror he walked past, and the photos of Remy were enough to make Sage sigh happily.

With nothing else to do, she set her phone down and picked up a book. At least she'd be able to rejoin everyone at dinnertime without it being weird. Part of her wondered if Remy was starting to enjoy her company. It mattered, more than maybe it should, that Remy respected her. Remy was clearly a really big deal, and if Sage could get her approval, it just might fill that bit of her that never felt like enough.

Chapter Ten

"I DON'T UNDERSTAND WHY you didn't let me know you were here," Remy said, leaning back and sipping her synth. "How long have you been in Bluffington?"

Geno stretched his long legs out in front of him. "Two years."

Remy blanched. "Geno—"

"These aren't the old days, Wind." His expression turned vampire neutral. "We move freely, thanks to you. There's no need to let another vampire know you're in their territory because we're always in each other's territory. I knew you were here, and I made the decision to stay out of your way. Let the universe bring us together when the time was right."

She set her glass down, his words not sitting right. There was a lie in the air. "We've known each other too long to play games, Valentino. What's going on?"

His eyes stayed on her, and she could see him thinking, debating. Although he kept it shuttered, she could feel the power pulsing deep within him. If he wasn't on their side, they'd just brought a wolf in with the sheep.

Finally, he sighed. "I've been doing my best to blend in. I look twenty-five, like your little human pet upstairs, and so I have to learn the era's jargon and act like other twenty-year-olds. I enjoy the act, for the most part, and when I tire of it, I go to other countries where that age is more mature. I was back in Romania when I caught you on the news, discussing vampire politics as though it was the most normal thing in the world." He shook his head and pressed a fingernail into the wood table. "I was angry. I could have blown through a town the way you used to. How dare you out us? How dare you bring our worlds together and shine the light on our shadows? How dare you take away our power and make us live like we're one of them?"

"Val—"

He waved her off. "But then I realized you weren't forcing anyone to come out. I could stay in the shadows if I wanted to. I'd been living among humans for the last century, and they barely glanced at me, except for my eyes and when I wanted to, I simply wore colored contacts." He fluttered his lashes, and she gave a small smile. "So I watched. I waited. I saw more and more vampires living out in the open, going about their lives. Drinking synthetic blood they bought from grocery stores instead of from willing, or unwilling, victims. We haven't lived this long by going against the grain, have we? So I joined in. I started in Madrid, moving among the elite vampire circles there, then went into Switzerland, where they arranged for vampire health care, the most unnecessary and unused health care system in history. But they were trying to be inclusive."

Remy laughed, her shoulders easing. "Okay. But why not come say hi, as a friend?"

His eyes narrowed ever so slightly. "Are we friends, Wind? I wasn't sure after the last time we parted."

The door opened, and Lars and Jet came in, both with neutral expressions. She waved them over. "Geno," she said, using his current name because that was how their customs worked, "this is Lars and Jet. They live here at the ranch and serve as the angel and demon on my shoulders."

"I'm both." Lars held out his hand. "Jet just sits there for the free ride."

Geno took his hand and kissed his knuckles. "Nice to officially meet you, angel."

Remy rolled her eyes hard enough for it to nearly be a sound when Lars looked like he might swoon.

Geno turned to Jet. "Given how smooth your friend's hands

are, I'm guessing you do more than ride our Wind."

Jet made a gagging sound. "The very notion has seared a part of my brain that will never be usable again." She slid into a chair at Remy's nod. "I understand you're helping solve our temporary communication issue?"

As Geno and the other two entered into easy conversation, Remy considered Geno's question before they'd been interrupted. Were they friends? She remembered the last time they'd been in one another's orbit and some pieces came together.

"Geno," she said, interrupting whatever they'd been saying. "Did you know Cadence was here?"

He looked genuinely surprised and then his expression flattened to neutral. "I didn't. Why do you ask?"

She folded her arms. "Because on the same day I find out one of the few other vampires on Earth as old as me is living nearby, I also find out my ex is in town. An ex you and I have in common, if I remember correctly."

He sighed softly, his gaze somewhere to the left of her instead of on her. "Ah, Wind. Still toying with human emotions when it comes to love and grudges."

"Not a grudge, Geno. As you say, that's long past. But I dislike coincidences when it comes to our kind. They usually end up causing blood loss at some point." She noticed the faint way Lars and Jet stiffened and moved away from the table. Now they understood there were nails in the roses.

He nodded, finally looking at her. "You're right. But I swear to you I didn't know she was in town. It isn't all that strange though, Remy. The human world has turned against us, as I feared it would one day, and now vampires are on the move again. Some coming here, where they think there's power in numbers, others going back to the old ways, finding safety in the shadows. We're bound to be seeing kin and clan we haven't seen in millennia."

She had to acknowledge that was true. Maybe it wasn't so odd. "I still don't understand why you didn't come let me know you were here."

His eyes narrowed ever so slightly and the tips of his fangs poked over his lip. "I don't have to check in with anyone, anywhere. If anything, they check in with me."

She raised her eyebrow. "And have they been checking in here with you in Bluff?"

There was a moment of tense silence as they stared one another down. Lars and Jet stood and moved away from the table, ready to back Remy in a fight if that's what it came down to.

And then, all at once, Geno threw back his head and laughed. "Ah, Wind. How I've missed feeling the raw power of someone like me." He slapped the table. "I wasn't sure of your welcome, that's why I didn't come. After Cadence and that whole mess, I went years wandering the globe, remembering the way you looked at me. I was lucky you didn't take my head from my shoulders that day. Would you want me living in your little human-vampire paradise? I didn't know, so I kept to myself. I knew we'd cross paths one day." He raised his hands. "Et voilà. Here we are."

She allowed a small smile, but the tension didn't leave her shoulders. "I appreciate you coming to help. None of the tech needs to be permanent; we just need something until this all blows over."

His expression twitched ever so slightly. "You think that will happen? I've already begun packing my belongings to head somewhere more...friendly."

Remy scrubbed her hands over her face and tilted her head toward the stairs. She could hear Sage coming down. Jet moved away to intercept her, if only to make sure she didn't say anything she shouldn't. "I don't know, Geno. Honestly, I hope so. I think it's good for vampires to be free and to be who they are without having to pretend or move every few years. For us to have communities like this where we're spread out but still available to each other and can understand what it is to live so long." She watched him for any sign of agreement or dissent, but he was a master at hiding what he was thinking.

Sage and Jet walked in, and Sage was clearly brimming with curiosity. All at once, Geno's entire demeanor changed. He slouched slightly, and a slack grin came over his face. "Awesome. I was hoping you'd come back. Want to help me get some of this stuff up and running? I could use someone's help who isn't a billion years old."

Sage bit her lip, a sign she was uncertain and one Remy found particularly cute. It was good she was thinking instead of just jumping in. Remy would have known if Sage had been close enough to listen in on the conversation, so she wasn't concerned. Not that they'd said anything of substance. Most of it had been sub-level threatening, the kind long-lived vampires were particularly good at.

Sage looked at Remy with the question in her eyes, and Remy gave her a quick smile.

"Actually, Sage asked if she could help me put together the evening meal. I hope you'll join us tonight?" Remy stood, the conversation over for now.

He tilted his head in understanding. "I'd love that. Man, to have dinner at Dark Haven with Remy Winslow and Sage Samara. Crazy!" He stood, looking every inch the too-relaxed twenty-something nerd. "I'll start setting up."

Remy caught Lars' eye and motioned, and Lars sidled up beside Geno.

"I, on the other hand, would love to come with you. Maybe you could explain how some of this works? I'm a petrified end user, but I'm not unwilling to learn." He lightly touched Geno's shoulder.

Remy winced inside. Lars' power was subtle, but if Geno felt him trying to use his powers of persuasion, Geno could cut him off at the knees, quite literally. But Geno just smiled back and started chatting as they headed toward the office.

Sage blew out a long breath. "You could slice the tension in here with a butterknife. Want to give me a heads-up?"

Remy put her arm around Sage's shoulders and instantly felt a little better when Sage's sweet, light energy touched her own. She breathed it in and let it settle her. "Lars told you about our eyes?" When Sage looked surprised, Remy grinned. "If someone directs thoughts at me, or is thinking too strongly of me, I know. When you came downstairs, Lars silently let me know he'd told you."

Sage stopped dead. "You can read my mind?" Her cheeks turned pink and her eyes were wide.

"Only if you're thinking too loudly about me." Remy looked down into Sage's pretty face and found she really, really wanted to kiss her. "Have you been thinking about me, Sage?" she whispered.

"I..." Sage swallowed hard, her gaze going to Remy's mouth and then back to her eyes. "I mean..."

Damn it. She backed up and let Sage see the desire in her eyes before she turned away. Nothing would come of it, but she didn't want Sage to feel unwanted. In fact, she very much wanted her to feel...wanted. "Trust me when I say that vampires who have lived as long as we have are complex, and you don't always know where we're coming from. You can trust me, and Lars, and Jet. But beyond us, I need you to be careful. Okay?" She led the way into the kitchen. The gate bell rang, and she turned to Jet. "Can you grab that?"

Jet shook her head and took Sage by the shoulder. "Nope. I have a feeling that's the guest you asked me to call, and I'm staying far, far away from her. All yours."

Remy understood and waved them off. She felt Sage's gaze on her, and the thought popped into her head like a text. *Come back soon.*

She grinned and looked over her shoulder, and saw Sage's surprised smile in turn. She shook her head and headed to the gate, where she saw Rac's truck idling, its windows so darkly tinted she couldn't see the driver. But she felt her. Rac's energy was dark and solid, like a six-foot ocean wave about to crash into the shore in the dead of night.

She opened the gate and waved her in, and Rac pulled up to the side of the ranch. She hopped out beneath an overhang and then leaned against the truck while Remy closed the gate.

She held out her hand and Remy took it, knowing what it was Rac was asking for. When she felt Rac's power shudder over her skin like sandpaper, she grimaced but let it ride. This was Rac's way of knowing friend from foe, and she insisted on it. She could read anyone's thoughts and know every one of their powers. She already knew Remy's, but now she was up to speed not only on all the problems but also on how Remy felt about them. It saved a lot of time, but fucking hell it was like being invaded by a swarm of intelligent bees.

She let go and nodded. "Well, that's a goddamn whole lot of stuff, isn't it?" She looked toward the house. "Valentino. I'd hoped he was a burned skeleton underground with all the other relics."

Remy shoved her hands into her pockets. "He's no worse than the rest of us, I don't think."

Rac narrowed her gaze and continued to stare at the house. "We've all done our share of wicked shit, Wind, but that doesn't mean we're wicked in our bones." She nodded toward the house. "That one will follow the person who offers him the easiest path."

"The same could have been said about both of us over the years. Anyway, he'll leave as soon as he's got the comms systems up and running. He said he's already packing to leave."

Rac shook her head. "Let's deal with the other problem for now. But, Wind," she looked directly at Remy with eyes that matched her own, "if he steps out of line, I'm going to deal with him too. You don't call in an exterminator and not let them kill *all* the vermin."

Remy looked at the ground and gave a quick nod. Arguing with Rac hadn't been a good idea in any century. As Remy led the way into the house, she wondered just how fucked the situation was about to become.

CHAPTER ELEVEN

SAGE BALANCED HER PHONE on a high shelf, tilting it downward so the video caught everything they were doing in the kitchen. Jet teased her and bumped her out of the way, and Sage wondered when she'd last had fun with people who weren't drinking or worried about what other people were thinking or doing. Of course, she was always aware of the camera and tried to keep it on her good side, but soon she managed to forget about it as Jet had her dig her hands into the coleslaw to mix it, mayo and all. Sage squealed a little at the mushy mess between her fingers, making Jet laugh.

The door opened, and she looked over her shoulder to see Remy come in, followed by Rac. She lifted a coleslaw-covered hand. "Hey, stranger! Good to see you!"

Rac, her braids tied back with a black band, shook her head. "I won't be eating any of that tonight, that's for sure." She nodded at Jet.

Sage glanced over when Jet didn't say anything and was stunned to see Jet's head bowed slightly, her eyes on the floor. Remy looked serious too. "Um, have I missed something? Did you become president or something since I last stayed at your inn?"

Rac turned to Remy. "Take me down to the markings."

Remy nodded and led the way out the back door without saying a word.

Sage wiped off her hands and turned to Jet. "What's going on?"

Jet blew out a soft breath. "Notice the eyes?"

"Yeah. So she's as old as Remy, like Geno. That doesn't seem so weird. Or is it?" Sage knew enough to know she still understood hardly anything about this community of vampires. But getting answers to questions felt damn near impossible.

"Rac isn't as old as Remy or Geno—she's older." Jet leaned against the counter, and her far-off gaze softened. "The oldest, in fact. You don't fuck with Rac. If you want to know who the leader of the vampires is, you just watched her walk out."

Sage blinked, taking that in. "Rac is the oldest vampire in existence? And she's running a B&B in the middle of nowhere?"

Jet seemed to come back to the moment, and she began to laugh. "When you say it that way, it does sound a little absurd." She turned back to the steak and let the blood from the raw slabs drip into small glasses. "She and Remy have been friends for a long time. Longer than I even know, probably. My understanding is Rac decided to come live here *because* Remy was at Dark Haven, but she likes her space too."

"And is she crazy powerful? Can she turn into all kinds of animals and read minds and stuff?" Sage looked at the back door like she could see Rac doing exactly that.

"And stuff." Jet pointed with her butcher knife at the vegetables. "Get to carrot-peeling, and stay away from the big scary vampires, okay?"

Sage started peeling but her thoughts were far from carrots. "What about Geno?"

"What about him?" Jet's tone was bland, a tell-tale sign she wasn't about to give up any more information.

"Is he really a friend? Or is that complicated too? Do any of you have non-complicated relationships? Is that possible when you live so long? I mean, I can barely have anything uncompl—" Sage, not paying attention, slipped with the peeler and caught her finger down the side. "Shit!" Blood welled and she gripped her finger, the pain making her eyes tear up. When there was no reply, she looked over at Jet, who stood frozen by the sink, her eyes glued to the blood dripping from Sage's finger. She had a death grip on the white marble countertop, and it began to crack. Sage turned away, but then the back door opened, and Remy and Rac came in. They both stopped, and Rac's eyes went a deeper red than the blood welling from Sage's finger. Remy's nose flared, and she looked from Sage's hand to her face. Whatever she saw in Sage's expression must have been enough to override the scent of fresh blood.

In an instant she was at Sage's side, and she'd wrapped a dishtowel around the finger, almost too tight. Her jaw was clenching. "Go. Now."

Sage, her knees weak as the feeling of danger slid over her soul, simply nodded and let Remy lead her upstairs by her shoulder. When they were in Remy's place with the door locked behind them, Remy leaned against it and closed her eyes.

"I'm sorry," Sage said softly. "I didn't mean—"

"No, Sage." Remy opened her eyes, and she looked so very, very tired. "It isn't your fault. Accidents happen, and humans are fragile. But fresh, healthy blood like yours..." She gave a wan smile and pushed away from the door. "We don't get a lot of that around here, and it's like putting a fresh kill in front of a hungry lion. Or bacon in front of a soon-to-be lapsed vegetarian. Same things, really."

Sage's finger throbbed beneath the towel. "I don't want to be any kind of kill or meat product if it's all the same to you." She held her hand behind her. "I can take care of this myself. Do you have any first aid stuff?"

"As you can probably imagine, we don't need any." Remy went into a room off the kitchen and came out with duct tape, then she took plastic wrap from the drawer. "Have a seat."

Sage shook her head and backed up a step. "Seriously, it's fine. I can handle it."

For a split second, Remy looked hurt. "I have plenty of self-control, Sage. It took me by surprise before, but I'm good now. Let me help. I swear I'd never hurt you."

Sage sat down and offered her hand. Blood had already soaked through the towel, and she hissed slightly when Remy knelt in front of her and peeled it away.

"It's shallow but long." Remy's touch was gentle as she turned it this way and that to check it. "You don't need stitches, but it's going to take a while to heal." Blood welled from it, and Remy closed her eyes for a moment.

"Remy," Sage said, "did you want to..." She tensed her hand in Remy's grip. "If it would make you feel better, I mean."

Remy's gaze was sharp as steel when she opened her eyes and looked up at Sage. "You don't know what you're offering. Don't ever, *ever* offer your blood to a vampire again, Sage."

She trembled under the heat of Remy's disapproval. "I'm sorry. Can you tell me why though?"

Remy sighed and gently cleaned the blood from Sage's hand. "If I tasted your blood, especially from an open wound, we'd be connected. I'd know where you were, what you were feeling, what you were thinking every minute of the day. When a vampire takes blood from a human, it creates a bond stronger than anything you can understand. It can die off with time if it's only a little and only once, but the more often it happens, the more bonded they become. Eventually, the human becomes a kind of...pet. The vampire can take over their willpower, make them do whatever they want. A kind of living puppet."

Sage gaped at her, and her pulse raced. "And does the human get anything out of it?"

Remy's laugh was brittle. "It depends on the vampire. If they're good, if they're caring, then it isn't so different from a relationship, just a lot more intense. If they're not? Then the human is used up, drained off, and usually dies."

Lightly, Sage touched Remy's cheek. "I have a feeling I know which one you'd be."

Remy tensed under her touch and gently took Sage's hand from her cheek. "You don't know me, Sage. Don't think for a second you do. You've seen my public face, and you've seen how I am with my few friends, but that doesn't tell you who I am. What I am, or what I've done." Her eyes went red, and her fangs extended. "I'm a vampire, and you should never forget it."

Sage leaned back, fear making it automatic, and Remy nodded as though she'd made her point. Her eyes went back to their usual pale blue and her fangs disappeared. She placed a clean paper towel over the cut, covered it with plastic wrap, then secured it with purple duct tape.

"That should hold it." She stood and moved away, not meeting Sage's gaze. "If it starts to bleed through, I need you to get up here right away, okay?"

Sage stood, but her legs were shaking. "Okay." She didn't want Remy to know how disturbed she was, how suddenly it felt a little too real. These little reminders weren't what she wanted to show her followers. But if she didn't, she wasn't really showing them the truth, was she?

She followed Remy back downstairs and into the kitchen, where Jet was still cooking. She was the only one there.

"All good?" Remy asked, standing slightly in front of Sage.

"Yeah." Jet looked up and although she smiled, it was tight. "Haven't had that happen in a while." She tapped the cracked counter with the knife. "We'll need to get a new countertop."

"Better than a new influencer." Remy grinned, and the tension left Jet's expression. She grinned back.

"I'm not easily replaceable." Sage looked around. "What should I do next?"

Jet carried over a huge bowl of oranges. "Nothing with a fucking blade, that's for sure."

Remy laughed, an open and honest sound that made Jet join in. When they settled, she asked where Rac had gone.

Jet sobered. "Said she wanted to look around a little more and she'd be back soon."

Remy ran her hand over her eyes. "And Geno?"

"He and Lars are in the living room talking about fashion in the Victorian era." Jet made a face. "I'd leave them to it if I were you."

Remy put on an apron and winked at Sage. "Then it looks like the three of us will be feeding the horde tonight."

They fell into an easy routine, and Remy even showed Sage how to make a special sauce for the steak, which wasn't really cooked so much as waved over the flame to lightly warm the outside, and then cut into strips. A good veterinarian could've revived it. It was fun, as long as Sage didn't stop to think about how she'd looked like food to a room of vampires not so long ago. Remy's warning continued to ring through her mind. Somehow though, she couldn't help but feel like she *did* know Remy, enough to know she was one of the good ones for sure. One she could depend on. One who would deny herself fresh blood from a human who'd willingly walked into a vampire encampment.

She shivered at the thought of Remy sucking on her finger, taking the blood on her lips. Of them being bonded, and Remy knowing just how often she thought of her hands on her.

She jumped when she felt Remy's breath on her ear.

"If you don't stop thinking those dirty thoughts so loudly, we're going to have a problem," she whispered in her ear. "Have mercy on a vampire, would you?"

She backed away, laughing as Sage's face heated to the point she must have looked like a tomato. "That's so unfair. If you can read my mind then I should be able to read yours."

Jet snorted. "Believe me, you don't want that kind of boring shit in your head. Unless you have trouble sleeping."

"Laugh it up. I can hear you too sometimes." Remy winked and then laughed as Jet made a gagging sound.

As they put things on serving dishes, Sage got up enough courage to ask a question on her mind. "Can I ask why Rac is here? You don't seem happy that she is. Like, how you'd treat a plumber who has to fix the toilet."

"Offensive, but often the reaction I've had over the last few centuries." Rac stood in the doorway, her arms crossed and a fraction of a smile on her lips.

"Oh god." Sage put her hand over her mouth. "I'm sorry, I didn't mean—"

"Yes, you did. Don't apologize for speaking truth. It diminishes you." Rac looked past Sage to the others. "Have you explained the situation?"

Remy stabbed at a piece of steak for no apparent reason. "I thought she'd be safer not knowing. We're dealing with it. That's cnough."

Raf looked at her like she might be the dumbest organic being on the planet. "Because ignorance and a lack of knowledge has always been the go-to to keep people safe. This human matters to vampire survival. Do you want me to do it for you?"

Jet let out a sound somewhere between a laugh and a rasp.

Remy finally stopped stabbing the steak. "I'll explain after dinner, once there are less ears with excellent hearing surrounding us." She picked up the platter of steak. "People will already know there's something going on with you here, and I don't want to tip our hand any further."

Rac nodded like she agreed and turned toward the dining room. Sage and Jet picked up a couple more platters and carried them out. Sage was surprised at the evening's turnout. Every seat in the large dining room was taken, as was the seating in the living room. A few people were even sitting on the stairs. And all of them were watching Rac.

The room went silent as Rac picked up a plate and began to fill it. She didn't acknowledge the tense atmosphere or speak to anyone. She simply sat down at the table and began to eat.

Remy cleared her throat. "You're acting like humans in front of a celebrity. Come on, dig in."

That seemed to lift the weird veil, and they began to move toward the food. But the seats next to Rac remained empty, even when there was standing room only. Sage stood in the corner, watching everything and taking it all in. Only then did she remember that she'd left her phone recording in the kitchen. It was probably still going and the battery would be dead soon. Damn. She would have liked to record what was happening right now. Community dinner with the vampires, and one clearly more important in some way than all the rest, felt special.

Remy and Jet filled their plates, and Remy looked over at Sage, then nodded toward the food and the table Rac was at. Sage took the hint and got a healthy serving of everything except the meat, which she wouldn't touch with someone else's hands, let alone her own. She sat beside Remy and stayed quiet, even though she had a million questions.

"How is the B&B going?" Remy asked between bites.

"Thanks to the influx of vampires because of humans being humans, it's full. I've even got a few people sharing a room." Rac looked over her shoulder at the vampires in the room. "Looks like you've got a fair gathering of new vamps as well."

Remy followed Rac's gaze. "It's good we put up those few extra cottages, and I've got bunks in the barn for when the extra hands come to help with the harvest crops. More hands on deck means we'll get more cottages up faster too. We can take more."

Rac ripped into a piece of steak and stared at Remy thoughtfully. "You know where this is likely to lead?"

Remy put her fork down. "I know where it *could* lead. I'm hoping it won't."

"Hope is what keeps us going through the centuries. Even a flicker can become a flame." She seemed to laugh when she saw Remy looking surprised. "If I'd had a real problem with you bringing vampires into the light, the Council and I would have stopped you. I agree that we deserve the option, but our legacy as monsters is as set in stone as the pyramids in Egypt. You might be fighting a losing battle, Wind." She shrugged. "Humans are humans, after all. You can only expect so much."

There it was again. That nickname that Remy was so adamant she didn't want to talk about, and yet so many of the vampires referred to her by it. Damned if Sage was going to give up trying to find out where it came from. "You say that like you weren't once human. I've heard several vampires talk like that about us. But surely if that's where you started, then you can't think we're so useless? I mean, were *you* so useless before you turned?" The words were out of Sage's mouth before she could think about them. She'd said as much before but not to a vampire of Rac's stature. She glared at Jet when she kicked her under the table.

Rac stared at her for a moment as she chewed. "You've got backbone. I'm not sure how smart you are, but you're brave, I'll give you that." She leaned back in her chair, her gaze laser-focused. "You're right. Most every vampire in this room was human at some point. For some, that was longer ago than they can remember. For others, it might be practically yesterday."

Conversations trailed off as Rac spoke, and she seemed to know that others were listening. There was something hypnotic about her voice, about the rhythm and tone of it that made Sage feel almost like she wanted to sway.

"But we're not human, are we? I know you want people to think we're not so different from them. You think you're helping by showing how *normal* we are. In fact, you said on one of your videos that it's mostly a dietary difference."

There was a titter of laughter, and Rac's smile acknowledged it. Sage felt her face flame with embarrassment. Okay, so she'd learned a bit more since she'd made that video.

"When we become vampires, Sage Samara, we are no longer human. We are *more* than human. We look like you, have jobs, have families." She smiled at two children playing by the stairs, and their mother bowed her head. "But when we become vampires, we realize how weak we were. How little we knew about the world, about ourselves, about what it means to be predator and prey. We comprehend so much more than we did as humans. When the magic, or virus, or god-touch, or whatever it is that shifts us into powerful, immortal predators takes over, we become *more*. And so, when we disparage humans, we don't do it from a place of hypocrisy. We do it from a place of understanding. We know what we were, and we know what we are. You, my dear, are Homo sapiens. We, on the other hand, are Homo lamia. We are a different species from the moment we become vampires." She raised her glass, which contained all the blood from the steak. "To vampires."

Everyone else raised their glasses of synth and repeated the cheers.

Sage pressed her hands between her knees to try and stem the trembling. The short speech had been delivered in a smooth, easy tone with no judgment or passion. It was matter-of-fact, like she was imparting simple information meant only to create understanding. But the words themselves and the passion in her eyes said far more. Sage looked at her plate, her appetite long gone. She'd wanted so bad to believe they were just like humans. She'd fought beside them, called for vampire rights, hell, she'd gotten this assignment so she could help the cause.

And now she was...nothing. A weaker species of a creature that walked on two legs and didn't have an iota of what made the vampires special.

Remy laid her arm casually across Sage's shoulders, surprising her.

"That doesn't mean we don't need humans on our side though. You were right to try to help us when we came out of the proverbial closet. And we appreciate it, we really do."

Tears welled in Sage's eyes, and she did her best to blink them away before they made her mascara run. The safety she felt under Remy's arm was nearly as surprising as Remy trying to make her feel better.

"That's true." Rac's gaze moved from Remy to Sage. "Once the human world became aware of us living among them, it was imperative they see us as less threatening, as less monstrous. As more like them, even if it isn't really true." She tilted her head toward Sage. "And a human who walks straight into the lion's den to show the world that they don't have to fear their neighborhood vampires is good PR, no doubt. You're brave, and you *are* helping."

Mollified slightly, Sage gave a small smile. "Thank you."

Conversation began to flow again, and much of it surrounded the politics that had brought so many of them together, but there was plenty of conversation about where people were from, if they knew this vampire or that one, and about all the other minutia of life. Remy's arm remained over her shoulders, and she leaned into her strength and support. Suddenly, she was exhausted. So much emotion was total overload.

"Come on. I'll take you to bed," Remy whispered in her ear and then grimaced. "I mean, I'll take you upstairs."

Sage grinned. "I like the first one better. Let's do that one."

Remy rolled her eyes and stood, taking Sage's hand in her own. "I'll be right back."

Sage was aware of the glances thrown their way as Remy led her through the crowd and up the stairs. It was both electrifying and a little disturbing. Did they think she was a pet, like the kind Remy had described? Or did they think Remy had a thing for her, that they were an item of sorts? That thought gave her a giddy feeling. Being Remy's plaything sounded just fine.

Remy threw open the door and gently pushed Sage into the room. "I need to teach you how to quiet your thoughts before you make me insane." She lifted her hand like she was going to touch Sage's face and then quickly withdrew it. "Get some sleep. I'll probably be in late, but we'll talk in the morning, okay?"

Sage bit her lip and took a step forward, but Remy stepped back.

"Night." She closed the door and the lock clicked into place.

Sage stood there for a minute at a loss. She was tired, yeah, but like a kid who didn't want to miss anything, she wished she was still downstairs listening to everything going on. A yawn overtook her, and she shrugged. There was always tomorrow. She headed to the guest room and found all her things already in it. When had Remy arranged for that? It didn't matter. At least she had her stuff.

With a start, she remembered her phone again. Considering it was something that hardly ever left her hand, it was surprising how she'd forgotten it today. She'd have to be sure to get it at breakfast in the morning though. Geno would probably have the internet up and running, which meant she could dive back into her socials and catch up with everything, not to mention post one of the huge number of videos she'd taken.

She yawned again and got out her pjs and toothbrush. After a quick shower, where she took the time to sniff the amber and musk bodywash Remy had on the shelf, she crawled into the big guest bed. It was incredibly dark, so much so she couldn't see her hand in front of her face, and she was reminded once again of the way they lived. No light would get into this room, and she would sleep undisturbed.

Just like a vampire.

Chapter Twelve

Shadows danced in the moonlight as the trees swayed in the breeze. Remy leaned against one, her arms folded, every one of her senses on high alert. It was late enough in the season that the smell of pine had given way to the scent of frost on wet earth, and the naked branches above her scratched at one another without their leaves to cushion them.

A sound, still a little way off, caught her attention and she glanced toward Rac, who crouched in the shadows nearby. A moonbeam slid over her face and highlighted her red eyes and white teeth. Remy was ready too, her power humming through her like old, ungrounded electricity. If they could finish this tonight, Sage could move back into her little cottage and out from under Remy's senses, which were driving her crazy.

A twig broke, a sign that the vampire coming toward them wasn't in full control. If they were, they'd be as silent as the wind over ice.

The figure came into view, weaving, their limbs jerky. Their eyes glowed a sickly pinkish red in the dark and drool ran in thick drops from their fangs. Remy shifted slightly so she could see them better, and she nearly groaned out loud.

It was Pam, the only mother on the compound. The one who'd birthed two children who were also vampires. Black lines ran up her neck and into her cheeks, and she growled and hissed at the air. Her claws looked twisted and grotesque as she clawed at the tree, mewling like she was in pain. Like an animal. Remy closed her eyes. An animal who had to be put down. Damn it.

She sensed the shift in the air and a moment later, there was the sharp snap of breaking bone, then the wet thud of a stake through the heart. She counted to three and then opened her eyes. Killing another vampire was forbidden by vampire law and if it was necessary, then Council permission had to be obtained first. Only one vampire had total authority to do so, and that was Rac. Every vampire knew that if Rac came for you, your time was up. Even clan leaders had to get the Council's permission to deal with a feral or outlaw vampire, which was a hell of a lot easier now than it had been before the invention of the phone.

Rac crouched beside the woman, tilting her head as she studied her face and then her hands. She pulled back her upper lip to expose her gums, which were threaded through with the same black that ran over her neck.

Remy knelt in the wet earth beside Rac. "What do you think?"

"Feral, definitely, but I think we've got a bigger problem." She turned Pam's head, gently, which was easy given her broken neck. "Look at the base of the skull."

Remy leaned down and frowned at the strange dark patch that looked like a root ball, out of which flowed the other black lines. "I've never seen anything like that."

"I have." Rac stood and looked around, clearly listening for any other vampires headed their way. "Back in the fourteen hundreds, a village created a poison and infected several humans with it, then they sent the humans as an offering to the castle where the vampires were living. They asked only that they be left alone. The vampires drank their victims dry, and every one of them ended up like this, until they eventually either killed themselves or were killed by a human who then had the ability to take them down. I found out about it when word reached me from one of our lamia-libres that they'd gone to the vampires' home and found it deserted."

"Diabolical." Remy brushed Pam's hair from her gaunt face. "Why's it only happening at night? The ferals I've come across before exhibited signs during the day too. I've been watching but haven't seen it in anyone. Hell, Pam and the kids were at breakfast this morning, and she seemed fine."

"Something to do with the poison, I imagine. We're strongest at night, and so when we're trying to fight it off, that's when it happens. At some point, it will probably manifest in the day too if it's allowed to get that far. Because it's not a regular feral infection, it will act differently." Rac turned and looked at the trees around them. "Based on the claw marks, I'm guessing there's at least another four, and they're probably at different stages."

Remy looked up from where she still knelt, mud oozing beneath her jeans. "Someone brought poison into Dark Haven."

"Maybe." Rac leaned against a tree. "Maybe it was in the food they ate. Or the synth they drank." She shrugged. "If any of the others aren't as far gone, maybe we can talk to them and try to get an answer. But in the meantime, I'll have this one's body sent to the lab. See if that tells us anything."

Remy pushed up, feeling even older than she was. "I'll have to ask for a different synth supplier. We've been supplementing our food with grocery-bought, but maybe we need to stop that and use only what we have here on the farm."

Rac's eyebrows rose. "With the new influx, do you have enough to feed that many?"

Remy fell in beside her as they began the walk back to the lodge. Rac's hand moved gently through the air as she levitated the body along behind them as easily as flying a kite.

"It will get tight, but I'm hoping the borders won't stay closed for long. If they do, then we'll have to evacuate people by water. I don't want to cause panic but not telling them seems irresponsible too." She waited, hoping for some guidance or even just an opinion, but Rac stayed silent.

They stopped at the edge of the woods. There were three different firepits going, and they were all surrounded by vampires making the most of the clear night and full moon. Rac and Remy turned and stayed in the tree line that led to the back of the lodge. Rac let the body float to the bed of her truck and laid it down gently.

With her hands on the edge of the truck bed, she said, "You know you need to check the kids."

Remy's stomach turned. "I know."

"And they're orphans now. You equipped to deal with that?" Rac asked as she got into her truck.

"Who the fuck is equipped to deal with vampire orphans?" Remy snapped. She held up her hands. "Sorry. I'll figure it out."

Rac tapped the steering wheel, looking through the windshield. "No one likes being the one in charge when shit goes sideways, Wind." She finally turned to look at Remy, her eyes still red, her fangs still out. "But you decided to open Dark Haven as a refuge, and now you need to keep them safe. I'll help in any way I can, but this is up to you. I expect you to do what you need to do."

She put the truck in gear, and Remy followed her to the gate to let her out and close up after her. She stayed there for a long time, thinking, letting her thoughts move from one problem to the next, trying to see any connections that might make sense. Her beautifully ordered world had keeled over and was taking on water. How was she going to keep them all from drowning?

***

Gritty eyes and a foul-tasting mouth were unpleasant bedfellows to wake to, and Remy shuffled to the bathroom for a hot shower. Without opening her eyes, she opened the door and heard an intake of breath, making her look.

Sage stood in front of the mirror, wearing nothing but a towel over her hair. Her big blue eyes were wide, and Remy couldn't help but look from her eyes to her neck, to her full, high breasts with dark pink nipples that hardened under her gaze. Her waist was trim, her stomach flat above a dark, trimmed triangle of hair that still glistened from the shower. Her legs were on the short side but looked strong enough to wrap around Remy's waist... Remy looked back into Sage's eyes and saw her desire mirrored there.

She needed this. She needed Sage on her back, screaming her name as she fucked her senseless...

"Fuck me backwards." Remy spun and went back to her room, slamming the door behind her and leaning against it. She bent over, putting her hands on her knees and forcing herself to get control. She moved back to her bed and flopped down on it. What had she done to deserve this torture? If there was a god or goddess of any kind, they were most definitely fucking with her.

There was a light tap on her door. "Um, the bathroom is free now."

She heard Sage walk away and forced herself to sit up. "Thanks," she called. She hadn't lived with anyone in so long, she'd forgotten how utterly inconvenient it could be. She ducked out of her room and nearly leapt into the bathroom, strangely aware of being in nothing but old boxers and a tank top that had seen better days. She couldn't deny that she cared what Sage thought, and she was too old for denial. The question she asked herself while she showered was why she needed Sage's approval. She was just a human passing through, and she'd be gone as soon as the borders opened. Yeah, there was a physical attraction between them, unquestionably. And under different circumstances, she might have considered enjoying Sage's company for a little while. But these were far from normal circumstances, and Sage was very public about every aspect of her life. Remy had no desire to be an internet topic of conversation for anything other than politics. And yet she couldn't deny that there was a connection of some kind. One she couldn't explain, and she disliked things she couldn't explain.

Settled and back in control, she wrapped a towel around her and got dressed in her room. Sage's thoughts were silent, which was a godsend right now. When she went into the kitchen, she found Sage reading a book at the breakfast table. She looked up and smiled shyly.

"Sorry. I'll lock the door next time."

Remy shook her head and moved to the fridge, where she poured herself a synth-orange juice mixture. "It's my fault. If I'd been halfway awake, I would've known you were in there."

There was a moment of awkward silence before Sage laughed softly. "At first I thought for sure I was going to need another shower because you were going to get me dirty again." When Remy blew out a breath, she smiled. "But then you looked like a teenager caught checking out the babysitter."

Remy laughed and let some of the sexual tension dissipate. "That's about how I felt too." She took a deep drink and felt the power run through her, erasing the rest of the tiredness from the night before. "You're a beautiful woman, Sage."

Sage's cheeks turned pink. "Then can I ask why we're not thrashing around in your bed right now? I mean, it looks like you want me, and you clearly know I want you."

"I like how straightforward you are. Women in other centuries would have died of shame before they admitted that they had sexual urges." Remy grinned.

"Well, answer my question about our sexual urges then." Sage drummed her fingers on the book.

"If you were a vampire, I'd have taken you on the bathroom floor. Up against the wall. In the hallway. All before we even made it to my bed." Remy reached across to stroke Sage's cheek with the back of her hand. "But you're not a vampire. You're a very sweet, very open human who will be going back to her very human world as soon as we can get you across the border."

Sage waited but when nothing else was forthcoming, she shook her head. "So? We're not pledging undying devotion. We're having what would probably be incredible sex and enjoying each other while I'm here. What's the problem with that? Do you not have sex with humans in general? Is that what you're saying?"

"That's part of it. I tend to stick with vampires when I desire company. We understand each other and our way of being. No worries about accidental bloodletting." She nodded toward Sage's still-wrapped finger and tried to figure out how to say the rest without sounding weak. "And the other part of it is that I don't want to get attached to you. I find sex incredibly emotional, which might not be a very butch thing to say in this era, but it's true. When I have sex with someone who is as sweet, passionate, and irksome as you, I don't just say thanks and look the other way in the morning."

"Is that all?" Sage looked a little hurt but mostly thoughtful.

"No." Remy came around the breakfast bar and tugged Sage's hair to expose her throat. "Humans are soft and full of the life that nourishes me. That *feeds* me. And although I haven't lost control in a very, very long time..." She bent her head and drew her teeth gently over Sage's throat. "I'm still overtly aware that I'm stronger and far more dangerous than you understand. And I won't put you in a position where I could hurt, or even kill you." She let go of Sage's hair and stepped away with Herculean effort. Sage's pulse was visible in her neck, and Remy could almost taste the intoxicating combination of fear and desire. She backed away. "Let's go out on the terrace. The daylight should kill my craving to drag you back to bed. And if it doesn't, I'll just step into the sun and melt away." She smiled and was relieved to see Sage smile back. The conversation they were going to have about the need for Sage to leave was going to be hard enough as it was.

Once they were settled in the big Adirondack chairs and Sage had pulled a blanket over her legs, Remy chose a place to start. "I assume you did a lot of research before you came on this adventure of yours." She waited for Sage to nod. "Did you come across the term feral?"

Sage shook her head. "Like, when something lives in the wild and can't be tamed?"

"Sort of." Remy took a sip of her morning synth as she corralled her thoughts. She had to deal with orphaned children today too. "When a vampire goes feral, it's a kind of sickness. A lot like cancer or something, but more insidious. The infected vampire stops functioning. They hallucinate, lose control of their powers, attack pretty much anything that moves, and they can't be reasoned with. The disease moves fast and can't be cured. They become incredibly dangerous to the world around them." She took a deep breath, picturing the vampire on the ground last night. "The vampire has to be put down."

Sage stared at her. "You have to kill them? Like…like an animal?"

Remy tilted her head. "I don't. Or not here, I don't. It isn't my job anymore. You see, vampire-on-vampire killing is pretty much our one sacred law. You can't do it, and if you do, it's a death sentence. In ancient history, only the oldest vampire in any community had the right to do it, and once the Vampire Council was established, you had to go to them with any issues that might result in the death of another vampire. Now, you can go to the oldest vampire in your area or to a clan leader, and both will take it to the Council."

Sage looked like she was putting the pieces together. "So you brought Rac here because you have feral vampires, and she's the only one allowed to deal with them."

Remy nodded, already wishing she could go back to bed.

"But everyone respects you. Until Rac got here, they all looked at you like they look at her. And your political standing too. I mean, you're clearly the one actually in charge. Why couldn't you do it on your own? Aside from it just being an age thing, I mean?"

"But it is an age thing. It's part of our laws and traditions. Rac is older than I am, and as the oldest vampire in our location, it's down to her to enforce the laws of the Council. If she wasn't here, I'd still call her and talk it through, and she'd take it to them. That keeps any vampire from making unilateral decisions."

"You said it's like an infection. Does that mean there's a sickness here? Can it spread?"

"No, I don't think so. Ferals tend to have something happen genetically. Something goes bad inside them. Like I said, it's like a cancer. Not contagious." She decided that Sage didn't need to know about the poison. This information was enough. She sighed and lowered her voice. "I'm telling you this because ferals are dangerous, Sage. They're dangerous to other vampires, but they'd suck you dry in the time it takes to eat an apple. You're in danger here, which is why I've said you have to stay with me. That way I know you're safe, and if you're always with me, Jet, or Lars, then we can make sure no one comes at you." She looked below at the vampires moving under the overhangs as they headed into the lodge for breakfast. "And there are a lot of new vampires here too. People I don't know, and likely more than a few who are well and truly pissed off at humans right now."

"And they don't want me in their business and reminding them that we're on different sides." Sage bit her lip. "I don't want to be a problem, especially when you've got so much going on. Is there any way I can help?"

How surprising. Sage seemed to have grown up a little in the short time she'd been there. Maybe she'd misjudged her a little.

Sage bit her lip. "I mean, Geno will have the internet hooked up, and I'll be able to launch videos. We could do interviews, you and I. And we could do them from up here, so I'd be safe."

And the notion that she understood deflated like a balloon. "You don't understand. We're in an incredibly delicate situation. One wrong move, one bit of video that could be misconstrued, and we go to war with the humans. Humans and vampires both die. Once this has blown over and you're back home, then you can do what you want. But the internet is a necessity right now, so I know what's going on outside Dark Haven. It isn't for you to go online and share what's going on here. The last thing I want out in the world is people seeing vampires huddled up in one big space, afraid and uncertain about their future."

"You said the videos I did from the hotel were useful." Sage drew her legs to her chest and wrapped her arms around them.

"You letting the world know you were safe was useful. And we may need to resort to that again if this goes on longer than it should. If we have to develop a political statement and use your platform to do it, then we'll do it as a group. We'll decide what's going to be said and shown." Remy stared at her intently. "Under no circumstances do you make that decision on your own."

Sage jerked back. "I don't work for you. I'm not one of your vampires to be ordered around. You can't tell me what I can and can't say. That's censorship, and if people knew that vampires were afraid—"

Remy stood abruptly. "You need to grow up, Sage. The world doesn't revolve around you and what *you* think should happen, or what people *should* think. You signed a contract saying you wouldn't post anything from here, and I expect you to abide by it, whether you like it or not. Clearly, you don't understand the larger implications at play, which means your voice in this matter needs to stay silent." She turned and went inside and was grateful when Sage didn't follow. She spoke over her shoulder. "Don't leave the lodge today without one of us by your side."

She finished getting ready and then went downstairs to breakfast. Jet and a couple others were already there, and the kitchen was a hive of production. It slowed when she entered, and a few heads bowed. She gave a smile and quick nod, and movement resumed.

"You look like you could take Rac's place right now," Jet said as she handed her a glass of synth.

Remy took it, and her stomach turned. "Where did we get this batch of synth?"

"It's left over from the last shipment. We're due a new one tomorrow, if the blockade lets it through. Why?" Jet's voice was quiet, as though she understood there was more to the question.

This was synth they'd had in store for several weeks, which meant it wasn't the source. Remy took a long drink and set it aside. "I'll tell you later. Is Lars around?"

Jet grinned. "He spent the night with Geno. They're having breakfast, looking very pleased with themselves."

Remy was about to ruin Lars' morning. "I'll go get him. Look, I could use someone to help me with all the shit going on and to make sure I don't miss anything. Would you mind?"

Jet looked a little offended. "Obviously. Like you have to ask. What do you need right away?"

Remy pinched the bridge of her nose as she thought. "I need you to get in touch with that vampire mom and son I went to see during the conference. They were supposed to be out here this week, but then everything went to hell. Find out where they are and see if you can get them here, by water if necessary. I have to go do something, and when I get back, let's sit down and lay out all the puzzle pieces."

Jet pulled a phone from her back pocket. "Will do. And this is for you from Geno. I've already given Dez Carmine your number, and I've put hers and the number for the White House in there too. He gave me and Lars new phones too, and those numbers are in there as well."

Remy squeezed her shoulder. "Thank you. That's one thing off my list already." She turned to go and stopped. "Oh—"

"I'll watch out for Sage too." Jet looked at her quizzically. "Is that part of your pent-up butch rage this morning?" She ducked her head a little. "Did she turn you down?" she whispered.

"On the contrary, she asked why we weren't already fucking like rabbits on Viagra." Remy rolled her eyes. "And apparently she wants to do a whole documentary about what's going on here."

"Ah." Jet backed away and grabbed a bowl full of cut fruit. "And Remy the hermit did not like that at all."

"Remy the hermit has good reason." She waved over her shoulder. "See you in a bit." She weaved her way through the vampires already in place, most not eating but clearly wanting community. She bent next to Lars, who was in the middle of some sickeningly sweet banter with Geno. "I need you."

He stopped mid-sentence and looked up, and whatever he saw in her expression stopped the lighthearted reply probably already on his lips. He dabbed at his mouth with a napkin, gave Geno a kiss on the cheek and stood. "I'm all yours."

Geno leaned back. "I'm happy to help too if you need an extra hand?"

The last person she wanted there was someone who'd once stabbed her in the back. As it was, she didn't even want him on the property. He had secrets, and she could feel them like pinpricks at the base of her neck. "We're good, thanks. And thanks for getting the tech set up. I'll be back in a while and maybe you could walk us through the particulars if there's anything I need to understand?"

He nodded, looking from her to Lars, but she didn't feel the need to explain what they were doing. She spoke to a few people on their way through the lodge but didn't stop to chat. Once they were outside and walking along the path that would take them to the cottage she really, really didn't want to go to, Lars touched her arm.

"How bad is it?" he asked.

She explained about the night before, including the aspect of poison.

He stopped and leaned against a pole, then shifted quickly when a sun ray caught his shoulder. "Pam was such a good mom. She was amazing in the garden." He put his hand on his chest and closed his eyes.

"I know. And now we need to go check on the kids."

His eyes opened wide. "Oh Jesus, Remy. If they show signs—"

"Let's just hope they don't, okay? But I'm going to need you to use your power to help me calm them down. I need to stay focused, and if I have to be inside their heads at the same time..."

He gave a small nod and fell into step with her. They didn't speak again until they got to the cottage. She took a deep breath and knocked.

A child of about nine opened the door, and a smaller child peeked out from behind him.

"Hi, Remy!" The smaller child ducked around her brother and threw herself against Remy's legs.

Remy hefted her into her arms. "Hey, kiddo. How are you this morning?"

"We're hungry." The older child, Jake, looked from Remy to Lars, his expression somber. "Mom didn't come home last night."

"Can we come in?" Lars asked, his hand on Jake's shoulder.

He swallowed and tears filled his eyes. Another unusual thing about born vampires. They could actually cry, whereas turned vampires couldn't.

"She's gone, isn't she?" he whispered. "I felt it, when she wasn't... here anymore."

Shala buried her head in Remy's shoulder and tears wet her neck. "She was acting icky. It scared us."

Remy and Lars went in and closed the door behind them. Remy sat with Shala on her lap, and really had no choice since the child didn't seem inclined to let go, and Lars sat beside Jake on the couch. Remy gently moved Shala's hair and looked at the back of her neck. Thankfully, there was no blackness. Lars glanced at Jake's neck and shook his head as well. Thank the dark gods for that. But what had gotten to their mother that hadn't gotten to them?

"Do you know if your mom ate or drank anything different recently? Anything at all that made her feel sick?"

The kids were quiet as they thought but then both shook their heads. Damn. Remy had been hoping for even a tiny lead.

"Did she go feral, Remy?" Jake asked.

"You know what that means?" Lars said, his hand still on Jake's shoulder. His power thrummed gently through the house.

"She wrote the word on a napkin a few weeks ago, right before she started acting weird and left the house one night. I looked it up in one of our history books." He pointed toward a textbook used in the schools on vampire history. "She knew what was happening, didn't she?"

Remy's heart ached for the mother who must have known what was coming but was powerless to stop it and too afraid to tell anyone. "It sounds like it. Did the note say anything else?"

He shook his head but got up and pulled it from a drawer in the kitchen, then handed it over.

It was as he said. The word feral was scribbled across it, barely legible. There was something about it though, something odd she couldn't put her finger on. She handed it to Lars, who glanced at it and set it down.

Shala cried quietly into Remy's neck, and she held her close. "What's going to happen to us, Remy?" she asked, her little voice muffled against Remy's shirt. "Are you going to make us go away?" She gave a quiet little sob. "I want my mommy."

"I know, little one. You're with family here, you know that. We'll take care of you, I promise." She looked at Lars, who, for all the calm he was emitting, looked stricken. "Let's go to the lodge and get you some breakfast, okay?"

The four of them walked to the lodge, and Lars kept hold of Jake's hand. If it weren't for Remy and Lars keeping the kids calm through their powers, both children would have been sobbing messes. And they could be, in order to grieve properly. But she needed to give them a safe space to do it, with an adult who could handle it.

They got to the lodge and a wave of silence followed them through the room. Pam had been popular, and everyone knew the special vampire children. The fact that they weren't with their mother and were clearly being calmed set every vampire in the room on edge. The fact that Rac had been there the day before and wasn't there now was quickly put into play as well. Remy could feel the links being made and the questions swiftly moving telepathically from vampire to vampire. Expressions varied from sympathy to fear to anger.

They got the kids settled at the table with Geno and Sage. Jet took in the scene and looked like she'd been struck. She dropped against the doorjamb and looked bleakly at Remy.

Remy turned to the room. "If you want to talk to me about this, let Jet know and she'll make sure we get time together. No rumors, no gossip. We have children to take care of, and if you have your own or if you have experience with kids, please let Jet know. If there's anything I feel you need to know, I'll call a community meeting. In the meantime, please sign up for work duty around the ranch. We could use the help with all the extra bodies around." She waited for anyone to speak, but no one did. Most looked down in deference, and some looked at the children, who were eating listlessly.

She turned to Jet, whose gaze remained glued to the kids. "Hey. You okay?"

Jet finally looked away. "I... Fuck. Pam?"

Sage left the table and joined them. "I'm a little confused. What happened to their mother?"

Remy couldn't bring herself to say the words out loud, where they took shape and created something even uglier. "You remember our discussion this morning, on the deck?"

Sage blinked and then went pale. "F—"

Remy held up her hand. "Yes."

"Oh." Sage looked back at the kids and her lip trembled. "What about their father?"

"Not in the picture. In fact, I could really use your help today, Sage." Remy touched her elbow to get her to focus. "Could you keep the kids upstairs with you? Young vampires sleep a lot during the day, so you shouldn't have much to do, but I'd like an adult with them."

Sage nodded quickly and dashed her hand over her eyes. "Of course. Yeah, obvs." She bit her lip and looked over her shoulder, then at Remy. "Could I ask Geno for an iPad or something, so they can watch movies? It might help keep their mind off things."

It made sense, in a way, but Remy didn't like it. "Their mom moved to Dark Haven because she wanted to keep them safe and away from all the chaos of the outside world. I'm not sure how she'd feel about us exposing them to it the moment she's gone and using media as a babysitter. Maybe you could find some books and read to them instead?"

Sage looked bemused but nodded. "I'll work something out."

"Thank you."

Remy went over to the children and squatted between them. "You're going to stay here in the lodge with my friend, Sage. Is that okay?"

Shala looked to her brother, who nodded. "Mom always said we had to do whatever you told us." His eyes filled with tears, and he put his arm around his little sister. "I'm scared, Remy. I want my mom." He began to cry, and his sister put her head on his arm and began to cry too.

Sage knelt beside them. "Hey. I lost my mom when I was little too. Let's go upstairs where we can talk and be away from everyone, okay?"

Shala looked up. "You don't have a mommy either?"

Sage touched her cheek. "Nope. I'll tell you about it if you want me to?"

The girl slid off her chair and hugged Sage but quickly pulled back, her eyes wide. She looked up at Remy. "She smells like synth. But better." Her brown eyes changed to red, and her tiny fangs poked out beneath her lip.

"Shit." Remy pulled Sage back and behind her, nearly sending her sprawling. She'd forgotten that the kids hadn't been around humans since their mom had brought them to the ranch when they were still little. Jake had only been three and Shala a newborn.

"I've got them." Jet finally moved away from the doorway and hefted Shala into her arms. "Come on. Let's go upstairs where it's quiet."

Shala looked down at Jake, her bottom lip quivering. "Did I do something bad?"

He looked from Remy to Jet, and there was a flicker of understanding in his eyes. Even child vampires understood that they were hunters who drank blood. And he'd been reading up on their history, which meant he knew what they usually hunted.

"No, honey." Jet bounced her a little. "You didn't do anything wrong. In fact, Sage is still going to come with us. Isn't she?" She looked over her shoulder at Remy.

"I'm not sure—"

"We have to learn sometime, don't we?" Jake stood and straightened his shoulders like he was trying to look more grown up. Although this had certainly forced him to do so. "One day we'll be out in the world. We can't always live here."

Remy held his shoulder. "You're going to be free to do anything you want when you're older. If you wanted to live out your existence here, you'd always find it was home." She turned to Sage, who looked a little miffed. "Go ahead, but watch yourself." Making a decision, she used her powers and spoke to Sage mentally. *These children haven't learned control yet, and they're going to be unstable emotionally. Even now, they're stronger than you. Understand?*

Sage's lips were pressed together, and her eyes never left Remy's. She gave a short nod and then motioned toward Jet, who led the children back through the crowd and up the stairs, with Sage following.

Remy breathed deeply and wanted nothing more than to sit down at the table and commiserate with Lars. But there was simply too much to do.

She jerked when someone else's thought entered her head.

A feral problem. Interesting. Just like old times.

Geno's grin was inscrutable, and she gritted her teeth. "Don't talk about things you don't understand." She stared at him pointedly and then turned to the kitchen. She needed to get outside to clear her mind. She left the lodge and headed toward the forest, and it was only as she was coming close to Lester's cottage that she slowed. He was sitting on his porch, his pale eyes gleaming in the shadows, his dark skin making him part of the shade. She often forgot about him because he kept to himself for the most part.

He waved her up. "Come, chérie. Sit with me." His soft voice carried on the autumn breeze.

She took the simple wood chair next to his and waited for the questions, but he simply continued to puff on a cigar and look placidly at the world. As the silence continued, her shoulders dropped, and she began to breathe properly again. His place at the edge of the living space of the ranch meant no one came by, no one wanted to talk. After a while longer, it no longer felt like chaos in her head. "Thank you."

He nodded. "You brought us here to escape the noise, but the noise has come to you, hasn't it?" He blew a smoke circle in the air. "The world always finds us, chérie, try as we might to pretend it can't. We must enjoy the moments of contentment in between." His soft French accent made it sound philosophical instead of bleak.

"Was I wrong, Lester?" she asked. "Did bringing the vampires into the human world put us in even more danger? Should I have let things stay the same?"

He puffed out a smoke circle, then waved his free hand and the circle became a picture in the air: a castle, with a rider heading toward it. "Do you know the first time I saw you?"

The smoke castle looked familiar, like a wispy memory. "No."

"It was fifteen twenty-six. San Miguel de Gualdape. Do you remember?"

She searched her memory but came up blank. "I'm sorry. I don't."

He nodded. "When we go through so much, it's hard to remember all the moments, isn't it? It was a revolt at a Spanish settlement. One hundred slaves from Africa and a large number of natives were being handled by fools who were starving them, watching as they died."

"You were a slave?"

His gaze slowly turned to her. "No, chérie. I was in the ship that brought them over. The second one, after the first one foundered. I'd been living in Spain and needed a change. So I put myself in the cargo, making sure I could get in and out to feed. Some of the crew, well, they got sick and fell overboard on the voyage." He shrugged slightly. "I followed the colony out of curiosity, and I freed those I could without calling attention to myself. But superstition was high, and the Africans feared me. Even then, my eyes looked like they do now."

If his eyes had been this pale five hundred years ago... "How old are you, Lester?"

He looked beyond her, toward the forest. "The first time I saw you, it was midnight. You rode past on a black horse, black as death, and I wondered if you were a ghost. But then I saw your eyes and knew you were like me." He threw his head back and laughed, surprising her. "You were the first! In all the years I'd wandered the earth, you were the first vampire I came across. We were so good at hiding, at being in the world but never part of it, that I truly thought I was alone."

"That must have been awful." She touched his arm and realized it was the first time she'd ever touched him. What would it be like to go so long without any touch at all?

"It was...soul destroying. I was not the man I am now." His eyes narrowed slightly as he seemed to gaze into the past. "But there you were. You saw what was happening. Maybe you'd been watching for some time, I don't know, and you rode right up to the house with some of the Spaniards in it, and you set it on fire. Just like that, you were a god dishing out punishment, and then the place was in the fires of hell, where it belonged. The slaves had already left their chains thanks to me, and I joined them as they razed it to the ground, and I fed well that night."

"But you didn't call out to me."

"You were gone like the ghost I thought you were. You rode away and left the flames burning behind you. But I never forgot your face." He turned to look at her. "And when I saw your face in the news, it was like a dark angel being returned to me. Living at night was easier in the new centuries and although I found more like us, I never fit into any clan. I'd grown so accustomed to moving I never grew roots. But then...you."

She was mesmerized by his story, by the smooth tone of his

voice and the way it carried with it the memories of the past. She remembered the night she'd set fire to the slavers' camp. She'd only been passing by but had seen other slave encampments elsewhere and was doing what she could without drawing attention. Not that it worked. Word spread and eventually she'd had to move on, knowing she'd done what she could.

"You were there, in front of the cameras, demanding that we be treated with respect. Not only were you not content with us continuing to live in the shadows, as creatures of the night, you were intent on us living as fully as we wanted to. You were riding your black horse once again, but this time it was for us." He turned away, his gaze back toward the land that was their home. "When I heard about Dark Haven, I knew it was where my roots would finally find a place to grow. If you hadn't stepped into the light, many of us would still be lost in the dark."

If Remy could cry, she would have broken down. As it was, her dry eyes ached with emotion. "I can't explain how much I needed to hear that."

His smile was faint. "You think I don't know?"

She laughed. "And that's why you don't want humans on our land."

His smile faded. "I've had more than my share of them over my lifetime. This community you built for us, where we can be safe and take part in the outside world if and when we wish, is something special. Sacred. And humans are threatening us once again, trying to wrest control of what they don't understand and letting fear rule them as it always does."

"I won't let them take this from us, Lester." Once again, she reached out to touch him, and this time he took her hand. "I promise, I'll fix this."

He squeezed her hand. "I know why they call you Wind. I heard whispers of it in the breeze when it was happening. I know you'll do everything you can." He let go of her hand and picked up his cigar. "But change is inevitable, Remy. We've seen it, you, me, and

Rac. We know there's no stopping it. We flow around it like water around rocks in a stream." His expression grew hard, his eyes narrow. "And if you need to fight, I will be at your side."

They sat there in silence for a while longer. Finally, she said, "Can I ask where you originally came from?"

He puffed on the cigar. "It's strange, isn't it, how we're so reluctant to talk of our origins? And why should that be? It gives no one power over us. It tells no one who we are, though it may suggest what we've been through." He tapped the ash from his cigar into an old-looking bit of tin. "France under Louie IX, chérie. And you?"

So he wasn't as old as she'd thought. Not as old as her. It was only fair she tell him, but he was right: it was hard to do. "Sweden. Viking age."

He stared at her for a long moment and then looked away. "What we've been through, eh?"

She stood and looked down at him. "Thank you, Lester. I hope you'll join in at the campfires some nights. I think the other vampires have a lot to learn from you."

"Is that a request, Remy?"

She considered it. "It is, Lester. I think it would be good for you too. But I could also use the eyes and ears of someone who understands how to really watch and listen."

He nodded and blew a smoke ring that became an eye. "Happy to help."

She squeezed his shoulder and left his cottage, feeling better and a little clearer, although she still had a lot to figure out. One thing was unequivocal though.

She would fight to her last breath to protect her community, and no one would stand in her way.

CHAPTER THIRTEEN

SAGE PLUGGED IN HER phone, which she'd remembered to grab when she'd first come down for breakfast. It was dead as a dodo, of course, and she found herself itching to get it up and running, not just to see what the video had captured while it had been recording but also to see what was going on in the world. Were her followers wondering where she was? Had the government decided to demand her back?

But all that would wait. Right now, there were two children crying in Remy's living room. She poured them glasses of synth, even though her stomach turned a little at the metallic odor, and she added a couple slices of orange like she'd seen Remy do. Maybe they'd like that. She brought them in, and the kids accepted the glasses but drank half-heartedly.

She desperately wanted to hug them, to wrap them up and tell them it would all be okay, somehow. But Remy's telepathic instruction had been clear. Unsettling and clear. So she curled up in the armchair instead. Jet sat on the floor in front of the kids, talking to them about this and that, mundane things.

Jake tapped Sage's arm. "You said you lost your mom."

"I did." Sage looked at Jet, who gave a faint nod of encouragement. "When I was ten—"

"I'm nine," he said.

"So, when I was about your age, there was a fire. I got out, but my mom didn't."

"You didn't have a daddy either?" Shala looked at her with watery eyes.

"Nope. My daddy died a few years earlier. He was sick, like

your mom."

"We didn't know our dad. Mom said he couldn't live the vampire life, and he had to go back to the human world." Jake's little brow furrowed. "But we were living in the human world, so I don't understand."

"Sometimes these things don't make any sense." Sage hadn't told anyone about her family history in a long time, and the words burned her throat. Jet was looking at her with sympathy, and she had to look away.

"Will it always hurt like this?" Jake asked, his lip trembling.

"Honestly?" She looked between them. "You're always going to miss her. You'll never forget her, and that way, she's always with you. Everything she taught you will stay in your heart. One day, you'll find that you can think of her without crying, and it doesn't hurt quite as much."

The kids didn't seem to know what to say to that, and Shala yawned.

"Come on, you two." Jet stood and held out her hands. "Let's get you some sleep."

Sage led the way to the room she'd been using. "They can sleep in here."

The kids clambered into the big bed and were quickly asleep. Jet pulled the blackout blinds down and closed the door behind her, leaving it cracked slightly.

They settled on the couch, and Jet rested her head on the back of it. "What a clusterfuck." She motioned at Sage. "Sounds like you know what they're going through."

"Yeah." She didn't feel the need to go into further detail.

"You did good."

Sage wrapped her arms around her knees. "Have you heard any more news?"

The door opened and Remy came in, looking a little better than she had when she'd left. Sage disliked the way they'd left things that morning, with what felt like bitter words and a lack of...of...she didn't know what. But it was missing.

Remy flopped onto the couch next to Jet. "They okay?"

Jet barely nodded. "When the anger sets in, we'll have to have someone psychically leash them, or take them out to the woods and let them vent. Or both. But for now, they're fine." She grinned and wearily lifted her head. "And they didn't want to eat Sage this time."

Sage winced. "Not funny."

"Kind of funny," Remy said with a smirk. "I made the suggestion without thinking, I'm sorry. I haven't lived among humans in so long, I forgot what it's like not to be able to control yourself around them. When I was dealing with the politics, I was so focused on the project that I didn't stop to think about food."

Sage sent a mental image of her and Remy fucking hard on the bed, and Remy glared at her.

"Knock it off."

Jet rolled her eyes and turned to Remy. "I think we need to lay some stuff out so we can get a handle on what needs to be done."

Remy pushed herself up from the couch and went to the desk, where she pulled a notebook and pen out and handed them to Jet. "Okay. First, did you manage to make that call this morning?"

Jet wrote something down and then put a check mark next to it. "I did, and I've made the arrangements. They're coming by boat around one in the morning, and I'll make sure I'm there to meet them. I've got someone setting up one of the extra cottages for them."

"Great, thank you. I'm thinking of asking her to take care of Pam's kids."

Jet's eyebrows rose. "That's a big ask. Come start a new life, and by the way, here are some orphans for you."

"Um? Hello?" Sage waved. "I'm still here. And apparently, I can't go anywhere without a bodyguard, so can you read me in?"

"Selma and Jimmy Artillo are vampires from outside the city, near the state border. Jimmy was attacked at a store, and he's an outcast in his high school. They're moving to the area, and they'll be staying here until we get them a place."

Sage blew out a breath. "Jet's right, but if she's already got a kid who's a vampire, she'll understand what they need, and that's a big part of the battle, right?"

Remy tilted her head and continued speaking to Jet. "Next. I need to get with Dez and see where things stand. Hopefully it'll be good news. After that, I need to set up a video conference with the clan leaders. I want them involved in evacuation for those who want to leave. They'll probably have good ideas about communities outside ours where we can go until..." She shrugged. "Until whatever happens, happens."

Jet wrote in what looked like scrawl.

"A laptop would make that a lot easier," Sage said, wondering how fast she could write by hand. She hadn't had to do it since before high school, since she'd had a laptop back then. Even her exams had all been on the computer.

"Sage, we discussed this." Remy rested her head against the sofa. "I don't want more tech here than we need. I know it's hard for you to understand, but try, okay?"

Sage crossed her arms and looked out the window. "Just because you're older than dirt doesn't mean you get to talk to me like I'm a child."

"To us, you are one." Jet gave her a sympathetic smile. "And Remy is definitely older than dirt."

"Fuck off, both of you." Remy nodded toward Jet's notepad. "Rac is coming back tomorrow night in case another feral or two come out. But she won't have the lab results on the vampire we sent out for a few more days, so I want to see where our synth lab is on production. We may need to switch."

Sage frowned. "Why would you need to switch synth because of a feral vampire? Didn't you say it was like an illness?"

Remy winced, but barely. "I didn't say it earlier, but it looks like this isn't the kind of feral we're used to. The vampire in question had been poisoned, and it caused feral-like symptoms."

Sage's heart raced a little faster. "And you think someone has poisoned your food supply? Oh my god. Are you in danger?"

Remy smiled, and her eyebrow lifted. *Your first concern is for me? That's sweet.*

Sage wasn't sure she'd ever get used to being spoken to telepathically, but she liked the tone of the thought that matched the slight glint in Remy's eyes.

"We're all in danger until we find out the source, the type of poison, and who the fuck would be so stupid." Jet shook her head and continued to scribble. "They have to know that if they get found out, they're in a world of hurt."

"Is there anything else I need to put on the list?" Remy asked Jet.

"Housing will need to be dealt with if this goes on more than a week. And we'll need to work out the food situation if you want to stop the trucks incoming." Jet tapped the pencil on the tablet. "What are you going to do about Geno?"

Remy ran her hand through her hair. "My instinct is to keep him close so I can keep an eye on him. His surprise that Cadence was here was genuine, but I don't like it. So my other instinct is to get him off our property."

"Split the difference then." Sage shrugged when they looked at her. "We're bound to have tech problems out here, and if he's as good as he says he is, then he'd be able to listen to any conversations anyway. So bring him here every few days, see what he knows, do your snooping thing in his head, and then send him away again."

Remy laughed dryly. "He won't like that, being told to come and go like a servant."

Sage shrugged again. "Then maybe he'll slip up if he's doing something nefarious."

Remy and Jet continued to talk about timings and what to do with the orphans and the influx of vampires still coming in. Meanwhile, Sage looked out the window and wondered if and when she'd be able to go home. She wasn't in a hurry, mind. She was happy to be where the action was, even if it scared the bejesus out of her sometimes. It was far better than her lonely apartment. And the memories brought up of losing her own family had reignited the flame of loneliness she usually managed to keep to an ember.

"Sage?"

She turned, startled. "Sorry, I was miles away. What did you say?"

"I said we need to be extra careful with you. Tempers are going to be running high, and I need to know you're safe. So you really do have to stay beside one of the three of us, okay? Please?"

Mollified at Remy's more gentle way of saying it this time, Sage nodded. "I don't intend to be anyone's meal, Remy. And I happen to really like the three of you." She grinned when Jet puffed up her chest. "But I don't want to be some kind of weird hanger-on either. I need to help, to be involved somehow. Please," she said, using the same tone Remy had.

There was silence for a moment as Jet and Remy both clearly thought about the problem.

"Here's the thing, Sage." Remy leaned forward, her hands planted on her thighs. "If you show too much of our fear and vulnerability to the human world, it could work against us. When everything was calm, we looked strong and capable. Now, we could easily look like targets or monsters. So you've got to be careful about what it is you show people." She looked at Jet, who nodded. "That means I'm not crazy about you posting videos while you're here unless they're to show the world you're still alive."

"But maybe this is your chance to leave your little screens behind for a while. Come help me with the garden or with building the new cottages. Get your hands dirty." Jet wiggled her eyebrows.

Sage bit her lip. "Okay. I can do that, but you have to let me help with the tech stuff when Geno isn't here. I know what I'm doing better than any of you." She looked between them and wondered if they were talking mind-to-mind. Their expressions weren't changing so she couldn't tell.

"That sounds like a good workaround." Remy stretched. "I'm going to go call Dez and find out where things stand. Maybe she'll tell me that everything has blown over, and everyone can go back to their lives, and they're sorry the wicked humans inconvenienced us." Her tone left no question what she thought of that possibility. "I need you two to stay with the kids until Selma and Jimmy get here. We can put the kids on the sofa bed, and he and Selma can have my room, since I'll be out with Rac for most of the night, most likely."

Sage bit her lip. "Why not put them in my room, put the kids on the sofa bed, and me in your room? That way you can still come to bed if you do get back in time."

Jet laugh-coughed and looked at the floor, her eyebrows high.

"That's fine too, as long as you keep your hands to yourself. I'm a delicate flower, and I refuse to be treated as anything other than the princess I am." Remy flipped back her non-existent long hair.

"I'll treat you just the way you deserve," Sage said solemnly.

"Okay." Jet stood and shoved Remy toward the door. "Any more pheromones in here and I'm going to need to go get my vibrator, and the thought of that having anything to do with you sets off my gag reflex."

Remy waved, and the door closed behind her.

Sage sat back, rather proud of herself for getting the stoic Remy to let loose with a little banter. It was almost like they were becoming friends.

Jet went to the bookshelf and pulled out an old Scrabble set. "I'm about to kick your ass."

"No fair." Sage settled at the table. "I can't possibly have the vocabulary of a vampire way older than me."

Jet grinned. "Why do you think I want to play?"

Sage began to set up and considered the weird sense of peace that had settled over her. Everything around her was chaos, and yet she felt more wanted, more at ease, more part of something than she had in a very, very long time. If only it could last.

Chapter Fourteen

"For the sake of all the fucks in the universe, Dez." Remy slapped a book on the table just to have something to take it out on. Being on a video call meant she couldn't hide her irritation.

"You need a TV over there, Remy. I need you or one of yours to be watching so you're always on top of things." Dez looked tired, though it only showed in her eyes, since her skin was unchanging. Her shoulders were slumped as she leaned back in her chair. "The military has been turning vampires away at our borders, saying no one goes in and no one goes out. And then they're escorting them away, but no one knows where the hell they've taken them. Footage only shows the cars sandwiched between military vehicles."

Remy allowed her fangs to grow with frustration and anger. "They wouldn't dare try anything."

Dez shook her head. "I wouldn't think so, but that alone is a gutsy move. Cornered vampires are going to fight, so it has to be for show. Otherwise, we'd be getting reports of dead military personnel strewn over the highway."

That was logical, but the situation was still out of control. "So what's the next step?"

"We've got a call with the president in a minute. I expect more platitudes and more of the same shit about staying calm and letting this blow over."

Remy waited, but Dez didn't say anything else. "And? What are we going to do? Just wait it out while vampires are going missing and have nowhere else to go? Are we going to tell the president to fuck off?"

Dez just raised her eyebrows.

"Yeah." Remy ran her hands through her hair. "Okay. We stay calm and keep things going for as long as we can. How is the city for supplies?"

Dez looked out her office window. "We're okay for now because supply trucks are still coming through. But if that stops, we'll be in trouble within a week, maybe two." She turned back to Remy. "How are you at the ranch?"

At least that was one area where Remy had the upper hand. "We've got the harvest to get in, and it's a good one this year so we'll have plenty of food, not that we need it, obviously. We don't have humans mixed in here like you do, and we could get by with just synth if we had to. It's a little crowded but with the extra hands, we can get more buildings up and running. We just had a shipment of wood, so we'll be fine on that end too." She didn't mention the feral problem. Dez had enough on her plate, and unless Remy could definitively say it was in the food supply, it wouldn't do any good to worry her.

"Good to know. I may end up on your doorstep." Dez gave her a wry smile. "Hey, the president is calling. Ready?"

Remy shrugged and waited. She breathed deeply and made sure her fangs were retracted. No need to look threatening from moment one. Not yet, anyway.

"Ms. Winslow, Ms. Carmine," the president said when he came on screen, his dark eyes guarded. "Thank you for taking the time."

"Mr. President, I assume you have good news for us," Dez said, jumping right in.

He sighed the sigh of the downtrodden. "I wish I did, Ms. Carmine. But I'm afraid the pain is still too fresh, and people are still too frightened. I imagine the vampires feel the same way, given some of them died as well."

"No, Mr. President. With all due respect, as a community we understood that this was two groups of people who were out for a fight. We didn't feel the need to round up all the humans and tell them to sit tight while the vampires got over their fear." Remy kept her tone neutral, but she knew full well that pretending things were fine wasn't going to make them so.

He blanched slightly. "It does sound pretty bad when you put it that way, Ms. Winslow." He peered more closely at her through the screen. "I've never asked, and I hope it isn't unprofessional, but how old are you?"

Remy peered back at him. "It is unprofessional and has nothing to do with this conversation, other than to say I've seen governments rise and fall, and I understand fear like you wouldn't possibly be able to. And I know that the way a government responds to attacks is the way the people will respond. So you deploying the military and escorting vampires away from safe haven is exactly what your people will think is the right thing to do."

"That sounded almost like a threat, Ms. Winslow." The president steepled his hands under his chin.

"It wasn't any such thing and you know it, John." Dez rubbed at her eyes. "You know Remy is talking logic. What's really going on?"

He pursed his lips, waved away someone off camera, and then turned fully to them. "I'm under a lot of pressure, Dez." His tone softened, as did his volume. "People were coming around to the idea of vampires among us, but that sliver of fear was just under the surface. Like living in a savannah. You know lions are out there, but you can roam about thinking you're safe until one pops up. But the attack has scared that sliver right into a javelin, and humans don't want to think they're prey."

"John, we've discussed this at length," Remy said. "You know full well we don't really drink from humans anymore, and certainly not those who are unwilling. The blood is too full of chemicals and imbalance. We've been drinking synth for decades. You signed a bill giving us rights, John. Are you really going to step aside and let all that work we did go to ground?"

His shoulders fell. "You're right, Remy. I forget, sometimes, those nights we spent talking. All I hear now is all these damn people who are supposed to be working for me filling my brain with so much static I can't think straight." He ran his hand over his face. "Okay. We've got to work together on this. I need more time to diffuse the situation. Can you give me that?"

Dez and Remy looked at one another. They'd discussed the supply and housing issue, so they could practically give him time. But on an emotional level, it was a different story.

"We need to see you making an effort publicly, John," Dez said. "Make a statement about the need for tolerance and understanding. Hell, get Remy back in front of the cameras to talk about what we want and who we are. People are used to seeing her up front."

Remy groaned. "God, I thought those days were behind me."

John nodded. "I think that's a good idea, Remy. Give it another week or so, and then we'll arrange for you to come to Washington, and we'll do a press conference."

Remy held up her hand. "In the meantime, your military at the border needs to stop whatever the hell it is they're doing with vampires trying to get into Bluff County. And what's that about anyway?"

He sat back and shook his head. "Hell if I know, honestly. General Cane is in charge and likes to make unilateral decisions. I only heard about it today myself, but I'll see to it that it stops." He looked beyond the camera, and his posture straightened. "Anyway, if you can keep things calm and even on your end, then we'll do so on ours. This will blow over in no time, and we'll be back to living together peacefully."

Clearly, he had an audience he needed to be in a mask for. Remy hated the politics of all of this down to her bone marrow. "You hold up your end of our deal, Mr. President, and we'll hold up ours. We'll be watching."

The president nodded and his screen went dark, leaving just her and Dez again. "What do you think?" Remy asked.

"I think his house isn't as in order as he thinks it is." Dez nodded at someone out of Remy's view. "I have to go. Is your tech all set up?"

Remy nodded and shook the phone slightly. "Obviously. I hate these things."

"Well, get used to it for a while. And all the vampires you've taken in will have them too, remember. Your world is about to shrink again, Remy. Sorry." Dez gave her a quick smile. "Let's talk tomorrow unless anything comes up."

Remy ended the call. She sat back, thinking. She disliked the idea of vampires being led away, and she had a feeling it wasn't just for show. Something bad was going on, and she needed to know what it was. Maybe, though, it would stop when the president gave the order. Still, the idea of not doing anything to check on the situation didn't sit right.

And it wasn't like she didn't have other things on her plate. She heaved herself from the chair and headed outside. The areas she passed were mostly empty, which was odd given the amount of people on the property now. When she got to the end of the main walkway, she saw why.

Under the large metal coverings that had been put in by cranes and which would be removed or moved to another building area later, vampires were working on five different cottages. Like ants, they moved over the properties swinging hammers, using drills, flinging cement, and best of all, laughing. Banter was loud and constant, and it seemed like damn near everyone on the ranch was helping out. She leaned against a post and watched, letting the sense of community fill the hole emerging in her soul. This was why she'd done it. Because her people deserved safety and happiness.

"Hey, Remy!" someone called out from a half-built roof. "You just going to stand there and watch like some wastrel god?"

Others laughed and joined in the teasing. She waved them off. "Looks like I'd just get in the way, and I need to go see how I'm going to feed you ungrateful lot." She took the jeers with good humor and set off toward the garden.

More vampires were gathered there, helping with the harvest, working beneath enormous shiftable gazebos. Working the harvest was harder, as it meant always being aware of where the sun was coming in, but these were clearly vampires who knew how to dance around the sunbeams, doing it like it was second nature. Which it was, in a way; that particular instinct seemed to show up the moment one turned from human to vampire.

She focused on what was actually being harvested and did some vague mental calculations. She'd have to talk to her crop manager to see if she was right, but it looked like they could hold out for a couple months if they had to. While eating real food wasn't necessary, it did make life a lot nicer. Dark gods forbid this went on that long though. She turned away, and then realized she wasn't sure where to go next. The vampires who'd been living on the ranch were clearly happy to take the refugees under their wings and get them involved without Remy needing to give any instruction. Housing was being taken care of, food was being taken care of... She thought of the synth lab. That needed to be ready to go, and she hadn't been out there in a while.

She headed to the stable and found Gabe inside. "Shouldn't you be out counting grains of wheat and logs of hay?"

Gabe grinned, her handsome face looking far less stressed than the last time Remy had seen her, after Sage had nearly run her off the road. "Thanks to the world's basic inability to live with difference, we've got so many people on hand I could delegate and give some attention to our other friends." She waved a grooming brush. "What brings you slumming?"

Remy laughed and held out her hand for the big black Friesian to nuzzle it. "You lot are making me think I live in an ivory tower."

Gabe scoffed. "You're the hardest working, most down-to-earth vampire I know. You should be despicably arrogant and intolerably difficult thanks to your looks and brains, but you aren't." She looked strangely serious for a moment. "If anyone can get us through this, you can."

"No pressure there." Remy pressed her forehead to the horse's, who snuffled at her. It brought back the memory Lester had reminded her of, on a slave plantation, where she'd ridden a black horse so much like this one. "Thanks for that vote of confidence though. I could use the bolstering these days."

Gabe made a noncommittal sound. "Glad it isn't me who has to deal with things. But don't let it go to your head." She gave a quick smile. "Something I can help with?"

Remy kept her hand on the horse's head, drawing strength and calm from it. "I need to take a ride out to the western edge."

"Okay. You taking Nero?"

"Yeah, if that's okay?"

Gabe shook her head. "Only you would ask if it's okay to take your own horse for a ride, weirdo." She hefted a saddle off the wall and shoved it into Remy's chest. "Stick to the trees today though. Sun's heavy."

Remy stood aside and let Gabe handle getting Nero, named after the planet in Remy's favorite sci-fi novel, ready for the ride. He pawed at the ground like he was ready to run, and Remy was most definitely ready to let him. She pulled on a leather riding jacket and a beanie that covered her ears and neck, then pulled up the snood to cover the bottom of her face. With her skin covered except for the narrow section of her eyes and nose, she climbed up and drank in how good it felt to have that much power under her. She stroked his neck. "Let's run."

He snorted and reared slightly, and they took off, quickly leaving the stable behind. She waved at Lester as she raced past his cottage and into the woods. The pounding of Nero's hooves made her thoughts slow and then disappear as she simply existed in the moment and the staccato, rhythmic beat. No politics, no worries about starvation or revolt, no feral vampires...nothing. Just her, the horse, the woods, the shadows, and the feeling of being completely at one with the world around her. They slowed to a walk, and she patted his neck.

As they moved through the forest and birds sang around them, she realized how long it had been since she'd used any of her powers beyond mind-to-mind communication. She hadn't needed to. Was she losing touch with her vampire self? Even when she'd set up the ranch and invited others, she'd never considered asking them about what types of powers they had or how often they used them. There was something private about it, much like talking about age and origin. Strange, the taboos they lived with and never really questioned.

She sighed as the concerns around life came rushing back in like a tide. Maybe she'd grown too far from what she was, and she was out of touch with the way vampires wanted to, and should, actually live. What if people accepted that there were predators among them? She let out a choked laugh, making Nero snort. As though they'd simply accept that without taking up arms. Every sci-fi and paranormal movie in history showed how humans dealt with the monsters among them. Only recently had the other side of the story begun to be shown, and she loved the new books coming out showing how the monsters and villains were often created by the circumstances and bastard humans around them.

But then there was Sage. Sweet, feisty, irritatingly positive Sage. Remy was doing everything in her power to keep her at a distance, but she felt her control slipping. For all that she showed Sage what she was and explained that Sage shouldn't expect anything other than...well, a monster, Sage seemed disinclined to give a hot damn. She'd melted into their community easily, talking and laughing, and not overly fazed even when threatened with being a meal. Remy found that she liked her, despite her naïveté and stubbornness. Or, maybe, because of them. Sage would be gone soon though, when the chaos faded, and Remy could go back to her somewhat lonely but reasonably fulfilling existence. Why didn't that feel like enough these days? The thought of Sage leaving, of never seeing her again, pained her in a way that was both illogical and frustrating. But it was true, nonetheless.

The synth lab came into view and she did a quick scan, using her extra senses. Five people inside, nothing to worry about on the perimeter. The six cottages in the back, where the lab team lived, were all empty. She needed to consider more security around the lab. The barbwire fencing and keycard entrance were good, but if things went really badly, she might need to post guards too. They couldn't be without the synth necessary for their survival.

She dismounted, keyed herself in, and led Nero inside. She didn't bother to tether him. He could roam and would come when she whistled. He gave her shoulder a shove with his head, and she rubbed his nose. "I'll be back soon."

He turned toward the small feeding area set up beyond the lab, and Remy headed inside. The air was cool, and she was glad for it as she stripped off her gear. It was necessary but riding at night would have been a lot easier. She left it all in the changing room at the front and donned a sterile jumpsuit from the cupboard.

When she finally entered the lab, they were clearly waiting for her, and they all stood. "Hello, everyone." She nodded at each of them. "Sorry I haven't been down in a while. I wanted to check in. Hope I'm not interrupting too much."

Raphael, the lead scientist, held out his hand. "It's good to see you, Remy. It's been too long."

His thick black hair was pulled back into a tight little bun, and his equally dark eyes made his words ring true.

"Thanks. How's everything going?" Remy moved toward the staff room and took a seat, and she was glad when all of them joined her and not just Raphael. In small groups like this one, it was important everyone felt heard and that she knew if anyone was unhappy.

"Things are going really well for the most part," Olivia, the second in command, said, pushing her glasses up her nose. She didn't need them, of course. Any illness or defect went away the moment they were turned, but she liked wearing them.

"For the most part?" Remy looked at the team. "Is there a problem?"

Elijah got up and pulled two small bottles from the fridge.

"We're having a little bit of a consistency issue." He held up the first bottle and pulled the cork out. "This is what we're going for."

He handed it over and Remy first sniffed and then tasted a small amount. She let it sit on her tongue and paid attention to the tang of it. It was smooth, and the iron content was just right. It was nicer than the real thing had been in recent decades. "Nice."

He opened the other and handed it to her. "Notice the difference."

She sniffed it and instantly could tell the difference. "Something's off." She took a small sip and grimaced. "It almost tastes dead."

They nodded, understanding her meaning. Blood from dead bodies quickly went sour and became almost undrinkable except under the most dire circumstances.

"Do you know what the problem is?" she asked, taking a sip of the original batch to get the taste out of her mouth.

"We think it's to do with the livestock." Olivia tilted her head toward the barns out back. "They're being delivered, but they don't look like they usually do. In order to make the mixture like the original, we need hematopoietic cells from healthy bovine stock that we then turn into the molecular structures we need. That hasn't been a problem, and we really thought we were ready to begin creating vats for large quantities."

"But?" Remy had so hoped this would be the one area where she'd have good news. So much for that.

"But the livestock we're getting isn't healthy. The supplier swears there's nothing different, but we can tell that isn't the case." Raphael's gaze was searching as he looked at her. "We made some calls to get a new supplier, but every one of them turned us down."

Remy felt the red seeping into her vision and took a deep breath. "The reason given?"

"Mad cow disease, a lack of available cattle, shutting down... We've been given all kinds of reasons." He crossed his arms, his gaze never wavering. "How bad is it, Remy?"

She looked at this invaluable small team of dedicated vampires who'd chosen to live onsite and devote themselves to creating something sustainable and innovative. They were just as much a part of Dark Haven as the others tending to the farms and building. "You haven't been offsite in a while?"

They shook their heads. "With the cold and dark days coming, we've been waiting so we can go out without having to worry about daylight," Olivia said.

Remy told them about what was happening in the real world, along their borders and in the wider government. They listened without interruption, but she could feel them becoming increasingly agitated. With a deep breath, she also told them about the feral issue. If anyone could help, it would be the scientists.

There was silence for a long moment after she finished, and it occurred to her to wonder if they'd stick around or if they'd want to relocate like so many others.

"I'm sorry I asked," Raphael finally said. The others smiled a little in response.

"Rac has sent the feral we dealt with the other night to her special lab," Remy said and tilted her head in acknowledgement at their grimaces. "I know, none of us want to ever head to Dr. Frank's place, but if anyone can figure out what's going on, it'll be him." The creepy old scientist liked playing with life and death scenarios, and it was well known you wanted to stay out of his orbit, whether you were dead or alive or anywhere in between.

"So we need to figure out how to get synth created in large quantity as soon as we can." Olivia steepled her fingertips under her chin. "But we can't get the main ingredient we need."

Remy stood. "I'll get a new herd delivered. I'll call Dez, and she'll call the president if necessary. Obviously, I won't tell them why we need the herd, and they'll assume it's just a food source for the ranch." She made eye contact with each of them. "We need to keep this lab as secret as possible for as long as possible. Let me know *anything* you need, any issues you're having, and anything I can help with. We're out of the luxury of time and I hate to ask, but

I'm going to need you to move as quickly as you can. I can't trust what we've got coming in from the outside, and we may need to become self-sustaining faster than we thought. And of course, if you think of anything that might help with the feral problem, I'd love to hear it."

They nodded, all of them clearly deep in thought.

Raphael walked with her to the door. "I'll send over a list of everything I'm going to need for actual distribution. If you get us the new herd and it's healthy, we should be up and running within the next two weeks. I'll make sure of it."

Remy shook his hand, relieved to have such a competent and dedicated team working on vampire behalf. "I'll find a way to get what you need." She hesitated. She couldn't very well ride out here every day. "In fact, let's start talking more regularly." She pulled the cell phone from the shelf she'd left it on just inside the front door. "I assume you all have one of these?"

He grinned. "Like most people on the planet outside of Amish vampire territory." He took it from her, entered the phone number into his own phone, and handed it back.

"Okay. I'll call you when I've got a line on a new herd coming in. I'll send over the herd from the ranch, but be careful and run tests just in case they've been tampered with. Give me a call every couple days to let me know where we stand, okay?"

He nodded and waved her off, and was already back in the lab while she got out of the jumpsuit and stuffed it in the wash bin. She went outside and sat on the stone bench under the overhang. Who was fucking with their supply chain? Were farmers being told not to supply to vampires, or was there a kind of species-phobia spreading that meant it wasn't just the government they were going to have to contend with? And did this somehow have to do with the feral poisoning?

She looked up from the spot on the ground she'd been staring at when a shadow fell over her. Nero huffed and bobbed his head.

"You're right. Sitting here navel-gazing isn't going to help us find answers." She caressed him and then pulled on the beanie and snood. "Let's go home."

The ride back was far more sedate, as though both of them were more than happy to spend time in the woods and away from the ranch itself. She puzzled through the many questions and finally pushed them aside. Instead, she concentrated on the smell of the autumn earth around her, the crunching of the leaves under Nero's hooves, the soft flutter of the last leaves falling, the creak of the branches, and the sound of the river flowing freely in the distance. This was her sanctuary, and nowhere she'd ever lived compared to the place of peace she'd created here. It would have been easier in a country other than America, which was still so young it continued to have the often disastrous teething problems other countries had endured and outgrown centuries ago. But they had the land here, the open space and the opportunity to enfold the vampire culture in a way that other countries, whose mythologies were so entrenched, occasionally found more difficult. Except perhaps in the Nordic countries, but those were always so cold. While she couldn't be in the sun, it didn't mean she wanted to freeze her tits off every day either.

Her thoughts turned, as they often did these days, to Sage. The attraction was intense, and although she'd had her share of women throughout the centuries, and plenty this year alone, something about Sage felt different. Why couldn't she understand what it was? Remy wanted her. Wanted to touch her, make her smile, feel her presence even in the rare times they were apart. Should she simply sleep with her and get it out of her system? Somehow, she had a feeling that wouldn't be a good idea. Let a woman under your skin, and you could have a hell of a time letting her go later. And Sage wasn't going to be around much longer. She circled the thoughts, but they simply led back to one another, a snake eating its tail.

They entered the ranch's primary area, and Lester wasn't on his porch. She wondered if he'd be among the others, as she'd asked him to be. As she saw this morning, community was going to be of utmost importance right now, and she didn't want anyone left out.

The sun had dropped below the trees, and she could hear voices all over the compound. Laughing, joking, giving instruction... It was more alive than it had been for a long time. The people who lived on the ranch gathered and were very much like a loose family, but this time of crisis seemed to have brought out a sense of really living. She shook her head at the irony.

She rode Nero to the stable and handed him off to one of Gabe's stable hands, a young man who still looked a little haunted by the life he'd left behind. It took time, sometimes decades, to come to terms with being a predator in a far more intense way than as just a carnivorous human.

Her skin felt tight, and she realized that she hadn't eaten since her synth at breakfast. The living room had a few people lounging and chatting, and she nodded at them, aware of the brief, silent respect before she went into the kitchen. She stopped and stared at the sight that greeted her.

Sage, Jet, and the two children were standing at the kitchen island, and each of them was covered in flour. They were laughing so hard Sage had tears in her eyes, and when Jet spotted her, an evil smile instantly spread across her face.

"Don't even think about it," Remy said, taking a step back.

Sage turned and let loose with a palm-full of flour, and it poofed right into Remy's face, making her cough.

The others descended into another bout of laughter, and Remy wiped the flour from her eyes. "What's gotten into you?"

Shala giggled. "We need to feed all the hungry people, but we decided that dessert is the most important thing to make first."

That definitely didn't answer the question. Remy looked at Jet. She found she couldn't look at Sage, because even with flour on her cheeks and in her hair, she was absurdly beautiful.

"We're baking cookies and having fun while we do it." Jet let a handful of flour run through her fingers and into the bowl. "You remember fun, don't you?"

Jake grinned and blew some flour at Sage, who batted it away, laughing. "Yeah, Remy, you remember fun, don't you?" he mimicked Jet's words, but they were infused with giggles.

Remy shook her head and grabbed a hand towel from the shelf. "Those cookies had better be the best tasting things in the world, or you'll be on cook duty for the next month!"

The kids giggled, and Jet got down to showing them the next steps.

Sage, wiping her face and hands on a towel, came over to Remy's side. "How was your day?" she asked. "Did you miss us?"

Without thinking, Remy put her hand to the bottom of Sage's back. "You mean, did I miss you?"

Sage leaned into her touch. "Obvs."

Remy slid her hand away, but really, she wanted to take Sage upstairs and shut out the world while she made Sage her own. The thought surprised her, and she shut it down. A little bit of time out in the wild and suddenly she was back to wanting intimacy, which she had no time for. "I learned a lot and have about fifty new things to deal with." She looked beyond Sage to the little group. "But right now, I need a drink, and we need to get dinner started." She raised her voice a little. "And now that we have a couple new super-cooks here with us, I bet dinner will be better than ever."

The kids glowed under her praise, and soon the kitchen was bustling with dinner prep. It wasn't long before Remy was overtly aware of Sage's presence, mainly because she made it a point to brush against her every time they were near each other. At one point, Remy entered the large fridge storage just to get herself under control.

"Hiding? Not very big, bad butch vampire of you." Sage came in and pulled the door nearly closed behind her.

"You're killing me." Remy backed up, her arms crossed. "And since I'm legally considered dead, that's something special."

Sage moved closer, almost like she was stalking her. Remy bumped into a shelf and couldn't get any further away. Sage didn't stop until the length of her body was pressed to Remy's, her hands on Remy's biceps. "I like being something special."

"Fuck, Sage," Remy whispered. "We can't do this."

Sage leaned in and brushed her lips to Remy's. "Clearly, that isn't true." She kissed her a little harder.

Undone, Remy slipped her hand around the back of Sage's neck and pulled her in hard. She thrust her tongue into Sage's mouth, demanding entrance, and spun so Sage was up against the shelving instead. She slid her free hand up Sage's shirt and caressed the smooth, soft skin until she got to Sage's breast. She thumbed her nipple and moaned when Sage jerked into her touch.

"I hate to interrupt what I could happily watch for hours, but I need the grapes, and they're right behind you."

Remy pulled away, breathless, and had to force herself to let go of Sage, who drooped a little against the shelves, her breathing ragged. Remy reached around her, giving Sage a look she hoped telegraphed what she really wanted to be doing, and grabbed the bag requested. She turned to Jet and shoved them into her chest as she left the fridge. "Fucking grapes," she mumbled.

Jet laughed. "Come on, Sage. You're going to turn into a popsicle in there without hot pants over there warming you up."

Sage came out rubbing her arms. "Your timing is shit."

"Agreed. But when a girl needs grapes..." Jet shrugged and wiggled her eyebrows.

Remy needed air. Actually, she needed to take Sage upstairs and fuck her senseless, but as she kept telling herself, that was a bad idea. Before she could escape, there was a tug on her shirt.

"I'm s'posed to set the table, but I can't reach," Shala said, her arms full of plates that looked too heavy for her.

It was just the douse of cold water Remy needed. "Well, I can reach, but I'm not very good at setting the table." She took the plates. "So how about I hold them, and you stand on the chair and put them where they're supposed to go?"

Without answering, Shala took hold of Remy's shirt and led her into the dining room.

Coward. She gritted her teeth at Sage's mental communication. She shouldn't be so good at it since she wasn't a vampire, but there was no denying their connection. She didn't bother to respond, because there was nothing to say that wouldn't incriminate her or be an outright lie. The fact was, she wanted Sage more than she'd wanted anyone in a while, and it irked her that was the case. She'd have to parse it out later. For now, she had a vampire community to feed.

Chapter Fifteen

Sage murmured appreciatively as Remy massaged her feet. The fire was roaring in the fireplace, the kids were sound asleep on the sofa bed, and Jet had gone back to her place for some sleep before she and Remy went to meet the newcomers at the dock in the early hours of the morning.

She wiggled her toes, wishing they were on a couch instead of separate comfy chairs, but she couldn't remember the last time she'd had a foot massage so this would be fine for the moment. "Can I ask you some things?"

Remy's fingers stilled for a moment and then continued. "You'll only end up asking later, so you may as well." Her small smile took any sting out of the words.

"I've heard that vampires can change shape, and that really old ones can be more than one thing." She waited a moment, but Remy kept rubbing her feet. "So I was wondering if you could tell me what shapes you can take?"

Remy was quiet for a minute. "I've heard that there *used* to be vampires who could change shape, but as far as I know, none have been able to do it for millennia. I certainly can't. Imagine trying to get all this bone and flesh to suddenly poof into a tiny bat." She shook her head. "It's another part of the monster mythology that's defined so much of our existence. An old, useless stereotype that does more harm than good. I wish it were true though."

Sage flexed her foot as a signal for her to keep going when Remy went quiet again. "But you do have powers. What are yours?"

"We all tend to be strong and incredibly fast. Most of us have telepathic abilities, and some of us can read minds in general, vampire or not." She grinned when Sage grunted. "And the longer we're around, the better we become at that. I could talk to the entire ranch all at once if I needed to. Some vampires can mesmerize, which is a dangerous thing, since that's essentially mind control. Yes, I can do that too. And our senses are heightened sometimes to the point it's painful. When I ride through the forest, I can practically taste the colors, and the scents caress my skin like a lover."

Sage listened intently. "What makes it so you have these extra powers? I mean..."

"You're basically asking what a vampire is." Remy's smile looked a little sad. "We don't know. A virus that mutates us into something else? We've done tests through the centuries and never found a difference to suggest that. Magic? Maybe. Maybe there really is something more to the universe around us, something we can't explain that lies in the realm of the mystical. Even now those are the only answers I can come up with. What I know is that if I drink real blood, freshly drawn, my heart starts to beat again, although it slows and stops eventually until I feed. Synth doesn't start our hearts, but it keeps us alive and strong. How do we live without a beating heart? Why does it start to beat when we drink human blood?" Remy shrugged. "All my powers are enhanced when I've had fresh human blood. And yet, if you drank it as a human, it wouldn't affect you that way. It's something to do with the transformation, with being made into this other species. I'm afraid I don't have a better answer than that." She looked up from Sage's foot. "What animal would you be, if you could change?"

Sage was melting under Remy's touch and feeling a little more animalistic by the minute. "I don't know. A unicorn, maybe?"

Remy laughed. "Maybe choose something that isn't extinct."

"Extinct?" Sage narrowed her eyes. "You're messing with me. They're mythical. Being young doesn't mean I'm dumb."

Remy shook her head, that small smile still on her lips. "Extinct. Just like there are horned whales, there were horned horses. It's not exactly a leap, is it, when you consider deer, and rhinos, and such. That strain just happened to die out, long before people were making records of that kind of thing." She sat back, her hands resting on Sage's feet. "Try again."

Sage thought about it. "I don't know. The only animals I've seen up close are skunks, and pigeons, and rats. And I don't want to be any of those." She closed her eyes and let images come to her. "I think I'd want to be a bird of some kind. I like the idea of flying and seeing everything going on under me."

Remy laughed. "Yeah, that sounds like you. Always watching and wondering, wanting to know what's going on."

Sage bit her lip. "Is that bad? I have to admit, I was so hyped to come to vampire country, but since I've been here, I feel so out of my league. I was somebody before I got here, and now I'm just this silly human in your way." She blinked back the tears. She hadn't meant to be quite so honest.

"Hey." Remy moved Sage's feet off her lap and knelt in front of her. "First of all, there's nothing wrong with growth and self-reflection. Second, it was really brave of you to come on this adventure, and I'm sorry you got stuck in the middle of our politics. But not once have you behaved in a way that isn't strong and capable. That's impressive." Remy gently wiped away a stray tear.

"But there's so much I don't know." Sage leaned into Remy's touch.

"There are still things I don't know, and I've been around a while." Remy sat back on her heels. "And if you knew everything, how boring would life become?"

Sage returned Remy's smile. How desperately she wanted to be wrapped in her arms, and surprisingly, not just for a rowdy roll in the sheets. Remy was kind and comforting, and that was something Sage hadn't had in a long time.

Remy pushed away and sat back in her chair, putting some distance between them. Sage put her feet back in Remy's lap, not for a massage, but just because she wanted the closeness. "Will you tell me more about yourself? Where you come from?" She pushed her foot into Remy's thigh. "Tell me a story." She grinned when Remy rolled her eyes.

"And you promise this doesn't leave this house?" Remy said, her expression wary.

"One hundred percent promise." Sage thrilled a little at getting a glimpse into Remy that other people, even other vampires, didn't.

Remy's gaze went a little vacant as she stared at the fireplace, the shadows flickering over her almost like they were inviting her to dance. "I was born a Viking in the year 802CE, under Uí Ímair's reign. My parents were both warriors and expected their children to be warriors too."

Remy's voice had a sing-song quality that wove a spell, and Sage wouldn't have been able to pull herself away if the building had been on fire. There was also the hint of an accent coming through that brought the story to life.

"My clan was nomadic. We raided other villages, sailed far and wide, and rarely stayed in one place for long. Other clans were more settled, and we'd often stay at camps that weren't ours, where there were farmers and craftswomen who had talent you can't imagine. When I was twenty-five, considered old back then, I took the vows of a warrior. I had a mate, a woman with two kids who'd been widowed a few years before. It was a good life. Hard, but wild and free." Remy's expression darkened. "And then came the fiercest battle we'd ever known. King Aethelwulf in Carhampton was waiting for us when we came ashore for a raid, and we sustained heavy losses. That was the night I died."

Sage nearly swayed with the timbre of Remy's voice, and the pictures in her mind were so vivid, it was like she was there. Was Remy sharing this event telepathically? It almost hurt to breathe, it was so real.

"I was mortally wounded, and I was laying in the mud, waiting to leave for Valhalla. I'd fought well and wasn't afraid to die. But a shadow came from the darkness, followed by more. They swarmed the fallen and those who weren't dead yet began to scream. It was the first time in my life I'd been afraid. And then one of those shadows leaned over me, teeth white as bleached bone, eyes redder than blood spilled on snow. And she looked at me, stared at me for what felt like years, and I couldn't say a thing. She yanked my head to the side and sank her fangs into my neck. The pain..." Remy's eyes flickered. "The pain was like nothing I'd ever experienced, and I deafened myself with my own screaming. And then..." She rubbed at her eyes. "She cut her wrist with her own fingernail and pressed it against my mouth. I knew what she was; all children grew up hearing the tales of the draugr who ate souls and only moved at night. I struggled, but I was too weak. Her blood slid down my throat. When I woke the next morning, I was surrounded by my dead clan, and although I wasn't alive, I also wasn't one of the dead."

Sage drew in a ragged breath. "That's... I don't know what to say. How did you figure out what you were? I mean, how to live? Keep living, I mean?"

Remy's voice was soft. "The hunger burns through you like fire. Believe me, you know what it is you want." She rubbed at her face again. "I found a boat and made my way home, the only one of the warriors on that raid to do so. I told my story but left out the draugr. I knew what their sentence would be. When I woke that night next to my mate, all I could see was her pulse, all I could smell was the blood pumping through her veins. It took every ounce of self-control to leave our tent, get back in a boat, and sail away."

"You didn't even get to say goodbye. Did you ever see her again?" Sage's heart hurt for the Remy of so long ago who'd lost everything.

"No. I never went back. I wouldn't put them in danger, and I was out of control a lot of the time back then. I went back to the battlefield where I'd been turned, but no matter how much I searched, I never did find the clan that swarmed us that night or the vampire who turned me. I allowed it to haunt me for years. I didn't understand why she turned me instead of letting me die. What did she see in me that night that made her think I deserved to be a vampire? I'll never know."

"So you went through it all alone." Sage leaned over and took Remy's hands in her own. "That must have been so lonely."

Remy was looking into Sage's eyes, and the look slowly turned from one of memory to one of desire. Sage's breath hitched. No one had ever looked at her the way Remy did, and it was quickly becoming a drug she couldn't get enough of.

A knock on the door startled them. Remy looked over her shoulder. "Is it time?"

Sage turned to see Jet leaning against the doorway, her expression shuttered. How long had she been there? Had she known Remy's story before, or had she just learned some of it?

Remy stood, giving Sage's hands a squeeze before letting them go. "And that, my dear, is the mostly untold history of Ulfhild Skógr, the battle wolf of the mountains who eventually went on to start a ranch in America where vampires could be safe." Her eyes flicked to Jet. "Now you know."

Jet nodded, her expression inscrutable. "Let's wake the kids," she said, gently touching their shoulders.

Sage knew it was dangerous to leave the children with her, but she wished it weren't the case. The poor things had been through so much. But with the feral situation, Remy was uncomfortable leaving Sage with anyone else on the ranch. Lars had been MIA since Geno's arrival, and it was assumed he was back at Geno's place. Remy lifted Jake into her arms and Jet took Shala, and Sage opened the door for them.

"Lock the door behind us, and I'll be back as soon as I can." Remy's gaze lingered on Sage for a second, and then they were gone.

Chapter Sixteen

REMY WAS GLAD SHE and Jet had the kind of strength that belonged to their kind. The kids were sleeping in their arms, their pale little cheeks pressed against their protector's shoulders. The night was cold and damp, and although they didn't feel the temperature changes like humans did, it wasn't exactly pleasant.

The boat dock was well hidden on the widest part of the river at the edge of the ranch's property. The sound of water lapping against the wood was the only thing to be heard. No nightbirds were calling, nothing was scurrying through the underbrush.

"Feel weird to you?" Jet asked, her jaw firmly set as she looked out at the water.

"A little. Maybe we should have left the kids with Sage after all." Remy shifted the child into a better position.

"No, you were right to bring them. One of them wakes up from a nightmare, or is hungry, and they go on the attack. Then we have a cute, dead internet celebrity on our hands, and you're all heartbroken and sad again." Jet shot her a quick grin and then turned her attention back to the water.

"That's rather hyperbolic, don't you think? Heartbroken?"

"Maybe. I've never seen you in love, so I don't know what it looks like. But I can tell you that you seem different around her. Hell, you even shared your origin story, and we all know that isn't given lightly. You're less...austere. Less distant."

Remy huffed. "I'm less distant because we're in the middle of a mess I had a big part in creating. I need to be with everyone right now. It has nothing to do with Sage." Even as she said the words, she knew full well they weren't true. But the thought of admitting to the truth made her itch.

"You've never struck me as someone who frolics in denial." Jet stiffened. "Hear it?"

Remy shifted into the shadows a little more. Soon though, the boat came into view, someone pulling hard at the oars. Remy looked at Jet, who looked equally concerned. This should be a motorboat, used for quick ins and outs.

It pulled up at the dock, and Remy could see that there were only three people onboard. She and Jet stepped out of the shadows. Jimmy leapt out first and then gave a hand to his mom. The driver handed up their luggage.

"Problem, Mark?" Remy asked softly.

He nodded and kept handing items up to the others. "Patrols on the water, every few miles along the shore as well. We can handle it, but we're keeping an eye and deciding what's best in the moment." He looked around, and apparently satisfied, looked up at Remy. "Could be you need to discourage retreat, Remy. Things are tight."

"If they catch people trying to come in or leave, what's the protocol?" Jet asked, nodding to Jimmy and Selma, who trudged up beside them.

He picked up an oar and leaned on it. "Whispers on the wind, but sounds like we've got a few unaccounted for. Escorted away and not seen again. There's an obvious effort to just turn them away at the big road closures, but at the little ones and on the water..." He shrugged.

"Okay. Get word to us if things change or if you need anything." Remy nodded to him, and he waved as he set off into the darkness, paddling so softly it sounded like nothing more than lapping water. She turned to Selma and Jimmy. "You two okay?"

"Tired but safe, thanks to you." Selma's smile looked like worn paper.

"What she's not saying is they spray-painted our house, and we found a gas can with a partially burned rag in it by the back door."

Jimmy's eyes were flint in the darkness. "If it had caught, they'd have burned us to the ground."

"Jesus." Jet flinched and shook her head. "Good thing you're here."

"Can I help?" Selma held out her arms, and Remy gladly transferred her little burden over.

"Thanks. Tell me what you need tonight, and I'll bring it back with us now. I'll have someone come get everything else and take it to the lodge for you later."

Jimmy took the child from Jet, and then she and Remy picked up the few items they said they needed in the immediate future. They walked back through the woods to the main house, and along the way, Remy explained the children's predicament and presence.

"So you're hoping that as someone experienced with vampire children, I can watch over them." Selma nuzzled the child's hair. "It's a wicked play, bringing them with you to the pick-up site."

"I know. I'm sorry. I don't mean to be manipulative, really. I just couldn't leave them alone."

Selma gave her a knowing look. "Let's talk about it more after we've had some rest."

Remy opened the door of the main lodge and led the way upstairs. It was a fair answer, and she couldn't very well expect Selma to make such an important decision when she'd barely arrived at the ranch and her life was already in flux.

They entered, and the kids were placed on the sofa bed. They hadn't even stirred. She let Selma and Jimmy into the guest room, which she already thought of as Sage's, and then waved Jet off. She stood outside her door, her hand on the doorknob. She could sleep in one of the chairs. She could sleep on the floor. Hell, she could sleep on a tree branch outside. But Sage was right there. On the other side of this door was someone who made her feel alive again. Even in the midst of everything going on, or maybe even because of it, she wanted the kind of comfort Sage was offering.

The door opened, and Sage stood there in a pair of Remy's

boxers and a tiny tank top. "You know it's creepy to stand outside someone's door, right?"

"Not if it's your own door, and you know going in might be a mistake." Remy barely kept from pulling Sage to her. Her hair was tousled like she'd been asleep, and what she was wearing was straight out of a lesbian romance novel.

"But it could be a mistake not to," Sage said and reached out to take Remy's hand.

She tugged, and Remy let herself be led inside. Sage turned to her as soon as the door was closed and pressed herself against Remy's body. Automatically Remy's arms went around her, pulling her close, her desire nearly unbearable. "I want you."

"Show me," Sage murmured against her lips.

That was all Remy needed. She lifted Sage, who wrapped her legs around Remy's waist, and the kiss was like a sharing of the air needed to live. She walked Sage back to the bed and laid her down. "I don't want to take my time, not right now. I want to fuck you until you beg me to stop."

The sound that came out of Sage was somewhere between a moan and sob. "God, yes, please. Now."

Remy pulled the boxers off and inhaled the scent of Sage's need. For a moment, she felt her fangs press against her lips, but she breathed deeply and centered herself. "I haven't been with a human in a long time."

"Then I'm honored. Stop talking." Sage pulled Remy's hand down her stomach.

Remy lay beside her and yanked the tank top up to reveal Sage's full breasts. She sucked Sage's nipple and felt herself respond as Sage cried out and arched into her, one hand grappling with the bed sheet, the other on the back of Remy's neck. She slipped her hand between Sage's legs and was instantly coated in hot, wet heat. "Fuck," she murmured and pushed inside.

Sage cried out, her body arching as she pressed down against Remy's fingers. "More."

Remy slid another finger in, and then another, filling Sage and pushing deep and hard, barely controlling her desire to fuck her as hard as she would a vampire.

"Please. Please, Remy." Sage's begging was almost incoherent and when she opened her eyes, there were tears in them. "Please don't hold back."

With a groan, Remy let go. She pushed hard and fast, fucking Sage with all the pent-up need she'd kept leashed for too long. She wrapped her arm around Sage's waist and held her firm as she felt Sage's desire building, tightening around Remy's fingers, her cries nearly sobs of release.

"Let go," Remy whispered into her hair. "Let go and give yourself to me."

Sage buried her face in Remy's shoulder and cried out as she came, flooding Remy's hand as she pushed deep and held still, taking Sage's offering and drinking it in. The emotion that rose like a tide made her push in that little bit more, made her pull Sage even tighter against her. The feel of her pulse pounding against Remy's chest made her ache and brought with it memories of feeding in the wild, of women writhing under her as she drank from them, making them feel good even as they were keeping her alive. But this...she hadn't felt this desire for ownership, for total surrender in hundreds of years.

But Sage wasn't hers. Why didn't that feel true?

She loosened her grip as Sage's breathing slowed. She shifted them, never quite letting go, until they were under the comforter. Sage snuggled in against her, her head on Remy's shoulder. Remy pulled her close and stared at the ceiling.

"Can we do that again?" Sage mumbled, her eyes closed.

"Why don't you sleep for a while first?" Remy kissed the top of Sage's head and wasn't surprised when she drifted off. Remy sighed. It was bound to happen, really. There was no denying the chemistry between them and in close quarters like this, under stressful circumstances, people often reached out for carnal comfort. She pressed her cheek to Sage's head. Somehow, this felt like more than that. A connection had been created, and it had already burrowed deep. Granted, she was likely just a passing interest for Sage, a girl's tale to tell at the bar when she was back in her own world.

Remy knew that this wouldn't be a night *she'd* forget. Whatever happened in the future, Sage would always be something special.

***

Remy woke at dawn to the sound of people in her house, an unusual occurrence that made her freeze for a millisecond before she remembered that they should, in fact, be there. Children's voices floated back, happy and high, and she relaxed and paid attention to her immediate issue.

Sage slept soundly, her hand tucked under her chin, her butt pressed to Remy's stomach. She was so beautiful, her pale hair light in the dark room. The comforter had fallen below her breasts, and Remy didn't bother to resist.

She bent and kissed her way along the side of her chest and then took a nipple in her mouth and bit lightly. Rewarded with a moan and Sage's hand on the back of her head, she continued her teasing, using her other hand to tweak and twist the other nipple, stopping sometimes to palm her breast and squeeze. Sage's breath quickened, and she turned more fully to Remy.

Remy pushed her back onto her stomach and placed hot kisses over her shoulders and neck as she slid her hand between Sage's legs. Slowly, she moved so she was kneeling behind Sage and then pulled her up so her ass was in the air. Leaning over her, she wrapped her arm around Sage's waist and then pushed into her.

Sage moaned into the pillow and pushed back into Remy's hand as she began to fuck her, deep and slow, twisting inside her, pressing against her G-spot, drawing every bit of need from her. She added another finger, and Sage pushed back harder.

"Please. Please, don't stop," Sage gasped. "Please, Remy. Please make me yours."

Remy growled, the animalistic part of her ready to grant Sage's request. "Show me you want me," she said, pushing deeper.

In response, Sage pushed back, drawing her deep, her soft cries driving Remy into a frenzy. She had to have her. All of her, every second of the day. Sage was hers, goddamnit.

Sage exploded as she called Remy's name. Remy kept going, fucking her until the tension left her body and her head dropped to the pillow. Remy pulled out gently, and Sage dropped to her side. Remy curled up against her, big spoon style.

"What does it mean?" Sage asked, her tone soft and uncertain.

"What does what mean?" Remy asked.

"What I'm feeling." She pulled Remy's arm even tighter, as though using it to ground herself. "Like I'll drown without you."

The words punctured the bubble of Remy's need and wariness set in. How to explain? She wasn't sure she knew herself. "Sleep, beautiful. We'll talk about it later."

Sage drifted back to sleep but Remy lay awake, wondering at what had happened between them. She didn't own Sage. Not in the typically vampire way, anyway. She hadn't taken Sage's blood, hadn't created that bond that meant Sage couldn't be without her. And yet, it felt an awful lot like that. The thought of Sage leaving now made her irrationally angry. Not wanting to end the perfect moment in a rage, she slowly disengaged and slipped from the bed. She tucked the comforter around Sage, then pulled on sweats and a sweatshirt and left the room, careful to shut the door silently.

In the living room, she found all four of her other guests gathered around the table. Selma was reading from a book, and the kids looked entranced. Jimmy was focused on his phone.

"Morning," she said. "Everyone okay?"

Jimmy looked up from his phone and gave her a devilish grin. "Some of us more than others."

"Jimmy!" Selma said, but she had laughter in her eyes. "I was explaining to the children, which you're clearly not used to having in your home, that Sage's muscles hurt, and you were helping massage them out, so she wasn't in pain."

If Remy could still blush, she would've been bright red. "I'm not used to having any guests, let alone tiny ones. Sorry about that." She grinned, unable to be completely abashed.

"No worries here," Jimmy said. "I'll store up those sounds for later use, thanks."

"Gross." Remy nodded toward his phone. "You're getting reception?"

He shrugged. "Yeah. Just signed onto your Dark Haven Wi-Fi. Is that okay?" Then came a look of understanding. "Oh. You aren't supposed to have any tech here, are you?"

"I don't, usually." Remy poured herself a glass of synth. She held up the container to ask if they wanted any and received several nods. "We've had it put in while we're dealing with all the political stuff. It'll be gone as soon as this blows over. Go ahead and use it but be careful about what you share." She didn't miss the look of uncertainty that passed between mother and son, but there wasn't much more she could say. It wasn't like she had any information to make them feel better. She handed them their glasses of synth and then looked at the kids. "And how are our little monsters this morning?"

"I miss my mommy," Shala said, resting her head against Selma's arm.

"Me too." Jake looked at Remy. "Are we going to live here with you from now on?"

Remy took a long sip of synth, trying to figure out how to respond.

"Actually," Selma said, "Jimmy and I were wondering if you want to come live with us? You see, we're new here, and we don't know our way around. But you do, so you could help us settle in. What do you think?"

Jake looked from her to Jimmy while Shala looked at him for

guidance. "Were you born a vampire? Like us?"

He shook his head. "No, buddy. But I was turned really young, when I was about your age, actually. So I know what it's like to be a vampire kid, and my mom understands how special we are."

Jake nodded solemnly. "We know Dark Haven like the back of our hands. Even the super-secret places. We'll make sure you fit in."

Jimmy gave his shoulder a squeeze. "Thanks. We can all start our new lives together."

It did Remy good to see that she'd been right about Jimmy and Selma. They belonged here, among their own kind. Shala climbed into Selma's lap, and she wrapped her arms around her and rocked her. She met Selma's gaze and gave her a short nod. Selma hummed a soft song while Jimmy showed Jake a game on his phone.

"We'll head over to your cottage after breakfast." She checked her watch. "In fact, I'll get it started so we can get going right after."

Jake looked up from Jimmy's phone. "Can we help again?" He was still in his pjs, which were covered in little pictures of Count von Count from Sesame Street.

"Why don't you all get ready and meet me down there?" Remy wanted a shower, but she needed to put a little distance between her and Sage, because what she really wanted was to wake her up and take her yet again.

"Sounds good." Selma set Shala on the couch and stretched. "Do we need to do anything about..." She tilted her head toward Remy's room.

"No, she'll come down when she's ready." She made a face that made the kids giggle. "Humans sleep way more than we do." She headed downstairs, their laughter still clear with the door shut.

She whistled as she started prepping in the kitchen, scrambling eggs and laying out bacon for the grill.

"If this is hell, I'd really appreciate you sending me back to the world where Remy was a silent, god-like presence instead of a whistling vampire in sweatpants. Because this will definitely ruin my existence." Lars swept in wearing a white three-piece suit, complete with a purple pocket square.

"Hello, Mr. Dapper. Nice of you to crawl out of bed for a visit." Remy continued to whistle as she cut the melon into flowery shapes.

"I'll have you know, the bed itself saw very little action." He perched on a stool and fanned himself with a napkin. "Your old friend is quite the romantic."

Remy stopped whistling. It would've been nice to have this serene morning of afterglow sex to herself. Such was life, though. "And did my 'old friend' explain some of our history?"

Lars tilted his head back and forth. "He alluded to it but sadly, I received no details." He paused, and his expression turned serious. "However, as your dutiful keeper of knowledge, I did hear a few things that haven't sat quite right."

Remy stopped cutting. "Like?"

He frowned, something he rarely did just in case a vampire could develop wrinkles. "He took a phone call in the other room one night, and it sounded like he was trying to placate someone. Telling them to be patient, to trust him. That kind of thing. I couldn't read him, and I couldn't hear who it was, but when he came back, his energy was off-kilter. The fucking then was positively feral." He gave a little shiver.

"I wouldn't put it past him to be involved in all this, although I can't see how he would be. It isn't like he's pulling the president's strings or poisoning our food supply. He doesn't have anything to do with either issue." She wondered, though, if that was true. He'd been around for a long time and could be devious if he wanted something. But what would he have to gain?

"Well, I'm happy to keep an eye on him and sacrifice my virtue for your needs, of course." He fluttered his eyelashes at her, making her laugh despite her unease.

"And I greatly appreciate your sacrifice, my lamb."

Before they could say anything else, the entourage from upstairs came in, the kids running right to Lars.

"Hi, Uncle Lars," Shala said, holding up her arms.

He lifted her into the air, careful to keep her clear of his white suit. "Hello, you darling thing."

He set her back down, and she climbed onto a stool and picked up a knife.

"Nope." Remy took the knife from her and stuck it in a melon. "You get to squeeze these," she nudged over the bowl of oranges, "into the synth so it's perfect for breakfast."

Shala jumped in without hesitation, laughing as the juice covered her hands and went everywhere but in the synth.

"And you get to cracking eggs," Remy said, handing Jake a carton and a bowl. She turned to Lars. "And you."

He gave an exaggerated bow. "Your wish is my command."

"Can you take Selma and Jimmy over to the Riverview cottage?" She looked at them. "That's one of our newest and largest. See if it works for you, and if it doesn't, just say so. It can be temporary while we build something that does work for you."

Selma leaned on the counter. "You say that like we'll be living here at Dark Haven."

Remy blinked and then flinched. "Damn. I'm really sorry. You're right, I did make that assumption. I guess because of the kids, I thought you'd want to stay here, where you could all be safe." She shook her head. "I'm sorry, Selma. I'm not a dictator. You're free to live wherever you want, of course."

Selma laughed. "I'm teasing you, Remy. We have a lot to think about, but staying here would make our lives a lot easier for a while. Thank you. And I'm looking forward to teaching next semester." She looked at Jimmy, who didn't say anything. There seemed to be a silent communication between them. "Things have been crazy, and it will be good to have the time and peace to decide what we really want to do down the road. Is that good with you?"

"Of course. We're just glad you're here and you're safe." Remy was thankful for Selma's measured, thoughtful response. In these times, when so many decisions were on her shoulders, it would be easy to forget that she didn't have to make them for everyone around her.

"We appreciate that." Selma turned to Lars. "Lead on, good sir."

Jimmy rolled his eyes in the way that only teenagers, all of them on the planet, could. The three of them traipsed out, leaving Remy to watch over the little ones. She moved around them, laughing and teaching, and something in her soul that had been untethered suddenly felt a little less loose in the wind.

Her skin twitched, and she looked up before Sage entered the room. She'd felt her, like a sunbeam just about to break through the clouds. That shouldn't be possible without a bonded connection, and she had no idea what to make of it. But at the shy, sweet smile Sage gave her, she lost all thought and didn't care about why. Dark gods, it felt good. "Hey, beautiful. You're up early." Remy came around the kitchen island and pulled her in for a kiss. It might not last, but she'd play the part of happy lover, however fleeting the moment might be.

"I was having weird dreams and when I woke up, you weren't there." She played with the string of Remy's hood. "I needed to be with you. Is that okay?"

Remy kissed her gently. "Of course it's okay."

"Sage, are your muscles okay now?" Shala said from her perch on the stool.

Sage looked at Remy in confusion, and Remy grinned. "They heard you making noises, and Selma explained that your muscles hurt, and I was helping you feel better."

Sage's cheeks turned a beautiful shade of pink, and her eyes went wide. "Oh... Yes, I'm feeling much better, thanks." Her grin made Remy want to drag her back upstairs.

But there wasn't time for that, and the distraction of arriving vampires was a good one. She and Sage worked on getting all the food out, and Remy briefly wondered where Jet was, as she usually made it a point to help with the meals. It wasn't like they weren't used to being up in the early hours of the morning. Hopefully there wasn't some emergency that Remy was yet to be made aware of.

The dining room and living room were crowded but the general mood seemed okay, and Remy walked through and chatted with people to make sure nothing was bubbling under the surface. A strange unease began to niggle at her. She looked around the room but couldn't see anything out of the ordinary.

"Vibe check all good?" Sage asked as she sat down beside Remy with a bowl of cereal.

Selma, Jimmy, and the children were sitting in the living room chatting with other vampires, and she smiled when she looked at them.

"If that means is everyone happy, then yes." Remy didn't bother with food. The unease was growing. and there was a flare of... panic? "I need to go check on something. Would you mind heading upstairs so I know you're safe?"

Sage grimaced and rolled her eyes. "I'm in a huge room of people. It isn't like anyone's going to attack me here, is it?" She drew her fingers along Remy's hand. "And if you told them I was spoken for..." She wiggled her eyebrows.

Remy pulled her hand away gently. "I know you're probably safe, but if I can go do what I need to without having to worry, it would make things easier. Please?"

Sage picked up her cereal bowl. "Okay, fine. But only because you look so hot when you beg."

There it was again, that desire to head straight to bed. "I wasn't the one begging," she whispered in Sage's ear before walking away. She waited by the front door until she saw Sage disappear at the top, then she headed outside.

She went to the large covering in the middle, where the various overhangs met and diverged. She closed her eyes and let her senses roam. Something was *wrong*. Like running your palm over a cactus, it pricked at her, alerting her. She turned and felt it grow, and she set off down the covered path that called to her. Belatedly, she realized it was the path to Jet's cottage, and she broke into a run. Dread snaked its way up her spine and a panic she hadn't felt in centuries made it hard to breathe.

Jet! Jet, can you hear me? Her mental call received no answer.

She bounded up the few stairs to Jet's door and swore. The door was open to the chill autumn wind. "Jet!"

Living room, dining room, kitchen… "Fuck." She knelt beside Jet's inert body in the bedroom. Her shirt was half on, as though she'd been in the middle of changing when someone had caught her off guard. Brackish blood congealed on the side of her head where she'd clearly been hit. Gently, Remy turned her over onto her back, and she stopped breathing at what she saw.

Blood covered the front of Jet's torso from what looked like multiple stab wounds. How much blood had she lost? Had they hit her heart? "Don't you dare die on me. Don't you fucking dare." She cradled Jet's head in her lap. *Lars, get every doctor on the ranch in motion. Send them to the new cottage that's nearly finished. Now.* Remy carefully lifted Jet into her arms. She was heavy, solid, and she didn't make a sound to show she wasn't truly dead.

Remy left the cottage and headed toward the place about to become a medical center. The pain of loss made her vision red, and the few vampires on the paths bowed their heads and looked away as she moved past them. *Don't you dare die on me. Whoever hurt you is going to wish for a swift death.* The door to the cottage was open, and she carried Jet into the kitchen and laid her on the center island. The necessary vampires flowed in behind her and went straight into emergency mode. Remy stepped back to give them room.

Someone had come into Dark Haven and hurt one of Remy's people.

Someone was going to die.

Chapter Seventeen

Sage had never, *ever* felt pain and rage like that which flooded through her while she was taking a shower. Like fire, it traveled over her veins and made her gasp for air. She dropped to her knees and let the tears flow, even though she had no idea what was going on.

Remy.

It took a minute to figure it out, and then she understood. Whatever it was Remy had gone to check on, it had gone bad. Really, really bad. Shaking, Sage got up and braced against the emotions that weren't actually hers. Was this what being with a vampire meant? That you felt everything they felt? She shuddered. Whoever was in Remy's way after this was in trouble, that was for sure, and she was damn glad it wasn't her.

She got dressed, having to stop occasionally to breathe deep. Maybe... She sat on the edge of the bed and closed her eyes. *Breathe.* She pictured trees moving softly in the wind, the ocean slowly moving onto and away from the beach, and she sent the images in the same way she'd sent the words, as though thinking them right into Remy's brain.

The rage began to recede. The feeling of...of...red? Could red be a feeling? It began to dim, and Sage could breathe a little easier. More importantly, she had a feeling that Remy was breathing easier.

Thank you.

Sage smiled as the thought filled her mind. *Are you okay? What's going on?*

There was no response but the emotion had settled, and Sage had to be okay with that. Briefly, she considered leaving the house and going in search of Remy, but the concern in Remy's eyes had been genuine. It wasn't controlling; she was literally worried. And why shouldn't she be? With feral vampires, poisonings, and military patrolling the borders, Remy had plenty to be worried about. Adding a fragile human into the mix probably wasn't the best thing ever.

Sage flopped back onto the bed that still smelled of sex, and her tummy flipped. Last night had been magical in the truest sense of the word. The way Remy had taken her, all dominant and intense, had melted Sage into the best kind of romantic ever. It was hot in a way she didn't think was possible outside movies. Her whole body had felt taken over, wanted, owned, desired...all the words she couldn't even think of right now. But more than that, it was like Remy had tied a string to her soul, tethering them together, demanding Sage's submission. But submission in a good way. A very good way.

She squeezed her legs together and smiled at the soreness. She'd begged Remy to take control. And, god, did it feel like she had. It was intense, and tears had flowed as she'd given herself over so completely for the first time. Sex was often fun and usually good enough, but it had never felt like it had last night. She'd wanted to become part of Remy, to hand over her heart and soul and say, "Keep me."

When she'd woken this morning to find herself alone, she'd had a momentary bout of panic. Had it been one-sided? Had Remy already left the bed because she didn't feel the same way? As she'd gotten ready, the doubts had multiplied, bringing her close to tears. But when she'd walked into the kitchen, they'd melted away like morning mist from the welcome in Remy's gaze. It had been hard to blink away the relief when Remy had put her arms around her and said she was glad Sage was there.

And now, banished to the house for her own safety, she found her desire to be at Remy's side caused an ache in her chest. What the hell was she going to do when she had to go back to her own life?

She considered the question as she continued staring at the ceiling. *Why* did she have to go back? She didn't have any family or friends who would miss her. Her apartment was okay, but it wasn't anything special. But she couldn't keep up her internet presence here, and wasn't that a huge part of who she was? What about the years she'd spent creating her brand? That was why she was here, after all. If it weren't for that, she'd never have crossed Remy's path. What would she do here at Dark Haven?

She pondered the question. Plenty of people lived here, tending the land, building, just...living. Could she get used to that? Thinking of the night with Remy, she decided there wasn't much she couldn't get used to if her nights were filled with that kind of passion.

She rose, tired of thinking about things that didn't have answers, and went about cleaning up the house. The kids were kids, and they'd left a bit of a mess. Sage stripped the beds and washed the sheets. She laughed at herself as she went about the domestic work she so often put off at home. Once all that was done, she sat on the couch and pulled out her phone, which was all charged up.

Strangely, even after just a few days without it, there was an alien feel to it, and she couldn't help but feel like she was going against Remy's wishes. But Geno had put the tech in, and it wasn't like Remy didn't know Sage had all these videos to share. Granted, she'd said she didn't want Sage to share things while she was on Dark Haven property... She sighed. Well, she could at least get them edited and ready in the draft folder, so she could share them later.

Time flew past as she edited a few of the original videos from the conference, cutting them, adding sound, changing filters to make everyone's face look just right, and getting them ready to put up. There were longer ones taken at Dark Haven, but she didn't want to look at them just yet. She still needed time to process, and she didn't want the videos interfering with that. It was a strange thought, and she wasn't sure what to make of it, but she let it go for the moment.

She couldn't wait to see what her followers thought, and she was a little surprised at how few comments there were asking if she was okay. Barely a couple thousand. *That's why you can't let up. You're forgotten the minute you're away too long. You become no one.*

She hit save on one of the videos she'd taken at the end of the conference, and then heard the sounds from downstairs indicating the lunch crowd coming in. Remy hadn't come back yet though. Making a decision, she got up and pulled her hair into a messy bun and put on her shoes. She wasn't going to be scared into being useless.

She made her way to the kitchen and was happy to have plenty of people say hi along the way. No one was getting food ready, and she quickly moved into action, pulling leftovers from the fridge and putting out several different jugs of synth, some of which had mint in them, others flavored with fruit. One was plain.

She chose to think of them as tomato juice, which made it easier. She'd probably never drink a Bloody Mary again though.

Soon, lunch was out, and she wiped the sweat from her brow. Still no Remy. Or Lars or Jet, for that matter. She looked out over the room but didn't see anyone she knew well enough to ask, so she shrugged. She tried to think a thought to Remy, but it was strange. When she'd sent the others there'd been a feeling, like a heatwave, that the thought rolled on. But now, the thought was just that. A thought that stayed in her brain with nowhere to go. She tried it again, just out of curiosity, and felt the beginning of a headache. Well, that was intense.

Knowing how Remy felt about her safety, Sage decided to eat alone in the kitchen. At least that way she wasn't going totally against Remy's wishes. It was lonely and made her think of how often she'd been fine eating alone in her apartment. But then, she always had the company of people online. She'd left her phone upstairs, again knowing how Remy felt about the use of them here. Now she was faced with her rampaging thoughts, and no one to talk them through with. Before, she would have turned to her ZimTak family and solicited advice from her thousands of followers. Now…she looked at the four walls and listened to the laughter in the other room. She was an outsider with no one to talk to, and it wasn't a feeling she liked in the least. She'd already had enough of it to last a lifetime.

When she finished eating, she started clean-up, and plenty of other vampires brought in dishes and began to help. Not once did Sage feel threatened or worried, and it gave her pause to wonder if maybe she and Remy really could make it work here after all. At some point, she wouldn't be an outsider anymore, right?

She laughed at herself. They'd known each other for what, a week? Had sex once. And here was Sage, planning her future life at Dark Haven. How utterly lesbian of her.

She was doing dishes and caught a piece of conversation behind her that made her stop to listen.

"She could be a little much sometimes, but who would dare take on Remy's second like that?" the person said in a gossipy whisper. "Don't they know that's a death sentence?"

"I don't know," someone else said. "Remy's soft now. She's probably spent more time with humans than vampires over the last few years."

"You didn't see her face." The first person gave a low whistle. "Death personified."

Their voices drifted off, and Sage turned away from the sink. Remy's second? Someone had hurt Jet? Goosebumps covered her skin. That explained the rage. But like the person said, who would dare? She leaned against the sink. The same person who was poisoning vampires and making them go feral. Had Jet figured out who that was?

Unease made her shiver. The feeling grew until goosebumps covered her arms, and she began to tremble. She wiped her hands, grabbed herself a soda, and took the stairs to Remy's place two at a time. Her palms were sweating and her heart was racing as she looked down the stairs behind her. No one was there, but she could swear she heard a soft, cynical laugh float through the air. She was reminded of her first night at Dark Haven, when she'd woken feeling certain she was in danger.

She went in and locked the door behind her. Fear slowly ebbed, and she sagged onto the couch. This was what Remy was afraid of. This was why she couldn't live at Dark Haven. No matter how easy things seemed on the surface, the reality was that she'd always live in fear of being prey. If someone could hurt Jet, a vampire, then what chance would a human like Sage have?

She curled up on the sofa and mindlessly scrolled ZimTak, liking and commenting here and there but not really engaging the way she usually did. She said nothing about her situation, mostly in deference to Remy's request, but also because it didn't feel right. Where was Remy? What was going on?

There was a knock at the door, and she automatically jumped up to answer it, and then skidded to a stop. Remy hadn't said anything about answering the door. But if someone wanted to come in, it wasn't like a door was going to stop them, was it? She bit her lip, locked in indecision. The knock came again, a little louder this time. She edged to the door.

"Who is it?" she asked, hoping her voice sounded more unafraid than she actually was.

"Geno, sweet lady."

Again, Sage hesitated. She was aware there was something off between him and Remy, but that didn't make him dangerous, did it? After all, he'd come to Dark Haven to help. Lars spent a lot of time with him, and Lars was one of Remy's closest friends. He wouldn't hang with someone who would go against Remy, right? She unlocked the door and cracked it open. "Hey there."

His eyebrows rose as he looked pointedly at the small opening. "You okay? Say coconut if you're being held hostage," he whispered.

She couldn't help but laugh. "No hostage situation here. I just have a feeling that Remy likes her private space private, you know?"

He nodded and held up his hands. "Hundred percent get it. No worries. Want to come down and talk tech? I can show you a couple things to try if it goes down, which it probably will way out here. Don't want to be without comms in these crazy days, right?"

She wavered. Remy had asked her to stay up here—safe. But it was true, she could be useful if things went wonky, and she really wanted to show Remy that there was more to her than her internet celebrity personality. "Yeah, okay. Let me grab my stuff, and I'll be right down."

"Cool. I'll pour the synth." He looked over his shoulder when he got to the stairs. "Kidding."

She ran back in, grabbed her shoes, a notebook, and her phone, and headed down to the living room. Geno was sipping synth in front of the fireplace, and from where she stood, he didn't look like the young tech geek from her generation. He sipped elegantly and appeared more sophisticated somehow. Even his body language was different. Was this what it was to be a vampire? To blend in so seamlessly that no one really knew who you were? Did you have to spend your whole existence as though you were on a stage? The notion that she too had a persona occurred to her, but that was something to think about later. Maybe. Or never. That could work too.

Sage plopped onto the other end of the couch and took a little pride in having startled him. "I thought vampires had super senses?"

He smiled, and she watched as his body language shifted to the one he used with her.

"We do, but we still have to be paying attention. My mind was elsewhere."

She searched his expression, but there was nothing at all there to read. "Do you know what's happened with Jet? I overheard something, but Remy hasn't come back in hours."

He sipped his synth, looking at her over the rim, and once

again, she saw someone else lurking behind his eyes. "What did you hear?"

She shook her head. "You vampires and your habit of answering questions with questions. Is that a survival tactic?"

He laughed. "It is. We understand the flow of information and how it can work for or against you. Now...I heard that Jet was injured, but I don't know how or why. Remy has gently requested that I only be here when necessary, so I'm not privy to all the goings on, I'm afraid."

There was the subtlest hint of irritation in his words, as though he wasn't used to being told where he could and couldn't be. "I wish she'd come back. I think if I ever felt as angry as Remy did, I'd burst into literal flames."

His eyebrows rose. "You felt her emotions?"

Somehow, she knew she shouldn't have said that, but she couldn't fathom why. "Isn't that normal? You guys talk to each other brain-to-brain all the time, don't you?"

"If we choose to." His accent was back, as was the different posture. His mask was slipping. "But emotions are different. If I wanted you to feel what I was feeling, I'd have to intentionally send that emotion to you. And it would be more difficult because you're human, and we aren't bonded."

Sage wanted to laugh and then understood. She was feeling his amusement, and she instantly wanted it to stop. There was an oily feel to it that made her feel...ick.

"See?" He flicked fluff off his jeans. "But if you felt Remy's emotion without her sending it at you, then that means...you've bonded." His smile didn't reach his eyes, but he was clearly searching her for bite marks. "Congratulations."

"I don't think... I mean, she didn't..." She shrugged. "From what I understand, you have to be bitten to be bonded, and she didn't do that."

He sipped his synth, his gaze never leaving her face. "Interesting."

Sage wanted to ask questions. God knew she had a ton. But

she got the distinct feeling that she shouldn't ask Geno any of them. Was that Remy's emotion rubbing off on her? She did a little mental digging but didn't find Remy's essence in her head. Was that even a thing? It was like there was a new language to learn.

"Now." Geno leaned forward and took a tablet off the table. "Let me show you some ins and outs so you can be part of this useful little community."

He took her through a variety of ports and apps, showing her the logins and options to try if things went down. She made copious notes, and he always slowed down enough to let her catch up. He also answered every question she asked, and he seemed surprised that she had more than a base knowledge already in place.

"Most end users don't have the kind of know-how you do. What gives?" he asked as he handed over the tablet. "Make sure you keep this close by so you can fix things quickly before they get out of hand."

She took the tablet and settled it on her lap. "I've always been really curious about everything, and I wanted to understand how we get the information we do. Like, it just shows up on my phone, right? But how? How does that info get to the phone at all, when it isn't even plugged in? So, I studied a lot until I understood. I had a lot of time on my hands after my mom..." No. She didn't want to share that piece of her history with him.

He handed her a glass of water from the table. "Impressive."

"Why did you go into technology?" She glanced at the door, wishing again that Remy would come in. Or anyone else, for that matter. The communal space was strangely empty today. "I mean, Remy went full tree-hugger, and you went full Steve Jobs."

He laughed, open and loud. "That describes Remy and me perfectly. It always has. She's always been a kind of homebody. She likes her friend groups small, and the world she inhabits has to be one she can control, where she can see every move on the board. I like the chaotic nature of life, the way it grows and changes. Technology is the next stage in evolution, and I wanted to be part of it from the beginning."

"How long have you known each other?" The question was out before she could take it back. It wasn't any of her business. But then, it kind of was, since she was staying here, and the point of coming to Dark Haven had been to interview people.

He leaned back and put his feet on the edge of the table. "We first crossed paths in Bulgaria in the year 917. I'd been wandering the world, such as it was back then, trying to find anyone like me. I'd become convinced I was the only one, a devil left behind when the others retreated to Hell. Wars were good places for the likes of me, where the dead were expected and never looked at too closely. The Battle of Anchialos was a bloody one, and I was more than happy to wade in. I stayed fed and commiserated with the dead who would get the peace I never would. I didn't know I could change them, fortunately, as my loneliness might have resulted in waves of vampires just to fill the void in my soul." He glanced at her and then away again. "I'd been a grave digger, and I was turned one night when I was digging a new grave. I didn't see my attacker, and I had assumed it was the Devil himself."

"It sounds like it was a lonely time for vampires." She didn't want to divulge anything Remy had told her, but she had to say something.

"Yes." He gave a wry grin. "You can't possibly imagine what it was like to have no true transport other than beasts of burden, boats, or your own feet. To have to carry messages across continents, to live through the plague and watch the bodies burn..."

She shuddered as the images seemed to fill the air around them. Her own fear of fire and the memories it evoked were ones she could do without.

"As I was saying, Remy had learned the value of battlefields for her survival too. But unlike me, she'd been a Viking and had a strength of character I'd never seen in another person, let alone embodied myself. She sat astride an enormous black horse on the edge of the battlefield, looking down on it as though she was a god above it all. I knew. The moment I saw her, I knew she was like me."

"And did you talk to her?"

His smile was tight. "No. I was going to find her as soon as I finished feeding, but by then she was gone, like a ghost at daylight. But now I knew I wasn't alone, and I began searching for her. I simply had to find her."

"And did you?"

"He did." Remy stood in the doorway, her arms crossed. "He tracked me to London."

"A particularly lovely brothel if I remember correctly." Geno's smile showed no sign of artifice now. It looked genuine. "I begged to talk to you, and you told me to wait until you'd conducted your other business."

Remy moved to sit on the arm of the couch behind Sage and lightly dropped her hand on Sage's shoulder. There was meaning to the gesture, and Sage saw Geno's eyes flick to the movement and then away again.

"We drank ourselves stupid for a long time, discussing what we were, what stories we'd heard, what news of a cure." Geno stared into the fire.

"And then we parted ways, coming across one another over the centuries here and there." Remy's tone was final, as though the story was over.

Sage looked up at her. "I heard something had happened to Jet. Is she okay?"

Remy's expression was shuttered as she looked down at Sage. "We'll see. Let's go upstairs."

Sage stood, and Geno held out the tablet. "Don't forget this."

Sage took it and hugged it to her. "Thanks for being so patient. I'll call if there's anything that stumps me."

He nodded but didn't rise. "I'll wait here for Lars."

Remy took Sage's hand. "He's going to be busy for a while. Best you head home instead of wasting time here."

His jaw clenched, and he stood slowly. "As the great leader

wishes."

Remy moved so Sage was behind her. "I assume you're not involved in this, Valentino."

"This, what?" he asked, his head tilted slightly.

Remy's hand tightened on Sage's, but Sage didn't say anything. The tension between the two was intense enough to make her want to duck, like there was something physical in the air.

"You've never played stupid before. Don't insult me by doing it now." Remy's voice dropped an octave.

"I wouldn't dream of it." He actually looked a little confused. "We've had our issues over the years, Remy, but I know where I stand."

She sighed and stepped back, pulling Sage gently with her. "Thanks for your help. Hopefully Lars will be free soon."

He raised his hand. "If there's anything more I can do, just let me know. I'm always happy to help."

Remy led Sage up the stairs, but Sage could feel his gaze on them like a strange touch against her hair. She glanced down as they went in, and he tilted his head, an odd smile on his lips.

"Phew." Sage shivered. "You guys are wicked intense."

Remy drew Sage into a hug and breathed her in. She didn't say anything, just held on tight, and Sage rested her head against Remy's shoulder, content to give comfort however Remy needed it. Finally, Remy pulled away.

"Is Jet okay?"

Remy headed to the kitchen and poured a tall glass of synth. She drank down half before turning to Sage. "She's been attacked. I found her stabbed and unconscious in her cottage."

Sage's knees went weak, and she slid into a kitchen chair. "And now?"

Remy leaned on the island, moving the glass from hand to hand. "She's on an IV transfusion. The docs think she'll pull through, but she lost a lot of blood. It'll take a while for her to be back to full strength."

Questions. Always so many questions, and Sage wasn't sure where to start. "Who would do such a thing? Do you think it's the same person behind the feral poisoning?"

Remy nodded. "I do. But they didn't mean to kill her. It was a message."

Sage took that in. "Weirdest question I've ever asked, but how do you kill a vampire? Is it true that it's a stake through the heart or whatever?" The very concept made her feel nauseous.

"That's one way. The other is beheading. Anything less, and we're basically badly wounded but still able to recover, eventually. If they wanted Jet dead, they would have known how to do it."

Sage frowned as a thought occurred to her. "What if they didn't know?" At Remy's look, she went on. "Do you check to make sure everyone here is actually a vampire? I mean, can you tell?"

Remy went still, and she stared out the window. "A human pretending to be a vampire so they could get inside our walls," she said softly, her expression thoughtful. "It would be a suicide mission, potentially. At some point, we'd catch the scent of their blood, feel their pulse as they walked by, that kind of thing."

"But..." Sage kept thinking, puzzling it out. "But with the influx of refugee vampires, is it possible that you allowed a human in, if they came with a vampire? Would they even question it, especially with me living in your house?" She was reminded of the conversation in the kitchen. "I overheard someone say you probably spend more time with humans than vampires these days."

Remy's gaze snapped to Sage. "Someone said that? When were you around anyone else?"

Sage flinched. "When you didn't come back for lunch, when no one did, I went downstairs to help. But it turned out no one showed, so I took care of the whole lunch thing."

Remy frowned. "And your chat with Geno?"

Sage blew out a breath. "After lunch, I had this weird feeling like I was being watched. Like the first night I was here, and I nearly had a full-on panic attack, like I was about to be chased through the woods like in some horror movie—"

"Did you see anyone?" Remy's grip was hard on the countertop.

"No. Just a feeling, both times." Sage shrugged like it hadn't been totally terrifying. "So I locked myself in here after lunch, and then Geno knocked and asked if we could talk. I wasn't going to, but then I figured you might really need me to know what the tech stuff was, and I didn't want to let you down, so I went out there, even though I kind of felt weird about it." She took a breath, growing more nervous with Remy's continued silence.

The air seemed to go out of Remy all at once, and she rested her head on her forearms. "Thank you for taking care of lunch," she said, her voice muffled by her position.

"Will you finish telling me about you and Geno?" Sage needed to understand the strange dynamic between them if she was going to be talking to him.

"Yeah. Let me shower and change, and then we'll talk." As she was walking toward the bathroom, she said, "I've asked a couple other people to take care of dinner tonight. We've got the night to ourselves."

The bathroom door closed, and Sage wondered just what those words meant. Having the night to themselves sounded heavenly, but Remy was worried and had an insane amount of things on her plate. Was it wrong of Sage to hope they ended up back in bed? Was it wrong to hope she got to know a whole lot more about Remy? She headed to the bathroom, stripping off her clothes as she did so. Distraction of a more physical nature was sure to help Remy's state of mind.

Chapter Eighteen

Remy stretched languidly, enjoying the afterglow of another bout of fast, hard sex. At some point, maybe they'd slow down enough to savor the moment, but this wasn't that point. Sage's head rested on her shoulder, and Remy felt the rhythmic beat of her heart like someone was tapping on Remy's soul. Fortunately, she was well past the age of losing control, but she couldn't deny that it still called, quietly but insistently, to the predator in her. She ran her fingers along Sage's back, liking the way she shivered a little every time Remy touched the sensitive part of her neck, just at the top of her spine.

"Now that we've cleared away some of the stress, tell me things."

Remy laughed. "What kind of things? How the taste of women has changed over the centuries?" She laughed harder when Sage pinched her side. "Or how I learned to fly planes in World War Two? Or maybe about the time I enjoyed the company of Catherine the Great until her tastes got a little too weird for even me?"

"All of those things and more." Sage ran her fingertips over Remy's abs. "Actually, I had a random thought today. How do you afford to keep up the ranch? I mean, all these people, the synth, the food… It must cost a fortune."

It was a strangely practical question and Remy couldn't help but be a little disappointed. Sage's questions were usually more interesting. "I think you already know the basics. I bought the land about forty years ago, when it was cheap because the land flooded a lot of the time. I saw the potential and understood the way climate was changing and knew it would be good one day. I just had to wait for the right time. We're completely off-grid. We have our own electric and water supplies, and we grow most of our own food. We're pretty much self-sufficient, so the cost is less than you might think."

"And do the vampires who live here have jobs?"

"Some do." She kissed the top of Sage's head as she thought. "They drive into the city and work just like normal people. But a lot of them live and work here, tending the gardens or fields. Like Gabe, for instance. She takes care of a lot of our farm stuff, as well as the horses. But it's well known that she's a great riding instructor, so she gives lessons at the community center in town a couple times a month."

"And what about you?" Sage shifted and leaned on her elbow to look at Remy. "Are you just so crazy wealthy that you can build all these houses and such and not have to worry about money running out?"

Remy palmed Sage's breast and ran her thumb over her puckered nipple. "Why? Are you sleeping with me for my money?"

Sage sighed happily and leaned into Remy's touch. "If that was the case, I would have asked before you chucked me into bed."

Remy laughed and pulled Sage down to rest against her again. "I am wealthy, yes. I've been poor, and I've been absurdly rich. I've lived in crypts with the rats and spiders, and I've lived in castles. Over the last century, I've invested wisely and kept a close eye on companies that were going to do well, and I got in early. When those paid off, I reinvested and built new investments. I also own a lot of property all over the world, and that means I've always got a steady income to support my own community."

Sage groaned. "That's so unromantic and basic. Like, I was hoping for some crazy tale about you having sold some gold from your time on a pirate ship."

"Well, I've done that too."

Once again, Sage lifted up so she could look into Remy's face. "What's it like? Getting to live so many lifetimes and do so many things? It must be amazing."

"It can be." Remy threw off the comforter and got out of bed. She stretched and very much liked the way Sage looked her over like she wanted to devour her. "Come on. I'm hungry, and we should hydrate you so I can make use of you again later."

Sage pulled on one of Remy's T-shirts and followed her into the kitchen.

Remy poured herself a glass of ice-cold synth and a glass of iced tea for Sage.

"Okay. So, tell me about you and Geno. What's the deal?"

Remy stoked the fire in the fireplace while Sage curled up on the sofa. "He already told you a lot of it."

"Yeah, but not the meat of it, right? Like, why you're so intense with each other. There's totally baggage there."

Remy blew on the fire to get it started and let the memories of her time with Geno flow forward. She sat on the couch and pulled Sage's legs over hers. It had been so long since she'd had intimate, firelit conversations with a half-naked woman draped over her, and she found that it felt good in a way she shouldn't get used to. "I said we'd met here and there over the years, and that was true. There was a time, though, when we were inseparable. We lived in a beautiful villa in Spain during the Age of Enlightenment. Philosophy, art, culture... It was a time of hope and beauty."

"And then?" Sage prompted when Remy drifted off.

"And one night, we attended a grand ball at one of the rich families' houses. Geno and I were well known as sophisticated aristocracy, and we were often in the company of people who wanted to be seen with us, although no one really knew us. We had our pick of bed mates, and we were always careful never to feed in the city we lived in. And then..." Remy took deep drink of her synth, and she could almost hear the music and chatter of that night. "A woman walked in, and I would have sworn she'd fallen from heaven. She was beautiful in a way that was almost painful. She had long, golden hair, eyes the color of a summer sky, and skin so pale and perfect, she could have been a painting."

"Maybe I don't want to hear this after all," Sage said, sliding her legs off Remy's lap.

"I'm pretty sure being jealous of a woman from a couple hundred years ago is irrational," Remy said, gently pulling Sage's legs back in place. "Geno noticed her too, and we approached her together. We did that sometimes, just to see which of us would be chosen."

"He's not gay?"

Remy grinned. "When you live for eternity, limiting yourself to a label can get tiresome."

Sage's eyes grew wide. "Were you with men too?"

Remy shuddered. "No, actually. I never did like them. But Geno wanted beauty and never cared what package it came in. That night, the woman chose me." And Remy had often wished ever since that it hadn't been the case. "We started seeing each other more formally, and it turned out she was an heiress with no family, which meant she was free to keep company with us."

"Did she know what you were?"

Remy sighed. "Not at first. But Geno brought someone home one night, even though we'd sworn never to feed where we lived, and she saw him feeding in the garden. She ran to me, but I couldn't lie to her. So I told her what we were, and she left."

"But she came back."

Remy nodded. "For two days, I thought my heart would break. I'd fallen in love with her. When she came back, the three of us talked late into the night." Remy tickled the bottom of Sage's foot. "She asked a lot of questions, like you do. By morning, she was back in bed beside me, and at breakfast, she made her demand."

Sage leaned forward. "What was it?"

"That we turn her. That I turn her, specifically. She wanted immortality. But I refused." Remy could still hear the ultimatum, the anger.

"Why?"

Remy looked at Sage, who looked so beautiful and young in

the firelight. "It sounds like a grand adventure, doesn't it? To learn and explore every part of the world, to have lovers through the centuries, and watch the world change in exciting ways. But there's a dark side no one thinks about." She took Sage's hand. "You watch *everyone* die, Sage. Everyone you care about ages, gets sick, gets old, and dies. Over and over again, you're alone. People fear you, abhor you, and you have to hide or lash out. You live through wars, plagues, global pandemics, every atrocity humans can think up to inflict on one another. It can become unbearable in every imaginable way. Almost no one can know what you really are, and if they do—"

"They can turn on you."

Remy tilted her head in acknowledgement. "I refused, and she threatened to denounce us. She said she'd tell everyone there were monsters living among them. Still, I refused. We could move again, if we needed to. We'd done it before, and I was thinking it might be time for Geno and me to part ways for a while anyway. We were getting on each other's nerves and having vicious fights. I left the house and headed into the mountains, where there's a beautiful cave system. I wanted darkness and to be alone with my thoughts."

Remy could hear the water lapping against the walls, see the way the reflections shifted lazily, and hear it drip from the stalactites. "When I got back, Geno was sitting on the couch with her head in his lap. He'd turned her because he didn't want to move again. He liked the way things were and thought it was better to have another of us than to move on. He thought we'd be a little family, together for eternity."

"You must've felt so betrayed. But were you a little relieved too? I mean, the two of you could be together forever now."

Remy shook her head, still aching at the pain of that night. "She didn't understand what she was asking for, and I'd made it clear what I wanted. What he'd done was wrong. In all the centuries we'd wandered the earth, neither of us had created another vampire. Even Geno, who was lonely and wanted to be loved like a tree wants sunlight, never did. We knew what it meant to take someone's life away like that. To know your existence would never end and to wonder at the pointlessness of it all. I left and went to Madrid, where I spent two weeks in a drunken stupor, trying to decide where to go next. When I figured it out, I sobered up and went back home to say my final goodbyes." She swallowed hard at the memory. "Geno was gone. The woman I'd loved had woken alone and hungry, and without anyone there to stop her, she'd gone into a nearby village and swept through it like death. Not only did she feed, but in some kind of strange defiance I've never really understood, she turned person after person, who then did the same. They had no one to tame them, no one to stop them. They'd been turned against their will and were filled with rage and confusion."

"Why did Geno leave?"

"Because he knew I'd be angry, and he always hated confrontation. He didn't know how to take care of her because he'd never turned anyone before, and he resented that I'd refused them." She shrugged. "Those sound like weak reasons, but that's all he gave me when I asked him about it later."

"And what about the village? And your girlfriend?"

Remy squeezed her eyes shut and cold spread through her. "I stopped them. I went through the village, and I killed every single one of them until the village was nothing but a pile of dead vampires. The last one was her. She'd become crazed, almost feral, and the woman I loved was gone."

"Wind," Sage said softly, her gaze on Remy's face. "That's where your nickname comes from. You went through it like a deadly wind."

"That's part of it." Remy sighed at the heaviness in her soul. "Once I informed the Vampire Council of what had happened, word got out and other clans started to contact me about communities out of control. I'd done it once, and I was instructed to do it a few more times. While we'd been alone for centuries, we'd now found plenty of others and vampires had begun to band together, so laws were put into place and communication became paramount." Remy rolled her neck, trying to rid herself of the scent of death, the screams of pain and fury. "Those who know me understand me. I'll do *anything* to protect our vampire communities, even if it means it's against the proliferation of our species. Even if it means dealing with our own. I was the Killing Wind, and if I came to their village, they knew what was going to happen."

Sage seemed to ponder that idea as she sat there silently looking at the fire. "You must be incredibly powerful. And that must have been harder than anyone can imagine."

Remy blinked away the memories. "Aside from Rac, I'm probably the most powerful vampire there is. It's not something to brag about, but my reputation was built over long, hard centuries. It's strange to become a legend while you're still alive."

"So, Rac is older than you?"

Remy grinned, letting the change in subject wipe away the last of the horrors. "What do you think Rac is short for?"

"Rachel? There's a vampire in novels named Rachel, isn't there?"

"There is. But that's not the answer." At Sage's puzzled look, Remy laughed. "Dracula ring any bells?"

Sage's eyes went wide. "But that was a guy. Vlad the Third. I read all about him in my research. I even did a paper on him for college."

"Then you know that when he was seventeen, Vlad was ousted from Wallachia and went traveling. What you definitely don't know is that when he was traveling, he came across an exceptionally old vampire who'd been living as a man in Moldavia. When the stupid boy got in a fight and got himself killed, our old vampire, who bore a striking likeness to him, simply took over his identity. She wore his clothes and because she'd been watching him, affected his mannerisms. It was almost absurdly easy for her to become him. She took over as the King of Wallachia, Vlad the Third, son of the Devil. Dracula."

Sage wiggled her toes under Remy's caress. "And the rest of the history about him? Her, I mean?"

Remy sighed. "A strange mixture of truth and falsehoods. Well before Vlad, Rac was a ruthless leader and was determined to create a better society than the one in place. No one realized that many of the people fighting in the region at the time were clans of vampires. Hence, all the impaling." She shook her head. "I disagreed with it, but it wasn't my place, and I was only there a short while before I moved on. The fourteen hundreds in that area of the world were full of superstition and ignorance, not to mention plague and severe overpopulation. In her own way, Rac was dealing with all of that, including vampires who'd banded together into violent military groups that raided and killed entire villages."

"Is she part of the Vampire Council you mentioned? Who are they?"

"You're insatiable." Remy slid her hand up Sage's thigh. "Anything other than information you're hungry for?"

Sage stopped her hand before it got any higher. "I've got you talking, *and* I've got you all to myself. Both things are rare, and I'm so not missing this opportunity. Keep going."

Remy sighed and dropped her head back against the chair. "The Vampire Council is made up of clan leaders from all over the world. They make the rules and keep the community in line. I had to work closely with them when I suggested we fight for our rights in the world and come out of hiding. And no, Rac isn't part of the Council, and neither am I. After Wallachia, where she was rumored to have had her head cut off, she went underground. I didn't hear anything about her for centuries, and I wondered if they had, in fact, cut off her head. But she resurfaced in the eighteen hundreds. The Council let me know, and I joined her on the excursion she was on. The HMS Beagle wasn't a cruise ship, I can tell you, but watching Darwin work was something else. He was a bit of a bastard, but I understood Rac's urge to travel with him—"

"This is surreal." Sage looked genuinely in awe. "You traveled with Charles Darwin."

Remy stopped to think. "Yeah. I guess I forget how much history I've lived through. Anyway, Rac had joined his geology team, which of course never gets mentioned along with "his" discoveries. But she didn't want acclaim, she was interested in the way he was changing the world with his insights. We spent months together, talking about what we'd seen and done, who we'd been with, and about the way the world was morphing into something new. It was good to be with someone who understood the world in the way I did. I'd come across more vampires over the years and spent time in different clans, but I never felt like a part of anything. Rac was like me that way. She'd never found a clan she wanted to stay with, and most were either afraid of her or afraid she'd take over."

"Did you stay together when you got back to England? And how did you feed if you spent huge amounts of time on a boat?"

Remy winced, knowing full well how an honest answer would sound. "We can feed without killing or turning people. We fed on the crew, taking only enough to keep ourselves going, and then we fed properly whenever we docked. The time to and from the Galapagos was hard, but it was made easier because we had each other." She looked at her watch and gently eased Sage's legs off her lap. "And that brings to an end our history lesson for the evening. Rac is going to be here soon, and we need to go out for a while."

"The ferals," Sage said, standing and stretching so the T-shirt rode up to her hips, showing she had nothing on beneath.

Remy pulled her close and kissed her hard. "Stay inside, okay?"

Sage leaned back, her eyes half-lidded. "Do you really have to go?"

"I do. But you know you can shout telepathically, and I'll come flying." She gripped Sage's bare ass in her hands and pulled their bodies together. "I'll be back as soon as I can." With a quick, hard kiss, she let go and went to quickly get dressed. If she lingered, she'd drop back into bed with Sage, and Rac didn't like being kept waiting. She emerged from the bedroom to find Sage lying face down on the sofa, her bare ass exposed to the moonlight.

"You'll be the death of me." Remy ran her finger down Sage's spine. "I'll be back soon." She left and laughed when she heard Sage's sigh of exasperation before the door closed behind her. She took the stairs down two at a time and strode quickly out to the gate. The moment the night air hit her, all the troubles surrounding her came rushing back in. She got to the gate just as Rac's truck pulled up, and she gave a brief wave as Rac drove past.

"You reek of sex." Rac leaned against the truck door, her gaze narrowed. "I can smell her on you like you've been rutting in a field."

"My rutting in a field days are long gone." Remy led the way toward the forest trail. "Maybe."

"You should have showered. Even a feral will smell you a mile off."

Remy thought about that. "It could be they'll be attracted by the scent of a human."

Rac didn't respond, and soon they were in the deep shadows of the forest heading toward the lake.

"Any news from the lab?"

"There's something wrong with the blood, but they don't know what it is."

Remy stiffened as she considered her own news.

"What is it?" Rac asked, clearly sensing her shift in mood.

"The lab thinks our synth has been tainted. They're not sure by whom, but the cattle we've been getting are weaker, sickly. But they can't put their finger on a poison."

Rac was silent as they moved swiftly toward the lake. "Coup?" she finally said, like a curse on the breeze.

"But why?" Remy ducked a low hanging branch. "There's nothing to take over here. Unassuming vampires who don't want to live among humans aren't exactly coup material."

They got to the lake and looked around. No one was there and although an owl called to its mate, all else was still.

"Take *you* out of a position of power, show the world our weaknesses, and you leave a void. We know what voids require." Rac's tone hinted at the centuries of power struggles they'd both been privy to.

"But there's you. And no one fucks with you." Remy glanced over her shoulder at a barely audible sound.

"We're too visible for me to do anything about a vampire uprising. The Council would have my head if the military didn't get to me first." Rac turned toward the forest, her gaze searching the shadows.

Remy thought about the history she'd shared with Sage, about all the time she'd spent with Rac over the years. "Have you ever bonded with a human without a blood bond?"

Rac crossed her arms and leaned against a tree. "Why?"

Remy just looked at her, not needing to explain herself. But when Rac simply returned her stare, she capitulated. Rac could wait out an apocalypse if she wanted to. "Something is different with Sage. She can link with me without me instigating it. When Jet was attacked—"

"Excuse me?" Rac pushed away from the tree. "That's a little more important than your sex life, I think."

That was true, and Remy should have led with that. "Sorry. You're right. Jet was attacked today. I felt it in the air, and I found her with a head wound and various stab wounds."

"A message." Rac's eyes narrowed thoughtfully.

"That's what I thought. Poison, ferals, an attack..."

"You've got a traitor in the ranks."

Remy sighed and rubbed the back of her neck. "Yeah. Sage wondered if a human could have gotten on the ranch, maybe as a vampire's partner."

"A human couldn't have taken Jet by surprise. She's too aware for that." Rac leaned against the tree again and looked up into the branches. "Don't let Sage's plebeian human thoughts mess up your intuition, Wind. What do your true senses tell you?"

True senses. That was a term Remy hadn't heard in a long, long time. Those were the senses you developed as a vampire, the deeper, darker ones that let you feel beneath the gossamer veil of people's thoughts and desires. She closed her eyes and sank into them, letting them flood her. Her energy rose and spread, flowing like silken mist through the forest and into the ranch. She pressed her boots into the ground and reached, sliding through the houses, listening to snippets of conversation, feeling the emotions that were mostly well contained. She flowed around the bodies at the campfire, most still and subdued, and she breathed in the layers of truth and lies unfolding around the flames. The more she let go, the more she felt and the more she heard, and the power she'd developed and honed over the centuries swept through her, achingly beautiful and so intense she wanted to challenge the stars to see who could burn brighter.

At a touch to her arm, she pulled back, bringing her energy slowly and carefully back to her, noting which vampires twitched at the ghost among them and who didn't. She opened her eyes, blinking against the half-moon light.

Rac removed her hand from Remy's arm. "We've got company." She moved into the forest where she became one of the shadows.

Remy swallowed and pressed the leftover energy throbbing through her into the ground. Branches snapped, and the sound of someone clumsily tramping through the undergrowth became clear. They were moving fast and coming directly toward Remy. They'd caught Sage's scent on her, no doubt.

She crouched, waiting, letting her vampire self take control. Exhilarated from letting her power flow, it was hard to stay still. But she didn't have to wait long.

A long haired, youngish vampire stumbled into the clearing, scratching at his arms, tugging at his hair, hissing and clearly confused. He scented the air like an animal, his chin raised, his eyes red and wild. Remy wanted to dart from the shadows, tackle him to the ground, and break his neck. The predator in her wanted to kill something like it hadn't in centuries.

He looked toward Remy and darted forward, searching for the scent of the human waiting to be food. Before she could rise to meet him, Rac stepped out from a tree behind him, grabbed him by the head, and twisted his neck in a brutal, quick motion until his spine snapped. She let go, and he dropped to the ground like a sack of skin. The silver stake she drove through his heart glinted in the moonlight as it stuck out of his chest.

Remy jumped up and nearly challenged Rac over the kill. *Her* kill.

Rac held up her hand. "Stop. Breathe. Pull back."

The directive, delivered with Rac's own brand of psychic power, slammed into Remy's skull and doubled her over. That forced her to breathe deeply, and as told, she grounded her energy properly. "Sorry." She pushed back to standing to find Rac bent next to the young vampire.

"You're out of practice," Rac said without looking up. "You've lived like a human for so long, you've forgotten how to be a vampire."

It was said without judgment, without rancor. It was a statement of fact, nothing else, and Remy felt it like a nail to her chest.

"Look." Rac motioned her over. "Look at the bruising at the base of his skull."

"The same as Pam's." Remy looked at him closely. "He's not one of mine. He could only have arrived with the refugee influx."

Rac stood, and with a flick of her hand, the body on the ground unwound like a grotesque mannequin and floated into the air behind her. "The fact that they're not running around all over the place means the poison is being given at intervals and only to select people. If he's not one of the vampires whose claw marks are in the trees already, then there's no telling how many ferals we really have here." She glanced at Remy. "You may need to disband or blow through your own clan."

The air left Remy's lungs. "I don't have a clan—"

"Don't be daft, Wind. Call this whatever you like, but everyone looks at you as a clan leader, whether you like it or not. And if you're going to protect your clan, you may have to cleanse it."

Remy shook her head vehemently. "I won't kill my own people."

"You have before." Remy looked at her sideways. "We've both done what we've had to do over the years. If this gets out of control and humans find out, or god forbid, are affected, then we're going to have to wage war, and there won't be any winners." Once again, they followed the tree line out of sight of the vampires milling around the moonlit ranch. "I'll come back tomorrow so we can talk about what steps we need to take." In a rare gesture of camaraderie, she put her hand on Remy's shoulder. "You're not alone, Wind. I'll be right beside you, but we have to put a stop to this."

Remy didn't have the words to respond. She opened the gate and watched Rac's taillights disappear into the night. She'd told Sage she'd do anything to protect her species, even if it meant killing her own. But she'd thought those days were long gone. Now she protected them with laws and politics.

Rac was right. She'd forgotten what it was to be a real vampire. She was Killing Wind. Death, destruction, dissolution. From now on, she couldn't afford to forget her true nature. She'd do what she had to, even if it meant losing everything she'd built.

Chapter Nineteen

Sage waited by the window, her back pressed to the wall. Her pulse raced and her heart beat like a bird against a cage. She willed it to slow, to be quiet so it couldn't be heard or smelled or whatever by every vampire on the ranch. Particularly the one messing with her right now.

After Remy had left, Sage had showered and opened a book on her iPad. But, restless and filled with thoughts a long way from the book on fashion through the ages, she'd gotten up and wandered Remy's place, touching this trinket or that one, wondering at their origin and thinking of all the stories Remy could tell her.

And then she began to tremble, almost before she was aware of the fear sliding over her like tar. Eerie laughter drifted through the room, seeming to come from everywhere at once. Her first instinct was to mentally call for Remy, but she was with Rac, dealing with something more serious than creepy laughter.

She pressed harder against the wall and focused on her breathing like she'd learned to in Sunday afternoon yoga class. The laughter grew and dimmed, and Sage refused to let the tears that began to well up fall. Closing her eyes, she tried to think about beaches, and sunrises, and rainbows. What she ended up picturing was horror movies where stupid people thought they were invincible and ended up chopped into bitty pieces.

The window beside her cracked in a jagged lightning bolt pattern, and she leapt away from it. She ran to Remy's room and crawled into the bed, drawing her knees to her chest and holding the pillow in front of her. It would do exactly zero good as protection, but it smelled like Remy and that helped a little.

The door crashed open, and she whimpered, closing her eyes so tightly it hurt.

"Sage!"

She let out a small sob of relief. "In here," she called, her voice shaky.

Remy threw the door open, her eyes blazing red, her teeth fully out. She looked around the room. "Are you okay? Are you hurt?"

Sage shook her head and gradually released her death grip on the pillow. Remy closed her eyes and tipped her head back, and her teeth receded. When she looked at Sage, her eyes were back to normal.

"Why didn't you call to me?" Remy asked, sitting on the edge of the bed and drawing Sage into her lap.

Sage curled into her and let the tears fall. "You were doing something important, and it was just...someone laughing." It sounded so stupid when she said it out loud.

"It wasn't though, was it?" Remy kissed the top of her head and gently caressed her back. "I felt it the moment I entered the lodge."

Sage shifted to look at her. "What was it? I don't think I've ever been so scared."

"Come on." Remy set Sage on her feet and took her hand. "Let's get you a hot drink. That's always good for calming people down."

Sage didn't argue. Remy's hand in hers felt right, and she knew she was safe.

Remy made a cup of instant coffee and handed it over, and although Sage winced a little at the bitter blandness, she was right. It did help soothe her nerves a little.

"You know how I said I could talk to the whole ranch at the same time if I needed to? Well, what you were hearing was kind of like that. A vampire was sending that laughter, that feeling of fear to you." Remy traced the crack in the window with her finger, her expression thoughtful.

Sage nodded, gripping the mug tightly. "Like Geno showing me how he could make me feel emotion if he wanted to."

Remy's eyebrow went up. "Oh, he did, did he?"

"Was that wrong? I didn't like the way it felt." Sage took in Remy's thoughtful expression, wondering what it meant.

"That's not surprising. Being forced to feel someone else's emotions, especially someone you're not connected to, is unnatural. And that's part of why the fear really touched you tonight. You weren't in actual danger, but someone was messing with you." She frowned. "With me. They were sending another message. They got to Jet, and they can get to you."

Sage shivered and pushed away the bile-inducing coffee. "If you'd heard their laugh or felt the emotion, would you know who it is?"

Remy scrubbed her hands over her face. "Only if I actually knew them." She leaned against the countertop, her expression unreadable. "You're not safe here, Sage. We need to get you home."

Sage's stomach dropped, and the tears began again. "Please don't send me away. Not yet. I'm not ready. It hasn't even been the full week we agreed on. I still have two more days."

With a soft groan, Remy moved around the counter and pulled Sage against her. "Let's go to bed. We can talk about things in the morning."

Sage followed, but her mind was spinning as her world spiraled out of her control. She truly didn't want to leave. But staying here was never the plan, and as she'd figured out only a short time ago, living here would always mean being prey. But already, she couldn't imagine being without Remy.

She curled up on her side and pushed against Remy when she slid in behind her and draped her arm around Sage's waist. She cried, and Remy just stroked her arm and let her cry herself out. There wasn't anything to say to make her feel better.

***

She woke with her head on Remy's chest and the weight of her arm reassuringly around her shoulders.

"Morning," Remy said softly.

Before Sage could reply, her stomach growled loudly.

Remy laughed. "I need to go get breakfast started. I'll bring you some food in a minute."

Sage shook her head, sat up, and stretched. "I'll come help. I don't want to waste a second with you." She murmured softly when Remy's hand slid up her back to the back of her neck and pulled her back down to the bed.

"I think we have a little time," Remy said, lightly biting Sage's bottom lip.

Sage shifted so that she was straddling Remy, her thighs spread. Remy slipped her hand between Sage's legs, brushed her clit with her thumb and used her other hand to begin tortuous strokes of her nipple.

"Please," Sage said, panting, her back arching. "Please, Remy. Again."

Remy didn't say anything, and her expression was unreadable. But the feeling of her fingers sliding into her, the way she filled her, the way her other hand left her breast to tangle in Sage's hair and pull her head back was all the answer Sage needed.

She rode Remy's fingers, begging wordlessly, and she let herself fall into the moment. Nothing mattered other than this, here. Nothing mattered more than the feel of Remy taking her, making her desire, making her need, making her beg. Remy pushed in harder, adding another finger, and Sage drove down on her, crying out in pleasure as the orgasm built.

Remy shifted so she was sitting up with Sage on her lap, her fingers still buried deep, and she held Sage to her as they moved in an ancient rhythm. Sage bit down on Remy's shoulder as the orgasm exploded through her, and she cried out Remy's name.

She tightened around Remy's fingers when she started to pull out, getting her to stay inside her. She didn't want to lose the connection.

"Tell me," Remy whispered against her hair.

"I don't know." Sage let the tears continue to fall as she tried to explain. "It's so...beautiful. So much. I feel like you took my soul and fixed it then put it back in, but with all the tears and cracks filled in. Like...like..." She took a shuddering breath. "Like being without you would break me into a million pieces."

Remy continued to hold her, rocking slightly, until Sage's body relaxed. She pulled out of her and drew her back into bed. They lay there for a long time in silence. Had Sage said something wrong? Self-doubt began to eat away at the beauty of what she'd felt. She'd been open and honest, but Remy remained silent. Of course she didn't feel the same way. She'd fucked Catherine the Great. Sage Samara from Canton didn't exactly cast the same shadow. Just as she was pulling into herself, thinking that she'd been foolish, Remy squeezed her shoulder.

"Shh." Remy kissed her head. "I felt it too. Don't shut down. I just don't understand it, and I don't like things I don't understand. I need to figure out what's going on, that's all." She moved to look down at Sage. "But I felt it too."

Sage couldn't help the little sob that came out, and Remy waited until she'd settled again.

"I'm afraid I really do need to get downstairs and make breakfast, beautiful." Remy sighed. "But if the offer is still available, I'll take you up on helping me." She grinned and brushed Sage's hair from her cheek. "I want you with me."

Sage gave a tearful smile and sat up. "We should probably shower."

Remy swept out of bed. "Definitely. And alone. Otherwise we're going to delay breakfast even further, and we don't want hungry vampires knocking on the door, do we?"

Sage shivered a little at the memory of the night before. "Nope. We don't want that."

Remy showered first, and Sage took the time to gather herself.

She'd never felt so exposed, so...was there a word for it? There had to be, but she couldn't fathom what it was. What was it when you felt like you'd connected to someone else's being? She smile-winced at the soreness between her legs, which was a welcome distraction from her thoughts. Remy exited the bathroom in record time, and Sage slipped by her with a quick kiss.

Once she was clean and dressed, she felt a little more composed. The house was empty, but Remy had left a note to join her in the kitchen. Sage closed the door behind her, sure to make certain it was closed after last night's weirdness, and joined Remy in the kitchen.

She looked up from the bowl of eggs she was mixing. "Hey, beautiful. You okay?"

Sage nodded shyly, feeling awkward in the wake of their morning's emotional sexy time. "What can I do?"

"If you could start getting the fruit ready, that would be great." Remy nodded toward the bags of fruit and bowls.

Sage went to work, and there was an uncomfortable silence now that hadn't existed before.

"You know a lot about me," Remy said, pouring the eggs into a pan. "I want to know more about you. Tell me about your life outside Dark Haven."

Sage bit her lip. How could she talk about what would now sound so mundane?

"Family?" Remy asked.

"Yeesh." Sage bit into a strawberry and liked the way Remy's gaze darkened a little. "If that's where you want to start. My dad died when I was little. Cancer. My mom didn't handle it well, and I kind of lost her too." She'd already mentioned this to Jet but telling Remy felt a little more important. "She drank a lot and worked even more. Functional alcoholic, they call it. I learned to take care of myself, and I spent a lot of time alone. I had a couple close friends, but their parents were always worried about it, and it made me feel weird, so I didn't spend a lot of time outside school with them."

Remy kept stirring the eggs and added spices to them. "I'm sorry. That must have been really hard. What happened after that?"

Sage swallowed. She pictured the night of the fire and let Remy into the memory. The smell of smoke, the fear, calling out for her mom, stumbling from the house, the fire department lights flashing through the night sky, her sitting wrapped in a blanket on the curb, crying as she watched the firefighters come out carrying a person who wasn't moving, and who never moved again. She thought all of that, sending it like she had the calming thoughts the other day.

Remy stilled, her eyes unfocused as she watched Sage's mental replay. Then she turned off the flame, set down the wooden spoon, and pulled Sage into a crushingly tight hug. "You're so strong."

The unexpected compliment made Sage blink and pull away. "I couldn't save her. I couldn't get her out. That doesn't feel very strong." The guilt that she'd been carrying for years finally spilled out.

"Sage, you were a *child*. Would you expect Jake or Shala to get an adult out of a burning building? Would you blame them when they couldn't? Maybe give yourself the same grace you'd give any other child." Remy's look of sympathy was genuine.

Sage sank into not just Remy's embrace but also her words. "Thank you."

They disengaged and went back to making breakfast, the awkwardness gone.

"That's why you refer to the people on the internet as your family and tell them you love them," Remy said thoughtfully, her eyes on what she was cooking. "Because you don't have an actual family to love."

Sage frowned. "Well, I mean, they kind of are my family. I mean, they care about me and what happens to me, you know. Isn't that what family is?"

Remy shrugged slightly. "I'm beginning to think family means different things to different people. To me, family is physical. They're around you, like here at the ranch. Jet, and Lars, and the others are my family. People I talk to, share my deepest fears and hopes with. I can tell them I love them because I know them and they know me. We've been through things and have more in common than what internet program we use."

"I share my life with my ZimTak family. And they share their stuff with me." Sage knew it wasn't the same, but she couldn't pinpoint why, and it felt a little like an attack on the way she was doing things.

"I think..." Remy tilted her head, still not looking at Sage. "I think family, to me, is deeper than that. Someone hurt Jet, and when I find out who it is, they'll have to deal with me. If Lars needed me, I'd be there. No questions. To me, that's love." She finally looked up. "Would your cyber family actually show up in person? If you were being kept here against your will, would the cyber people band together to get you out? Will they prove their love by standing at your side when things go from bad to worse?"

Sage knew the answer but wouldn't say it out loud. She couldn't. "I'd never ask anyone to put themselves in danger for me. I wouldn't expect it, and I wouldn't want it. Being family doesn't mean that. And you can love people for just being around." That most definitely didn't sound right.

Remy's expression remained thoughtful. "I guess we all have to decide what it means to us. To me, calling someone family is saying they're your innermost circle. Chosen or biological, it doesn't matter. I don't understand how you can have an innermost circle of people you don't actually know, let alone love them." Her gaze was penetrating. "Or love people who don't really know you. It cheapens it, doesn't it? If you can tell the whole world, people you don't know, that you love them, how is that different from telling the person you want to spend your life with?" She shrugged. "Seems to me that word should be reserved for the people and moments that truly deserve it."

Lars came in looking tired and wearing jeans and a T-shirt. "Good morning, sexed-up sexpots." He poured himself a large glass of synth.

"Jet okay?" Remy asked, slowly looking away from Sage to Lars.

"I was at her bedside all night, and I've set two vampires to guard her." When Remy moved toward the door, he held up his hand. "I bonded with two of our own vampires and set them as guards."

Remy froze and looked at him in surprise. "An extreme measure."

"Extreme times." He drank deeply and looked a little more like himself when he finished the glass and then poured himself another.

"What does it mean when you bond with each other?" Sage asked, glad for the move away from her idea of family. Apparently she needed to think about her idea of love too.

"We don't drink from each other. We've got dead blood, and unless we've just had a fresh meal," Remy grinned a little at Sage's wince, "the blood isn't good for us. But a small bite and drink will bond us. We can speak easily to each other and read each other's minds."

Sage looked at Lars. "So you'd know if they were going to do something stupid. But that means they can also read your mind, doesn't it?"

He nodded. "It does, my sweet little flesh bag. And that's why Remy says it's extreme. No one likes someone poking around in their head. But we need a break, and we need to know Jet is safe."

Remy pulled him into a hug and thumped his back. "You're a good man. I don't care what anyone says."

He pushed her away with a huff. "Everyone says I'm fucking magnificent, my dear."

The sound of voices filtered back to them, and all three of them went to work, quickly filling trays and bringing them out to the vampires gathering for breakfast. Sage missed the fun banter and sensual touches, but Remy seemed focused on other things, a world away from what they'd shared that morning. When they sat for breakfast, Sage was surprised when Remy faced the room before sitting down beside her.

The room went quiet immediately, and everyone turned to her

expectantly. She hadn't even needed to clear her throat or ask for their attention. Impressive, as always.

"I hope you're all settling in. I know we're hoping for a quick resolution, and I'm still working on it. But I got an important reminder last night, and I've made a few decisions." She scanned the room for a moment. "I've received word that there are patrols on the water, watching for vampires coming to or from the compound. Some of ours are reported to have gone missing."

A wave of dissention began, and a few people even stood up.

"Wait." Remy didn't move, didn't raise her hands, didn't raise her voice. But the room went silent and those few who'd stood sat back down. "We're going to be a little less reactive and a little more proactive now. We're vampires, and as such, we have powers available to us that we don't always give full rein to because of an awareness of the balance we need to strike to live among the humans. But here at Dark Haven, we're not among humans." She glanced at Sage and gave her a tiny smile. "Mostly." She looked back at the assembled vampires. "I'd like to put together a small team to patrol our shores, and I want a separate small team who are willing to take on spy duties to see who is taking vampires near the militarized borders and where they're taking them. That could be dangerous if you get caught. But I'm not asking you to do it at half strength. I'd like you to use the full extent of your powers in an effort to forestall any further danger and to help those of us who may be in need." She paused as she looked around the room, and not one person looked away. "If you'd like to be on either of these teams, please put your name on a list by the door, and we'll get in touch."

Lars stood. "In Jet's lazy absence, I shall be standing beside our clan leader. Feel free to discuss these things with me."

Remy looked at him gratefully. "Until we understand what's happening along our borders, I'd like those of you on the relocation list to reconsider, just momentarily. You're safe here—"

"Jet wasn't safe here." A vampire in the back stood slowly,

looking uncertain about challenging the boss. "Sorry to interrupt, but...Remy, what's going on?"

Sage, unsure what to do but knowing that her first instinct, which was to jump up and defend how hard Remy was working to keep them safe, wasn't it, simply pressed her foot against Remy's. It was a small, probably silly show of support, but she didn't know what else to do. And she had a feeling a human standing up to defend Remy wouldn't go over well either.

"You're right, Quinn." Remy looked around, her jaw set and her eyes hard and tinted pink. "I believe there's a traitor among us. Someone who wants to break down everything we've built. Someone with an agenda I can't quite figure out right now. Jet was attacked as a message to me, by someone who is playing a game they're not going to win." Remy's eyes went a little redder. "When I figure out the game being played, I can assure you that I will put an end to it."

Sage pressed her foot a little closer to Remy's. *Maybe tell them they're still safe? That it isn't their heads you want to rip off?*

Remy's eyes twitched only slightly as she heard Sage's thought. "But I believe this person's game is being played with me alone. Those closest to me should be careful, and those who aren't close to me should, of course, be watchful. As I said before, you can stay or you can go, but going right now could be far more dangerous until we have answers." Her eyes returned to their regular color. "I am going to do everything possible to fix things. But I can't do it alone. Be my eyes and ears, and if you have anything I need to know, come find me or Lars."

He nodded beside her but didn't say anything more. Remy gave a curt nod and then turned and sat down. "Thank you," she murmured to Sage, before taking a sip of synth.

"Anytime." She meant it, although she wasn't certain what, exactly, it meant.

Remy turned to Lars and gave him a questioning look.

"Well, we didn't talk about it, but everyone knows I'm actually your favorite." He took a big bite of eggs and dabbed at his mouth with his napkin. "And you need family beside you right now."

Sage looked quickly at Remy, who seemed equally puzzled.

"Were you listening to our conversation earlier?" Remy asked.

He looked between them. "What conversation?" When neither of them answered, he shook his head. "I don't know what emotional nonsense you're wafting between you, but I consider you family. And Jet is our family." He waved in the vague direction of the room. "And the others who live here are our family. We need each other right now. That doesn't seem like such an outlandish thing to say, does it?"

Remy shook her head and poked her fork at her food. "It isn't. We just happened to be talking about the issue of family before you came in."

He gave an elegant shrug. "Synchronicity, my dear. If something like that comes up in such a way, it's often good to listen." He put down his napkin and clasped his hands. "Now. What can I do to help our dour and yet sexy leader?"

Sage didn't agree with the dour part, but he definitely had the sexy part nailed. Seeing Remy speak so confidently was a huge turn-on, even if there was an us versus them feel to what she'd said.

"I want a meeting with the clan leaders after lunch. I think Jet already let them know, but can you follow up?" Remy pinched the bridge of her nose, her eyes closed. "I want those teams set up by the end of the day, too." She opened her eyes and took a deep breath. "And I want to talk to Dez about getting Sage out of here. Publicly."

Sage froze, and her stomach dropped. "What?"

Lars patted her hand. "Save the emotional outburst for when I'm gone, lovely." He stood. "I'll leave you to your shenanigans and get on with my serious duties." He gave a mock salute and left the table.

Remy took her plate and headed for the kitchen without a word.

Sage, shaking, picked up her own dishes and followed. "Want

to explain what that's about?" She set the plates down, and they rattled at her trembling. "After this morning—"

"After this morning, it's even clearer." Remy stood with her back to Sage, looking out the window. "I don't understand our bond, Sage. Maybe at some point I'll be able to figure out what it is, what it means. But right now, it means one thing: you're in danger because of your proximity to me, and I won't let anything happen to you because of it."

Sage crossed her arms, fury building. "And what about my say in this? What about what I want?"

Remy turned and mirrored Sage's body language. "I'm sorry, but what you want right now doesn't matter. You'll walk out of here in full view of the world, safe and sound, and it will be known you're no longer part of my world. Then I can stop worrying about you being someone's meal or about you being used against me."

"So what we have doesn't mean anything to you?"

Remy sighed, and her arms dropped. "It means more to me than you know, Sage. But Rac showed me last night that I've let myself become too human. I've dimmed what I am, and I'm going to have to get back to that part of me who was—is—Wind. I don't want you here for that. And, frankly, I can't let your human assumptions and logic get in the way—"

Sage jerked back. "In the way? I've been trying to help." She stepped away when Remy reached out. "No, thanks. You've made your position clear." She wiped away tears of anger and hurt. "I want to go sit with Jet. That way I can be out of the way while you do all your important vampire stuff that I'm so clearly not a part of."

"We knew it wouldn't work, Sage." Remy shook her head slightly and looked away. "Fine. I'll have Lars take you over. But you'll have to wait there until one of us comes to get you."

Sage moved toward the door. "Whatevs. I'm going to get some stuff to keep my basic human mind busy while I'm with her." She stopped at the door and swallowed hard. "I..." Her voice cracked, and she took another deep breath. "I thought we had something special."

"It was good, Sage. And special. But it isn't special enough to bring you into my world. You don't belong here, beautiful. You never will. That's simply the fact." Remy's tone was flat, emotionless. "One day, this will just be another story among the other stories of your life. A week of something unusual and exciting."

Sage barely kept the sob from escaping. "You know what? You really don't remember what it is to be human. Because let me tell you something." She looked over her shoulder to see Remy staring at the floor. "Whatever this is between us is undeniable, even though it has happened crazy fast, and the fact that you're throwing it away proves you don't remember what it is to..." She couldn't say the words. "I can't pretend it won't tear me apart. No matter what you think."

She turned and ran upstairs, ignoring the glances and whispers around her. She threw herself on the couch and let the sobs come. She'd let herself believe, just for a moment, that she had found her place and her person. The deeper sense that Remy was right, that she didn't belong here, wasn't fair. It wasn't *fair*. What she'd felt, what Remy said she'd felt...didn't that mean there was something there worth fighting for? Was she being ridiculous? Only a few days ago, she'd been pondering the fact that she couldn't be prey living among predators. Now she was upset she couldn't stay, that Remy had made that decision too.

She sat up and wiped away the tears. After splashing some water on her face, she got a drink and tried to regain her footing. Remy was fighting for her family. And right now, and maybe not ever, Sage wasn't part of it. It hurt in a way she'd never known and wasn't sure what to do with. So, for now, she'd go sit with Jet and hope that, somehow, something would happen to not make it feel like she was drowning.

Chapter Twenty

Remy squatted in the kitchen, trying to breathe past Sage's pain. Sage would have no idea that Remy could feel every tear, every sob, every ounce of hurt and abandonment that was running through her. She took it all, letting it flow as a reminder of the depth of what they'd shared, whatever it was.

It was true. The sex this morning had been something else. Something beyond anything she'd felt since she was reborn a vampire. They'd blended, their souls entwined and their desire matched only by the need that filled them both. She'd never possessed someone the way she'd possessed Sage, the way she'd taken her and invited her into the essence of who and what she was. She'd never felt compelled to hold someone so tight and practically demand the release of not just their body, but their soul as well. She'd needed it, that total loss of control, of submission. And just as surely as Sage had given herself to her, Remy had lost a piece of herself to Sage, too. Sage wouldn't know that, of course. But Remy had felt part of her slip into Sage's being, making them one.

It was a bond stronger than any vampire-human bond she'd ever heard of. No blood exchange had been necessary. What the holy fuck did it mean, and how was she going to deal with it? Not having Sage beside her was going to drive her into a feral rage, she just knew it.

Sage's pain began to ebb slightly, and Remy slowly rose from where she crouched on the floor. She could breathe again, and she mentally called Lars to come get Sage and take her to Jet. She received a vague confirmation and turned back to work.

The monotony of clearing up breakfast and having brief, surface conversations with people eased some of the emotional chaos, helping her refocus on her day.

She stopped for a moment when she felt Sage leave the house. Like a string being pulled, it tugged taut, making her skin feel too tight and making it harder to breathe easily. What the hell was she going to do and how would she feel when Sage wasn't even in Bluffington State anymore? It would feel like steel wire wrapped around a finger, cutting off the circulation. But it wouldn't be her finger. It would be the heart she'd not given to anyone in centuries.

Clean-up done, she went upstairs to her desk and made the call she was dreading, just to get it over with. When Dez picked up, her feeling of dread worsened. "What is it?" she asked without any preliminaries.

"Two dead vampires washed up on North Bay shore. Their necks were broken, and they'd been staked."

Remy slumped in her chair. "And?"

"And they were two of the vampires who'd been reported missing after they'd been escorted away from the border."

"General Cane?"

Dez nodded. "Probably on his orders. I really don't think the president would condone this. I'm sure Cane will say he and his men had nothing to do with it."

Remy thought of the power she'd used last night that swept through the forest, through the ranch, and how it burned through her. "Maybe it's time we remind them that we're stronger than they are."

Dez ran her hands through her long hair. Dark circles under her eyes underscored her own part in this drama. "There was a time I would have told you to hold your horses. But I don't know anymore, Remy. I genuinely don't know what to do. We said we'd give him time, and it's only been a week. That's not giving him time. But if they're killing vampires..." She shook her head, looking as defeated as Remy felt.

"I've organized teams to patrol our borders and to begin a counter patrol of the military zones to find out what's going on. Maybe that's where we start. Gather information so we know what we're really dealing with. I feel like it's tied into what I'm dealing with here." She gave Dez a brief rundown.

"It seems awfully coincidental that we have a sudden military problem and you have an uprising and poison problem at Dark Haven." Dez steepled her fingers under her chin. "But it could be that someone is just taking advantage of the political issue to fan some flames."

Remy held up her hands. "And that's the question, isn't it? Are they related, or are they two issues overlapping? I think..." She drifted off as she sifted through the questions. "I think if we find at least one person involved, we'll be able to tug on that thread until we find the source of the knot."

Dez nodded. "How can I help?"

Remy thought for a minute, and Dez let her ruminate in peace. "We need information that isn't being given freely. Do you have contacts who can slip into the shadows? Let's see what we can get from conversations and meetings we aren't part of. As I said to my folks here this morning, let's get proactive."

Dez nodded, already writing. "I'll let you know what I find out. You called me. Was there something else to talk about?"

Remy hesitated. "Sage Samara."

Dez put her pen down. "Is she giving you a headache? I know she's over the top and having a human there right now can't be easy."

Remy's chest ached and she had to force the words out. "I don't think she's safe here, Dez. Someone already hurt Jet to get to me, and—"

"And you're afraid they'll use Sage as a political pawn. They hurt her, they make us look even worse and make the situation untenable, pushing us to war." Dez let out a whoosh of air. "The thing is, Remy, they know all that. They knew it the moment they closed the border and said they wouldn't let her out. She's been a game piece since the moment this kicked off. Nothing has changed."

Everything had changed, but Remy wasn't about to tell Dez that she'd bonded with the very human who could push them to war. "Then I might work on getting her out by other means. Put her on a boat. Hell, I'll carry her through the treetops if I have to. Then she can make a public statement that she's out of Dark Haven, and they won't be able to use her anymore."

Dez tilted her head, and Remy could see she was wondering if there was more to it. "Okay. That's a plan, but if it goes wrong and you're caught sneaking her out, who's to say they won't kill her anyway and make it look like the vampires did it? If she isn't shown leaving on camera, in public, then I think it's still too much of a risk."

Remy deflated. She hadn't thought of that possibility, and she should have. She just wanted Sage safe, goddamnit. Somehow, she had to get Sage out of here and back where she belonged.

"I think that's the least of your worries right now, Remy." Dez's tone was soft, like she understood more than Remy had said out loud. "As long as she's under your care, she has a good chance of being okay. Right now, we need to find out who's behind your chaos at Dark Haven, and who's pulling the strings here. I'm going to have some people find the survivors of the original fight that started all this bullshit. I'll have them questioned and see if it was a plant of some kind."

Remy nodded slowly. "The fight between humans and vampires might have been set up to get all this rolling. By someone who doesn't want us living in peace together."

"And that could be on either side. Or both, working together to keep us apart." Dez shrugged, looking even more tired now. "Let's get our people out there finding answers. I'll be in touch."

She logged off, and Remy sat back as a larger picture began to unfold. Pieces began sliding together, creating an image that made her blood begin to boil. It made sense, but it was a long game that had required meticulous planning as well as people willing to sacrifice themselves.

The question was, who had put everything in motion? And what was she going to do with them when she figured it out?

***

She sat in the main area of the lodge, waiting as the seven clan leaders arranged themselves around the table in solemn silence. All wore the purple band around their upper arms, but one also wore a slim red band that sat above it.

She nodded at him. "I wasn't aware we had a member of the Council in the area."

"My name is Vanquil. I made it across the border before the military closed it off. I'm lodging at the hotel." He bowed his head slightly. "It is my honor to meet you, ancient one."

"Thank you for coming, Vanquil." She nodded at the others as well. "Thank you all for coming. I'm sorry it's been a few days, but as you can imagine, there's a lot going on."

When she thought about Rac's assertion that a lack of knowledge and understanding of a situation had never done anyone any good, Remy plunged in and gave the clan leaders a full rundown of the entire situation, including the ferals and the potential poisoning. They listened intently, clearly growing more and more ill at ease. When she finished, she put her hands flat on the table. "Now you know how dire the situation is. Someone powerful, or maybe even a group of people, are working to set us at odds. And the enemy is both on the inside and the outside."

There was silence for a while as the Council members processed what she'd said.

"What do you need from us?" Vanquil asked. "How would you like to proceed?"

"I need information, but the last thing we need is vampires turning on each other. So the person gathering the information needs to be discreet. They need to be unobtrusive and able to keep things to themselves. They need to be people you trust implicitly. Right now, that's the most important thing. The other thing I need to know is which clans are open to taking in refugees. There are vampires who don't want to stay at Dark Haven, but right now I can't get them out safely. So are your clans open, and can you provide them housing until they choose to move on?"

There was some shuffling, and a few clan leaders didn't meet her gaze.

"Remy, if I may speak for my clan and, I think, a few of the others." Ashari was a clan leader from a clan at the far edge of the county, a woman with a reputation for being tough but fair. "Given what you've said, I believe we're concerned that we could be letting the snakes into our gardens, should we welcome vampires we don't know who turn out to be poisonous."

There were a few small nods of agreement.

Remy looked around. "I understand your line of thinking. But I feel certain their aggression is directed at Dark Haven right now. Disrupting smaller clans won't have the same effect."

"Because someone wishes to unseat you." Vanquil's eyes were narrowed thoughtfully. "If they managed to unhinge you, to make you lash out, then it's possible both vampires and humans could turn against you."

"And as the face of the political movement, it could be most disastrous if it's you, specifically, they discredit." Ashari looked at the others. "Which means it is true that we would not be as likely to have the disruptors eager to leave Dark Haven, and we could welcome new vampires into our clans without excessive worry."

Remy let them take the time to think. Bringing new vampires into a clan was always something to take seriously. Clans were family. They lived together, supported each other, and would die together if it came to war. Like any chosen family, you had to believe in them. Plenty of vampires lived outside of clans on their own, but it meant a lack of community as well as safety. That thought took her back to Sage, and she pushed it away. She couldn't be unfocused right now.

"Our clan will take new families who wish to live near the border." Ashari placed her hand on the table, palm up. It was a signal of trust, like a human giving their open wrist to a vampire.

The other clan leaders followed her example, including Vanquil. Remy made notes of where their clans were located and how many spaces they had available. It was tradition for any clan to have extra housing in case of emergency. She also noted any caveats, like the clan who drank synth and ate only a vegetarian diet.

"Remy, your success or failure affects all of us," Vanquil said, sitting back. "If you are uprooted, if it is seen that the human with you dies by the hand of a vampire, if the poisoner manages to create more ferals than you can handle, then all of us are at risk."

Remy nodded, uncertain where he was headed. All that had been made clear.

"As such, the Council has asked me to let you know that we will back whatever decisions you make. You've eschewed your rightful place on the Council, but there's no question that you have always had vampire interests at heart. You are one of the strongest, oldest, and wisest among us, and as such, the Council will sanction whatever means you feel necessary to keep us from war."

The weight of the statement was heavy on Remy's shoulders. They were giving her free rein to do whatever she deemed essential. If that meant killing other vampires, she didn't have to ask for anyone's go ahead. Rac had always been the one with the Council's blessing on that. Now, Remy had it too. She didn't want it, but so be it. "Thank you, Vanquil. Please tell the Council that I'll do my best to be worthy of that trust."

He nodded, and everyone stood to leave. Remy let them know she'd be in touch when she had names and numbers, and she had to admit it was easier with a cell phone and computer than it would have been if she had to drive to each clan for a discussion. But thinking like that was a slippery slope. Following that path would end with a FacePlant account or whatever it was called.

The clan leaders left, and Remy closed the gate after the last vehicle. Not one of them rode a horse, or walked, or even rode a bike. She thought of the teasing about their Amish vampire ways and understood just how odd they must seem to the outside world. Once again, that line of thinking returned her to Sage.

Beautiful, passionate, naïve, sweet Sage. She made Remy feel like she could conquer the world and like she was tearing it apart at the same time. She still believed it would be better to get Sage out of vampire territory and back to her human habitat, but it was true that the risk involved was extensive. Remy was powerful, no question, and the likelihood of someone sneaking up on them or having the strength to take her on was about as likely as bees learning to use chopsticks. *But.* There was always the possibility, however slim, that having Sage with her would distract her. *But.* Sage here at Dark Haven was already a huge distraction, and if someone hurt her here, there would also be consequences.

Remy rested her arms on the gate, wishing for the briefest moment that she could simply leave it all behind. She'd never been someone who ran from trouble. She might not like conflict, but she didn't back down from it either. She'd always done what was necessary, and she'd do it again now.

She pushed away from the gate and headed toward the lodge. The question was, what was necessary? Which path would lead to the right decision? What questions would lead to the answers that would stop the chaos? She stood on the deck, trying to decide what to do next. The list was overwhelming.

Jet's awake, grumpy bear leader of ours.

Lars' communication made her smile a little. Sage would be there too, and that would be hard, but what wasn't right now? She headed along the covered walkways she'd designed with sacred geometry in mind. The idea that everything was connected in some way had always appealed to her, and she'd seen plenty of evidence of it throughout history. It was those connections she was looking for now. Maybe if she could sit with them the way she'd sat with the idea for constructing Dark Haven, she'd garner some insights.

She arrived at Jet's cottage and heard them speaking inside. Instead of going in, she sat down on the step to listen. It was eavesdropping, without question, but right now she didn't care.

"What about you, darling girl?" Lars asked in his gossipy tone. "We know you and Remy have become friends of the bumping uglies variety, but do you have anyone back home pining away for your return?"

Remy tensed. She hadn't even considered that Sage might be with someone.

"I've had various situationships. Nothing serious until Remy." Her voice shook a little.

"Situationships. Interesting word. I like it. Completely lacks the integrity of relationship and suggests more than a hookup." Lars sounded genuinely approving. "And do you have one of these situationships in motion back home?"

Remy admired his persistence. No doubt he'd heard her arrive and was fishing on her behalf. She didn't mind.

"Not right now. Not in a while, actually. I hook up with the occasional ZimTakker, and a couple lasted more than a week or two, but I've been working hard on my brand and building my platform, and I don't...didn't have time for that kind of thing." Sage hesitated. "And I guess, if I'm honest, my connections always felt a little flat. Like, we both totally knew it was temporary. I never got with anyone who liked drama. And it wasn't like they were desperate to hang around either."

The loneliness in her voice was unmistakable, even though she'd tried to keep her tone upbeat.

"Why don't you meet real people in bars or pottery classes like we used to?" Jet's voice was gravelly and tired.

"You guys out here with your buggies and horses are so cute." She rolled her eyes. "My generation is way too anxiety-driven for bars and in-person hookups. We're all about the tech. We video chat when we're feeling really brave but generally we're happy reading books, going to therapy, cheering each other on through social media, and drinking coffee. We do enjoy coffee shops."

"Doesn't that mean you're alone more often than not?" Lars asked. "Surely that only feeds the anxiety."

Remy could almost picture Sage shrugging and looking embarrassed.

"Maybe? I mean, it's just the way things are."

"The way things are implies you don't have a choice," Jet said. "But you do. Look at what Remy has done. The way things were didn't work for her or for vampires in general. So she changed it. And when she decided she didn't like the way the world was impacting her, she changed the way she lived in it. You choose the way you live, Sage. Not the other way around."

"Okay. That's enough vampiric philosophy for you today. We need to get going and let Jet rest."

Remy stood, understanding that Lars was giving her a cue. She turned and opened the door as they were moving toward it.

You're welcome.

Remy tilted her head in response to Lars statement. *Nosy little flower, aren't you?*

Well, now you have one less excuse to be a Shakespearean farce of a character, Romeo.

She barely refrained from rolling her eyes and took Sage's hand. "Are you okay?"

Sage didn't make eye contact. "Sure. Why wouldn't I be?" Her tone was flat, and her hand in Remy's was limp.

Remy desperately wanted to pull Sage to her, to tell her it would be okay, that they could take their time and see where this went. But she couldn't in good conscience do so, and it was unfair to give mixed messages. She let go of Sage's hand. "I'll see you back at the house."

Sage turned away without answering, and Lars gave a little

pout and patted his heart. Remy moved to Jet's side and sat down beside her. She didn't say anything until she heard Lars and Sage walk off down the path.

"You're an idiot," Jet said, her eyes closed.

"You're the one who got stabbed in your own house. What kind of vampire are you?" Remy's tone was light, but she took in Jet's pallor, and it made the anger rise again.

"I didn't hear them, Wind."

Remy stiffened. Jet was one of the few people who didn't use the old nickname. It spoke volumes about her feelings of being caught unaware. "What do you mean? Not at all?"

"The first moment I knew someone was in my house was when they stabbed me in the side." Jet's eyes opened, and she rolled her head on the pillow to look at Remy. "There was no warning. No smell, no sound. I didn't feel them *right behind me*."

Remy leaned back in her chair. "How is that possible?" It ruled out the idea of it being a human, just as Rac had said. No human could move silently or without the scent of their blood being immediately in play.

"I don't know. But that was in my pocket." She looked at a piece of paper on the table beside her.

Remy picked it up and was instantly aware of the strange scent. It was the same one she'd picked up before.

This is a warning. It's time to take our place at the top of the food chain. Don't stand in the way.

It was succinct and unimaginative as notes from villains went. Remy tossed it on the table and then sniffed her fingertips. "That scent. There's something about it."

Jet nodded, her eyes closed again. "I didn't smell it when I was attacked, but I can smell it on the paper."

Remy patted her leg and stood. "I'll let you sleep. Don't die on me, and don't get all comfy and lazy in here while we stress out beyond your door."

Jet's eyes fluttered open. "Be careful, Remy. This vampire could be stronger than you." Her eyes shut again, and her breathing slowed.

Remy went out and motioned at the vampires who'd been chosen to guard Jet's cottage. They'd been waiting under the longer walkway leading to the lodge, in order to give Jet and her visitors some privacy. "Anything at all strange, any vague sense that something isn't right, even if you're not sure what it is, you get hold of Lars. Okay?"

They nodded and stationed themselves at Jet's cottage, one at the front door and one in the back.

Now where? Once again, Remy stood still, waiting for some inspiration to strike. She was so tired, and all she wanted to do was take Sage to bed and sleep between bouts of sex. That wasn't going to keep them from going to war.

She headed into the lodge and looked at the lists of vampires volunteering for the two teams she'd asked for. It was heartening to see that both pages were full. They'd have their pick. She looked at the stairs and debated going back out. But Lars would have a better idea of who the best vampires for this job were going to be, and he was with Sage at her place. So be it.

She went upstairs. Lars was draped over the armchair, reading a magazine. At Remy's look, he tilted his head toward her bedroom. "She's gone for a nap. Tuckered out from all the crying, poor thing. You big, bad butch vampire, breaking that girl's heart." He fluttered his eyelashes, clearly enjoying her irritation.

She held up the pages. "I need your help deciding who to put on the teams."

He undraped himself from the chair and took the pages. "You pour the synth."

They sat at the kitchen table and worked through the lists until they had six people for each group. Enough to cover large areas, but not so many that would draw attention. They were also all old enough to know how to handle themselves around humans.

"Jet told you she didn't hear her attacker?" Remy asked,

stretching out her back after being hunched over the table.

"She did." Lars drained the last of his glass. "I can't fathom who could manage that, or how."

"Sage heard weird laughter a few times, like someone was messing with her. Yesterday I came in sure she was about to be someone's dinner, but there wasn't anyone here. Just a sense, like knowing the monster is in the closet."

"Apt phrasing, my dear." Lars pulled on his jacket. "I'm off to Geno's tonight. I'll send him your love."

"Be careful, okay?"

He nodded, his expression turning serious. "I know what we're looking for, and I know how to get information from people. I'll always come back to you, wifey."

She shook her head and smiled as he left.

"Remy?"

Sage's soft voice came from behind her like a caress. She turned in her seat to look at her, and her heart lurched. Once again, Sage was wearing Remy's shorts, but this time she was in her T-shirt too. She looked so small, so fragile and vulnerable.

"Fuck it." Remy rose, went to Sage, and led her into the bedroom.

Sage crawled into bed, her eyes wide and watching Remy's every move as though worried she'd disappear. Remy undressed quickly, throwing her clothes in a pile, and then got in beside Sage and pulled her close. Sage nestled in beside her.

"I don't understand what I'm feeling. Or what's going on." Sage sounded forlorn.

"I know, babe. It's confusing, isn't it?" Remy stroked Sage's soft hair, liking the way it felt as it rested against her skin. "I'm confused too, for the record. I've never had this happen."

"Really?" Sage drew little circles on Remy's stomach. "Never?"

"Never." Remy thought back over the centuries. "I've bonded with a few humans, of course. And I've had relationships. But this connection we have is new, and I'm not sure how to handle it." She kissed Sage's head and rested her cheek against her silky hair. "I don't want you to go, Sage. To be clear, and so you understand, this scares the shit out of me. I don't know what it is or how to deal with it, but that doesn't mean I don't want you here."

Sage lifted her head so she could look into Remy's eyes. "But?"

"But you're in danger, sweetheart. Aside from all the other stuff, apart from you being human and in the midst of vampires, aside from our vastly different lifestyles, aside from our age differences—"

"Enough with the asides." Sage frowned.

"Aside from that stuff, which we might be able to work around, you're in danger. Not movie-style stuff. The kind that would mean you ceased to exist. And it isn't just that." Remy ran her hand over Sage's cheek. "Because I care about you, and probably every vampire here knows it, you could be used against me. Because I couldn't let anything happen to you, Sage. Not just because of the political fallout, but because..." she swallowed hard at the thought of Sage injured, or worse, "because I think I might go insane if anything happened to you. I'd lose my mind. And I have too many people counting on me for me to lose my mind over a woman I've just met but can't get enough of."

Sage looked surprised. "Really?"

Her sweet vulnerability made Remy smile. "I told you, of course it mattered to me. But in the big picture, I have to make choices. I've had to sacrifice a lot over the years, and I've never been responsible for so many vampires all at once. If we go to war, we all lose. The president knows that, but other people are pulling strings, and they're damn good at it." Once again, she caressed Sage's face. "Maybe when this is all over, we can figure things out."

Sage closed her eyes and pressed her cheek against Remy's hand. "When you say it's either war between our species or my need to stay beside you, it sounds pretty selfish." She opened her eyes and bit her lip. "I've been thinking a lot about this, and I need you to hear me." She waited until Remy nodded. "If things go really bad, you know, if they do get to me—" She shook her head when Remy started to speak. "Listen to me. If it happens, I want you to turn me."

"Sage—"

"No. Listen. I'm not asking you to do it just because I want to live forever or whatever other reasons people have given you. I've heard you, and I understand what you mean about the dying and all the bad stuff. But there's a lot of good stuff too, and I think maybe you've forgotten that. And that stuff would make it worth it. Not to mention getting to be under and over and around you all the time." She gave a small smile. "And I'm saying it so you know you have my consent, just in case things literally go to shit."

Remy sighed. "Thank you for making that clear, in spite of your misuse of the word literally. I won't do it, but thank you." She pulled her close. "Let's get some sleep. I'll wake you up nicely so you start your day the right way." She gave her a slow, lingering kiss. At some point, she needed to talk to Rac, or maybe Lester, about the kind of bond they had. But, for now, having Sage in her arms tonight was all she wanted.

Chapter Twenty-One

Sage reluctantly agreed to stay in the house, sit with Jet, or to call Lars if she wanted to go somewhere else. Remy, Lars, and Jet often met at Jet's bedside and talked through the various issues. They'd organized the teams and had sent them out on their scouting missions but after a week, there was nothing to report. Remy had taken the note left at Jet's attack to Rac's place, and Rac had sent it on to the lab she used. Remy's synth lab wouldn't have the kind of tech needed to find whatever it was they could smell. Sage had tried, but the only thing she could smell gave her a strange memory of pie. Remy had said that wasn't hugely useful.

Sage listened in to all their meetings and was always welcome at the table, but the situation felt so much bigger than she could deal with. Sometimes she'd make a remark that they bounced off of but generally, she was content to listen. She so wanted to be recording all of it, not just to share it with the world but also so she could remember every moment if and when she went back to her own little bubble beyond vampire country.

The clans had reported back to Remy, but only with a repeat of the information Lars had heard at the conference. Whispers were in the air about someone who thought vampires deserved better than what they'd been given and was urging them to step up. But no one could pinpoint the origin of the whispers. Dez's people had come up empty too. The vampires from the brawl had been questioned, but no one seemed to know how the old-fashioned rumble had been organized. It was as though a fight had been agreed on and showing up meant proving you were a vampire unwilling to kneel to humans. Some, apparently, even regretted having joined in.

Remy and Rac had been to the forest and dealt with two more feral vampires who had been too far gone to question. Remy had come back with their deaths on her shoulders. And although Rac's lab results on the poison had come back, they showed a complicated chemical compound they hadn't seen before. They were still analyzing it.

Sage flopped onto the couch with her phone and got caught up on the ZimTak happenings. She refrained from checking in or even commenting on anyone's feed, simply out of respect for Remy's wishes. She realized she hadn't looked at the footage she'd taken when she'd arrived, and she opened the videos and began the tedious editing process.

There was a super long video, and she realized it was from the time she'd put it on in the kitchen and then left it there. Curious, she played it, and there was nothing of interest for a long time. And then...

"What the hell," she murmured, sitting up and paying closer attention. When it finished, she sat back as various pieces of the puzzle slid into view.

Remy, I need you guys back here.

She'd become used to the telepathic communication, or mind Zoom, as she thought of it, and liked the way it felt when Remy's words came back to her. Like silk running over her brain or something.

Remy's footsteps pounded up the stairs, and she flung the door open, looking around wildly. "Are you okay?"

"I'm fine." Sage held up her phone. "But I've got something you need to see right away."

Remy sighed and sagged against the door. "Jesus, Sage. I thought you were in trouble."

"Sorry. I should have been clearer. But I promise this is worth it."

Lars came up behind Remy, far more sedately. "You're making the place look messy. At least get out of my way." He pushed at her arm, and Remy moved away from the doorjamb to sit beside Sage.

"So, one day I put my phone on video and set it up on a shelf in the kitchen, you know, just to record a day-in-the-life kind of vibe. But then things went crazy, and I left it there. Totally forgot about it."

Remy's eyebrows were furrowed. "And?"

"And..." Sage handed over the phone and hit play. "Before it died, it caught something weird."

The three of them watched in silence as a group of three female vampires slipped in the back door and stood talking in the kitchen, their furtive looks showing they didn't want to be found.

"Do you know them?" Lars asked.

Remy shook her head. "Not ours."

"Thing is, I saw them at the *VCN* conference." Sage pointed at one of them. "This one told me I shouldn't be there, that vores didn't have any place at the *VCN*. I seriously thought she was going to come at me. And she was with those other two at the time."

"The day you were in the bathroom crying," Remy said, glancing at her.

"It freaked me out, honestly." Sage shrugged, a little embarrassed. "But watch what happens next."

Another minute later, the door opened.

"The snake shows itself," Lars said softly.

"Fucking Cadence. How did she get into Dark Haven without us noticing? And what is she doing—"

"Look, there." Sage interrupted and tapped Remy's hand.

Cadence pulled a small, opaque bag from her pocket and handed it to the woman who'd threatened Sage. That woman, in turn, opened the fridge and took out a tray of steak marinating for the following day. She opened it and sprinkled something from the bag on one of the pieces of meat, then recovered it and put it back. She did the same with two of the clean glasses in the cupboard.

"They poisoned bits of food and tableware. Turning vampires feral little by little." Remy's jaw was tight, her eyes red. "Why not poison us all at once?"

"Because it's a game. Cadence has always been a game player. You should remember that." Lars' tone was unusually flat and hard.

The others watched and didn't appear to say anything as it was done. Then the woman handed the bag back to Cadence, who gave a full-fanged smile and said something else the phone didn't catch.

"Is there a way to turn up the volume?" Remy asked, turning the phone sideways.

"I've tried. They were talking too quietly for it to pick it up, and the phone was about to die. Sorry."

Remy gave a short nod and then leaned forward. "What the fuck?"

Cadence disappeared. She didn't walk out with the others or go out another door. She was simply there one second and then gone the next.

"That's not possible." Lars leaned closer. "We can't do that. Can we?" He looked at Remy, his expression showing his bemusement.

"I've heard there were vampires who could, before I was born. But I haven't seen one do it in my lifetime. Maybe Rac has." Remy looked at Sage. "Could you call her and ask her to come over, please? I want her to see this before I make a move." She turned to Lars. "I need you to go down and clear out the fridge. Trash everything that could possibly be tampered with and get all the dishes out and put them outside." She looked at the phone, which she'd paused on the three vampires. "We need to find them. I haven't seen them at meals, but that could be because they've holed up in a cottage. Cadence may have ways of getting onto the property, but there's no way those three could."

"The kids." Sage mentally went through the vampires she'd met as she sent a text to Rac. "Jake, Shala, and Jimmy could wander the entire ranch and not raise suspicion, because that's what kids do, and Jimmy is new here. Show them the pictures of the people we're looking for and see if they come across them."

Remy winced. "I don't like the idea of using kids as spies."

"But they're just looking. We'll tell them not to engage in any way. They're smart." Sage could imagine how proud Jake in particular would be to be helping catch the people who'd hurt his mom.

"Okay." Lars stood, wiping his hands on his linen trousers. "We have more answers than we've had this whole time. I'll go get the kids so you can put them to work, then I'll get to the kitchen." He left without another word.

Remy held the phone loosely, her gaze trained out the window.

"So…" Sage bit her lip, unsure if she should ask. "I remember her standing up at the conference and thinking she's the kind of ex who slashes your tires, but she's put that idea to shame. What's her damage?"

Remy sat back, her gaze still unfocused. "We were together for a couple years before I came to build Dark Haven. We were living in Back Bay, Boston, in a home her family had owned since the eighteenth century. She was a young vampire, only about twenty-five years old in vampire terms, and she was in love with the power. It's one thing to turn a regular person into a vampire. But when you turn a sociopath into one, it's a different thing altogether."

"Did you know she was a sociopath when you got together?" Sage asked.

Remy's look of incredulity could have curdled milk. "Of course. That's my type, you know. Sociopathic women who use you as an emotional punching bag." She shook her head. "Obviously not. I learned the painful way, and you'd think after living so long that I'd be able to walk away from that kind of nonsense. But maybe the need for someone to change is hardwired into who we are." She looked at the phone and rewound it to a frozen image of Cadence. "I cared for her, but she was a manipulator of a grand design. One I hadn't seen since Mussolini."

"Was Mussolini a vampire?"

Remy rolled her eyes. "No. He was quite publicly shot and then hung upside down and stoned. Maybe that's what I'll do with

Cadence when I get my hands on her. Anyway, she pushed me too far one day when we got into an argument about vampire politics, among other things like the fact that she was also sleeping with Geno, and I said I was done with her. It took a while, but she finally got the message that I meant it, although like you said, she did slash my tires more than once. And she took a baseball bat to my car. Have you ever seen a vampire use a baseball bat to crush something? Needless to say, I had to get a new car. But I never dreamed she'd do something like this. Not go after innocent vampires. I don't get it." She hit play on the video and kept going over the moment she vanished. "How is she doing that?" she muttered.

There was a knock at the door and Rac came striding in. She held out her hand, and Remy passed her the phone without comment.

Sage watched, mesmerized, as Rac's face changed from angular normality to "monster you don't fuck with" in the blink of an eye. Her eyes went a deep, magenta red and her fangs came out, her cheekbones seeming to sharpen. She looked at Remy. "Do you know where she is?"

Remy stood. "No, but why don't we see if we can find out?"

Just as they were heading to the door, there was another knock. Remy opened it to find one of the vampires on the military border patrol team standing there.

Sage got up and moved closer so she didn't miss anything.

He held up his phone. "I've got something you should see, from the early morning patrol." He handed it over and Remy, Rac, and Sage leaned in to watch.

"Fucking woman. I'm going to rip her head off," Remy said, her calm tone undermined by the words themselves.

It was simply a fact, devoid of emotion, and it made Sage shudder.

Cadence was talking to someone who looked like a guy in charge. He wore full military fatigues and had the stance of someone used to being listened to. Cadence laughed, touched his arm, flipped her hair, and then turned to pull a plant from the backseat of her car. She held it out, and he motioned another soldier over to take it. She opened the trunk, and the view was momentarily obscured until the vampire doing the recording moved slowly to a better position.

"Well, that isn't good." Rac folded her arms as they continued to watch.

The trunk was full of plants, and she also took out a box and held up the same kind of opaque bag she'd had in Remy's kitchen. She dropped it back in the box and handed it over to a soldier. With a final flip of her hair and an insincere wave, she got back in the car and drove off. The vampire doing the recording shifted once again, and they watched as the soldiers fanned out into the border of the forest and began planting the small, wide-leaved plants in various locations. Not in a line, but in a kind of jagged crisscross pattern.

"Whatever they put on the food looked like it was dried. Will the real plants do the same thing?" Sage asked, even though the tension around her was enough to make her want to curl into a ball in the corner.

"Cadence must think so, or they wouldn't be doing that." Rac turned to Remy. "How, exactly, did you piss this one off?"

Remy nodded at the vampire who'd taken the video. "Thanks. Make sure your team stays far away from that stuff until we know what it is."

He leaned over and picked up a bag from beside the door. "We will, but I managed to grab a freshly planted one." He shook his head quickly. "I didn't touch it with my hands, I wrapped it in my sweatshirt and then threw the sweatshirt out after I put it in here."

Rac took it from him, and Remy shook his hand. "Good job. What you've done is exactly what we needed."

He gave an informal salute and jogged off down the stairs.

Sage reached for the plant. "Since this is supposed to turn you into something that could totally kill the rest of us and probably the entire planet, and since you're, you know, *you*, I'll just take that."

Rac tilted her head and gave her a wry grin. "Glad to know someone still appreciates me."

Remy watched the bag like it could turn into something she could kill. "Be careful, Sage."

"Really? I thought I'd go dissect it on our bed." Sage stepped back from them and carefully opened the bag, then lifted out the plant, which was surprisingly heavy. Broad, flat leaves were interspersed with small, fan-like ones, which were topped with small white flowers. Thick stems had a deepish red tint underlying the green.

Sage sniffed it lightly. "See?" she said, looking closer. "It smells kind of like pie."

"Pie that turns vampires feral." Rac sniffed the air, and she snarled and tossed her head. "Putrid. Let's go. Sage, put that away. See if you can find a box or something to put it in so I can get it to the lab when we get back."

Sage eased it back into the bag and tied it closed. She held up her wrist. "Um...ow." Small white blisters were breaking out along her vein.

"Hot water and soap. Now!" Remy stepped forward, but Rac jerked her back.

"Good idea, Wind. Get close enough to let it infect you so that you turn feral and kill not only the human in front of you, but everyone else in your sanctuary." Rac tugged her toward the door.

"Go. I'll wash it off and be fine. It isn't like I ate it." Sage waved them off, but her wrist was on fire. She did her best to shut down her thoughts so Remy wouldn't take the risk.

Remy hesitated, her gaze moving from Sage's swelling wrist to her face. "Please take care of that quickly. I'd send a doc over but—"

"But the docs are vampires too." Sage nodded and began walking backward to the sink. "Go. I've got this. Do what you need to do."

Remy shook off Rac's hand. "Fine. Goddamnit. I knew I

should've gotten you out of here. I knew, but I was too stupid... When I get back, we're getting you home."

The door closed behind them, and Sage quickly set down the bag and rushed to the sink. A weird piece of an old article on what to do about poison ivy came back to her, and she went to the fridge instead. Remy didn't drink milk, but she'd had some brought in for Sage's coffee. Over a bowl sitting on the counter, Sage tipped the carton over her wrist, letting the liquid course over the swollen white blisters, and she sighed in almost instant relief. She dipped a paper towel into the remaining milk and wrapped it around her wrist. While it didn't look like poison ivy, it was clearly the same kind of skin irritant.

We're getting you home. Sage resisted brushing the tears away, just in case she hadn't quite removed all the poison. How could the back-and-forth continue? One minute, she wanted to stay and Remy wanted her to stay, the next, they both knew it was dangerous for her to do so. They hardly knew one another, and yet it was like she'd known her forever, like she'd just been waiting around in her apartment until the day her car broke down and she met Remy for the first time. That seemed like a million years ago. She felt different now. Attached and cared for, not alone and hoping someone in the cyber world would be there to chat. Could she somehow convince Remy to give them a chance if they figured out how to stop Cadence? What if they didn't stop her? What if there was war? Remy would leave Sage behind, no question. She'd think it was too dangerous to keep her around. Maybe that was true. A human living among vampires in a human-vampire war wasn't going to be a welcome addition, other than as sustenance.

She took a long, ragged breath. One thing at a time. For the moment, she was here, in the middle of a crisis and helping out. They'd have to deal with the fallout later.

She pulled up her laptop and began an image search for the plant on the counter, but nothing seemed to match. When she thought she'd found the right one, it didn't have flowers, or the ones with the flowers didn't have the strangely colored stem. On a whim, she typed in plants used in pies. "Yes!" she said, looking closer.

Rhubarb. That was the strange pie scent, but she'd only had it once. The stems were kind of red, like rhubarb. But not exactly, so maybe it was just a type of it. She took screenshots to show Rac and Remy when they got back. And then she sat there, uncertain what to do next. She went through the rest of the videos but nothing strange came up, and she hadn't done a lot of videoing even after Geno had set up the tech, as she'd been too busy with Remy, both in and out of bed.

She opened the app and hit record. "Hey, ZimTak fam. Wow. Total whirlwind, right? Military at the borders, politics gone totally cosmic—"

She stopped the recording. It didn't feel right. It was the same tone she always used, but it felt...false. She wanted to be authentic, and without being able to talk about what was really going on, what could she say? She went out onto the terrace, leaned on the railing, and looked over the ranch. Because of the network of covered walkways, she couldn't see anyone, and the day was too bright to be out in the open. Where had Rac and Remy gone? She hadn't heard them say anything about where they'd begin their search.

She went back in and opened the app again. "Hey, ZimTak fam." She took a deep breath and considered what Remy had said about love and family, then started over. "Hey, everyone. I'm not really sure what to say, other than I'm fine. More than fine, really. I've learned so much about myself here. Someone told me recently that knowing how things are doesn't mean you have to accept that as set in stone. I mean, like, you can change things and make them better. You just have to decide what you want, right? And then figure out how to make it happen." She hesitated. "I want more, I think. More adventure. More time away from my screen. Maybe I'll even set up a group to get together and do stuff out in the world. I don't know. I just know that...well..." She swallowed against the rising emotion. "I know I've actually been pretty lonely, and I bet some of you out there have been too. I hope, one day—"

A noise, like sand dropping on the hardwood floor, made her stop and look around. Fear, cold and terrible, flooded her as she sensed something else, something bad, way too close. Her heart raced and, shaking, she lowered her phone. "Hello?" She meant to say it confidently, but it came out in a strangled whisper.

"Hello."

The whisper came from right behind her ear and before she could scream, before she could call for Remy, pain shot through her neck, blinding her, and she slumped to the floor, the last thing in her vision was red eyes and fangs dripping with blood.

Her blood.

Chapter Twenty-Two

Remy pounded on Geno's door, standing as close to it as she could. His shaded porch wasn't quite large enough to cover them from the angle of the sun at this time of year. Was it intentional to set any visitor on edge before they'd even stepped beyond the doorway?

He answered, making sure to stay well back from the light. "This is a surprise." He motioned her in, and she quickly slipped past.

"Is it?" She took off her cowboy hat and tapped it against her thigh. "You had to know I'd show up eventually, when it became clear my people were being poisoned."

To his credit, he looked genuinely surprised. He walked away into the living room and sat down, his legs crossed, and his fingers steepled under his chin. "I think it's probably impossible to fully trust someone when you've seen them at their utter worst, but in all the time you've known me, have I ever injured another of our kind?"

She sat opposite him and let her senses have free rein. He didn't so much as bat an eyelid as she sent her power cascading through the room, over and around him, up the stairs. It wasn't the freeing experience it had been in the woods but rather the kind of concentrated effort she'd learned so long ago. No one else was in the house.

Except Rac, of course, who made her way in from the kitchen.

Geno's eyebrows went up as she sat next to Remy, and his widening pupils were the only giveaway that he was afraid now. "I helped when you asked and haven't gone against your wishes in any way. But you seem to be accusing me of something, and you've brought the Impaler with you. Forgive me, but I'm a little behind the ball and more than a little concerned."

Remy noticed the way his pulse was beating in his neck. "You've fed on someone recently."

He tilted his head. "Turning a human is against the law. Feeding on one who consents isn't. As you know, there are humans who live here in Bluffington as well, and many are...enthusiasts of our kind."

That was true enough, and Lars had filled her in numerous times on his nights out in the kind of den where that relationship took place. "When did you last see Cadence?"

This time, his gaze shuttered. "Why do you ask?"

She leaned forward, allowing her power to ease from her fingers so that the tips began to crack the wood of his coffee table. Rac didn't move, but Remy felt her power begin to slip through the air like coalescing silver.

"Okay. No need to get twitchy." Geno held up his hand. "I saw her just after the *VCN* conference. She stopped by when it was over, and we had a chat."

"About?" The wood splintered a little more under her fingers. "Don't make me repeat myself, Valentino."

He glanced at the table and then back at her. He settled against the couch, his hands flat on his thighs. "She started with a rant about vampires not having our rightful place in the world, which obviously moved on to you and how you'd dampened what we are so you could fit in and have a simple life, which you were forcing on the rest of us. Same old Cadence, but this time she was more enthralled with the idea and clearly more intent on being active about change." His fingers twitched slightly, giving away his continued worry about Rac being there. "She said she had a plan, and she wanted my assistance. Given my age and understanding of you, she felt my input would be useful."

"Her plan being?" Rac asked, her voice low.

"I don't know." He looked between them. "I told her I didn't want any part of anything that would piss you off. I explained, not very politely, mind you, that she'd never truly understood the depths of what you are and the power you contain. I told her she was mad to go against you, and by proxy, the Impaler." He sighed, and his shoulders dropped. "She called me a coward, said I'd always been your chihuahua and that I deserved whatever might befall me when she was in charge."

"Do you know where we can find her?"

He shook his head but got up and went to a table by the wall. He returned with a business card. "She left me this and said I should call when I changed my mind and understood the consequences of not joining her."

Remy read the card. *Next Step Botanical Chemistry.* There was a phone number and address, but both were Boston-based. "Well, that explains one aspect but not where she is now." She handed the card to Rac, who grunted and set it down. "Why didn't you come to me?"

Geno sat on the sofa's arm. "You know how I feel about confrontation, Remy. That hasn't changed in millennia. So I suppose she's right. Call it cowardly if you will."

Remy stood. "I will. Conflict or not, you should have told me, or at least Lars, that she'd come to you with something like this. Do you know how many vampires she's already hurt? Do you have any idea what this could lead to?"

He shrank away and folded his arms, his gaze averted to the floor. "You and I have history, and I know I've let you down repeatedly throughout the years, Remy. But I've never had anything but respect for you, regardless of how strained things have been between us through the centuries." He finally looked at her. "You asked why I moved here? Because I missed you. My first friend, oftentimes my only friend. You started a beautiful life, a community I couldn't be part of because of our past, and you were the most lauded vampire in history, the rest of us nothing but shadows in your light. But at least this way, I could be close, I could watch you, pretend that I was still in your orbit. I wasn't completely on the outside. But if I brought trouble to your doorstep, I thought you might make me go away. And I couldn't bear that idea. So I stayed silent and on the sidelines, hoping she'd just go away when she finally realized she simply wasn't as powerful as you." He blanched when Rac shifted. "I'm sorry. I was wrong. I didn't know what to do for the best, so I did nothing."

Remy stared at him for a long moment, trying to decide whether he was being genuine or if he was playing her. "Let me in your head."

He winced. "Is that truly necessary?"

Rac leaned forward, just enough to make him flinch. "If you want to live to see another moonrise, yes."

He held up his hands in surrender.

Remy concentrated and let her power snake into his head. This way, she would know for certain if he was lying. She let her subconscious roam, not looking for anything specific but rather sifting through memories here and there, through his thoughts as they flitted past. And what she saw was truth. He was lonely, despite other vampires around him. The years of living had overwhelmed him, nearly broken him, and pushed him into the kind of immortal madness many of the oldest of them eventually fell to. She found the conversation with Cadence and focused in on it. Cadence's eyes were lit with an almost fanatical gleam as she raved about not being able to feed how and when she wanted, about the fact that some of the best minds in the world were going to waste because they were being allowed to age and die. She said a queen, like there was in ancient times, would bring them all together and create a new world where vampires were in charge. And she heard Geno's response, that he wouldn't be part of anything that harmed Remy or took the choice from other vampires. It wasn't conflict that had made him shy away, it was his old, deep respect for their friendship and his own creation without consent. She was about to leave his mind when she remembered what Lars had told her, and she searched for the phone conversation he'd overheard, where Geno was telling someone to be patient. That gave her no further information though.

She pulled away, leaving his mind, and he blinked like he'd just woken.

"I always have disliked the way that feels. Like someone is unthreading your mind." He rubbed at his eyes. "Satisfied?"

"She's staying at the Ashford." She looked Geno in the eye. "The conversation you were having with someone about being patient. What was that about?"

His eyes widened slightly. "It has nothing to do with this—"

"Answer." Rac's tone left no room for negotiation.

"I'm working on a tech deal." He looked between them. "A company I've been under contract with for a long time wants to be the primary provider to vampire territories. Immortal subscribers sounds really good to their bottom line. I said I'd put it to you and to Dez, but then everything went tits up here, and I've refused to broach the subject, given the whole could-go-to-war issue."

"How plebeian." Rac stood and turned to go.

Remy placed her hand on Geno's shoulder. "I'm sorry the years have been so hard. When all this is over, we'll have a true talk, okay?"

He nodded. "Can I help with anything in the meantime?"

She debated. His loneliness was deep, but how close had he come to breaking? "Not yet, but I'll let you know if that changes."

He looked disappointed but didn't press the issue.

Rac stopped at the door. "How do you know where she is?"

"I saw the conversation she was having with Geno. The Ashford has a distinctive key card, and it was sticking out of her purse on the table behind her."

Rac nodded but didn't say anything further until they got to the car, moving fast because even the late autumn sun burned. Remy got the truck on the road and headed toward the hotel. Her mind was whirling. "She's doing all this so we go to war and vampires are forced to fight back. So we can prove how powerful we are and become what she wanted us to be even back when we were dating. And I damn well bet she has someone in mind for the position of queen."

"And you gave her the vehicle for her plan when you brought vampires out into the open." Rac shook her head. "You might have won the difficult ex award."

"Batshit rabid, more like." Remy tapped the steering wheel. "Ideas on next steps?"

"Even if we go in and take her down right now, she's clearly already put bigger things in motion, since the military are planting toxic bushes along the vampire borders. We need to encourage her to give us details of *all* things in motion."

Remy glanced over. "Encourage?"

Rac met her gaze evenly. "Not gently." She looked back out the window. "I'll take care of it."

They were silent, and Remy was remembering her time with Cadence. It was gaslighting chaos, and Cadence had been the epitome of a power-hungry vampire chafing at the boundaries placed on her behavior, even back then.

"You asked me the other night about bonding with a human without blood." Rac broke the silence as they entered the more urban area of the county.

"Do you know anything? Have you done it?"

Rac shifted and pulled some papers from her back pocket. "I brought these for you to look over. They're rubbings taken from the cuneiform clay tablets written in Uruk in the fifth century. I came across them when I was dealing with a similar situation."

The truck swerved as Remy looked at her. "You've had this happen?"

Rac nodded, continuing to look out the side window. "Once. I was inhabiting a cave with a clan in Guyaju, China. In a nearby village, there was a woman whose beauty rivaled anything in the known universe. The first time I saw her, it was like something had burrowed under my skin. I had to see her again, and our connection was a chemical fire right from the start. After we had sex, it was like an addiction. Every fiber of my being called to her and strangely, she felt the same way. No blood bond, but one just as strong. Maybe stronger."

"What happened? What did you do?"

Rac's jaw clenched. "My clan grew suspicious of my constant wandering into the village, and her family suspected I was something other than human. Both groups began to whisper in our ears, to sow doubts. My clan was worried I'd bring attention to us and get us all killed as we slept through the day, and her people were worried I was a demon, luring her into darkness."

Remy waited, understanding that Rac was reliving the time she'd had something so special.

"I started searching for answers." She waved the pages. "I hardly found anything, but in this ancient text I found a mention of demons bonding with humans. Unlike other superstitious or religious texts, this one almost seemed like it might have been written by one of us. It suggested it could have to do with reincarnation, though I found that unlikely, as I'd never felt that way before. But it also suggested it was an element of the magic in us, creating the energies and source of the person born *just* for us, only once in our lifetime."

Remy laughed dryly. "A soulmate reward for being a vampire?"

"Maybe." Rac finally looked at her. "But a soulmate created by virtue of us being here for so long. We spend centuries wishing for the right person, thinking about the kind of person we want to be with. We essentially manifest them into being. They're quite literally ours. It may sound ludicrous, but when you've felt it, it's hard not to believe it."

Remy pondered that. "Did you tell your manifested soulmate that?"

Rac's sigh came from a deeply injured place inside her. "She refused to stop seeing me, and her people killed her in order to keep her from being dragged to the underworld."

"Fucking hell." Remy thought of anything happening to Sage

and couldn't imagine the pain Rac must have felt. "What did you do?"

"I left." She gave a wry smile at Remy's look of disbelief. "They were wrong, and they took my one chance at happiness. Maybe I'll manifest her again one day. The universe's energies will combine to give me back my Jia Li again. But even then, I understood that they did it because they cared for her, and because we were the monsters, not them." At Remy's look, she shrugged. "We were, back then. Barely civilized, living in caves, sleeping in coffins, coming out only at night. It's no wonder there's so much misinformation about us." She sighed and tapped the dashboard. "If you've got what I had, Wind, don't lose it. Don't run, and don't let the world take her from you. This is your chance for a mate who will cleanse your soul and make you see beauty again."

"And the danger she's in? The fact that she's living among predators? What if I can't protect her?" Just seeing the rash on Sage's arm had made her panic. Real danger could make her go feral.

Rac huffed. "Please. Do you know how dangerous this world is anyway? She could get hit and killed by a motorized scooter while she's walking to the coffee shop. She could be on a hijacked plane or in a store when some human asshole comes in with a semi-automatic and starts shooting because he's pissed off about his kid reading a banned book or the fact that someone altered his favorite peanut butter. Is her risk a little higher if she stays with you? Yes. But she's at risk without you too."

Remy considered the options and eventually accepted that there was truth to what Rac was saying. They pulled into the underground parking at the hotel, and she turned off the ignition. "Did you ever consider turning her?"

Rac looked at her, expressionless. "Yes. And there might have come a time that I did, because I didn't want to be without her, and I truly felt we were meant for one another. Losing her took the most human part of me, the part that was still good and wanted to see what the world would become. If I'd done it sooner, she might still be with me now." She gripped Remy's shoulder. "If this is true, if it isn't simply something born of the tumult around us right now, then be wary of time, Wind. We never know when we won't have another chance."

She got out of the truck and slammed the door. Remy waited a moment, trying to ground herself, trying to focus on the moment. Rac had given her a lot to think about, but this wasn't the time or place to work out her love life.

She joined Rac at the elevator, and they entered the pristine, wide-open lobby.

"Should I ask why you recognized the key card of one of the most exclusive hotels in the area?" Rac asked with a subtle grin.

"Not unless you want the tawdry details that go with it. Suffice to say—"

"Ms. Winslow." The receptionist gave her a sultry smile. "It has been far too long. Do you have a reservation tonight?" Her gaze flicked to Rac and the confusion was clear in her eyes, though she did her best to hide it. Clearly, she knew Remy's type, and Rac most certainly wasn't it.

"No, Yasmin, no reservation today." She rested her arms on the desk and gave her a lazy grin when she saw Yasmin's gaze take in her muscled arms. "Actually, I need your help." At Yasmin's returned smile, she shook her head. "Not that kind, not tonight. I'm looking for someone I think is staying here."

Yasmin bit her lip, looking a little sheepish. "Ms. Winslow, you know we guard our clientele's privacy."

Remy took her hand and kissed it, feeling almost like she was betraying Sage, but she needed to play this game. "Yasmin, beautiful darling, you know full well I wouldn't ask if it wasn't of the utmost importance." She ignored the slight scoffing sound behind her.

Yasmin glanced around and then took her hand from Remy's. She turned the screen, moving it so Remy could see it if she looked closely. "I'm sorry, I can't help." Her fingers hovered over the keyboard, and she looked at Remy expectantly.

Remy gave Cadence's name, and Yasmin continued to look at Remy and tell her that privacy at the Ashford was of paramount importance while her fingers flew over the keyboard. Cadence's reservation appeared on the screen. Remy made a note of the room number and moved away from the counter.

"I understand, Yasmin, and your dedication to your clients is most impressive." She allowed the double meaning to enter her tone and smiled when Yasmin flushed. "We'll have a meal on the rooftop terrace since we're already here."

Yasmin smiled and waved them toward the elevator. Without a room key, they wouldn't be able to go anywhere, but Yasmin put in the floor number they needed and told them to have a nice lunch.

"Do you ever get tired of women fawning over you that way?" Rac asked, leaning against the glass wall.

"Hey, I live at Dark Haven so I have space and privacy. But I come here to work off energy occasionally." Remy looked her over. "How long has it been since you worked off that kind of energy?"

"I run a bed and breakfast for vampires. Believe me, I'm getting more than you are." Rac's expression turned serious. "This could get messy. Are you prepared? Or do you want me to go in on my own?"

"My thing with her was a long time ago, and she's hurt my people. I'm fine." Remy hesitated. "But that thing she does, where she just disappears..."

Rac shook her head and faced the opening doors. "I can do it too. You could, if you really let yourself be the vampire you are. But you've always held back so you don't go too far." She glanced at her and led the way toward Cadence's room. "It does speak to her power though."

They stood outside Cadence's room, listening with their extra senses.

"She isn't here." Rac held her hand over the door handle for a moment until it bent, twisted, and the lock popped open.

They went in and found an empty room. No clothes, the bed made, the shower toiletries untouched.

Nothing, except a cell phone, sitting in the middle of the pristine bed. A cell phone in a bright pink case Remy had seen in her own home not so long ago. She stared at it, and Rac moved around her to pick it up. It lit up at her touch, and a video opened.

Remy slumped against the wall as it played. Sage was doing one of her videos where she talked to the screen, and presumably whoever was watching, about how she'd changed since her time at Dark Haven, but it was interrupted when Sage clearly heard or felt something and lowered the phone, her expression one of obvious fear. And then the phone fell to the floor, and Sage screamed.

The phone moved again, and this time Cadence's face came on. "Hello, lover. It seems we're at an impasse. This fragile, irksome little human has become quite the marker in our game, hasn't she?" She moved the phone to take in Sage's inert body on the floor, blood smeared across her neck. "If she dies on your watch, then the human community will be out for blood, so to speak. They'll come at us, and we'll have no option but to defend ourselves." The camera came back to Cadence. "And when they find out that this pretty little thing was turned by feral vampires who are out of control, well..." She shrugged elegantly, a cruel twist to her lips. "And then the vampires won't trust you anymore, will they, *Wind*? Our great defender, the leader who brought us into the world to live more like humans, will be the last vampire they'll listen to when the humans start their war against us and vampires begin dying. Including, of course, those who have been found staked on the riverbanks. Such a shame, that."

The camera shifted again, and Cadence's heel pressed against Sage's wrist, digging into the skin. "I've heard whispers, Remy, that this is your plaything. If you want your toy back before I make the next move and either kill her or make her one of us, then I suggest you simply...go away." She shifted the phone so it focused on her eyes. "Go away, Remy. Go live in a cave in the desert where you can be all alone and live like you don't have the power of gods running through your veins. Go pretend you're not better than them and they aren't just waiting to be servants to a better species. Go away, and I'll spare her life. I'll send her home, and you can pine away for her like I did for you, once upon a time. So, I guess you don't really get her back, but you'll know she's alive somewhere without you. How romantic." She made a show of looking at her watch. "I'll give you twenty-four hours, mostly so you can think about what I'm doing to your friend. I'll have someone watch you get on a plane, and then I'll get to work creating the kind of world vampires should live in, the kind that the world owes us." She focused again on Sage. "Say bye-bye."

The screen went dark, and Remy felt the air go out of her. The world around her had a pinkish tinge and moved unsteadily. *Sage.* Sage had been fed on by a power-crazed monster who now had her at her mercy.

She jerked when Rac punched her shoulder, hard.

"Come on."

She followed Rac from the room, numb, and started to consider where she'd fly to. Somewhere gray. The UK, maybe. Climate change had made it warmer but cloudier, and they got less rain but rarely saw the sun. She'd find a place in Scotland, perhaps in the Highlands where the population was sparse.

"Stop it." Rac got in the driver's seat of the truck and took the keys from Remy. "You're not going anywhere. We're going to find Cadence, we're going to tear her arms off and rip her teeth out, and then we're going to fix things."

"She's right, Rac. Sage could send the pieces flying."

"Bullshit. Sage is what she's using to get to you. But she doesn't understand that you're not alone, and she's overreached. You're far stronger than she could ever hope to be."

Remy tried calling to Sage telepathically but was meant with blankness. "Sage's still unconscious, I think."

"Good. Then her smart mouth won't get her in any more trouble." Rac glanced at her. "We'll get her back. But you're going to have to reach for the woman who was the Killing Wind. There's no going back now."

Remy nodded and released the fear, instead filling with rage. How dare Cadence touch a hair on Sage's head? She wanted to play this game? So be it. Remy would remind her just what it meant to truly be a vampire.

Chapter Twenty-Three

Before she was fully conscious, Sage couldn't help the gasp of pain that escaped her. Fire, like a hundred stinging wasps, covered the side of her neck and shoulder. She went to touch it but couldn't move her hand.

Slowly, she opened her eyes and groaned. She was lying on cold concrete, her hands tied behind her, and rope around her ankles. She tugged on her hands, and that moved her feet. She'd been hogtied. Tears welled and fell as the pain ran through her whole body like a lit fuse.

"Oh, good. I prefer it when my food is aware it's food. Far more entertaining and tasty that way."

Sage tilted her head and squinted against the bare bulb backlighting the person with a voice she recognized. "What have you done?"

Cadence squatted in front of her and gently wiped a piece of hair away from Sage's cheek, laughing when she jerked away as best she could. "I've simply moved you to a different square on the chess board, my dear. Remy should have known better than to allow you into the game, but she's always been too fond of humans and too unable to embrace her true nature."

"We barely know each other. She won't change anything because of me." Even when she said it, she knew full well it wasn't true, and she knew the reasons why. They'd discussed them at length, but Sage hadn't really thought she'd become an actual pawn. What had been theoretical now burned like she'd been...

"Did you poison me?" she whispered. She wouldn't be able to withstand it the way the vampires did, not for days and days. Hell, she might not make it through the night.

"In a manner of speaking." Cadence moved away and pulled up a chair where she could look down and force her into an awkward position to look back at her. "A vampire can make a bite the most beautiful thing you've ever experienced, like you've entered a state of nirvana, and keep you there right to the point of your death. They can make it sexual, so you have the most exquisite orgasm you've ever experienced." She grinned and showed her teeth. "Or you can make it hurt so your victim cries, and begs, and promises to do anything you want. That one is my favorite. But because you're special and I'm a sadist, I added a little of my special botanical formula to the area where I drank from you. Not for any purpose, just because I wanted to."

"You sick bitch," Sage bit out, trying not to cry or writhe. "When Remy gets hold of you—"

"Silly thing. Remy is going to be on a plane tomorrow, heading off to live in a cave or coffin or something, where she belongs. If, of course, we don't manage to end her pathetic existence first. That will leave the rest of us to get on with the war that's been brewing for quite a while now." She leaned down, and her gaze was like nails on Sage's skin. "Now, I'm happy to give you the choice, Sage Samara, internet *personality*. You can live on as a human and watch as we change the world, where you'll become a servant if you're lucky or sustenance if you're not, or you can become one of us, and I'll teach you everything you need to know. You can be my apprentice." She grinned and slid her heel over Sage's thigh. "And since you like women, I can even teach you some things in that realm too."

Don't provoke her. Don't be stupid. Sage kept the mantra running through her head, but her mouth opened anyway. "Psycho and bitchy aren't my type. You're short a lightbulb if you think I'd want anything to do with you. At least on the other side I can fight against you."

Cadence's smile was as evil as could be imagined. "Well, then

I should probably just kill you, shouldn't I? Save myself the hassle down the road."

Sage's heart lurched but Cadence laughed.

"However, I need to keep you alive until I know Remy has left. She's soft, and she has a real issue with having the lives of humans on her hands." She rolled her eyes. "You should have seen how angry she'd get every time I'd feed and leave the body by the rose bushes in the garden." She shrugged. "They were good for the roses, and the apology sex after was explosive. She really knows how to enjoy a woman's body, doesn't she?"

Sage didn't respond. What could she say that wouldn't get her killed? Tentatively, she tried to reach out telepathically to Remy, but there was nothing beyond her own thoughts.

Cadence tutted. "I shouldn't be surprised that Remy taught you how to call to her. But you see, I've got you in a place no one will find you." She stood. "Scream all you want. Silently, if you must, but I prefer it out loud so it gives me the happy goosebumps." She gave a little shiver. "Now, I have plans to see to. Don't worry, I'll make sure to feed and water you like any good bit of cattle." She waved and closed a huge metal door behind her.

Sage let the tension out of her body and allowed the tears to flow. The idea that she was going to be used against Remy was awful enough, but the idea of Remy leaving so Sage would never see her again was far worse. This had been exactly what Remy had been worried about happening, but Sage had practically begged her not to send her away. She'd been selfish, and now the world would pay for it. She turned, forcing herself onto her other side, and sighed gratefully when her neck and shoulder pressed against the cold concrete, giving her a measure of relief.

She continued to shift awkwardly, shuffling this way and that, until she got a full sense of where she was being held. The walls were concrete, and a few chairs and broken bits of furniture had been shoved against them. There were no windows and no door other than the one Cadence had left through. Sage stared at the broken furniture and tools, trying to make sense of them. Soon, though, her eyes drifted shut. The pain and exertion of moving while bound was exhausting. She still felt the tears dripping off her cheek as she fell into a pain-filled limbo.

***

The door opened with a bang, startling her and making her jerk. She groaned at the numbness in her legs and arms and the stiffness in her neck.

It was the woman from the video, the one who had placed the poison in the food and on the glasses. She put a bowl of something on the floor, as well as a plastic cup of water. Without a word, she jerked Sage onto her stomach, slamming the air from her lungs.

"Shut up." She held a lethal-looking blade in front of Sage's face.

Sage whimpered in relief when the rope attaching her wrists to her ankles was cut, immediately easing the tension in her shoulders. The woman cut the rope between her wrists and pushed her onto her back.

Sage gingerly moved her arms in front of her, pins and needles making her eyes water.

"Sit up."

Sage tried, but everything hurt and was too stiff for her to move. The woman grabbed her shoulder and jerked her upright to a sitting position, making her cry out despite her desire not to make a sound.

The woman roughly removed the rope around her wrists and put zip ties on instead, and then used that rope to create a kind of collar around Sage's neck, the end of which she threw over the thick wooden beam above them. She tied it in an intricate knot. There was no way Sage could reach it, even if she could stand. But at least she had more freedom of movement. That was something.

"How long will I be here?" she asked, her voice raspy.

"As long as you need to be." The woman didn't look at her again as she slammed the door behind her.

Sage scooted to the water and drank gratefully but forced herself not to drink it all. Who knew when she'd get more. The food was just cold oatmeal, but she used her fingers to scoop it out and felt marginally better for eating it. On a whim, she took the last scoop and spread it over the worst of the pain in her neck. It wasn't long before it soothed the skin, taking it from agonizing to awful. She sat against the wall and closed her eyes, thinking about her predicament.

First things first.

She studied the rope around her ankles. It was thick and looked new, and the knots were a lot like the one she now had tied around her neck. She felt it against her when she swallowed, but other than that, it wasn't too tight. She began to pick at the knots around her ankle and her fingertips quickly grew sore, but she didn't care. She kept at it, trying to ignore the pain in her neck, and shoulder, and now her fingertips. When her fingertips began to bleed with little progress on the knot, she stopped and flexed the spasms out of her hands. With them bound together, the movements were awkward and slow. Using the wall, she pushed herself up to standing and stretched her back. She twisted and turned, doing the yoga poses she could remember to ease her back, even though she couldn't move her legs properly.

Now that she was standing, she could look around properly. Spying a section of broken wood she thought she could reach, she hopped toward it, careful not to lose her balance, as falling forward would mean the rope around her neck tightening in a way that wouldn't be good. When she got close, she bent forward, moving what few pieces she could reach. None of them were really sharp, but maybe if she could break one somehow, she could use it to get through the rope.

There were pieces of desk legs, not even whole ones. The back of a chair, half a tabletop. Most of it was just out of reach, but she managed to sit down and drag a desk leg toward her with her feet stretched out in front of her. She shifted and took it in her hands. It was hefty—

She fell forward, dizziness assailing her. The room spun, and her stomach lurched. She turned just in time to vomit porridge and water against the wall. She crawled back to where the rope was loosest around her neck and rested on the floor. Eventually the room stopped spinning, and she took a deep, shaky breath. Was it the poison? Shaking, she pushed herself back to sitting and retrieved the desk leg. She held it between her feet and slammed it against the floor, but she was too weak for it to do any real damage. She tried again and again, but exhaustion took over, and she curled up on her side, the desk leg tucked against her stomach. She'd try again soon.

When she woke, nothing had changed. She finished the little bit of water left and squeezed her eyes shut against the blinding headache that felt like it was going to force its way out of her skull.

The door opened, and Cadence came in with two other vampires behind her. She wrinkled her nose and wafted her hand in the air. "Humans. Such revolting creatures with all their bodily fluids." She bent over Sage, who didn't move. "Hmm. She's more susceptible than the others. Ah, well. If we lose this one, we'll simply drop her body at the border and let the press know that their darling internet star was killed at Dark Haven. It will break Remy, and hopefully she'll then start breaking necks." Cadence laughed at her own stupid humor.

Sage swore and tried to lash out, but she didn't so much as twitch away.

"I've decided I like you. You're a fighter. I'm going to make you my human pet if you survive this. I haven't had one in ages, and breaking one like you will be fun. Not to mention, we can show all your followers, or *fam*, as you call them, what they have to look forward to." She ran her hand over Sage's hair in a parody of gentleness. "You can see firsthand the world I'll create with Remy out of the way when the clans bow to me."

"You really think you can take on Remy?" Sage rasped, although the headache was receding. "She's way better than you ever hope to be. You're salty because she kept you in line for so long, and you didn't have what it took to go all Disney villain while you were still with her." Sage flinched when Cadence raised her hand but relaxed when she pulled it back.

"Your smart mouth is going to be shut once you're at my feet." She moved away and nodded toward one of the others, who put down another bowl and cup of water. "Enjoy the silence. We're off to take over the world. Try not to die before I can enjoy you more fully." Her laugh echoed against the walls long after the door slammed shut behind them.

Sage uncurled and put the wood between her feet again. No way in hell was she going to sit here and wait to be rescued. Remy needed her. For what, she had no idea. Maybe she'd just be in the way. But whatever, she was going to get the hell out of here.

Chapter Twenty-Four

REMY STARED AT THE blood on the floor that they hadn't had time to clean up yet. There wasn't a lot of it but enough to make the rage inside her build into an inferno. Somewhere, Sage was hurt. Had she been turned? Unlikely. Cadence would want to keep her weak, and new vampires were unpredictable. At least there was that bit of fortune. She kept trying to mentally reach her, but she was met with blank space.

"She's tough, Remy." Jet still sounded tired but was healing well. By next week she'd be back to her old self. "She'd survived a hell of a lot before she got here. She can survive a little vampire kidnapping."

Remy rolled her eyes, but it was true. Sage had been through her own kind of hell. As long as she didn't give up, she'd be okay. And Remy would make Cadence pay in ways she hadn't even finished conjuring up yet.

There was a knock at the door, and Lars answered. He and Jet had been in her place, waiting with an update, and Rac filled them in on what they'd learned. Lars had cleared out the kitchen and checked in with the teams. The coastline patrol had seen boats moving along the tree line, clearly watching for anyone trying to leave.

Jimmy and the kids came in. Shala ran to Remy, who picked her up. "You guys okay?" she asked.

Jimmy nodded and handed her his phone. "Check out the pics. There are three vampires living in number twelve. They're new, according to the neighbors, and they don't mix with anyone else. But we saw them leave a little while ago."

Remy checked the photos with her free hand. It was the three Sage had caught on camera in the kitchen. "That's them. Good work." She handed back his phone.

"Remy?" Jake was looking at the blood on the floor. "Is Sage hurt?"

"We think so, buddy." There was no point in lying to him. "Someone came in and took her, but we don't know where."

Shala wriggled in Remy's arms, and she set her down. "We know all the super-secret places, Remy! We can find her." She looked toward her brother, who was frowning.

He turned to Jimmy. "Remember that place we showed you? The one across the bridge and through the forest, over past the wind turbines?"

Jimmy nodded and turned to Remy. "It's an old factory of some kind. Mostly a ruin, but it looked like someone had been there. There were tire tracks and some trash. I thought maybe it was just some people passing through."

"First of all, how did you get all the way out there without covering? Second, can you show us where it is?" Remy didn't want to take them, but she also didn't want to waste time searching when they knew where it was.

"We used brellas and wore hats, the way mommy taught us to." Shala took Jake's hand. "And we stayed in the trees."

Jimmy zipped up his sweatshirt and pulled a floppy hat out of his pocket. "I can show you if you want them to stay here."

"Hey!" Jake said. "We're the ones who showed it to you."

Remy knelt in front of him. "I have another job for you. It's important, and I wouldn't trust anyone else." She waited as he looked at her intently. "Jet has been hurt too, and she's pretty weak right now. I need someone to guard her and make sure she's safe. Can you do that?"

He looked past her to Jet, who was propped on the couch. "I can do that."

"Good man. You know how to call me with your thoughts?"

He nodded. "We've been practicing with Jimmy."

"Okay. Anything gets scary here, and you shout really loud with your mind. I'll come back so fast, you'll be amazed."

He grinned. "I bet I wouldn't."

"Let's go." Rac tousled his hair on her way past, and he smoothed it back into place with a look of irritation.

Remy, Lars, and Rac followed Jimmy out of the main lodge and down the primary covered walkway that led through the courtyard and beyond the cottages. When they got to the bridge they drew on their hats, and Jimmy opened a black umbrella to cover him fully. They moved quickly across the open grassland to the thicket of trees, and then through the forest to the edge where it opened again. Three huge wind turbines turned lazily as the vampires moved silently through the trees.

"There," whispered Jimmy, pointing.

Remy took in the ruined area. She'd forgotten it was there. It had been derelict long before the ranch land had become available, and it hadn't been part of the area for Dark Haven. At the far edge of the ranch's property, it had been abandoned for years before she'd bought the property.

"I can't sense anyone," Rac murmured, her gaze sweeping over the ruins.

"Feel the ground," Lars said, bending and putting his hand to the dirt.

Rac did as he suggested and looked up at Remy. "Underground rooms."

Remy turned to Jimmy. "I need you to go back to my place and tell Jet what we're doing. And I need you to get your mom to go over there to help with Shala and Jake." She gripped his shoulder. "Jimmy, if we don't come back, I need you and your mom to tell everyone at Dark Haven to run. Get the kids and get out of there as fast as you can and get as far away from Bluffington as you can. Understand?"

He nodded, wide-eyed. "But come back, okay?"

She released his shoulder and gave him a little push. "Go."

He took off the way they'd come, and Remy turned to Rac. "I want to run in there and tear the place apart, but that's probably stupid. Right? They may not even be there. Her using a place so close to the farm would be absurd."

Rac shrugged. "Who knows what's going through her mind? It may be part of the game that excites her. There also aren't a lot of underground spaces in the area because of the water table. Finding somewhere Sage couldn't call you would be hard." She squinted at the space and moved out of a sunbeam. "There are three of us, and although Lars might get dirty and bitch about his dry-cleaning, I think we can handle anyone who might be in there." She put her hand against Remy's chest. "Remember what you are. Remember who you are, and what they're trying to take from you."

Fury, red and blinding, built within her, and she let her power free. Not the way she had in the forest, not in the way she had at Geno's. She let it free like she had when she'd swept through out-of-control villages, the way she had when she'd first been turned and hadn't learned to control herself yet. She set off at a run and was nearly airborne as she flew toward the ruin.

Sage simply had to be there. If she wasn't, Remy wasn't sure where she'd look next. But she did know she'd find Cadence and slowly rip her apart until she found out.

Chapter Twenty-Five

Sage fumbled the wood she'd been trying to break into something sharp. It dropped from her hands and onto the floor, where it got caught in a concrete whirlpool that swirled with the colors of the rainbow. She'd vomited until her stomach muscles ached, and the long, angry red lines making their way down her arms had begun to fascinate her, moving in a pulsing rhythm that matched her heartbeat, which was becoming more erratic with every soft thump.

I'll just sleep for a minute. She curled into an uncomfortable ball and watched as the walls danced a kind of strange jig. Maybe if they leapt high enough, she could slip under and run into the forest? She could picture it: the waving grass, the bright green leaves, the fairies that flew from flower to flower, picking up pollen and dropping it at the fairy factories. She could be one of them, maybe.

She turned her face, too exhausted to sit up, and let the bile spew from her mouth and dribble down her cheek. It stank, and she wearily rolled away to face the angry dust motes that formed faces under the harsh lighting. She made faces back at them, or at least thought she did.

From a long way away, she heard voices. Shouts. Was that god talking? It wasn't surprising that the deity had multiple voices. Why hadn't anyone thought of that before? It was nice that one of them sounded like Remy. She was a kind of god in her own way. A dark one who was really good at sexy-time. If that was the heaven she was going to go to, that would be okay.

Tears slid down her cheeks. But she didn't want to leave here yet. There were fairies and pretty lights, and there was Remy. *I'm in love with a vampire.* The thought made her giggle. Who knew that's where she'd end up? Dying on a swirly concrete floor after having made love to a vampire who made her question her whole existence. And she'd been doing a lot of that questioning in her time in this big box of disco concrete. Maybe, once Remy was a god and she was with her in a place where they were safe, she could talk to her about her thoughts.

She sighed and closed her eyes, only vaguely aware of the door crashing open. She didn't like the person who kept coming in that door. She was mean and said mean things. When Sage felt hands on her shoulders, she tried to shake them off, but it didn't work.

The itchy rope left her neck, the hard plastic left her wrists, and suddenly her ankles swung separately. She felt weightless, like a kid on a swing at the highest point, right before it began to fall back again.

Her eyes fluttered open, and she looked into Remy's face. "Hello, God. Do you have coffee here?"

***

Sage's stomach hurt. That was the first thing she knew. The second was that everything else hurt too. There wasn't an inch of her that didn't feel like it had been dragged through gravel.

The third thing, though, was far worse.

Cadence's laugh sent chills up her spine. Her eyes fluttered open, and she was surprised to see she wasn't on a concrete floor anymore. The burning sensation had passed, but she was so exhausted it was painful. Her head was resting against...

"You found me." Her throat hurt as the words made their way out. Remy cradled her in her arms like she didn't weigh a thing, and although Remy's arms tightened around her in response, she didn't look away from whatever she was staring at.

Sage rolled her head to look and wished she hadn't.

Cadence and her three cronies were standing on the other side of the couch. The three lackwits were holding the children, long blades at their throats. Jake and Shala continued to hold hands, and Jimmy looked helpless and scared. Cadence held what almost looked like a sword at Jet's neck, and the look of fury in Jet's eyes was unmistakable.

Instinctively, she knew that any kind of telepathic communication would be overheard by Cadence. She'd known Sage was trying to call for Remy in the concrete room, and Sage had a feeling she'd know now. They'd have to communicate like normal people. "Set me down," Sage whispered. "It's okay."

Slowly, Remy set Sage on her feet. She teetered for a moment, and Remy gently pulled her behind her, where Sage could hold onto the kitchen island. Rac and Lars stood beside Remy, and the rage coming off all three of them should have burned a hole right through Cadence and the others.

"You would kill children? Even for you, that's beyond the pale."

Cadence looked at the kids. "Something you've never understood, Remy, is that a good leader has to do what they have to do. The sacrifice of a few vampires is worth saving all of us."

"You don't need to save us, Cadence. We're not in danger. Or we weren't until you started a war. What makes you think you'll get away with this?"

She laughed, an unhinged, high-pitched sound. "I already have, lover. The US military is mine to command, and there are more vampires on my side than yours. The others will fall at my feet in gratitude once they see how powerful we are, once they're able to be themselves in every way." She tilted her head and looked Remy over like she was a meal. "You and I could have ruled them all. The queen and her consort. But you were never strong enough, and you still aren't." Her gaze flicked to Sage, who shrank behind Remy. "You let your emotions get in the way, and you live like a revolting, weak little human. You had such potential." She shrugged. "Once we're done with you, we'll kill everyone who kowtowed to you, like

Geno and your little family here at Dark Haven."

Sage moved out from behind Remy but kept hold of the counter, afraid she'd drop if she let go even for a second.

"You said you wanted me as a pet. I'll come to you willingly if you let the kids go."

"No." Remy's tone was flat and uncompromising. "That isn't going to happen."

Sage ignored her. "You want followers, don't you? Aren't vampire children the perfect way for you to start? Why kill off vampires you can raise to be loyal to you? I could help take care of them until they were the age to be useful to you. Just let me protect them now, until you're done."

Cadence stared at the children thoughtfully. The blade against Jet's throat pressed closer, and black blood began to seep down her neck. "You're right. After we've killed you all, we'll put them in a home for vampire children. We'll train our own beautiful killing machines. Sage, you lovely little beast. What a diabolical idea. I knew you'd make a fine pet. Good thing Remy seems to have kept the poison from killing you. How did she do that, I wonder?" She put her finger to her lips like she was thinking.

"It doesn't matter." It did, and Sage had a feeling she knew what Remy had done. "Let the children go."

Cadence's eyes narrowed. "We'll have to work on your manners." She nodded at the three beside her. "Let them go."

The three kids ran to Remy, who motioned them to stand back with Sage. They pressed against her, even Jimmy, who pulled Jake behind him. All three were shaking, and Shala was crying softly. Sage wanted to hold her but wasn't strong enough, so she simply pressed Shala close.

"Now." Cadence pressed the blade into Jet's neck. "Let's finish this, shall we? We've got work to do. I promised General Cane I'd turn him as soon as I was finished with you. The very first Vampire General. He's quite excited, as you can imagine."

Get down!

Remy's shout in Sage's mind, and clearly in the children's as well, made them drop to the floor. Sage scooted to the far corner, dragging them with her, and the four of them huddled against the cupboards as the world around them splintered into a surreal landscape of violence.

She pulled Shala into her lap, and Jake pressed his face against her arm. She and Jimmy watched as Remy and Rac seemed to evaporate. Where they'd been was a shimmer, like a heatwave off a road, and that shimmer shot forward. The sword flew out of Cadence's hand, and Jet fell to her knees and crawled out of the way. And then Cadence was a shimmer of air, and when one shimmer crashed into the other, thunder boomed through the room, shattering the windows. Sage pulled the kids tight as Shala screamed, and Jimmy pressed Jake closer.

Lars began what looked like hand-to-hand combat with the other three vampires, and just when Sage thought he might be outnumbered, Jet pressed her back to his, and they fought like they'd done it a hundred times before. Remy's door crashed open, and Jimmy's mother stood on the other side, her eyes red, her fangs out, and behind her were the Dark Haven vampires, including Lester.

They streamed in, and it wasn't long before the three vampires were face down on the floor with multiple vampires kneeling on their backs.

But still, Rac and Remy spun in a vicious dance with Cadence. Blood droplets flung through the air, painting the walls and broken glass in a grotesque mural. If Sage looked hard enough, she could see their bodies as though they dissolved and reformed as they whirled, fangs out, eyes flashing red in the shimmer, only to disappear again.

Just when Sage thought she might pass out from holding her breath, the three bodies had form again. Rac bent over, her hands on her knees. Blood streamed from cuts on both cheeks. It dripped from her hand... She was missing a finger.

Remy had her knee in Cadence's back, her hand in her hair so her head was pulled back hard enough to snap her neck. Remy was bleeding from several places too, and there was a large patch spreading on her chest. She was in full vampire mode, and it was both impressive and terrifying.

Cadence looked at Sage from her awkward position, and blood dripped from her fangs. "You're going to die anyway. One way or another. The great Killing Wind will still lose."

Remy pulled harder, and Cadence hissed. "Say what you want, I'm not going to kill you quickly." Remy looked at the others. "Thank you."

Jimmy's mom was one of the ones kneeling on a vampire. "He managed to call to me as soon as they stepped inside. I gathered the others when we figured out what was happening."

Remy pushed harder when Cadence struggled beneath her. "You all understand what has to happen."

There was an uncomfortable silence, but no one denied it. Lester, his eyes narrowed as he looked at the vampire beneath him, said, "They deserve no less. Vampires like these are the reason my clan was taken from me so long ago."

Selma looked at Jimmy and then to Remy. "I should take the kids."

Remy nodded, and her red gaze turned to Sage. "You too."

Her face twitched when Sage started to argue but then just gave a short nod. In truth, she didn't want to see what was about to happen. She stood slowly with Jimmy's help, and the two little ones stayed close as they made their way to the door. Selma relinquished her place to another vampire and moved to Sage's side. She draped her arm around Sage's waist and took her weight.

Sage looked over her shoulder at Remy, who continued to watch her, her expression inscrutable. *Whatever you have to do, do it and come get me. I love you.*

Remy's expression didn't change, and the door closed behind them.

Chapter Twenty-Six

Remy took in the people around her. Family and clan. "I need time." She looked at Rac. "*We* need time," she said. She didn't need to do this alone. Rac tilted her head slightly in acknowledgment.

Lars, Jet, and Lester, each kneeling on a traitor, looked back at her calmly. Jet had a sickly pallor and clearly needed to rest.

"Take them downstairs and guard them with everything you have. And be aware of any we might have missed. I'll get to them after we've dealt with their idiotic leader. Jet, I need you to go find Sage and the rest and stay with them, please." That would give Jet the break she needed without acknowledging she looked like she was about to drop. They'd look after her.

The traitors were jerked to their feet and dragged from the room. Not one of them said a word, though their hatred burned brightly in their eyes. They were bruising, which meant they'd fed on human blood recently. It was another question to add to the list. Lester bowed his head as he closed the door behind them, his look of respect and understanding letting her know she was right to do what needed to be done.

Once they were gone, she jerked Cadence to her feet. Rac pulled the rope they'd taken off Sage from the counter and they quickly bound Cadence. When she began to struggle, Remy knocked the air out of her so they could finish binding her. She pulled the rope particularly tight around her neck until Cadence grunted and coughed.

Remy sat opposite her with the rope wrapped around her fist. "You understand how this is going to go."

Cadence glared at her. "It's too far gone. Even when you kill me, someone else will take my place."

Rac shook her head and broken glass crunched under her boots as she moved to sit beside Cadence on the couch. Remy didn't miss the way she flinched aside. Bravado or not, she was scared.

"If you had any idea how many times we've heard that over the centuries." Rac looked at Remy. "It's never true though, is it?"

Remy wanted this over with. "It's never true. Ever. Not once have we taken down a despot and had someone who stepped into their shoes. The tangled webs they create unravel, and life goes back to normal. And that's what's going to happen here. We'll take down General Cane and expose what you've done, and life will go back to being what it was." She looked around at the broken glass and remnants of her living room. "We'll need to do some clean-up, but ultimately you'll be a footnote, nothing more."

Cadence jerked against her bonds, and Rac put her hand on Cadence's leg. She stopped moving immediately and swallowed hard. "Just kill me already. If you don't, I'll escape, and I won't give you a second chance like I did your little pet Jet."

"I'm afraid that won't happen." Remy stood and jerked on the rope, forcing Cadence to her feet. The confirmation that she'd been the one to hurt Jet was the final feather on the scale. "But it will be less unpleasant if you give us all the details we don't already know. What is the plant made of? How much did you make? Is there an antidote? Are there other military advisors in your pocket? I want the names of all the vampires who were willing to follow you. Every single one who was willing to kill other vampires in order to buy into your crazy vampire kingdom plan."

Cadence hissed and fought, but with Rac behind her and Remy in front, there was no way for her to win. But as they edged her onto the deck, where the sun was shining and the overhang had come down, she began to fight like a trapped animal. This time, Rac clamped her hands on the sides of Cadence's head, and Cadence slumped, whimpering as Rac's power flooded her mind.

Remy took her bound hands and spun her so her back was in the sun, releasing Rac's grip.

Cadence swore as the sun touched her bare skin, and it began to redden and welt. Blisters appeared, and she fought to move back into the shade. But Remy held firm. "Information, Cadence. All of it."

The hours wore on as they got the information they needed, though it came in dribs and drabs, and she had to speak through blistered lips. Remy shut down all emotion until the end. When there clearly wasn't any more for Cadence to tell them, Rac bowed her head and backed away into the room.

Remy stepped onto the balcony, holding Cadence in front of her. The sun had shifted far enough that she could stand in the open now. She took a deep breath, but before she could speak, Cadence gave a hoarse laugh.

"She's still going to die. Your little pet. I know you, Remy, and you haven't turned a human in all your time here. You won't do it now, and the poison will continue to eat her from the inside. You can watch her die, and that's my final gift. I loved you, and you left me. Now you'll know what it feels like." She spit blood onto the fractured wood at their feet.

Remy, barely controlling her desire to rip Cadence's arms off and throw them at her feet while she screamed, turned toward the ranch. She could feel her people down there, listening, waiting. "Cadence Taylor, you have been charged with the willful murder of vampires, with the intent to poison and murder innumerable more in order to declare yourself queen of the vampires. Your intent to murder and enslave humans has also been verified. The Vampire Council has sanctioned my ability to discharge punishment, and I sentence you, and all those who followed you, to death."

Remy grabbed Cadence's head, looked into eyes filled with hatred and fear, and twisted until her neck snapped. She continued to twist until Cadence's head remained in her hands while her body dropped at Remy's feet.

She dropped the head beside the body and moved to the railing. The sun had set, and everyone was standing in the courtyard below, watching in silence. She waited a long time, trying to find the words she knew needed to be said to calm and soothe the people who depended on her. She thought of Sage, and how open and honest she was. "Taking a life is a horrific act. Sickening, demeaning, and it always comes with a cost. We are vampires. We are remarkable in so many ways, and there's no shame in what we are. We've often taken lives throughout the centuries, usually in order for us to continue to live. We have synth now, and killing is no longer necessary. It's a choice, and one I've never chosen lightly. I know many of you don't care about the power or about the ways we're superior to our human brethren. Like me, you simply want to live and enjoy life." She was glad to see many people nodding in agreement.

There was movement, and Sage and Jet, leaning on each other, came out from under the walkway. Remy met her gaze but didn't lose focus.

"I have always fought for us, and that will never stop. We follow the rules of the world we live in. To some degree, we always have. Otherwise the world would be nothing but vampires. But we've even evolved from our ancestors. We change with the world we inhabit. We do this so our world doesn't devolve into the kind of chaos that this group of traitorous vampires was hoping for. We do it so we can live out in the open, in peace, or even continue to enjoy solitary lives the way we used to, but without fear of being hunted. We can live the way we want to, and that's because we don't have a single leader, but a Council devoted to our safety and continued existence."

She took a shaky breath, exhaustion, both physical and emotional, stealing up on her. She saw Sage and Jet moving slowly through the crowd toward the lodge doors.

"We don't have prisons. We don't have a legal system with lots of red tape. When a vampire hurts other vampires, when they set out with the intention to destroy our world, they are dealt with quickly." She could feel Cadence's empty eyes staring up at her, and she shifted so she couldn't see them. "My only aspiration is to keep our communities and families safe. We have the answers we need in order to put a stop to everything this group did, and there will be no mercy for the people who hurt those we love, who intended to enslave or kill anyone who didn't agree with them." She'd run out of words and wasn't sure what else to say.

Maybe tell them they'll be able to go back to their lives, and you're happy to talk to them if anyone is weirded out by all this?

She smiled internally at Sage's advice. "We're here for you. Me, Rac, Lars, Jet...and the rest of the Dark Haven family. If you need to talk, if you're upset or scared, don't hold it in. Talk it out so it doesn't fester." She raised her hand. "Stronger together."

The repeated response was resounding, and she nodded and turned to go inside. Jet and Sage were sitting on kitchen stools, both looking like they might fall off them any second. "Come on, you two." Remy put her arm around Sage, and Rac walked beside Jet as they headed toward the bedrooms. Jet let herself into the guest room and fell on the bed with a groan.

Remy opened the door to her room and helped Sage crawl into bed. "How are you feeling?" With a tenderness she didn't know existed inside her, she caressed Sage's cheek, Cadence's words echoing in her heart.

"Like gum stuck to a snowplow's tire." Sage closed her eyes and held Remy's hand. "You can't stay, can you?"

"Not right now, sweetheart." Remy kissed her forehead. "I have a lot to deal with, but I'll come check on you in a little while." The last thing in the world she wanted to do was leave Sage's side, but she was safe for the moment, and Remy still had traitors downstairs to deal with.

"Before you go...why do you still drive that truck?" Sage's eyelids fluttered. "Lars told me to ask you, and when I was on that floor, it occurred to me I'd never know."

Remy perched on the edge of the bed. What a strange thing for Sage to have wondered when she was in that state. "I bought it new in 1954, and I thought it was the sexiest thing I'd ever seen. I've had it all this time, and it's the only thing that has never changed."

"That's sweet. And kind of sad." Sage's head lolled a little. "What did she mean?" Sage opened her eyes, clearly with effort. "She said I was going to die either way."

"Don't think about it right now. Close your eyes and sleep, and I'll be back as quickly as I can."

Sage's breathing slowed, and she drifted off. She must have been exhausted not to argue a point she wouldn't have let go if she'd felt up to it. Remy touched her forehead, which was starting to grow warm again. How much time did she have before she had to make a decision she didn't want to make?

She forced herself off the bed and out of her house. Prepared to deal with the three traitors waiting, she was relieved to see their prone bodies already in a row on the grass out back, their heads twisted at awkward angles and gaping holes in their chests where their hearts had been. The place was empty except for Rac, who sat at the table, letting one of the doctors see to the stump of her pinky finger. Somehow Cadence had managed to bite it off while they fought.

"Didn't anyone ever tell you not to stick your hand in a vampire's mouth?" Remy rested her head on her forearms.

"I must've missed that lesson. I wish we could grow back body parts. I'll miss that little finger."

"Done. Remy?" The doc looked pointedly at the huge blood stain on Remy's shirt. "I have a feeling I should look at that."

Remy, too tired to argue, pulled off her shirt and sports bra. She'd stopped being modest a long, long time ago. The slash started just below her collarbone and went to just above her ribs. The doctor cleaned it up and put in some stitches where it was deepest, and then with a squeeze of her shoulder, left them alone.

She put her shirt back on, and they sat in silence for a long time.

"I suggest we divide and conquer." Rac finally shifted, stretching her legs out in front of her.

"Nice choice of words." Remy lifted her head from her arms. "Go on."

"You need to go call Dez and fill her in. Probably get the president on the line too. That's your thing. I'll take a team and head to the military zone to see if Cane is there, and I'll take him into the forest and deal with him."

"Make sure no cameras catch you." She wasn't about to tell Rac how to dole out punishment. She'd been doing it far longer than Remy.

"I suggest we start there and see where that takes us with the humans. Then we'll deal with the list of names Cadence gave us and weed out the vampire trash."

Remy pushed herself up from the table, only willpower keeping her going. "Let's do it."

Rac stood like she was feeling her age. "And Sage? What are you going to do about that?"

Remy swallowed hard and nearly sat down again. "I don't know."

"Well, you know my thoughts on it." Rac turned toward the door. "But you're the one who has to live with your decision."

She walked out, leaving Remy at the bottom of the stairs. They'd stopped the bad guys. Why did it feel like her world was still ending?

Chapter Twenty-Seven

Sage woke, dizzy and confused, but knowing she was safe. Her neck had started to burn again. What had made it stop before? She couldn't remember.

The murmur of voices made its way back to her, and she inched her way out of bed, her whole body aching like she'd turned ninety overnight. She slipped on the slippers sitting by the bedside and shuffled into the living room.

Remy was sitting at the computer talking to the mayor and the President of the United States. Sage brushed debris off the couch and sat down gingerly, out of camera shot. She ignored the blood-splattered walls and glass, as well as the cold coming in from the holes where windows had once been.

"We've dealt with General Cane our way." Remy's tone suggested she didn't require their approval. "He'd given the orders to kill several of the vampires they'd turned away at the border, as well as a few they found on the bay. More were being held in a shipping container. His intention was to become a vampire and then develop a vampire military to take over the government by force." She shrugged. "He won't be doing that now, but I suggest you try to find out if he had anyone willingly following him. The soldiers planting the toxic bush were likely just following orders."

The president, looking somewhat shell-shocked, shook his head. "If word of this got out, humans would worry that the vampires would eventually overturn the government. Hell, that they'd take over the world."

"But they'd also be told that it was vampires who stopped them from trying. Not humans. We continue to police our own and wouldn't allow anything like that to happen." Dez's gaze was intense. "If it's going to come out at all, then it should be the whole story, should it not?"

"Of course, of course. But maybe it's better that it doesn't come out at all?" He settled back in his chair and toyed with a pen. "Maybe, because we understand how all this began, we make that statement we discussed. We say long and intensive discussion has shown that we have nothing to fear from each other, and that we're removing all military patrols. That vampire rights remain in effect, and we should return to normal."

"Fine with me." Remy glanced over her shoulder at Sage and gave her a quick smile before turning back to her conversation. "We also need that plant analyzed and an antidote created as soon as possible. I have a couple infected vampires here who need help."

He wrote something down. "I'll have a lab team out there by morning to pull up all the plants and get them out of there." He hesitated. "You said we should find out who might be helping the general. Do you know who was helping Cadence Taylor?"

"We do. And we're dealing with it." Again, Remy's flat tone let him know he shouldn't ask more questions.

"Very well. I'll schedule the press conference for the day after tomorrow, if that's okay?"

Dez and Remy nodded, and the president left the conversation.

"My contacts already found some of Cadence's followers since our last conversation." Dez held up a piece of paper. "I'll email you the addresses."

"I'll send you the names of the others so you can get me addresses. Rac and I will take it from there."

Dez shifted and looked away. "I'm glad I'm not you. And that I'm not one of the people you're searching for."

"Yeah. I know what you mean." Remy tapped the table. "Send me a plane ticket for Washington when you have one?"

"Will do. I'll come with you." Dez looked at the camera again. "What are you going to do about Sage Samara?"

Remy sighed, and Sage waited anxiously for her answer.

"I'll let you know." She signed off and turned to Sage. "You shouldn't be out of bed, beautiful. Not with all this glass around. Come on." Remy walked over the remains of her living room, scooped Sage into her arms, and carried her back to the bedroom. After settling Sage in, Remy stripped down and got in next to her.

Sage curled against her, trying to ignore the burning in her neck and the sweat beading on her brow. "Will you tell me now?"

Remy's arm tightened around her. "When we found you, it was almost too late. The poison is meant for vampires, and as such, it's incredibly potent. The fact that you hung on as long as you did defies explanation. But you were delirious, and before I got you back to the lodge, I felt you slipping away." Her chest shuddered under Sage's cheek. "I was going to lose you before we got you home."

"But I woke up here." Sage frowned, trying to understand through her confusion.

"I opened my wrist and gave you some of my blood. Not a lot, not enough to turn you. Just enough to give your body the strength to keep going until we could find a cure."

"You saved me." She shivered even though she was sweating. "But I'm still sick."

"There isn't an antidote, Sage. When she bit you, she took a lot of your blood, weakening you and making it hard for your system to recover. Then she rubbed the poison into the open wound. In addition to the pain it caused, it began to shut down your body."

"And it's still shutting down." Sage blinked back the tears. They wouldn't do any good now. "So I'm dying."

"The president is sending a team to begin working on an antidote. Rac has sent the plant to her lab too, and while the scientist there is a nutcase of the highest order, he's also the most brilliant mind I've ever known. We'll cure you, honey. We just have to be strong and wait it out."

Sage relaxed into Remy's side. "What if I run out of time?"

Remy kissed the top of her head. "I'll keep giving you little bits of my blood to keep you going."

"What if I run out of time," Sage said again. "My body will shut down. Would you rather me die and be without me than make me a vampire?"

"Sage," Remy whispered. "You don't understand what you're asking me to do. I've never, in all my time here, turned a human. It's a curse, sweetheart. What makes life beautiful is its finality. You cherish it more because your time will eventually end."

"That's bullshit," Sage murmured. "You cherish what you find beautiful, and if you stop finding beauty, then there's nothing to cherish." She shuddered as a stab of pain ran through her. "Love is beautiful. And I love you. You're right. I told the ZimTak people I loved them. But I didn't know...I didn't know what it really meant till you. Those strangers aren't my family. You are. I love you, Remy." She didn't want to sleep. She wanted every last second with Remy's arms wrapped around her. But as she drifted off, she was glad to at least have that as her last feeling.

***

Remy cried.

She hadn't cried in a long, long time. But as she held Sage and felt her slipping away, she cried for what she could have had. What they could have had together. What might have been. Sage had given her consent before, but did she really understand what it meant? She couldn't possibly understand what it was to look into the void of infinity. What that did to your soul. Was Sage right though? Was there beauty she simply didn't see anymore? Her family and their life at Dark Haven was special and beautiful. Sure, they all carried the baggage of the centuries, but how could they not after living so fully? Maybe that wasn't such a terrible thing after all.

There was a knock at the door, and Remy carefully slid away

from Sage, trying not to cause her any more pain, and went to answer it.

She narrowed her eyes when she saw it was Geno standing beside the door, which was hanging off its hinges. He looked past her and raised his eyebrows.

"I'm not a fan of your new décor."

"What is it, Geno?"

"Will you come downstairs, please?"

Lars moved up beside him and placed his hand on Geno's back. "I'll stay with Sage, Remy."

Remy shrugged and followed Geno downstairs. The scent of blood hit her hard, and she hissed and stepped back. "What have you done?"

He held up his hand. "Wait. Hear me out." He motioned to the four people sitting at the table, silk blindfolds around their eyes and bite marks on their arms and necks. "Remember I said there were enthusiasts who spent time in our company? Humans who enjoy serving us of their own free will? A fetish, to be sure, but one that serves us well."

Remy nodded, her jaw clenching as the smell of fresh blood assaulted her.

"I brought them here after Lars told me about the battle, and about how some of you were injured. Including Jet." He touched her arm and pulled away when she looked at him. "Remy, synth isn't going to help you heal. It won't help the others who were hurt either, but this will. I've even delivered a few willing hosts to Rac, who accepted them because she understands what we need." He looked from the humans to Remy. "Rac said to tell you to remember what you've learned about yourself, whatever that means."

"We're not turning them. And they're here because they want to be." Remy repeated the phrases and looked into his mind. He was telling the truth.

She didn't waste any more time. He was right. Synth kept them alive, but it didn't have the potency or healing effect that the real thing did. She sat beside a large man and sank her fangs into his neck. She made sure it didn't hurt, and she drank deeply, feeling the strength pour back into her like tar had been turned to fine wine. She stopped and sent him to sleep.

She waited as her strength returned, along with clarity of thought and focus. "Thank you, Geno. You're right, I needed that."

He looked like a child receiving praise from a parent. "Any time."

"Make sure they get back safe and human, okay?" She started to leave, and he touched her arm again.

"Lars told me about Sage. I'm sorry." He looked at the floor, his hands shoved in his pockets. "I really like her. And...Remy, you've been alone for as long as I've known you. Even when you found love, it wasn't like this. It wasn't what I see, what I feel in your mind when you think of her. I know you have your values and standards, and that's always kept you safe. But maybe it's time to stop wandering the world alone. Once, this one time, may be all you ever need."

His words hit their mark, as did the images he sent of the many, many times he'd seen her alone, walking on beaches, looking out over castles, drinking in pubs. All of it, alone.

"You'll continue your situationship with Lars?" she asked.

He nodded and grinned. "I do love the way she uses language."

"I'm giving you leave to come and go from Dark Haven as you wish. Do anything stupid, and we're going to have a problem." She knew she'd done the right thing when his face lit up. "I'm hoping being part of a clan that's settled will give you something you've been searching for. Maybe something we've both been searching for." Indeed, what they'd built here could be a bulwark against the loneliness they'd both suffered from over the centuries.

She patted his shoulder and headed back upstairs. Before she could go in, Lars stepped in front of her.

"Jet's sitting with her." His gaze searched Remy's. "She's leaving us, Wind."

Remy shoved past and ran to Sage's bedside. Jet was on the

other side, holding her hand.

"Hey," Remy said, brushing the hair from Sage's face. "Hey, baby. Come on." Remy shook as she pressed on Sage's shoulder. "Sage, please."

Lars and Jet stayed silent as Remy pleaded with Sage to wake up, to keep fighting.

"We'll leave you to it," Jet said, standing up and moving away. "Whatever you do, we'll be here for you after." They left the room.

Remy pressed her head to Sage's chest and could barely hear her heart beating any more. The poison slid over her neck and face, creating angry red and black lines.

If the universe creates something just for you, who the hell are you to turn it down?

Rac's voice came into her head, and that was all she said.

Was it true? Had Sage come into existence just so they could be together? If she had to face a future without Sage, she might as well walk into the sun and stake herself right now. Instead, she could have a life filled with the love she'd never expected to have.

"I love you too, beautiful." She opened the vein in her wrist and pressed it to Sage's lips.

Chapter Twenty-Eight

Sage sat in the shade of the newly repaired overhang above the terrace. The autumn colors of the leaves interspersed among the evergreens were so brilliant and bold, she could practically feel them. The scent of damp ground mixed with a light rain created the essence of a world getting ready to hibernate. Even from up here she could hear the community moving, talking, and laughing from wherever they were on the ranch.

It was overwhelming in the best way.

Her body still ached, but nothing like it had only a week ago when she'd been about to die. The thought still made her feel sick. She'd been so close to Death, who'd been right there about to take her hand. But Remy had pulled her back.

She looked up as Remy leaned down to kiss her and then took the seat beside her.

"You okay?" she asked, as she had every day, several times a day since Remy had turned her from human to vampire.

"If I said no, what would you do?" Sage stretched, her T-shirt riding up, and she liked the way Remy looked her over.

"I don't know." Remy continued to look at her intently. "I know you said you're okay with it, that I did what you wanted, but what if you change your mind? What if you grow to hate me, to hate being a vampire? It would crush me." She swallowed and studied her hands.

"Enough of this." Sage stood and looked down at her. "No one knows the future, Remy. When I took the opportunity to interview vampires, did I think I'd wake up one day needing blood like I needed air? Nope. Did I think I'd find the love of my life, the person who makes me want to wake up every day? Nope. But here we are." She leaned down and gave Remy a long, lingering kiss. "And right here is where I want to be. I love you."

Remy stood and pulled her into a tight embrace. "I couldn't be without you. I love you more than I thought possible."

Sage pulled away, walking them backward into the house. "Then it's damn well time you showed me." They hadn't had sex since she'd woken, a newborn ravenous vampire. Granted, she'd had to heal from the poison, and she'd gagged a couple times when she'd first had blood, brought to her by Geno, fresh from the willing host living at his home. She'd quickly grown used to it, and the switch to synth had been a little disappointing, but Remy said she didn't want Sage getting too used to the real thing, which made sense.

But Sage craved the intimacy they'd had before, the bond that had created something between them that couldn't be broken. Remy had been cautious, almost too sweet, and Sage wanted... fierce.

With that in mind, she kissed Remy hard, pressing their bodies together, her legs on either side of Remy's so she could feel Sage's heat. "Stop treating me like I'll break," she murmured against Remy's lips. "Fuck me the way you want to. The way I need you to."

Remy moaned and turned to push Sage onto the bed. She lowered herself over her, her gaze hungry. She jerked on the thin shorts and they tore away, and she shoved Sage's T-shirt up to expose her breasts. She sucked on Sage's nipple.

Sage pushed into her, against her, pulling hard on her shoulders. "Show me," she gasped, her back already arching. "Show me what I am to you."

A growl reverberated through Remy's chest, and she pulled Sage's legs over her shoulders. She entered her fast and hard, filling her, fucking her, and the energy surrounding them left no doubts.

Sage's orgasm slammed through her harder than any she'd

ever had, and her body was alive, every nerve ending attuned to Remy.

Remy let her legs down and was instantly back inside her, her mouth hot as she covered Sage's neck, chest, breasts, and stomach with kisses and nips. She pushed harder, deeper, and Sage begged her not to stop.

Remy moved to cover Sage's body with her one. "Mine. You're mine, forever." Her breath was hot against Sage's ear as she fucked her into another orgasm and then another. Their kisses were hot and hard, and Sage basked in the way her body could take this intensity, this beautiful inferno of desire. She sucked on Remy's neck, her nails clawing down her back, and Remy continued to fuck her the way she wanted to, the way they both needed it to be.

Eventually they settled, satiated for the moment, and Sage lay in Remy's arms. Even the smell of sex was stronger, more potent, and Sage knew she'd never get enough.

"Are you ready for your interview tonight?" Remy asked, her fingertips trailing lightly over Sage's spine.

"I think so?" Sage raised up on her elbow to look into Remy's beautiful eyes, which were filled with love. "I mean, I was used to being on camera, but it was always on my terms, you know? I decided what I wanted to share and used the filters and effects that made me look my best. But this time I'll be on the other side, and I can't really control what she'll ask."

"Madison Ford is an excellent investigative journalist. She's not some creep out to make you fall." Remy shifted the covers off. "I need to replenish my energy. And yours." She winked and headed to the kitchen.

Sage lay back, thinking about how her life had changed, and how it was going to continue to change. Remy and Dez had met with the president and run the press conference as planned. The twenty or so military personnel who'd followed Cane had been taken into custody, but Sage had no idea what had actually happened to them, nor did she care. Rac and Remy had gone through the list of names and rooted out Cadence's followers, those who hadn't already fled anyway. They weren't concerned about the others. As they said, it took a real piece of work to think they could lead the world to a new way of being. The borders were open, and many of the refugees living in Bluffington had moved on. Of the ones at Dark Haven, about half chose to stay, and building work was nearly constant as they created housing across the river. There was more than enough room. She was glad Selma and Jimmy had decided to stay too. Shala and Jake deserved to keep the family they'd grown up with, and as the next step in vampire evolution, it was also important to keep an eye on them. Selma happily taught at the local high school, where Jimmy had made friends who often came back to hang out with him at Dark Haven.

The lab at Dark Haven was now up and running, and they were producing their own synth so that they were no longer dependent on outside sources. After coming so close to a civil war, Remy had decided that being fully off-grid was even more important. She'd taken several acres of land and turned them into cow pastures, so they'd have fresh meat too. Outside suppliers were no longer necessary, and there'd been a not-so-subtle boycott of the farms who'd turned against the vampires. Several of them were now making the kinds of ads that said they were there for "everybody who liked fresh meat."

The results had come back from Rac's lab too. Dr. Frank had listed out the plants used to create the super poison, which were rhubarb—which Sage found vindicating—as well as hogweed, white hemlock, and jimsonweed. He'd also created an antidote, which every vampire on the ranch had been given, just in case they weren't showing symptoms yet. There hadn't been another feral since, much to Remy's relief.

Remy had received a red arm band in the mail with a note saying she'd been given a place on the Council whether she attended the meetings or not. She put it in a drawer and ignored the message.

At the press conference, Remy had been asked about Sage

Samara's well-being, as Sage hadn't been heard from or seen in quite some time. Remy said she'd let Sage speak for herself when she was ready to do so, and although that had raised plenty of questions, it was the only way to buy them time. The interview tonight was Sage's coming-out party, so to speak. She'd toyed with posting a video to her ZimTak followers, but it felt too momentous, too serious to do on that platform. When Madison Ford had reached out, they knew it was the right path to take.

Remy came in and handed her a glass of synth. "I thought you might want to go into town and do some shopping."

Sage sipped, grateful that Remy had put in extra slices of orange. She still wasn't quite used to the tang. "I'd love that." She kicked off the blanket and lay there naked, sipping her drink. "We haven't talked about what's next."

"Next?" Remy continued to stand beside the bed, and given her expression, it wouldn't be long before she was making Sage her own again.

"Where I'm going to live."

Remy's gaze snapped up to hers. "What do you mean?"

"Well," Sage said, rolling over onto her stomach and looking at Remy over her shoulder. "Just because you love me doesn't mean you want me living with you yet. We could take it slow—"

Remy set down her glass and pressed the length of her body to Sage's. She moved her hair aside. "Are you seriously asking me if I want you to live with me? After all this?"

"A girl shouldn't make assumptions," Sage whispered as Remy bit her earlobe.

"My girl should." Remy shifted so she was lying beside her and tugged until Sage was facing her. "Sage, if it isn't clear, I want you at my side. I want to wake up to you every morning for the rest of history, until this big blue ball plummets into the sun. You were meant for me. We were meant for each other, and I'll do my utmost to make sure you know how much I love you for as long as we're both here."

Sage pushed on Remy's chest until she was on her back. "Well, when you put it that way, I guess we'll have to make a trip to go get my stuff." Straddling her, she leaned down and gave her a languid kiss. "But you have to promise you'll let me show you all the beautiful things in the world even if you've already seen them—because you haven't seen them with me." She began a slow, steady rocking against Remy's hand, which was now between her legs.

"I have the most beautiful thing in the world right here."

***

Sage tried some deep breathing and wiped her hands on her slacks. She didn't have sweaty palms, she just felt like she should. After all the time she'd spent building her platform as an influencer, she realized how small-time she was compared to a journalist like Madison. She'd covered religious wars and organ-trafficking gangs...and now she wanted an insider's look at the vampire-human conflict, which had almost caused a civil war. It was a far cry from the fashion and makeup tips Sage had been giving on ZimTak.

"Ready?" Madison asked, giving Sage a sympathetic smile.

"I think so. Maybe? Probably not, no." She swallowed and reminded herself that she was powerful and brave. Remy's words, not hers.

"I've seen your ZimTak." Madison nodded to someone who handed her some paper.

Sage's stomach fell. "I worked really hard on it."

"I can tell. You were always honest. Maybe a little too much focus on the positive for my taste." Madison smiled. "But you clearly believed in what you were saying. Do the same now, and we'll have a great interview."

The camera guy gave the signal and counted down, and Madison looked at the camera. "Good evening. The last month was one full of uncertainty, questions, and fear. Many of us wondered if we were on the brink of civil war. One which, frankly, would have been disastrous for everyone involved. Last week, that period of strife came to a sudden end when President Smith, the mayor of Bluffington County, Dez Carmine, and vampire spokesperson Remy Winslow held a press conference, confirming that there was no danger. All military convoys were pulled from vampire territories, and all three leaders assured us that the fight between humans and vampires which started off the cascade of chaos had been in ignorance, not unlike rival gangs." She turned to face a different camera angle. "Throughout the mounting tension, one person was involved from both sides. Tonight, I welcome our guest Sage Samara, internet influencer who went into vampire territory in order to get the truth."

It sounded so noble the way Madison put it. She smiled when Madison turned to her. She and Remy had talked through what she could and couldn't say, and she buzzed through it in her head.

"Sage, we know from your ZimTak videos that you've been a proponent of vampire rights from the beginning. What made you decide to cross the border and interview people from their community personally, despite the danger?"

Sage laughed. "Ironically, I didn't think there was any danger. I was convinced they weren't all that different from us. I thought they were being unfairly targeted, and I wanted to be a voice for change."

"Your answer suggests you were wrong?"

Sage nodded slowly. "I was. The fact is, they are different. We are different, I should say. And pretending there aren't differences when there obviously are doesn't do anyone any good. I was in danger, yes, but not from them. I was in danger because I went in intending to speak for a group of people who had their own voice. Instead of standing aside and using my platform so they could be heard on their own merit, I spoke from a place as an outsider."

"We?" Madison's eyes narrowed. "You said, 'We are different.' Are you saying you're no longer human?"

This was it. Sage looked Madison in the eye and stayed calm. "That's correct." There was shuffling among the crew that stopped quickly when Madison motioned with her hand.

"As you can imagine, that puts things in a different light. Can you tell us what transpired?"

"I was dying." Sage looked at the camera instead of at Madison. "A disgruntled vampire decided she wanted to take what Remy Winslow had created. In an effort to undermine her, she created a toxic plant meant to harm vampires and weaken Remy's political position. However, I came into contact with the plant, and it immediately began to shut down my system. During my stay at Dark Haven, I'd told Remy in no uncertain terms that if it came to civil war, if something happened to me, that I'd want her to turn me. I didn't want to die, I wanted to fight." Sage smiled softly, thinking back to that conversation that felt a million years ago. "We fell in love, you see. It wasn't just some notion of living forever, because every book and movie about that in history shows you it isn't all fun and games. I wanted to be with Remy, and I was happy to do that as a human."

"But you were poisoned and dying?" Madison prompted her, never looking away.

"I was very close to dead. Remy had my consent but didn't want to do it. She had never turned a human, in all her time on earth. But I'd made my wishes clear." Sage shrugged and smiled. "She kept me from dying, and I'll always be grateful for that."

"And the vampire who tried to overthrow Remy Winslow? Where is she now?"

"She was dealt with by the Vampire Council, who doesn't tolerate that kind of behavior. Madison, I truly believe that we can all live together. I believed it before I went to Dark Haven, and I still believe it now. Yes, we're different. Yes, difference can be scary when you don't understand something and there's lots of misinformation out there. But that's what interviews like this are for. To help people understand each other and build bridges."

Madison asked a few more questions that Sage answered according to what Remy had suggested and then Madison sat back.

"What's next for you, Sage? I imagine life is very different now."

"It isn't that different, really. I'll be living at Dark Haven, but I'll be working from the mayor's office in the city. I'm the new social media coordinator, and I'll continue to use my ZimTak platform to show people real life in vampire country. There aren't a ton of vampire influencers, but I'm hoping we'll see more. I've turned down the corporate sponsorships offered, so I can keep my platform as authentic as possible." She laughed. "Dark Haven remains an off-grid ranch with no internet or TV, and as much as it drove me crazy at first, I've really begun to cherish the way there's no noise at the end of my workday. Just me and my family at Dark Haven."

"We could all use some of that, I think." Madison thanked her and ended the interview. She took off her mic and the crew began doing what the crew does. Madison leaned forward. "I'm well aware there's more to the story than you're sharing." She raised her eyebrows and waited, but Sage just smiled sweetly and didn't say anything. "Okay. Not everything is meant for public consumption. But if you ever change your mind, you know where to find me."

Sage shook her hand. "You know, you could come to Dark Haven if you wanted to. We allow the occasional human in now, since we need to show that we really can live together. Come to dinner with Elodie next week? I hear she might be taking a vampire role in her next film."

Madison's surprise was evident. "I'd love to. Thank you."

Sage left the studio and walked out into the fresh night air. The moon was full, and she wished she could fly up and touch it. "Hey, stud. Give a girl a ride?" she said as she walked up to Remy, who was leaning against her truck.

"Anywhere, anytime, and as hard as you like." Remy pulled her into a rough kiss. "You were fantastic."

"I was, wasn't I?" Sage laughed when Remy pinched her side.

"I've invited Madison to dinner next week."

Remy sighed and pulled open the passenger door. "Of course you did. And what about her high-profile partner?"

"Nothing wrong with high profile, gorgeous." Sage turned to her in the driver's seat as they set off. "Thank you."

Remy took her hand while keeping one on the steering wheel. "For?"

"For giving me the world. For loving me enough to cross a line you'd never crossed before." She squeezed Remy's hand. "For giving us an eternity of beauty."

Remy kissed Sage's hand. "To the end, beautiful."

Sage stared out at the full moon and drank in the things she never would have been able to see as a human. The trees with their night critters jumping through the branches, the owls flying low to catch their prey, the way the sky felt like she could wrap it in her arms. This was her world. Dark Haven was her home, and the vampires there were her family. Remy was her soulmate, and she was going to cherish every moment of the future that was theirs for the taking.

Other Great Butterworth Books

Stolen Ambition by Robyn Nyx
Daughters of two worlds collide in a dangerous game of ambition and love.
Available on Amazon (ASIN B09QRSKBVP)

An Art to Love by Helena Harte
Second chances are an art form.
Available on Amazon (ASIN B0B1CD8Y42)

Where the Heart Leads by Ally McGuire
A writer. A celebrity. And a secret that could break their hearts.
Available on Amazon (ASIN B0BWFX5W9L)

Green for Love by E.V. Bancroft
All's fair in love and eco-war.
Available from Amazon (ASIN B0C28F7PX5)

Call of Love by Lee Haven
Separated by fear. Reunited by fate. Will they get a second chance at life and love?
Available from Amazon (ASIN B09CLK91N5)

Cabin Fever by Addison M Conley
She goes for the money, but will she stay for something deeper?
Available on Amazon (ASIN B0BQWY45GH)

Zamira Saliev: A Dept. 6 Operation by Valden Bush
They're both running from their pasts. Together, they might make a new future.
Available from Amazon (ASIN B0BHJKHK6S)

The Helion Band by AJ Mason
Rose's only crime was to show kindness to her royal mistress...
Available from Amazon (ASIN B09YM6TYFQ)

That Boy of Yours Wants Looking At by Simon Smalley
A gloriously colourful and heart-rending memoir.
Available from Amazon (ASIN B09HSN9NM8)

What's Your Story?

Global Wordsmiths, CIC, provides an all-encompassing service for all writers, ranging from basic proofreading and cover design to development editing, typesetting, and eBook services. A major part of our work is charity and community focused, delivering writing projects to under-served and under-represented groups across Nottinghamshire, giving voice to the voiceless and visibility to the unseen.

To learn more about what we offer, visit: www.globalwords.co.uk

A selection of books by Global Words Press:
Desire, Love, Identity: with the National Justice Museum
Aventuras en México: Farmilo Primary School
Times Past: with The Workhouse, National Trust
Young at Heart with AGE UK
In Different Shoes: Stories of Trans Lives

Self-published authors working with Global Wordsmiths:
Steve Bailey
Ravenna Castle
Jackie D
CJ DeBarra
Dee Griffiths
Iona Kane
Maggie McIntyre
Emma Nichols
Dani Lovelady Ryan
Erin Zak

www.ingramcontent.com/pod-product-compliance
Lightning Source LLC
Chambersburg PA
CBHW070431170726
48291CB00002B/450